Fire STUDY

"You need my permission to exit the Keep," Roze said. "This is *my* domain. I'm in charge of all magicians, including you, Soulfinder." Her hands smacked her chair's arms. "If *I* had control of the Council, you would be taken to the Keep's cells to await execution. No good has ever come from a Soulfinder."

The other Masters gaped at Roze in shock. She remained incensed. "Just look at our history. Every Soulfinder has craved power. Magical power. Political power. Power over people's souls. Yelena will be no different. Sure now she plays at being a Liaison and has agreed to my training. It's only a matter of time."

Looking over her shoulder, she gave me a pointed stare. *Keep out of Sitia's affairs. And you might be the only Soulfinder in history to live past the age of twenty-five.*

Go take another look at your history books, Roze, I said. *The demise of a Soulfinder is always reported along with the death of a Master Magician.*

Roze ignored me as she left the meeting room.

Fire STUDY
Maria V. Snyder

MIRA

MIRA is a registered trademark of Harlequin Enterprises Limited, used under licence.

Published in Great Britain 2009
MIRA Books, Eton House, 18-24 Paradise Road,
Richmond, Surrey, TW9 1SR

© Maria V. Snyder 2008

ISBN 978 0 7783 0265 0

59-0209

Printed in Great Britain
by Clays Ltd, St Ives plc

THE TERRITORY OF IXIA

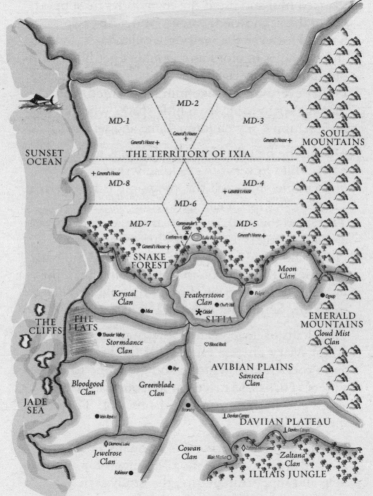

ACKNOWLEDGEMENTS

By this time you all should know how wonderful my husband, Rodney, can be. After all, I have thanked him and listed the many ways he supports me in the acknowledgements of my first two books. However, the writing wouldn't get done and the holes in plot logic wouldn't get filled without him. So once again, thanks go to him, because I don't ever want to take him for granted. And thanks also go to my two little sparks who fire my imagination – my children, Luke and Jenna.

One of the best decisions I've made is to attend Seton Hill University's graduate writing programme. Through this programme, I've learned so much and met a talented group of writers. Thanks to them all, and special thanks go to my critique partners, Diana Botsford, Kimberley Howe and Jason Jack Miller, who helped me with this book. Kim, I hope this reads better than the ingredients on a frozen dinner! I would also like to thank my Seton Hill mentor, David Bischoff.

First drafts of novels can be pretty rough, but my editor, Mary Theresa Hussey, has the knowledge and experience to wade in and guide me to calmer waters. Thanks, Matrice, for all your hard work and the smiley faces on my manuscript. They keep me going!

Thanks go to Catherine Burke, Selma Leung, Anna Baggaley, and Belinda Mountain for all their help and support in getting the Study series noticed in the UK. The MIRA Books staff in Surrey has been so enthusiastic and great fun to work with – thanks to all!

Many thanks to Henry Steadman, who did a fantastic job with the cover art for all three Study books. I love them – they are perfect!

Researching for a book is always fun, and this time I enrolled in a glass-blowing class. My appreciation for glass art rose considerably as I struggled to craft simple items from molten glass. Thanks go to my teacher and glass artist, Helen Tegeler, whose patient instruction not only added to my knowledge of glass for this book, but made the experience a blast.

And, finally, heartfelt thanks go to my army of Book Commandos! They're out in the trenches promoting and recommending my books to all who will listen, affixing stickers, and handing out bookmarks. Thanks to my Aunt Bette, whose efforts in the field earned her the rank of General. The Commander would be proud.

To my parents, James and Vincenza,
for your constant support and encouragement
in all my endeavours. You sparked the fire.

I

"THAT'S PATHETIC, YELENA," Dax complained. "An all-powerful Soulfinder who isn't all-powerful. Where's the fun in that?" He threw up his long thin arms in mock frustration.

"Sorry to disappoint you, but *I'm* not the one who attached the 'all-powerful' to the title." I pulled a black strand of hair from my eyes. Dax and I had been working on expanding my magical abilities without success. As we practiced on the ground floor of Irys's Keep tower—well, mine too, since she has given me three floors to use—I tried not to let my own aggravation interfere with the lessons.

Dax was attempting to teach me how to move objects with magic. He had rearranged the furniture, lined up the plush armchairs in neat rows and turned the couch over on its side with his power. My efforts to restore Irys's cozy layout and to stop an end table from chasing me failed. Though not from lack of trying—my shirt clung to my sweaty skin.

A sudden chill shook me. Despite a small fire in the hearth, the rugs and the closed shutters, the living room was icy. The white marble walls, while wonderful during the hot season, sucked all the heat from the air throughout the cold season. I imagined the room's warmth following the stone's green veins and escaping outside.

Dax Greenblade, my friend, tugged his tunic down. Tall and lean, his physique matched a typical Greenblade Clan member. He reminded me of a blade of grass, including a sharp edge—his tongue.

"Obviously you have no ability to move objects, so let's try fire. Even a baby can light a fire!" Dax placed a candle on the table.

"A baby? Now you're really exaggerating. Again." A person's ability to access the power source and perform magic manifested at puberty.

"Details. Details." Dax waved a hand as if shooing a fly. "Now concentrate on lighting this candle."

I cocked an eyebrow at him. So far, all my efforts on inanimate items were for naught. I could heal my friend's body, hear his thoughts and even see his soul, but when I reached for a thread of magic and tried to use it to move a chair, nothing happened.

Dax held up three tan fingers. "Three reasons why you should be able to do this. One, you're powerful. Two, you're tenacious. And three, you've beat Ferde, the Soulstealer."

Who had escaped, and was free to start another soul-stealing spree. "Reminding me of Ferde is helping me how…?"

"It's *supposed* to be a pep talk. Do you want me to list all the heroic deeds you've—"

"No. Let's get on with the lesson." The last thing I wanted was to hear Dax recite the latest gossip. The news about my being a Soulfinder had spread through the Magician's Keep like dandelion seeds carried by a strong wind. And I still couldn't think about the title without a cringe of doubt, worry and fear touching my heart.

I pushed all distracting thoughts aside and connected to the power source. The power blanketed the world, but only magicians could pull threads of magic from it to use. I gathered a strand to me and directed it to the candle, willing a flame to form.

Nothing.

"Try harder," Dax said.

Increasing the power, I aimed again.

Behind the candle, Dax's face turned red and he sputtered as if suppressing a cough. A flash seared my eyes as the wick ignited.

"That's rude." His outraged expression was comical.

"You wanted it lit."

"Yeah, but I didn't want to do it for you!" He glanced around the room as if seeking the patience to deal with an unruly child. "Zaltanas and their weird powers, forcing *me* to light the candle. Pah! To think I wanted to live vicariously through your adventures."

"Watch what you say about my clan. Or I'll…" I cast about for a good threat.

"You'll what?"

"I'll tell Second Magician where you disappear to every time he pulls one of those old books off his shelf." Bain was Dax's mentor, and, while the Second Magician delighted in ancient history, Dax would rather learn the newest dance steps.

"Okay, okay. You win and you've proved your point. No ability to light a fire. I'll stick to translating ancient languages."

Dax made a dour face. "And you stick to finding souls." He teased, but I sensed an undercurrent to his words.

His uneasiness over my abilities was for excellent reasons. The last Soulfinder was born in Sitia about a hundred and fifty years ago. During his short life, he had turned his enemies into mindless slaves and almost succeeded in his quest to rule the country. Most Sitians didn't react well to the news about another Soulfinder.

The awkward moment passed as a mischievous glint lit Dax's bottle-green eyes. "I'd better go. I have to study. We have a history test tomorrow. Remember?"

I groaned, thinking of the large tome waiting for me.

"Your knowledge of Sitian history is also pathetic."

"Two reasons." I held up my fingers. "One, Ferde Daviian. Two, the Sitian Council."

Dax gestured with his hand.

Before he could say anything, I said, "I know. Details, details."

He smiled and wrapped his cloak around him, letting in a gust of arctic wind as he left. The flames in the hearth pulsed for a moment before settling. I drew closer, warming my hands over the fire. My thoughts returned to those two reasons.

Ferde was a member of the unsanctioned Daviian Clan, who were a renegade group of the Sandseed Clan. The Daviians wanted more from life than wandering the Avibian Plains and telling stories. On a power quest, Ferde had kidnapped and tortured twelve girls to steal their souls and increase his magical power. Valek and I had stopped him before he could complete his quest.

An ache for Valek pumped in my heart. I touched his butterfly pendant hanging from my neck. He had returned to Ixia a month ago, but I missed him more each day. Perhaps I should get myself into a life-threatening situation. He had a knack for showing up when I most needed him.

Unfortunately, those times were fraught with danger and there hadn't been many chances to just be with each other. I longed to be assigned a boring diplomatic mission to Ixia.

The Sitian Council wouldn't approve the trip until they decided what to do with me. Eleven clan leaders and four Master Magicians comprised the Council, and they had argued about my new role of Soulfinder all this past month. Of the four Masters, Irys Jewelrose, Fourth Magician, was my strongest supporter and Roze Featherstone, First Magician, was my strongest detractor.

I stared at the fire, following the dance of flames along the logs. My thoughts lingered on Roze. The randomness of the blaze stopped. The flames moved with a purpose, divided and gestured as if on a stage.

Odd. I blinked. Instead of returning to normal, the blaze grew until it filled my vision and blocked out the rest of the room. The bright patterns of color stabbed my eyes. I closed them, but the image remained. Apprehension rolled along my skin. Despite my strong mental barrier, a magician wove magic around me.

Caught, I watched as the fire scene transformed into a lifelike picture of me. Flame Me bent over a prone body. A soul rose from the body, which I then inhaled. The soulless body stood and Flame Me pointed to another figure. Turning, the body stalked the new person and then strangled him.

Alarmed, I tried to stop the fire vision to no avail. I was forced to observe myself make more soulless people, who all went on a massive killing spree. An opposing army attacked. Fire swords flashed. Flames of blood splattered. I would have been impressed with the magician's level of artistic detail if I hadn't been horrified by the blazing carnage.

In time, my army was extinguished and I was caught in a net of fire. Flame Me was dragged, chained to a post and doused with oil.

I snapped back to my body. Standing next to the hearth, I still felt the web of magic around me. It contracted and tiny flames erupted on my clothes.

And spread.

I couldn't stop the advance with my power. Cursing my lack of fire skill, I wondered why I didn't possess this magical talent.

An answer echoed in my mind. *Because we need a way to kill you.*

I stumbled away from the blaze. Sweat poured down my back as the sound of sizzling blood vibrated in my ears. All moisture fled my mouth and my heart cooked in my chest. The hot air seared my throat. The smell of charred flesh filled my nose and my stomach heaved. Pain assaulted every inch of my skin.

No air to scream.

I rolled around the floor, trying to smother the fire.

I burned.

The magical attack stopped, releasing me from the torment. I dropped to the floor and breathed in the cool air.

"Yelena, what happened?" Irys touched an icy hand to my forehead. "Are you all right?"

My mentor and friend peered down at me. Concern lined her face and filled her emerald eyes.

"I'm fine." My voice croaked, setting off a coughing fit. Irys helped me sit up.

"Look at your clothes. Did you set yourself on fire?"

Black soot streaked the fabric and burn holes peppered my sleeves and skirt/pants. Beyond repair, I would have to ask my cousin, Nutty, to sew me another set. I sighed. I should just order a hundred of the cotton tunics and skirt/pants from her to save time. Events, including magical attacks, conspired to keep my life interesting.

"A magician sent me a message through the fire," I explained. Even though I knew Roze possessed the strongest magic in Sitia, and could bypass my mental defenses, I didn't want to accuse her without proof.

Before Irys could question me further, I asked, "How did the Council session go?" I hadn't been allowed to attend. Although the rainy weather wasn't conducive for walking to the Council Hall, it still rankled.

The Council wanted me well-versed in all the issues they dealt with on a daily basis as part of my training to be a Liaison between them and the Territory of Ixia. My training as a Soulfinder, though, remained a subject the Council hadn't agreed on. According to Irys's theory, my reluctance to begin learning could be the cause of the Council's indecision. I thought they worried I would follow the same path as the Soulfinder from long ago once I discovered the extent of my powers.

"The session…" Her lips twisted in a wry smile. "Good and bad. The Council has agreed to support your training." She paused.

I steeled myself for the next bit of news.

"Roze was…upset about the decision."

"Upset?"

"Fiercely opposed."

At least now I knew the motive behind my fire message.

"She still thinks you're a threat. So the Council has agreed to let Roze train you."

I scrambled to my feet. "No."

"It's the only way."

I bit back a reply. There were other options. There had to be. I was in the Magician's Keep, surrounded by magicians of various skill levels. There had to be another who could work with me. "What about you or Bain?"

"They wanted a mentor who was impartial. Out of the four Masters, that left Roze."

"But she's not—"

"I know. This could be beneficial. Working with Roze, you'll be able to convince her you're not out to rule the country. She'll understand your desire to help both Sitia and Ixia."

My doubtful expression remained.

"She doesn't like you, but her passion for keeping Sitia a safe and free place to live will override any personal feelings."

Irys handed me a scroll, stopping my sarcastic comment on Roze's personal feelings. "This arrived during the Council session."

I opened the message. In tight-printed letters was an order from Moon Man. It read, *Yelena, I have found what you seek. Come.*

2

THE MESSAGE I HELD WAS typical for Moon Man, my Sandseed Story Weaver and friend. Cryptic and vague. I imagined he had written the note with a devilish grin on his face. As my Story Weaver, he knew I sought many things. Knowledge about Soulfinders and finding a balance between Sitia and Ixia resided at the top of my list. A quiet vacation would be nice, too, but I felt certain he referred to Ferde.

Ferde Daviian, the Soulstealer, and killer of eleven girls had escaped from the Magician's Keep cells with Cahil Ixia's help. After the Council failed to recapture him, they debated for an entire month about how to find them both.

My frustration mounted with every delay. Ferde was weak from when I had pulled the souls—his source of magical power—from him during our fight. But all it would take was another girl's murder for him to regain some of his strength. So far, no one had been reported missing, but the knowledge that he remained free clawed at my heart.

To avoid imagining the horror Ferde might cause, I focused

on the message in my hand. Moon Man hadn't specified to come alone, but I dismissed the notion to tell the Council as soon as the thought formed in my mind. By the time they decided what to do, Ferde would be long gone. I would go without informing them. Irys would call it my rush-into-a-situation-and-hope-for-the-best method. With only a few minor mishaps, it had worked in the past. And at this point, rushing off held more appeal.

Irys had moved away when I unrolled the message, but, by the way she held herself so still, I knew she was curious. I told her about the note.

"We should inform the Council," she said.

"So they could do what? Debate every possible issue for another month? The message invited me. If I need your help, I'll send for you." I sensed her resolve softening.

"You should not go alone."

"Fine. I'll take Leif with me."

After a moment's hesitation, Irys agreed. As a Council member, she wasn't happy about it, but she had learned to trust my judgment.

My brother, Leif, would probably be as glad as I was to get away from both the Keep and the Citadel. Roze Featherstone's growing animosity toward me put Leif in a difficult situation. Apprenticed to Roze while training at the Magician's Keep, he had become one of her aides upon graduation. His magical skill of sensing someone's emotions helped Roze determine a person's guilt in a crime, and his magic also aided victims in remembering details about what had happened to them.

Leif's first reaction to my reappearance in Sitia after a fourteen-year absence had been immediate hatred. He had convinced himself that my kidnapping to the Territory of Ixia had been done to spite him and my return from the north had been an Ixian plot to spy on Sitia.

"At least we should tell the Master Magicians about Moon Man's message," Irys said. "I'm sure Roze would like to know when she can begin your training."

I frowned at her, and considered telling her about Roze's petty fire attack. No. I would deal with Roze on my own. Unfortunately, I would have plenty of time with her.

"We're having a Masters meeting at the administration building this afternoon. It will be the perfect time to inform them about your plans."

I scowled, but she remained steadfast.

"Good. I'll see you later," she said.

Irys sailed out of the tower before I could voice my protest. I could still reach her with my mind, though. Our minds always remained linked. The connection was as if we both stood in the same room. We each had our own private thoughts, but if I "spoke" to Irys, she would hear me. If she did probe into my deeper thoughts and memories, it would be considered a breach in the magician's Ethical Code.

My horse, Kiki, and I shared the same connection. A mental call to Kiki was all that was needed for her to "hear" me. Communicating with Leif or my friend Dax proved more difficult; I had to consciously pull power and seek them. And, once found, they had to allow me access through their mental defenses and into their thoughts.

Although I possessed the ability to take a shortcut to their thoughts and emotions through their souls, the Sitians considered the skill a breach of the Ethical Code. I had scared Roze by using it to protect myself against her. Even with all her power, she couldn't stop me from touching her essence.

Anxiety rolled in my stomach. My new title of Soulfinder didn't sit well with me, either. I shied away from that line of speculation as I wrapped my cloak around me before leaving the tower.

On my way across the Keep's campus, my attention returned to my musings about mental communication. My link with Valek couldn't be considered a magical connection. To me, Valek's mind was unreachable, but he had the uncanny ability to know when I needed him and *he* would connect with me. He had saved my life many times through that bond.

Turning Valek's snake bracelet around my wrist, I pondered our relationship until a biting wind laced with icy needles drove away all warm thoughts about him. The cold season had descended on northern Sitia with a vengeance. I shuffled through slushy puddles and shielded my face from the sleet. The Keep's white marble buildings were splattered with mud and looked gray in the weak light, reflecting the miserable day with perfection.

Spending most of my twenty-one years in northern Ixia, I had endured this type of weather for only a few days during the cooling season. Then the cold air would drive the dampness away. But, according to Irys, this horrid mess was a typical Sitian day during the cold season, and snow was a rare event that seldom lasted more than a night.

I trudged toward the Keep's administration building, ignoring the hostile stares from the students who hurried between classes. One of the results of capturing Ferde had been the immediate change in my status from an apprentice of the Keep to a Magician's Aide. Since Irys and I had agreed to a partnership, she offered to share her tower. I had accepted with relief, glad to be away from the cold censure of my fellow students.

Their scorn was nothing in comparison to Roze's fury when I entered the Masters' meeting room. I braced myself for her outburst, but Irys jumped from her seat at the long table and explained why I had come.

"...note from a Sandseed Story Weaver," Irys said. "He may have located Ferde and Cahil."

The corners of Roze's mouth pulled down with disdain. "Impossible. Crossing the Avibian Plains to return to his clan in the Daviian Plateau would be suicide. And it's too obvious. Cahil is probably taking Ferde to either the Stormdance or the Bloodgood lands. Cahil has many supporters there."

Roze had been Cahil's champion in the Council. Cahil had been raised by soldiers who had fled the takeover in Ixia. They convinced Cahil that he was the nephew of the dead King of Ixia and should inherit the throne. He had worked hard to gain supporters and attempted to build an army to defeat the Commander of Ixia. However, once he discovered he was really born to a common soldier, he rescued Ferde and disappeared.

Roze had encouraged Cahil. They held the same belief that it was just a matter of time before Commander Ambrose set his sights on conquering Sitia.

"Cahil could bypass the plains to get to the plateau," Zitora Cowan, Third Magician, offered. Her honey-brown eyes held concern, but as the youngest of the four Master Magicians her suggestions tended to be ignored by the others.

"Then how would this Moon Man know? The Sandseeds don't venture out of the plains unless it's absolutely necessary," Roze said.

"That's what they want us to believe," Irys said. "I wouldn't put it past them to have a few scouts around."

"Either way," Bain Bloodgood, Second Magician, said, "we must consider all options. Obvious or not, someone needs to confirm that Cahil and Ferde are not in the plateau." With his white hair and flowing robes, Bain's appearance matched what I had assumed to be a traditional magician's uniform. Wisdom radiated from his wrinkled face.

"I'm going," I declared.

"We should send soldiers with her," Zitora said.

"Leif should go," Bain added. "As cousins of the Sandseed, Yelena and Leif will be welcomed in the plains."

Roze ran her slender fingers along the short white strands of her hair and frowned, appearing to be deep in thought. With the colder temperatures, Roze had stopped wearing the sleeveless dresses she preferred and exchanged them for long-sleeved gowns. The deep navy hue of the garment absorbed the light and almost matched her dark skin. Moon Man had the same skin tone, and I wondered what color his hair would be if he hadn't shaved it off.

"I'm not sending anyone," Roze finally said. "It's a waste of time and resources."

"I'm going. I don't need your permission." I stood, preparing to leave.

"You need my permission to exit the Keep," Roze said. "This is *my* domain. I'm in charge of all magicians, including you, Soulfinder." Her hands smacked her chair's arms. "If *I* had control of the Council, you would be taken to the Keep's cells to await execution. No good has ever come from a Soulfinder."

The other Masters gaped at Roze in shock. She remained incensed. "Just look at our history. Every Soulfinder has craved power. Magical power. Political power. Power over people's souls. Yelena will be no different. Sure now she plays at being a Liaison and has agreed to my training. It's only a matter of time. Already…" Roze gestured to the doorway. "Already she wants to run off before I can begin lesson one."

Her words echoed through the stunned silence. Roze glanced around at their horrified expressions and smoothed the wrinkles from her gown. Her dislike of me was well-known, but this time she had gone too far.

"Roze, that was quite—"

She raised her hand, stopping Bain from the rest of his lecture. "You know the history. You have been warned many, many times, so I will say no more about it." She rose from her seat. Towering a good seven inches above me, she peered down. "Go, then. Take Leif with you. Consider it your first lesson. A lesson in futility. When you return, you'll be mine."

Roze made to leave, but I caught a thread of her thoughts in my mind.

…*should keep her occupied and out of my way*.

Roze paused before she exited. Looking over her shoulder, she gave me a pointed stare. *Keep out of Sitia's affairs. And you might be the only Soulfinder in history to live past the age of twenty-five.*

Go take another look at your history books, Roze, I said. *The demise of a Soulfinder is always reported along with the death of a Master Magician.*

Roze ignored me as she left the meeting room, ending the session.

* * *

I went to find Leif. His quarters were near the apprentice's wing on the east side of the Keep's campus. He lived in the Magician's building, which housed those who had graduated from the Keep and were now either teaching new students or working as aides to the Master Magicians.

The rest of the magicians who had also completed the curriculum were assigned to different towns to serve the citizens of Sitia. The Council tried to have a healer in every town, but the magicians with rare powers—like the ability to read ancient languages or find lost items—moved from place to place as needed.

Magicians with strong powers took the Master-level test before leaving the Keep. In the past twenty years, only Zitora had passed, bringing the number of Masters to four. In Sitia's history, there never had been more than four Masters at one time.

Irys thought a Soulfinder could be strong enough to take the Master's test. I disagreed. They already had the maximum, and I lacked the basic magical skills of lighting fires and moving objects—skills all the Masters possessed.

Besides, being a Soulfinder was bad enough, having to endure and fail the Master test would be too much to bear. Or so I guessed. The rumors about the test sounded horrific.

Before I even reached Leif's door, it swung open and my brother stuck his head out. The rain soaked his short black hair in an instant. I shooed him back as I hurried into his living room, dripping muddy slush onto his clean floor.

His apartment was tidy and sparsely furnished. The only hint of his personality could be gleaned from the few paintings that decorated the room. A detailed rendering of a rare Ylang-Ylang flower indigenous to the Illiais Jungle, a painting of a strangler fig suffocating a dying mahogany tree and a picture of a tree leopard crouched on a branch hung on his walls.

Leif scanned my bedraggled appearance with resignation. His jade-colored eyes were the only feature that matched my own. His stocky body and square jaw were the complete opposite of my oval face and thin build.

"It can't be good news," Leif said. "I'd doubt you would brave the weather just to say hello."

"You opened the door before I could knock," I said. "You must know something's up."

Leif wiped the rain from his face. "I smelled you coming."

"Smelled?"

"You reek of Lavender. Do you bathe in Mother's perfume or just wash your cloak with it?" he teased.

"How mundane. I was thinking of something a little more magical."

"Why waste the energy on using magic when you don't have to? Although…"

Leif's eyes grew distant and I felt the slight tingle of power being pulled.

"Apprehension. Excitement. Annoyance. Anger," Leif said. "I take it the Council hasn't voted to make you Queen of Sitia yet?"

When I didn't answer, he said, "Don't worry, little sister, you're still the princess of our family. We both know Mother and Father love you best."

His words held an edge, and I remembered it hadn't been long since he had wanted to see me dead.

"Esau and Perl love us equally. You really do need me around to correct your misconceptions. I've proved you wrong before. I can do it again."

Leif put his hands on his hips and raised one dubious eyebrow.

"You said I was afraid to come back to the Keep. Well—" I spread my arms wide, flinging drops of water onto Leif's green tunic "—here I am."

"You are here. I'll grant you that. But are you unafraid?"

"I already have a mother and a Story Weaver. *Your* job is to be the annoying older brother. Stick to what you know."

"Ohhh. I've hit a nerve."

"I don't want to argue with you. Here." I pulled Moon Man's note from my cloak's pocket and handed it to him.

He unfolded the damp paper, scanning the message. "Ferde," he said, coming to the same conclusion. "Have you told the Council?"

"No. The Masters know." I filled Leif in on what had happened in the meeting room, omitting my "exchange" with Roze Featherstone.

Leif's wide shoulders drooped. After a long moment, he said, "Master Featherstone doesn't believe Ferde and Cahil are going to the Daviian Plateau. She doesn't trust me anymore."

"You don't know that for—"

"She thinks Cahil is headed in another direction. Normally she would send me to determine his location and send for her. Together, we would confront him. Now I get assigned the wild-valmur chase."

"Valmur?" It took me a moment to connect the name with the small, long-tailed creature that lived in the jungle.

"Remember? We used to chase them through the trees. They were so fast and quick, we never caught one. But sit down and hold a piece of sap candy and they'll jump right into your lap and follow you around all day."

When I failed to respond, Leif cringed with guilt. "That must have been after…"

After I had been kidnapped and taken to Ixia. Although I could imagine a young Leif scampering through the jungle's canopy after a fleet-footed valmur.

The Zaltana Clan's homestead had been built high in the tree branches, and my father had joked that the children learned to climb before they could walk.

"Roze could be wrong about Cahil's intentions. So pack some of that sap candy. We might need it," I said.

Leif shivered. "At least it will be warmer in the plains, and the plateau is farther south."

I left Leif's quarters, heading to my tower to pack some supplies. The sleet blew sideways and tiny daggers of ice stung my face as I hurried through the storm. Irys was waiting for me in the receiving room just past the oversize tower entrance. The flames in the hearth pulsed with the rush of cold air slipping around the doors as I fought to close them against the wind.

I hustled to the fire and held my hands out. The prospect of traveling in such weather was unappealing.

"Does Leif know how to light fires?" I asked Irys.

"I think so. But no matter how skilled he is, wet wood won't ignite."

"Great," I muttered. Steam floated from my soaked cloak.

I draped the soggy garment around a chair then dragged it closer to the fire.

"When are you leaving?" Irys asked.

"Right away." My stomach grumbled and I realized I had missed lunch. I sighed, knowing dinner would probably be a cold slice of cheese and mushy bread.

"I'm meeting Leif in the barn. Oh snake spit!" I remembered a couple of commitments.

"Irys, can you tell Gelsi and Dax I'll start their training when I get back?"

"What training? Not magic—"

"No, no. Self-defense training." I pointed to my bow. The five-foot-long staff of ebony wood was still threaded through its holder on my backpack. Drops of water beaded and gleamed on the weapon.

I pulled it free, feeling the solid weight of the staff in my hands. Underneath the ebony surface of the bow was a gold-colored wood. Pictures of me as a child, of the jungle, my family, and so on had been etched into the wood. Even Kiki's loving eyes had been included in the story of my life. The bow moved smoothly in my hands. A gift from a master crafts-woman of the Sandseed Clan who had also raised Kiki.

"And Bain knows that you won't be at his morning lesson," Irys said. "But he said—"

"Don't tell me he assigned homework," I pleaded. Just thinking about lugging the heavy history tome made my back hurt.

Irys smiled. "He said that he would help you catch up on your studies when you return."

Relieved, I picked up my pack, sorting the contents to see what other supplies we would need.

"Anything else?" Irys asked.

"No. What are you going to tell the Council?" I asked.

"That Roze has assigned you to learn about your magic from the Story Weavers. The first documented Soulfinder in Sitia was a Sandseed. Did you know that?"

"No." I was surprised but shouldn't have been. After all, what I knew about Soulfinders wouldn't fill a page in one of Master Bain's history books.

When I finished packing, I said goodbye to Irys and muscled my way through the wind to the dining hall. The kitchen staff always had a supply of travel rations on hand for the magicians. I grabbed enough food to last us a week.

As I drew closer to the stables, I could see a few brave horse heads poking out of their stalls. Kiki's copper-and-white face was unmistakable even in the murky half-light.

She nickered in greeting and I opened my mind to her.

We go? she asked.

Yes. I'm sorry to take you out on such a horrible day, I said.

Not bad with Lavender Lady.

Lavender Lady was the name the horses had given me. They named the people around them just like we would name a pet. I had to smile, though, remembering Leif's comment about my bathing in the pungent herb.

Lavender smell like… Kiki didn't have the words to describe her emotions. A mental image of a bushy blue-gray lavender plant with its long purple cluster of flowers formed in Kiki's mind. Feelings of contentment and security accompanied the image.

The main corridor of the stable echoed as if empty despite the pile of feed bags nearby. The thick supporting beams of the building stood like soldiers between the stalls and the end of the row disappeared into the gloom.

Leif? I asked Kiki.

Sad Man in tack room, Kiki said.

Thanks. I ambled toward the back of the barn, inhaling the familiar aroma of leather and saddle soap. The dry smell of straw scratched my throat and clung to the earthy scent of manure.

Tracker, too.

Who?

But before Kiki could answer I spotted Captain Marrok in the tack room with Leif. The sharp tip of Marrok's sword was aimed at Leif's chest.

3

"STAY BACK, YELENA," Marrok ordered. "Answer me, Leif."

Leif's face had paled, but his jaw was set in a stubborn line. His gaze met mine, questioning.

"What do you want, Marrok?" I asked.

The bruises on Marrok's face had faded, but his right eye was still puffy and raw despite Healer Hayes's efforts to repair his broken cheekbone.

"I want to find Cahil," Marrok said.

"We *all* want to find him. Why are you threatening *my* brother?" I used a stern tone to remind Marrok that he now dealt with me. Having an infamous reputation had a few advantages.

Marrok looked at me. "He works with First Magician. She's in charge of the search. If she has any clue as to where to find Cahil, she'll send Leif." He gestured to the bridles in Leif's hands. "On a day like today, he's not going to the market or out for a pleasure ride. But he won't tell me where he's going."

It continued to amaze me just how fast news and gossip traveled through the Keep's guards.

"Did you ask him before or after you pulled your sword?"

The tip of Marrok's blade wavered. "Why does it matter?" he asked.

"Because most people are more willing to cooperate if they don't have a weapon pointed at their chest." Realizing that Marrok was a career soldier who did most of his talking with his sword, I switched tactics.

"Why didn't you plan to follow Leif?" Marrok's tracking abilities had impressed the horses so much that they had given him the name Tracker.

Marrok touched his cheek and winced. I could guess his thoughts. Marrok had followed Cahil with the utmost loyalty, but Cahil had beaten and tortured him to find out the truth about his common heritage, leaving Marrok for dead.

The soldier sheathed his sword in one quick motion as if he had made a decision. "I can't follow Leif. He would sense me with his magic and confuse my mind."

"I can't do that," Leif said.

"Truly?" Marrok rested his hand near his sword, considering.

"But I can," I said.

Marrok's attention snapped back to me.

"Marrok, you're hardly fit for travel. And I can't let you kill Cahil. The Sitian Council wants to talk to him first." *I* wanted to talk to him.

"I don't seek revenge," Marrok said.

"Then what do you want?"

"To help." Marrok gripped the hilt of his weapon.

"What?" Leif and I said at the same time.

"Sitia *needs* Cahil. Only the Council and the Masters know he doesn't have royal blood. Ixia is a real threat to Sitia's way of life. Sitia needs a figurehead to rally behind. Someone to lead them into battle."

"But he aided in Ferde's escape," I said. "And Ferde could be torturing and raping another girl as we speak!"

"Cahil was just confused and overwhelmed by learning the truth of his birth. I raised him. I know him better than anyone. He probably already regrets his rashness. Ferde is most likely dead. If I get a chance to talk to Cahil, I'm positive he would come back without a fight, and we can work this out with the Council."

Power brushed me.

"He's sincere about his intentions," Leif said.

But what about Cahil's intentions? I had seen him be ruthless and opportunistic in his quest to build an army, but never rash. However, I had only known him for two seasons. I considered using magic to see Marrok's memories of Cahil, but that would be a breach in the magician's Ethical Code unless he gave me his consent. So I asked for it.

"Go ahead," Marrok said, meeting my gaze.

Pain lingered in his blue-gray eyes. His short gray hair had turned completely white since Cahil's attack.

Granting me permission was enough to convince me of his sincerity, but despite his good intentions he still wanted to build an army and attack Ixia. And that ran counter to what I believed. Ixia and Sitia just needed to understand each other and work together. A war would help no one.

Do I leave Marrok here to influence the Council toward an attack, or take him with me? His skills as a tracker would be an added benefit.

"If I allow you to come with us, you must obey *all* my orders. Agreed?" I asked.

Marrok straightened as if he stood in a military formation. "Yes, sir."

"Are you strong enough to ride?"

"Yes, but I don't have a horse."

"That's all right. I'll find you a Sandseed horse. All you'll need to do is hold on." I grinned, thinking of Kiki's special gust-of-wind gait.

Leif laughed and his body relaxed with the release of the tension. "Good luck convincing the Stable Master to loan you his horse."

"What do you mean?" I asked.

"Garnet is the only other horse in the Keep's stables bred by the Sandseeds."

I wilted in defeat just thinking about the stubborn, cranky Stable Master. Now what? No other horse breed would be able to keep up with us.

Honey, Kiki said in my mind.

Honey?

Avibian honey. Chief Man love honey.

Which meant, if I offered to bring some Avibian honey back for the Stable Master, he might lend me his horse.

We left the Citadel through the south gate and headed down the valley road. Farm fields peppered with corn stubble and wagon ruts swept out from the right side of the road. The Avibian Plains dominated the left side.

The long grasses of the plains had turned from yellow and red to brown in the cold weather. The rains created extensive puddles, transforming the rolling landscape into a marshland and scenting the air with a damp smell of earthy decay.

Leif rode Rusalka, and Marrok had a death grip on Garnet's reins. His nervousness affected the tall horse, who jittered to the side at every noise.

Kiki slowed so I could talk to him. "Marrok, relax. I'm the one who promised to bring back a case of Avibian honey plus clean the Stable Master's tack for three weeks."

He barked out a laugh but kept his tight grip.

Time to switch tactics. I reached for the blanket of power hovering over the world and pulled a thread of magic, linking my mind with Garnet's. The horse missed Chief Man and didn't like this stranger on his back, but he settled when I showed him our destination.

Home, Garnet agreed. He wanted to go. *Pain.*

Marrok's rigid hold hurt Garnet's mouth, and I knew Marrok wouldn't relax even if I threatened to leave him behind. Sighing, I made light contact with Marrok's mind. His worry and fear focused more on Cahil than on himself. His apprehension came from not feeling in control of the powerful horse underneath him despite the fact that he held Garnet's reins. And also from not being in charge of the situation, having to take orders from *her.*

A dark undercurrent to his thoughts about me pulled a warning bell in my mind, and I would have liked to explore deeper. He had given me permission to see his memories of Cahil, but he hadn't given me carte blanche to probe. Instead, I sent him some calming thoughts. Even though he couldn't hear my words he should be able to react to the soothing tone.

After a while, Marrok no longer held himself so rigid, and

his body moved with Garnet's motion. When Garnet felt comfortable, Kiki turned east into the plains. Mud splashed from her hooves as she increased her pace. I gave Leif and Marrok the signal to let the horses have control.

Please find Moon Man. Fast, I said to Kiki.

With a slight hop, she broke into her gust-of-wind gait. Rusalka and Garnet followed. I felt carried by a river of air. The plains blurred under Kiki's hooves at a rate about twice a full-speed gallop.

Only Sandseed horses could achieve this gait, and only when they rode in the Avibian Plains. It had to be a magical skill, but I couldn't tell if Kiki pulled power. I would have to ask Moon Man about it when we found him.

The plains encompassed a massive section of eastern Sitia. Located to the southeast of the Citadel, it stretched all the way to the base of the Emerald Mountains in the east, and down to the Daviian Plateau to the south.

On a normal horse, it took about five to seven days to cross the plains. The Sandseeds were the only clan to live within the borders, and their Story Weavers had shielded their lands with a powerful protective magic. Any stranger who ventured into the plains without Sandseed permission became lost. The magic would confuse the stranger's mind and he would travel in circles until he either stumbled out of the plains or ran out of water and died.

Magicians with strong powers could travel without being affected by the magic, but the Story Weavers always knew when someone crossed into their land. As distant cousins of the Sandseeds, the Zaltana Clan members could also travel the plains unharmed. The other clans avoided the area altogether.

Since Marrok rode on a Sandseed horse the protection didn't attack him and we were able to ride all night. Kiki finally stopped for a rest at sunrise.

While Leif collected firewood, I rubbed the horses down and fed them. Marrok helped Leif, but I could see exhaustion etched in his pale face.

The rain and sleet had slowed during the night, but gray clouds sealed the sky. Our campsite had plenty of grass for the horses. It was on a high spot in the plains next to a rocky outcropping with a few scrub trees growing nearby, and was a solid place for us to stand without sinking ankle-deep into the mud.

Our cloaks were soaked, so I tied my rope between two trees to hang the wet garments. Leif and Marrok found a few dry branches. Making a tent of the twigs, Leif stared at the wood and small flames sprang to life.

"Show-off," I said.

He smiled as he filled a pot with water for tea. "You're jealous."

"You're right. I am." I growled in frustration. Leif and I were both born to the same parents, yet we had different magical powers. Our father, Esau, had no overt magic, just a flair for finding and using the plants and trees of the jungle for food, medicines and his inventions. Perl, our mother, could only sense if a person had magical abilities.

So how did Leif get the magical abilities to light fires and sense a person's life force while I could affect their souls? With my magic, I could force Leif to light a fire, but couldn't do it on my own. I wondered if anyone in Sitian history had studied the relationship between magic and birth parents. Bain Bloodgood, Second Magician, would probably know. He owned a copy of almost every book in Sitia.

Marrok fell asleep as soon as we finished eating our break-fast of bread and cheese. Leif and I remained by the fire.

"Did you put something in his tea?" I asked.

"Some fiddlewood bark to help him heal."

Wrinkles and scars lined Marrok's face. Through the yellowed bruises along his jaw, I spotted some white stubble. His swollen eye oozed blood and tears. Red streaks painted his right cheek. Healer Hayes hadn't allowed me to help with Marrok's recovery. He had only let me assist with minor injuries. Another who feared my powers.

I touched Marrok's forehead. His skin felt hot and dry. The fetid smell of rotten flesh emanated from him. I reached for the power source and felt the Sandseeds' protective magic watching me for signs of threat. Gathering magic, I projected a thread to him, revealing the muscles and bone underneath Marrok's skin. His injuries pulsed with a red light. His cheek-bone had been shattered and some bone fragments had gotten into his eye, affecting his vision. Small dark growths of an in-fection dotted the ruined area.

I concentrated on the injury until his pain transferred to my own face. A sharp needle of pain stabbed my right eye as my vision dulled and tears welled. Curling into a ball, I pushed against the onslaught, channeling the magic from the power source through my body. The flow chugged, and I strained. All of a sudden the current of magic moved with ease as if someone had removed a beaver's dam, washing away the pain. Relief swept through me. I relaxed.

"Do you think that was a good idea?" Leif asked when I opened my eyes.

"The wound was infected."

"But you used all your energy."

"I…" I sat up, feeling tired but not exhausted. "I—"

"Had help," a voice snapped out of nowhere.

Leif jerked upright in surprise, but I recognized the deep masculine tone. Moon Man appeared next to the fire as if he had formed from the rising heat and ashes. His bald head gleamed in the sunlight.

In deference to the chill, Moon Man wore a long-sleeved tan tunic and dark brown pants that matched the color of his skin, but no shoes.

"No paint?" I asked Moon Man. The first time I had met him he had coalesced out of a beam of moonlight covered only with indigo dye. He had claimed to be my Story Weaver and proceeded to show me my life's story and unlocked my childhood memories. Six years of living with my mother, father and brother had been suppressed by a magician named Mogkan so I wouldn't long for my family after Mogkan had kidnapped me.

Moon Man smiled. "I did not have time to cover my skin. And it is a good thing I came when I did." His tone conveyed his displeasure. "Or you would have spent all your strength."

"Not all," I countered, sounding like a belligerent child.

"Have you become an all-powerful Soulfinder already?" He widened his eyes in mock amazement. "I will bow down before you, Oh Great One." He bent at the waist.

"All right, enough," I said, laughing. "I should have thought it through before healing Marrok. Happy now?"

He sighed dramatically. "I would be content if I thought you learned a lesson and would not do it again. However, I am well aware that you will continue to rush right into situations. It is weaved into your life's pattern. There is no hope for you."

"Is that why you sent for me? To tell me I'm hopeless?"

Moon Man sobered. "I wish. We had heard that the Soulstealer had escaped from the Magician's Keep with Cahil's help. One of our Story Weavers scouting in the Daviian Plateau sensed a stranger traveling with one of the Vermin."

"Are Cahil and Ferde in the plateau?" Leif asked.

"We think so, but we want Yelena to identify the Soulstealer."

"Why?" I asked. The Sandseeds didn't waste time on trials and incarceration. They executed criminals on capture.

However, the Daviian Vermin had been very hard to find, and they had powerful magicians. The Vermin were a group of Sandseed youths who had become discontented with the Sandseed lifestyle of keeping to themselves and limiting contact with the other clans. The Vermin wanted the Sandseed Story Weavers to use their great powers to guide all of Sitia and not just the inhabitants of the plains.

They had broken from the Sandseed Clan and settled in the Daviian Plateau, becoming the Daviian Clan. The plateau's dry and inhospitable soil made farming a nightmare, so the Daviians stole from the Sandseeds, and earned the nickname of Vermin. The Sandseeds also referred to the Vermin's magicians as Warpers, since they used their magic for selfish reasons.

"You need to identify the Soulstealer because he may have harvested more souls, and only you can release those souls before we kill him," Moon Man said with a flat and emotionless voice.

I grabbed his arm. "Have you found any bodies?"

"No. But I am concerned about what we will discover when we raid their camp."

The horror of the last two seasons threatened to overwhelm me. Eleven girls mutilated and raped by Ferde so he could steal their souls and gain more magical power. Valek and I had stopped him before he could collect the final soul. If he had succeeded, Sitia and Ixia would now be his to rule. Instead, I had released all those souls to the sky. To think that he might have started again was unbearable.

"You've found their camp?" Leif asked.

"Yes. We put our lives on hold," Moon Man said. "The warriors of the clan have done a complete sweep of the plateau. We found a large encampment on the southern edge near the border of the Illiais Jungle."

And close to my family. I must have gasped because Moon Man touched my shoulder and squeezed.

"Do not worry about your clan. Every Sandseed warrior is ready to attack if the Vermin show any signs of departing their camp. We will leave when the horses are rested."

I paced around the campfire, knowing I should get some sleep but unable to still my racing thoughts. Leif groomed the horses and Marrok slept. Moon Man reclined next to the fire, staring at the sky.

Marrok woke as the sky darkened. His eye had stopped weeping blood, and the swelling was gone. He probed his cheek with a finger. Amazement lit his face until he spotted Moon Man standing next to him. He jumped to his feet and pulled his sword, brandishing the weapon at the Story Weaver. Even armed, Marrok looked slight next to the muscular Sandseed, who towered six inches over him.

Moon Man laughed. "I see you are feeling better. Come. We have plans to make."

The four of us sat around the fire while Leif made dinner. Marrok settled next to me, and from the corner of my eye I could see that whenever Marrok touch his cheek, he stared at Moon Man with a fearful fascination. And his right hand never strayed far from the hilt of his sword.

"We will leave at dawn," Moon Man said.

"Why does everything have to start at dawn?" I asked. "The horses have good night vision."

"That will give the horses a full day to recover. I will be riding with you on Kiki. She is the strongest. And once we reach the plateau, there will be no rest stops until we join the others."

"And then what?" I asked.

"Then we will attack. You are to stay close to me and the other Story Weavers. The Soulstealer will be protected along with the Warpers. Once we break through the outer guards, then the hard part begins."

"Dealing with the Warpers," I said.

He nodded.

"Can't you move the Void again?" Leif asked.

The Void was a hole in the power blanket where no magic existed. The last time the Sandseeds had uncovered a Vermin hideout, it had been protected by a shield of magic that created an illusion. The camp appeared to be occupied by only a few warriors. When the Sandseeds had moved the Void over the Vermin, the illusion was broken. Unfortunately, the encampment held four times the number of soldiers, and we had been vastly outnumbered.

"They are aware of that trick and will be alerted to our presence if we try to move the power blanket," Moon Man said.

"Then how are you going to beat the Warpers?" I asked, worried. If the Vermin had access to magic it would be a difficult battle.

"All the Sandseed Story Weavers will link together and form a strong magical net that will seize them and prevent them from using their magic. We will hold them long enough for you to find the Soulstealer."

Breaking his silence, Marrok asked, "What about Cahil?"

"He helped the Soulstealer escape. He should be punished," Moon Man said.

"The Council wants to talk to him," I said.

"And then *they* will decide what to do with him," Leif added.

Moon Man shrugged. "He is not a Vermin. I will tell the others not to kill him, but in a large battle it might be hard."

"He's probably with the Daviian leaders," Marrok said.

"Marrok—you and Leif find Cahil and take him north of the fighting and I'll rendezvous with you after the battle."

"Yes, sir," Marrok said.

Leif nodded, but I could see a question in his eyes.

Problem? I asked in his mind.

What if Cahil convinces Marrok not to take him back to the Council? What if they join together and I'm outnumbered?

Good point. I'll ask Moon Man to—

Assign one of my warriors to stay with Leif, Moon Man said.

I jerked in surprise. I hadn't felt Moon Man draw power to link with us.

What else can you do? I asked.

I am not telling you. It would destroy my mysterious Story Weaver persona.

★ ★ ★

The next morning we saddled the horses and made our way south toward the plateau. Even with the weight of two riders, Kiki easily carried us. Stopping only once for a warm dinner and sleep, we reached the border in two days. At sunset on the second day, we stopped to rest the horses at the edge of the plains.

The flat expanse of the plateau stretched to the horizon. A few brown clumps of grass clung to the sunbaked surface. While the plains had a few trees, rolling hills, rocks and sandstone protrusions, the plateau had bristle bushes, coarse sand and a few stunted spine trees.

We had left the cold, cloudy weather behind. The afternoon sun had warmed the land enough for me to take off my cloak, but as the light slipped into the darkness, a cool breeze stirred to life.

Moon Man left to find his scout. Even at this distance from the Vermin camp, it was too risky to make a fire. I shivered as I ate my dinner of hard cheese and stale bread.

Moon Man returned with another Sandseed.

"This is Tauno," Moon Man said. "He will show us the way through the plateau."

I peered at the small man armed with a bow and arrows. Only an inch taller than me, he wore short pants despite the chilly air. His skin had been painted, but in the dim light I couldn't discern the colors.

"We will leave when the moon is a quarter up," Tauno said.

Traveling at night was a good idea, but I wondered what the warriors did during the day. "How do the Sandseeds stay hidden in the plateau?" I asked.

Tauno gestured to his skin. "We blend in. And hide our thoughts behind the Story Weavers' null shield."

I looked at Moon Man.

"A null shield blocks magic," Moon Man explained. "If you were to scan the plateau with your magic, you would not sense any living creature behind the null shield."

"Doesn't using magic to create the shield alert the Vermin?" I asked.

"Not when it is done properly. It was completed before the Story Weavers left the plains."

"What about the Story Weavers behind the shield? Can they use magic?" Leif asked.

"Magic can not penetrate the shield. It does not block our vision or hearing, just protects us from being discovered by magical means."

As we prepared to travel, I thought about what Moon Man had said, and realized that there were many things I still didn't know about magic. Too many. And the thought of learning more with Roze quelled my curiosity.

When the moon had traveled through a quarter of the black sky, Tauno said, "It is time to go."

The muscles along my spine tightened in apprehension as Moon Man settled behind me on Kiki's saddle. What if my lack of magical knowledge caused me to endanger our mission?

No sense worrying about it now. I pulled in a deep breath, steadied my nerves and glanced at my companions. Tauno sat with Marrok on Garnet's back. From the pained expression on Marrok's face, I knew he wasn't happy about sharing his mount with a Sandseed warrior. And to make it worse, Tauno insisted on being in front and holding Garnet's reins.

To stay behind the null shield, our path through the plateau had to be precise. Tauno led us. The soft crunch of the horses' hooves on hard sand was the only sound.

The moon crawled along the sky. At one point I wanted to yell out and urge Kiki into a gallop just to break the tension that pressed around us.

When the blackness in the sky eased in the east, Tauno stopped and dismounted. We ate a quick breakfast and fed the horses. As the day brightened, I saw how well Tauno blended in with the plateau. He had camouflaged himself with the plateau's colors of gray and tan.

"We walk from here," Tauno said. "We will leave the horses. Take only what you need."

The clear sky promised a warm day so I removed my cloak and stowed it in my backpack. Dry air laced with a fine grit blew, scratching at the back of my throat. I decided I needed my switchblade. Strapping the sheath around my right thigh, I removed the weapon and triggered the blade. I treated the tip of the blade with some Curare. The muscle-paralyzing drug would come in handy if Cahil wouldn't cooperate. After I retracted the blade, I positioned the weapon in its holder through a hole in my skirt/pants pocket. I wrapped my long black hair into a bun and used my lock picks to keep the hair in place. Finally, I grabbed my bow.

Dressed for battle, though, didn't mean I was prepared for battle. I hoped I would be able to find Cahil and Ferde and take them without killing anyone. But the grim knowledge that I would kill to save myself formed a knot in my throat.

Tauno scanned our clothes and weapons. Leif's machete hung from his waist. He wore a green tunic and pants. Marrok had strapped his sword onto his belt. The dark brown scabbard matched his pants. I realized that we had all dressed in the colors of the earth, and, while we didn't blend in as well as Tauno, we wouldn't stand out either.

We tied our packs and supplies onto the horses' saddles, then left the horses to graze on what little grass they could find, and walked south. The plateau appeared deserted. The need to search the area with magic crept along my skin, and I tried to ignore the desire. Connecting with the life around me had become almost instinctive and I felt exposed and out of sorts by not knowing what breathed nearby.

Taking a circuitous path, Tauno eventually stopped. He pointed to a cluster of spine trees. "Just beyond that copse is the camp," he whispered.

I searched the plateau. Where was the Sandseed army? The earth undulated as if the sand had liquefied. The waves on the ground grew. I clamped a hand over my mouth to stifle a cry of surprise. Row upon row of Sandseed warriors stood. Camouflaged to match the sand, they had been lying on the ground in front of us and I hadn't noticed them.

Moon Man smiled his amusement at my dismay. "You have been relying on your magical senses and have forgotten about your physical senses."

Before I could respond, we were joined by four Sandseeds. Though they dressed the same as the warriors, these Sandseeds held themselves with authority. They issued orders and power radiated from them. Story Weavers.

A male Story Weaver handed Moon Man a scimitar. His sharp gaze pierced me as he studied my features. "This is the Soulfinder?" Doubt laced his words, but he spoke softly. "She is not what I expected."

"What did you expect?" I asked.

"A large dark-skinned woman. You look like you could not survive a sandstorm let alone find and release a soul."

"It's a good thing you're not my Story Weaver. You're easily distracted by the pattern of the cloth and can't see the quality of the threads."

"Well done," Moon Man said to me. "Reed, show us the camp."

The Story Weaver led us to the trees. Through the spiky needles on the branches, I saw the Daviian camp.

The air shimmered around the camp as if a bubble of heat had gotten trapped near the ground. A large cook fire burned in the central area. Many people scurried about either helping with breakfast or eating it. Tents fanned from the area, extending out until they reached the edge of the plateau.

Squinting in the sunlight, I looked beyond the encampment's border. Just the tops of the trees in the Illiais Jungle were visible. They reminded me of a time when I had stood on a platform built near the peak of the tallest tree in the jungle and had seen the flat expanse of the plateau for the first time. The sheer rock drop-off into the jungle had appeared to be an impossible climb. So why set up camp there? I wondered.

Moon Man leaned next to me. "The camp is an illusion."

"Do you have enough warriors to attack?" I asked, thinking the illusion hid many more Vermin.

"Every one."

"All—" The Sandseeds yelled a battle cry and dashed toward the camp.

Moon Man grabbed my arm, pulling me with him. "Stay with me."

With Leif and Marrok right behind us, we followed the Sandseeds. When the first warriors crossed into the illusion, they disappeared from sight for a moment. The sound of rushing water reached my ears as the chimera dissipated.

I blinked a few times to adjust my vision to what the Daviians had concealed. The central fire remained the same. But instead of many Vermin around the flames, there stood only one man. The rest of the camp was empty.

4

WHEN THE ILLUSION disappeared, so did the expanse of tents and all the Daviians. The lone man standing by the fire collapsed before the Sandseed warriors could reach him.

Evidence that a large army had camped here was imprinted on the ground. Although, by the time the Sandseed leaders restored order to the milling warriors, many of the Daviian tracks had been ruined.

And the only witness had taken poison.

"One of their Warpers," Moon Man said, nudging the corpse with his bare foot. "He held the illusion and killed himself once it broke."

"If you can clear the area, I might be able to tell you where they've gone," Marrok said.

The Sandseed warriors returned to the copse of spine trees. Moon Man and I stayed by the fire as Marrok and Leif circled the camp. Marrok looked for physical evidence while Leif used his magic to smell the intentions of the Daviians.

I projected my mental awareness as far as I could. If I sought a specific person, then I could reach them from far away, but with a general search my magic could only extend about ten miles. I reached no one in the plateau, and the bounty of life in the jungle was too overwhelming to sort out.

When they had finished their circuit, Marrok and Leif returned. Their glum expressions reflected bad news.

"They've been gone for days. The majority of the tracks head east and west," Marrok reported. "But I found some metal spikes with rope fibers in the ground near the edge of the plateau. A few Vermin could have climbed down into the jungle."

I touched Leif's arm. "The Zaltanas?"

"If the Vermin can even find our homestead among the trees, they're still well protected," he said.

"Even from one of the Warpers?" I asked.

Leif blanched.

"Are the ropes still there?" I asked Marrok.

"No. The others must have waited and either cut the rope or taken it along with them," Marrok said.

"Do you know how many went down?" Moon Man asked.

"No."

Leif said, "There were so many scents and emotions mixed together. The need for stealth and urgency predominated. They moved with a purpose and felt confident. The eastern group, though, had the most men and they…" Leif closed his eyes and sniffed the breeze. "I don't know. I need to follow their trail for a while."

Marrok led Leif to the eastern tracks. I asked Kiki and the other horses to come to us. While waiting for them, Moon Man and the other Story Weavers split the warriors into two groups, and sent two scouts, one to the west and the other to the east.

But what about those that went down the rope to the jungle? What about Cahil and Ferde? Were they even with the Daviians? And, if so, which way had they gone?

When the horses arrived, I grabbed my pack off Kiki's saddle. Opening it, I pulled my rope out and headed for the rim of the plateau. I found one of the metal spikes Marrok had mentioned and tied the end of the rope to it. On my belly, I inched closer to the edge until I could see down into the jungle.

The sides of the cliff appeared to be smooth, with no hand-holds in sight. I tossed the rope over, but knew it wouldn't reach the bottom far below. The end stopped a quarter of the way down. Even with a longer rope, the climb looked dangerous. Water sprayed out of fissures in the rock face about halfway down. The stones below glistened.

I considered the descent. A desperate person might attempt it, but Leif's assessment of the Vermin hadn't included desperation.

Moon Man waited for me by the horses.

"When the scouts return, we will set out," he said.

A notion that had been bothering me finally clicked. "Your people have swept the plateau and have been watching the camp. How could the Vermin slip away without you knowing?"

"A few of their Warpers had been Story Weavers. They must have learned to make a null shield."

"That would only hide their presence from a magical search. What about seeing them?"

Before Moon Man could answer, a shout rang out. Leif, Marrok and the scout ran toward us.

"Found a trench," Marrok panted.

"Heading east then north." The scout gestured.

"Ill intent," Leif said.

North toward the Avibian Plains. Toward the Sandseeds' unprotected lands because their warriors were here in the plateau. Every one.

Moon Man covered his face with his hands as if he needed to block out the distractions and think.

The second scout arrived from the west. Puffs of sand from his passage reached us before he did.

"Another trench?" Marrok asked.

"The trail ends. They doubled back." The scout reported.

Moon Man dropped his hands and began shouting orders, sending the warriors northeast at a run, ordering the Story Weavers to make contact with the people who stayed behind on the plains.

"Come on," he said, turning to join the others.

"No," I said.

He stopped and looked back. "What?"

"Too obvious. I don't think Cahil would go along with that."

"Then where did he go?" Moon Man demanded.

"The bulk of the Daviians went east, but I think a smaller group either went west or south."

"My people are in trouble," Moon Man said.

"And so are mine," I replied. "You go with your warriors. If I'm wrong, we'll catch up with you."

"And if you are right, then what?"

Then what, indeed. There were only three of us.

"I will go with you," Moon Man said. He called one of the

Story Weavers and a touch of magic pricked my skin as they linked their minds.

Not wanting to intrude on their mental conversation, I focused on finding Cahil. I examined the edge of the plateau. A branch from one of the tall jungle trees reached toward the cliff. I could use my grapple and rope and hook it—

No, Leif said in my mind. *Suicide.*

I frowned at him. *But I could swing—*

No.

Nutty could do it. Our cousin climbed trees as if valmur blood coursed through her veins.

You're not Nutty.

I reluctantly abandoned that course of action. Even if I could swing to the tree, I doubted anyone else would follow me. Then I would be alone. I berated myself for being worried about being on my own: living in Sitia had made me soft.

It has made you smarter, Leif said. Then he added, *not much smarter, but we can still hope for improvement.*

"Where to?" Tauno asked as he joined our group.

I looked at Moon Man.

He shrugged. "He is better at scouting than fighting. We will need him," he said with certainty.

I sighed at the implication. "West."

Perhaps we would find a better way down into the jungle or, failing that, we would follow the plateau's edge west toward the Cowan Clan's lands. Once in Cowan land, we would turn south into the forest then loop east into the Illiais Jungle. And hope we weren't too late.

We mounted the horses. Tauno and Marrok once again led us. The point where the Daviians had turned around was obvious even to me. The hard-packed sand had been scuffed where they stopped, and only flat unblemished sand continued westward.

Tauno halted the horses and waited for more instructions.

"A ruse. I can smell deceit and smugness," Leif said.

"Why so smug?" I asked. "Laying a false trail is a basic strategy."

"It could be Cahil," Marrok said. "He tends to think he is smarter than everyone. Perhaps he thought this would fool the Sandseeds into sending half their warriors in the wrong direction."

I projected my magical awareness over the smooth sand. A few mice skittered into the open, searching for food. A snake curled on a warm rock, basking in the afternoon sun. I encountered a strange dark mind.

I withdrew my awareness and scanned the plateau. Sure enough there was a small area a few feet away where the sand looked pliant, as if it had been dug up and packed back down. I slid off Kiki and walked over to the patch. The sand felt spongy beneath my boots.

"A Vermin must have buried something there," Marrok said.

Tauno snorted with disgust. "You have probably found one of their waste pits."

With Moon Man still on her back, Kiki came closer. *Smell damp,* she said.

Bad damp or good damp? I asked.

Just damp.

Taking my grapple out of my pack, I started to dig. The others watched me with various expressions of amusement, distaste and curiosity.

When I had dug down about a foot, my grapple struck something hard. "Help me clear the sand."

My reluctant audience joined me. But eventually we un-covered a flat piece of wood.

Marrok rapped his knuckles on it and proclaimed it the top of a box. Working faster to remove the sand, we sought the edges. The round lid was about two feet in diameter.

While Tauno and Moon Man discussed why the Vermin would bury a circle box, I found the lip and pried the top up. A gulp of air almost sucked the lid back down.

Everyone was stunned into silence. The lid covered a hole in the ground. And, judging by the pull of air into its depths, a very deep hole.

THE SUNLIGHT ILLUMINATED a few feet of the hole. Below the lip a couple rough steps had been cut into the sandstone.

"Can you sense anyone in there?" Leif asked.

Pulling a thread of power, I projected into the darkness. My awareness touched many of those dark minds, but no people.

"Bats," I said. "Lots of bats. You?"

"Just smug satisfaction."

"Could this be another false trail?" Marrok asked.

"Or a trap?" Tauno asked. He glanced around with quick furtive movements as if worried the sand would erupt with Vermin.

"One of us needs to go inside and report back," Moon Man said, looking at Tauno. "I knew we would need a scout."

Tauno jerked as if he had stepped on a hot coal. Sweat ran down his face. He swallowed. "I will need a light."

Leif retrieved his saddlebags and removed one of his cooking sticks. "This won't burn long," he said. He set the end on fire and handed the stick to Tauno.

With the flaming stick to lead the way, the Sandseed scout crawled into the opening headfirst. Tempted to link my mind with his to see what he found, I forced myself to focus instead on the ground beneath my feet, trying to discover a sign of life that would indicate the end of the cave.

The jungle's pulse throbbed in my soul, but I couldn't tell if it came from an opening below the ground or just from being so close to it on the plateau.

Waiting proved difficult. I imagined all types of hazards in Tauno's way and was convinced he had fallen and broken a leg or worse when he appeared at the hole's opening.

"The steps lead to a big cavern with many tunnels and ledges. I spotted a few footprints in the dirt, but had to come back before my light died," Tauno said. "I also heard water gurgling nearby."

Now we knew. Vermin had gone through the cave.

"Leif, what do you need to make a light last longer?" I asked him.

"You're not thinking about going in there, are you?" Marrok asked, sounding horrified.

"Of course. You want to find Cahil, don't you?"

"What makes you so certain he went that way?"

I looked at Leif. Together we said, "Smug satisfaction."

While Leif and Tauno returned to the Daviian camp for firewood, Moon Man and I discussed what to do with the horses. We would need Marrok's tracking skills and Tauno's keen sense of direction to find our way through the cavern. Leif and I needed to take Cahil back to the Council, so that left Moon Man.

"I am not staying behind," Moon Man said.

"Someone needs to feed and water the horses," I said.

Kiki snorted at me. I opened my mind to her.

Don't need, she said. *We wait then go.*

Go where?

Market. An image of the Illiais Market formed in my mind. As the main southern trading post for Sitia, the market was tucked between the western edge of the Illiais Jungle and Cowan Clan lands.

How do you know about the market? I asked.

Know land like know grass.

I smiled. Kiki's concise view of life kept surprising me with its many layers of emotion. If I could view the world the same way, I knew it would make my life easier.

Moon Man had been watching me. "Perhaps Kiki should mentor you."

"On what? How to become a Soulfinder?"

"No. You *are* a Soulfinder. She can help you *be* a Soulfinder."

"More cryptic Story Weaver advice?"

"No. Clear as air." Moon Man drew a deep breath and grinned at me. "Let us get the horses ready."

We removed their bridles and reins and packed the tack into their saddlebags. When Leif and Tauno returned, we sorted our supplies, distributing them among our packs and repacking the rest into the saddlebags. The horses would keep their saddles on, but we made sure nothing would hang down or impede their motion.

My pack weighed heavier than usual, but I had an uneasy intuition we might need a few of the items inside.

When we were ready, Leif lit the firewood torches dipped in the plant oil he had stored in Rusalka's saddlebags. He left most of his odd concoctions and medicines behind, boasting he could find anything we needed in the jungle.

"*If* we find a way out," Marrok muttered. "What will we do if we become lost in the caves?"

"That will not happen," Moon Man said. "I will mark our way with paint. If we can not find our way through, we will return to the plateau. The horses will wait until Yelena tells them to go."

Moon Man wrapped his muscular arm around Marrok's shoulders. Marrok tensed as if he expected a blow.

"Trust yourself, Tracker. You have never been lost," Moon Man said.

"I have never been inside a cave."

"Then it will be a new experience for both of us." Moon Man's eyes glinted with anticipation, but Marrok hunched his back.

I wasn't a stranger to small dark places. Before becoming the Commander's food taster, I had spent a year in the Commander's dungeon awaiting execution. While I wasn't anxious to return to a confined space, I would push past my nerves to recapture Ferde.

"There are a few caves in the jungle," Leif said. "Most of them are used as dens by the tree leopards and are avoided, but I've explored some." His gaze met mine and, by the sad smile, I knew he had searched those caves looking for me.

Tauno and Marrok each held a torch. With Tauno leading the way, I followed, crawling headfirst through the small opening. Leif was close behind, then Marrok and finally Moon Man.

The torchlight illuminated the three-foot-wide tunnel. Shovel marks scraped the rough walls, indicating the space had been dug. The steps turned into bumps that helped slow our progress as we slid down the sloped passageway. I coughed as the dust of our passing mixed with the steady flow of cool damp air.

When we reached the cavern, the tightness around my ribs eased. Tauno's light reflected off stones resembling teeth. A few of these hung from the ceiling and others rose from the ground as if we stood inside the mouth of a giant beast.

"Don't move," Marrok ordered as he examined the floor.

Shadows danced on the pockmarked walls as Marrok searched for signs. Deep wells of blackness indicated other tunnels, and small puddles of water peppered the floor. Dripping and running water filled the air with a pleasant hum that countered the unpleasant wet mineral smell mixed with a sharp animal musk.

Moon Man hunched his shoulders and short breaths punctuated his breathing.

"Is something wrong?" I asked him.

"The walls press on me. I feel squeezed. No doubt my imagination." He went to mark the tunnel to the surface with red paint.

"This way," Marrok said. Amplified by either the stone walls or by fear, his voice sounded louder than usual. He showed us a series of ledges descending down a chute.

The smell rising from the chute turned sharp and rank. I gagged. Tauno climbed down. The ledges turned out to be large chucks of rocks stacked crookedly on top of one another. In certain places he hung over the side and dropped down. We followed and with some mumbling and cursing we caught up to Tauno.

He waited on the last visible ledge. Beyond him, the chute ended in a pit of blackness. Tauno dropped his torch. It landed on a rock floor far below.

"Too far to jump," Tauno said.

I pulled the grapple from my pack and wedged the metal hooks into a crack, glad I had decided to bring it along. Tying the rope onto the hook, I tested the grapple's grip. Secure for now, but Moon Man braced himself and gripped the rope when Tauno swung over the edge and descended.

Moon Man's forehead dripped with sweat despite the cool air. His uneven breathing echoed off the walls. When Tauno reached near the bottom, Moon Man released the rope. The grapple held Tauno's weight. He jumped the last bit and picked up the torch, exploring the area before giving us the all-clear signal. One by one we joined him at the bottom of the chute. We left the grapple in place in case we needed to return.

"I have some good news and some bad," Tauno said.

"Just tell us," Marrok barked.

"There is a way out of this chamber, but I doubt Moon Man or Leif will fit." Tauno showed us a small opening. The torch's flame flickered in the breeze coming from the channel.

I looked at Leif. Even though Marrok was taller than him, Leif had wide shoulders. How had Cahil and Ferde fit through? Or had they traveled a different way? It was hard to judge size based on a memory. Perhaps they hadn't encountered any trouble.

"First explore the tunnel. See what's on the other side," I instructed.

Tauno disappeared into the hole with a quick grace. Leif crouched next to the opening, examining it.

"I have more plant oil," Leif said. "Perhaps we can grease our skin and slide through?" He stepped back when Tauno's light brightened the passageway.

"It gets wider about ten feet down and ends in another cavern," Tauno said. Black foul-smelling muck covered his feet. When questioned about the mud, he wiggled his toes. "The source of the stench. Bat guano. Lots of it."

Those ten feet took us the longest to traverse. And I despaired at the amount of time we used to squeeze two grown men through a narrow space. It might be impossible to catch up with Cahil and the others. And Moon Man's panic attack when he had become wedged for a moment had set everyone's mood on edge.

Standing ankle deep in bat droppings, we made for a miserable group. My dismay reflected in everyone's face. And it wasn't due to the putrid and acidic smell. Leif's shoulders were scratched raw and bloody, and the skin on Moon Man's arms looked shredded. Blood dripped from his hands.

Moon Man's breathing rasped. "Go back. We should…go back." He panted. "Bad idea. Bad idea. Bad idea."

I suppressed my worries about Cahil. Connecting with the power source, I gathered a fiber of magic and sought Moon Man's mind. A claustrophobic fear had pushed logic and reason aside. I probed deeper into his thoughts to find the strong unflappable Story Weaver, reminding him of the importance of our journey. A Sandseed Story Weaver would not let himself panic. Moon Man's breathing settled as calm reclaimed his emotions. I withdrew from his mind.

"I am sorry. I do not like this cave," Moon Man said.

"No one does," Leif muttered.

Keeping my thread of magic, I focused on Moon Man's arms. Large chunks of his skin had been gouged out. My upper limbs burned with pain as I concentrated on his injuries. When I could no longer endure the stinging fire, I used magic to push it away from me. I swayed with relief and would have fallen to the floor if Leif hadn't grabbed me.

Moon Man examined his arms. "I could not lend you my strength this time," he said. "Your magic held me immobile."

"What's this?" Leif asked.

He raised my hand into the light. Blood streaked my skin, but I couldn't find any damage. When I had helped Tula, one of Ferde's victims and Opal's sister, Irys had speculated that I had assumed her injuries then healed myself. I guessed it had been the same with Marrok's crushed cheek. But seeing the physical evidence turned Irys's theory into reality. I stared at the blood and felt light-headed.

"That's interesting," Leif said.

"Interesting in a good way or bad?" I asked.

"I don't know. No one has done that before."

I appealed to Moon Man.

"A couple Story Weavers have the power to heal, but not like that," he said. "Perhaps it is something only a Soulfinder can do."

"Perhaps? You don't know? Then why have you led me to believe you know everything about me?" I demanded.

He rubbed his newly healed arm. "I am your Story Weaver. I do know everything about you. However, I do not know everything about Soulfinders. Do you define yourself strictly by that title?"

"No." I avoided the title.

"Well then," he said, as if that settled the matter.

"Let's go," Marrok said through his shirt. He had covered his nose and mouth to block the smell. "The Daviians' trail through this muck is easy to follow."

With Marrok in the lead, we stepped with care. About halfway through the bats' cavern, I sensed an awakening. Sending a thin tendril of power, I linked with the dark minds above me as they floated toward a collective consciousness. Their need for food pushed at me, and, through them, I felt the exact location of each bat, of each wall, of each exit, of each rock, and each figure below. They launched.

"Duck!" I yelled as the cloud of flying creatures descended.

The drone of beating wings reached a crescendo as black bodies flew around us. The air swirled and filled with bats. They deftly avoided knocking into us or each other as they headed toward the exit, seeking the insects and berries of the jungle.

My mind traveled with them. The instinctual exodus of thousands of bats flying through the tight tunnels of the cave was as organized as a military attack. And like any well-planned event, it took time for all the bats to leave.

The muscles in my legs burned when I finally straightened. The flapping and fluttering sounds echoed from the tunnels then faded. I looked at my companions. No one appeared to be hurt, although a few of us were splattered with dung.

Marrok had dropped his torch, and his arms covered his head. He puffed with alarm.

"Captain Marrok," I said, hoping to calm him. "Give me your torch."

My order pierced his panic. He picked up the unlit stick. "Why?"

"Because the bats have shown me the way out." I cringed as my hand closed on the muck-covered handle. "Leif, can you relight this?"

Leif nodded. Flames grew. When the torch burned on its own, he asked, "How far to the jungle?"

"Not far." I led the group, setting a quick pace. No one complained. All were as eager as I to exit the cave.

The sound of rushing water and a glorious freshness to the air were the only signs we had reached our destination. The day had turned into night while we had traveled through the cave.

From the bats, I knew water flowed along the floor of the exit and dropped down about twenty feet to the jungle. The waterfall splashed onto a tumble of rocks.

The others followed me to the edge of the stream. We doused the torches and waited for our eyes to adjust to the weak moonlight. I scanned the jungle below with my magic, searching for signs of an ambush and for tree leopards. Necklace snakes were also a danger to us, but the only life I touched were small creatures scurrying through the underbrush.

"Prepare to get wet," I said before wading into the cold knee-deep water.

My boots filled immediately as I sloshed to the edge. There were plenty of rocks below to climb on, but they were either under the water or wet. I eased off my backpack and threw it down, aiming for a dry spot on the rocky bank.

"Be careful," I instructed.

I turned around and crouched, leaning into the force of the water. Keeping my face above the stream, I stuck my feet over the edge and felt for a foothold. By the time I reached the bottom, my clothes were soaked. At least the water had washed away the foul-smelling dung.

Once everyone climbed down, we stood dripping and shivering on the bank.

"Now what?" Leif asked.

"It's too dark to see trail signs," Marrok said. "Unless we make more torches."

I looked at our ragtag group. I had a dry change of clothes in my backpack, but Tauno and Moon Man had nothing with them. The bank was big enough for a fire. "We need to dry off and get some rest."

"You need to die," a loud voice said from the jungle.

6

ARROWS RAINED DOWN. Tauno cried out as one pierced his shoulder.

"Find cover," Marrok ordered. An arrow jutted from his thigh.

We scrambled for the underbrush. Moon Man dragged Tauno with him. Marrok fell. An arrow whizzed by my ear and thudded into a tree trunk. Another slammed into my backpack before I dived under a bush.

I scanned the treetops with my magic, but couldn't sense anyone.

"Null shield," Moon Man shouted. "No magic."

Marrok lay in the open, unmoving. Arrows continued to fly, but they missed him. He stared at the sky.

"Curare!" I yelled. "The arrows are laced with Curare."

The ambushers wanted to paralyze us, not kill us. At least not yet. The memory of being completely helpless from the drug washed over me. Alea Daviian had wanted revenge for her brother's death, so she had pricked me with Curare and carted me to the plateau to torture and kill me.

Leif yelped nearby. An arrow had nicked his cheek. "Theobroma?" he asked before his face froze.

Of course! My father's Theobroma, which had saved me from Alea. I ripped open my pack, searching for the antidote to Curare. The rain of arrows slowed, and a rustling noise from above meant our attackers were climbing down. Probably to take better aim. I found the brown lumps of Theobroma and put one into my mouth, immediately chewing and swallowing it.

Moon Man cursed and I broke cover to run to him. An arrow hit my back. The force slammed me to the ground. Pain rippled through my body.

"Yelena!" Moon Man grabbed my outstretched arm and pulled me to him.

"Here." I panted as the Curare numbed the throb in my lower back. "Eat this."

He ate the Theobroma lump without a moment's hesitation. An arrow's shaft had pinned his tunic to a tree.

I lost feeling in my legs. "Are you hit?"

He ripped his shirt free and examined the skin along his right side. "No."

"Pretend to be," I whispered. "Wait for my signal."

Sudden understanding flashed in his deep brown eyes. He broke the shaft off the arrow that had missed him, and swiped blood from my back. Lying down, he held the shaft between two bloody fingers of his left hand which he placed on his stomach, making it look like the arrow had pierced his gut. His right hand gripped his scimitar.

Men called as they reached the jungle floor. Before they could discover me, I put my right hand into my pant's pocket, palming the handle of my switchblade. Numbness spread throughout my torso, but the Theobroma countered the Curare's effects to a point where limited movement remained. Even so, I lay still, pretending to be paralyzed.

"I found one," a man said.

"Over here's another."

"I found two," a rough voice right above me said.

"That's the rest of them. Make sure they're incapacitated before you drag them out. Dump them beside their companion in the clearing," said a fourth voice.

The rough-voiced man kicked me in the ribs. Pain ringed my chest and stomach. I clamped my teeth together to suppress a grunt. When he grabbed my ankles and hauled me through the bushes and over the uneven stones of the bank, I was a bit glad for the Curare in my body. It dulled the burning sting as the left side of my face and ear were rubbed raw by the ground.

The Curare also dulled my emotions. I knew I should be terrified, yet felt only mild concern. Curare's ability to paralyze my magic remained the most frightening aspect of the drug. Even though the Theobroma counteracted it, Theobroma had its own side effect. The antidote opened a person's mind to magical influence. While I could use magic, now I had no defense against another's magic.

Marrok still lay where he had fallen. The loud scrape of Moon Man's weapon on the ground reached me before he was dropped beside me.

"His fingers are frozen around the handle," one of the men said.

"A lot of good it will do him," another joked.

Listening to their voices, I counted five men. Two against

five. Not bad odds unless my legs remained numb. Then Moon Man would be on his own.

Once the men brought Leif and Tauno to the bank, the leader of the attackers dropped the null shield. It felt as if a curtain had been yanked back, revealing what lurked behind. All five men's thoughts were open to me now.

Their leader shouted orders. "Prepare the prisoners for the Kirakawa ritual," he said.

"We should not feed these men to it," Rough Voice said. "We should use their blood for ourselves. You should stay."

My gaze met Moon Man's. We needed to act soon. I suppressed the desire to make mental contact with the Story Weaver. Their leader had to be a strong Warper to have created such a subtle null shield. There was a chance he would "hear" us.

The crunch of gravel under boots neared. My stomach tightened.

"I have orders to bring the woman to Jal," the leader said from above me. "Jal has special plans for her."

Without warning, the arrow in my back was yanked out. I bit my tongue to keep from yelling. The leader knelt next to me. He held the arrow, examining the weapon. My blood stained the smooth metal tip. At least the tip wasn't barbed. Strange I should worry about that.

"Too bad," Rough Voice said. "Think of the power you could have if *you* performed Kirakawa on her. You might become stronger than Jal. *You* could lead our clan."

My lower back pulsed with pain. The Theobroma was working. Another minute and I should regain the use of my legs.

"She is powerful," the leader agreed. "But I do not know

the binding rite yet. Once I bring her to Jal, I hope to be rewarded and allowed to ascend to the next level."

He smoothed tendrils of hair from my face. I made a conscious effort not to flinch as his fingers caressed my cheek.

"Are the rumors true? Are you really a Soulfinder?" he whispered to me. He stroked my arm in a possessive way. "Perhaps I can siphon a cup of your blood before I deliver you to Jal." He reached for the knife hanging from his belt.

I moved. Pulling my switchblade from my pocket, I triggered the blade and rolled over, slicing his stomach open. But instead of falling back in surprise, he leaned forward and wrapped his hands around my neck.

A blur of motion beside me, and Moon Man leaped to his feet, swinging his scimitar in a deadly arc through Rough Voice.

I struggled with the leader. His weight trapped my arms. The pressure from his thumbs closed my windpipe. He attempted to connect with my mind, and would have succeeded with his magical attack if the Curare on my switchblade hadn't worked so fast to paralyze his power.

One problem remained. Trapped under the frozen Vermin, I couldn't breathe.

Moon Man, I called. *Help!*

One minute. The clang of weapons split the air.

I'll be dead in a minute. Just push him off. A brief flurry of steel hitting steel was followed by silence. The man on me fell to the side. I freed my arms and pried his hands from my neck.

Moon Man reengaged in the battle. He fought three men. One man's decapitated head rested next to me. Lovely.

My short blade wouldn't last against their long scimitars and my bow was in the jungle with my pack. Gathering power, I sent a light touch to one man's mind. Relieved he wasn't a Warper, I sent him puzzling images to distract him.

He dropped out of the fight with Moon Man and stared at my approach with a baffled expression. The man raised his sword a second too late. I stepped close to him and nicked his arm with my switchblade, hoping Curare still clung to my blade. Unable to use his sword, the man dropped his weapon and lunged. His intent to subdue me rang clear in his mind, but I deepened my mental connection and forced him to sleep.

With only two attackers left, Moon Man had both their heads off in short order. He strode over to the man sleeping at my feet and raised his scimitar.

"Stop," I said. "When he wakes, we can question him about Cahil's plans."

"The other?"

"Paralyzed."

Moon Man rolled the leader over. The blood from his stomach wound had pooled on the rocks. After touching the man's neck and face, Moon Man said, "He is gone."

The cut was deeper than I thought. A felt a tinge of guilt as I scowled at the body. The leader probably had more information than the other man.

"It is a good thing. He was a Warper. We would not have gotten anything from him except trouble."

I looked at the scattered carnage. The headless bodies cast macabre shadows in the pale moonlight. The side of my face and the wound in my back throbbed. The cool night air felt icy on my wet clothes. Tauno and Marrok both needed medical attention, and we couldn't go anywhere until the Curare wore off. And the thought of spending the night surrounded by corpses...

"I will take care of them," Moon Man said, reading my thoughts. "And I will build a fire. You take care of the wounded. Including you."

Pulling the arrows from Marrok's thigh and Tauno's shoulder, I gathered power but couldn't assume their injuries. The Curare in their bodies blocked my magic. An interesting discovery. It seemed when under the influence of the drug, a person couldn't do magic or be affected by it.

I mulled over the implications as I searched in my pack. Finding a few lumps of Theobroma, I gave it to Moon Man to melt over the fire and feed to our paralyzed companions. From my own experience with Curare, I knew the drug didn't affect the body's ability to swallow, breathe and hear. So I told them what I planned to do.

The last of my energy faded after healing my own wound. I curled into a ball on the ground and fell asleep.

When I woke, watery streaks of color painted the sky. Moon Man sat cross-legged next to a fire, cooking a divine-smelling hunk of meat. My stomach grumbled in anticipation.

I checked on the others. Marrok, Leif and Tauno still slept. Leif's cut had scabbed over, but I would need to heal Marrok's and Tauno's wounds. Moon Man had tied the Daviian prisoner's arms and legs with some jungle vines even though the Vermin remained unconscious.

Moon Man gestured for me to join him. "Eat first before you heal them." He handed me a sliver of meat speared on a stick. When I sniffed at the offering, he said, "Do not analyze it. It is hot and nourishing. That is all you need to know."

"Why do *you* get to decide what I need to know? Why can't you just give me the information I ask for?" My frustration extended beyond the mystery meat.

"That would be too easy."

"What's wrong with easy? I can understand if the most stressful aspect of my life was worrying about Bain's next history test, but lives are at stake. Ferde could be stealing another's soul and I might have the power to stop him."

"What do you want? For me to tell you to do this or do that and wa-lah!" Moon Man flourished his hand in the air. "Instant success!"

"Yes. That is exactly what I want. Please, tell me."

A thoughtful expression settled on his face. "When you were training to be the Commander's food taster, would you know what the poison My Love tasted like if Valek had just described it to you?"

"Yes." There was no mistaking the sour-apple taste.

"Would you trust your life on that knowledge? Or others?"

I opened my mouth to reply but paused. Now I couldn't remember the poisons I hadn't tasted or smelled. But I'll never forget the tartness of My Love, the rancid orange flavor of Butterfly's Dust, and the bitter thickness of White Fright.

"I'm talking about magic. Testing food for poisons is different."

"Is it?"

I pounded my fist on the ground. "Do Story Weavers sign a contract or make a blood oath to be difficult and stubborn and a pain in the ass?"

A serene smile spread on his face. "No. Each Story Weaver chooses how he will guide his charges. Think about it, Yelena. You do not respond well to orders. Now eat your meat before it gets cold."

Stifling my desire to fling the food into the fire and prove the insufferably smug Story Weaver right about my inability to take orders, I bit off a large chunk.

Spiced with pepper, the oily meat tasted like duck. Moon Man fed me two more pieces before he would let me return to the sleeping men and heal them. Tired, I snoozed by the fire.

When everyone had roused and gathered around the campfire to eat, we discussed our next move.

"Do you think they would set more ambushes in the jungle? Leave more Warpers in our path?" I asked Moon Man.

He considered my question. "It is possible. They left one at the camp who sacrificed himself. This one was supposed to come back. Our spies have determined the Daviian Vermin have about ten Warpers—eight now. Two are very powerful, and the rest have various lesser talents."

"The ambush leader had enough magic to create and hold a null shield."

Moon Man turned the meat roasting over the fire. "A valid and alarming point. Which means they might have been performing Kirakawa for some time."

"What's Kirakawa?" Leif asked.

"It is an ancient ritual. It has many steps and rites. When done correctly, it transfers the life energy of one person to another. All living beings have the ability to use magic, but most cannot connect to the power source. A person performing Kirakawa will either increase their magical power or gain the ability to connect with the power source, and therefore become a Warper.

"Their leader mentioned levels and a binding rite. They are probably using the Kirakawa to grant certain members magical abilities and increase certain Warpers' powers. Their leader would not want all the clan members to be equally powerful."

"How is the Kirakawa different than the Efe ritual Ferde used?" Leif rubbed the cut on his cheek.

"The Efe ritual binds a person's soul to the practitioner, increasing their power. While blood is needed, it isn't the medium holding the power in Efe. The soul carries the power. And the person performing the ritual must be a magician."

"It sounds like anyone can use this Kirakawa to gain power," Leif said.

"*If* they knew the proper steps. With the Kirakawa, the victim's soul is trapped in blood. It is gruesome, too. The victim's stomach is cut open and the heart is removed while the victim is still living. The Kirakawa is also more complex than the Efe ritual."

"Could any magician use Efe? Or just the Soulstealer?" I asked.

"A Soulfinder could, but no one else. Is that a straight enough answer for you, Yelena?"

I didn't dignify his comment with a reply. Instead, I asked about Mogkan, Alea's brother. In Ixia, he had captured over thirty people, turning them into mindless slaves so he could siphon their power and augment his own. Valek and I had eventually stopped him from gaining control of Ixia, which explained Alea's desire for revenge.

"Mogkan tortured them both physically and mentally until they could no longer bear to be aware of their surroundings. They retreated within themselves and just became a conduit for him to exploit. Their magic remained in their bodies."

The implications over the different ways for people to abuse power raced through my mind. "Going back to the Kirakawa. If the Daviian Vermin have been performing it for a while, then they could have more than eight Warpers."

Moon Man nodded. "Many more."

Paranoia sizzled up my spine. Convinced Warpers surrounded us, my desire to return my friends to the safety of the plateau pressed between my shoulder blades.

However, if the Daviians wanted to find more victims for their ritual, the Zaltana Clan teemed with people and magicians. With the Warpers using a null shield, the clan would have no warning. Fingers of desperate fear squeezed my stomach as the images of my mother and father being mutilated filled my mind.

7

"HOW DO YOU COUNTER the null shield?" I asked
Moon Man, failing to keep the panic out of my voice. The
jungle around us darkened and I imagined predators lurking
behind every tree and bush. Only the small fire we huddled
around gave off any light.

"Magic cannot pierce the shield, but find a way around the
shield's edges and you can use your magic."

"What are the shield's dimensions?"

"Depends on the strength of the builder. The one we used
in the plateau was as tall as a man astride a horse, and as wide
as thirty men. But we had four Story Weavers combine their
powers to build it. For one Warper, the shield would have to
be smaller."

I looked up at the trees. The ambush had come from above.
Would they use the same tactic for another ambush? No. If the
first attempt hadn't worked, then a different strategy would be
used. Being higher than your target had many advantages, and
if I climbed into the tree canopy, I might be able to get past

the edges of another null shield and discover where another ambush lurked.

Knowing my next move helped to dampen my terror for my family. I made contact with Kiki, projecting my awareness up toward the plateau.

Any trouble? I asked.

No. Bored, she replied. *Go?*

Yes. I'll meet you at the Illiais Market rendezvous location.

I then told my plan to the others.

"Not without me," Leif said. "I grew up in the jungle. I know every leaf and tree." His body stiffened with determination.

"That is why you need to stay with them. To show them the way to the homestead. To help them avoid predators."

Leif crossed his arms over his broad chest. But he knew I made sense, so he couldn't argue.

"I need to question our prisoner before I go. There could be a chance the other Vermin might not be targeting my family."

The man groaned and blinked at me when I woke him from his deep sleep. Moon Man had been right to tie his arms. There hadn't been enough Curare left on my blade to paralyze him.

The Vermin's tunic and pants had been ripped, and I glimpsed portions of blackish-red tattoos on his brown skin. Moon Man reached over and ripped the man's right sleeve off.

The Story Weaver pointed to the symbols on the man's arm. "He has made the proper blood sacrifice to prepare for the Kirakawa ritual. That ink in his skin has been mixed with blood." Moon Man's shoulders dropped as if he grieved. "The Sandseeds were wise to banish the old rituals."

"You were misguided and fooled into following the teachings of Guyan," the prisoner said. "Not wise but weak and pitiful, giving up your power to become docile pathetic Story Weavers instead of—"

Moon Man grabbed the man by the throat and lifted him off the ground. *Docile* and *weak* were not words I would have used to describe the Story Weaver.

"Where did you get the instructions?" Moon Man asked, shaking him.

The man smiled. "I am not telling you."

"Instructions?" I asked.

"The details for the old rituals had been lost to time. At one point in history, we knew how to perform many different rituals to increase our power. Our clan passes information down to our children through teaching stories. Once Guyan became our leader, the evil ones who knew the required steps were killed. The information should have died with them." He dropped the Daviian to the ground.

I remembered Dax reading a bunch of ancient tomes when we had tried to interpret Ferde's tattoos to discover why Ferde had been raping and killing those girls.

"There were a few books in the Magician's Keep. A Sandseed might have written the instructions and symbols down before they died. Perhaps there is another copy that the Vermin are using." I turned to the man. "I guess you're not going to tell us what the Vermin's plans are either?"

He met my gaze and sneered. It was all I needed. My family could be in danger. I sent a rope of power toward his mind and rifled through his thoughts and memories, extracting the information I needed. I suppressed the pang of guilt and my recollections of when Roze Featherstone had tried to examine my mind in a similar fashion. She had thought I was a spy from

Ixia, and the Ethical Code didn't apply to spies or criminals. I could argue the same in my defense. Did that make me the same as Roze? Perhaps. The thought made me uncomfortable.

Besides a few horrid memories of watching an initial level of the Kirakawa ritual, the man knew almost nothing. Ordered to stay behind and ambush anyone who came out of the caves, his small unit had scheduled a rendezvous with the larger jungle group at a later time. Where and when the meeting would be, he had no idea. And, more important, he didn't know what the others planned to do.

He had a few tidbits of information. I confirmed that both Cahil and Ferde had come this way and they traveled with a group of twelve Vermin.

"Fourteen is not enough to win in an attack on the Zaltanas," Leif said, pride in his voice.

I agreed. "But winning isn't everything."

My anxiety to leave increased a hundredfold. A group of Vermin had entered the jungle and my clan could be in trouble. Images of my father and mother being captured and staked to the ground replayed in my mind. The thought of my cousin Nutty climbing without care through the trees and falling into a trap, hurried my preparations.

I shouldered my pack, threading my bow through its holder. "What about our prisoner?" I asked Moon Man.

"I will take care of him."

"How?"

"You do not want to know."

"Yes, I do. I want you to tell me everything!"

Moon Man sighed. "The Vermin were once a part of the

Sandseed clan. They are our wayward kin, and they are infesting the rest of Sitia. How we deal with them is in accordance to our laws, and it is the proper way to take care of Vermin."

"And that would be?"

"You exterminate them."

A protest perched on my lips. What about those members who might have been misguided? But my question remained unvoiced. Now wasn't the best time to argue crime and punishment.

Instead, I gazed at the tall trees, looking for a way up into the canopy, wishing I hadn't left my grapple and rope in the cave. I found a long vine and used it to climb into the higher branches. After a moment to reorient myself—the Zaltana homestead was to the west—I swung over to the next tree.

I kept my magical senses tuned to the life around me, seeking the Daviians and other predators as I traveled toward home. The web of branches and crowded trees slowed my progress. After a few hours, my sweat-soaked clothes were ripped, and my skin burned and itched from innumerable cuts and insect bites.

Resting on the branch of a hawthorn tree, I scanned the area between me and Moon Man. There was no sign of any intelligent life so I linked my mind with Moon Man's and Leif's.

You will be safe to travel to this area, I said, picturing the small clearing below. *Stay there until I contact you again.*

They agreed.

After I rested, I pushed my way through the jungle's canopy, staying alert to any sign of the Daviians. The rhythm of climbing from tree to tree combined with the steady pulse of the jungle's undisturbed life force. When an out-of-tune presence plucked at my senses, my energies focused on the distant ripple. Engrossed, I concentrated on discovering the source. A man in the tree canopy. Before I could determine if he was friend or foe, my left hand grasped a smooth and pliant branch. Surprised, I jerked my awareness back and my mind connected with a hunter lurking in the trees.

The leaves rustled with movement. The terrifying rasp of a stirring snake surrounded me. The limb under my feet softened. I scrambled for a solid branch, and touched nothing but the snake's dry coils. The necklace snake's coloring blended with the jungle's greenery so well that I couldn't determine where the rest of it lay.

I closed my eyes and projected into the snake's mind. It had looped part of its body between two branches, creating a flat net now closing around me. Pulling my switchblade from my pocket, I triggered the blade.

When the heavy coils of the snake dropped onto my shoulders, I knew I had mere seconds before the predator would wrap around my throat like a necklace and choke me to death. I sensed satisfaction from the snake as it moved to tighten its hold.

I stabbed my knife into the snake's thick body. Would the Curare on the blade affect the creature? Mild pain from the thrust registered in the snake's mind, but it considered the wound minor.

The snake contracted around me, trapping my legs and left arm. I realized the necklace snake held me aloft. If I cut through its coils, I would plummet to the ground.

Another loop brushed my face as the snake tried to

encircle my neck. I pushed it away with my free arm. A coil slid up my back.

Deciding the odds of surviving a fall were better than dying by strangulation, I stabbed my blade in the nearest coil with the intention of sawing through it. Before I applied more pressure, the creature stopped.

Perhaps Curare had paralyzed the snake. I pulled the blade out and the snake resumed its tightening. The Curare hadn't worked. But when I reinserted the knife, the creature paused. Odd. I must have found a vulnerable area. We were at an impasse.

Through my link with its mind, I sensed the snake's hunger warring with its desire to live. I tried to control the predator's will, but our minds were too incompatible. Even though I could feel its intentions, I couldn't direct its movements.

I wanted to avoid killing the snake, but I could see no other way. Once dead, I should be able to cut my way back into the trees.

"Hello. Is someone in there?" a man's voice asked.

My struggle with the snake had seized all my attention. Cursing myself for forgetting the man, I directed my mind into the tree canopy and encountered the well-protected thoughts of another magician. But Warper or Story Weaver, I couldn't tell.

"Has the snake got your tongue?" He laughed at his own joke. "I know you're there. I felt your power. If you don't belong in the jungle, I'll gladly let the snakes have you for dinner."

"Snakes?" I asked. His speech patterns sounded familiar. Not Daviian. Not Sandseed. I hoped Zaltana.

"Your necklace snake has sent a call for help. You might kill this one and untangle yourself, but by then its kin will be here to finish the job."

I scanned the jungle canopy and, sure enough, I felt five other snakes moving toward me.

"What if I do belong in the jungle?" I asked.

"Then I'll help you. But you'd better make a strong case. Strange things have been happening lately."

I thought fast. "I'm Yelena Liana Zaltana. Daughter of Esau and Perl and sister to Leif."

"Common knowledge. You have to do better."

Soul mate to Valek, the scourge of Sitia, I thought, but knew that wouldn't help my case. I searched my mind for a bit of information only the Zaltanas knew. The problem was, since I had been raised in Ixia, I knew only a few things about my lost clan.

"I could send you on a wild-valmur chase, but wouldn't it be easier if I gave you a piece of sap candy?" I held my breath, waiting.

Just when I was convinced I would have to cut my way out of the snake before its brothers arrived, a low drumbeat throbbed. More beats followed. The vibrations pulsed through the snake.

The snake relaxed. A gap appeared above my head and a green painted face smiled down at me.

He extended his hand, which was also camouflaged. "Grab on."

I clasped his wrist. He pulled me from the snake's net and onto a solid branch. Relief puddled in my knees and I had to sit down.

The man's clothes matched the jungle's colors and patterns. He placed a leather drum on the branch and played another song. The snake unraveled and disappeared into the jungle.

"That should hold them off for a while," he said.

From his clothes and dyed-olive hair color, I knew the man had to be a Zaltana. I thanked him for helping me.

His answering nod reminded me of someone. "Who are you?" I asked.

"Your cousin, Chestnut. I was out on patrol when you were here the last time so I didn't get a chance to meet you."

After living in Ixia for fourteen years, I had finally returned to a home I hadn't known existed. It had been such an emotional whirlwind, and I had met so many cousins, aunts and uncles it was unlikely I would have remembered him even if I had been introduced to him.

Seeing no sign of recognition on my face, he added, "I'm one of Nutty's brothers."

Nutty's stories about her siblings had been humorous and I remembered a game I used to play with her against her brothers before my kidnapping.

"How did you control the snake?" I asked.

"I'm a snake charmer," he said as if the title explained everything. But when I failed to respond, he said, "It's part of my magic. The necklace snakes are very hard to spot. Not only do they blend in so well, but also they mask their life energy. Even if you're able to sense the other jungle animals you probably wouldn't feel the snakes. Not until it was too late." He rubbed his hands together in appreciation. "They usually hunt alone, but if one gets into trouble it can call to the others with a low sound we can't hear. My magic allows me to locate the snakes and hear their calls. And my drum is my way to talk to them. It doesn't work on the other animals." He shrugged. "But I keep the snakes away from our homestead."

"You were out on patrol when you heard my snake?" Funny how I had become possessive of the creature that had tried to squash and eat me.

"Yes. Although, when I left this morning, I had hoped to find more than snakes." He gave me an odd look. "I guess I just did. Why are you here, Yelena?"

"I'm following a group of people who had been living in the plateau," I said. "They came through here. Has anyone seen them?" But what I really wanted to ask was had they attacked the clan? Were my mother and father okay?

"Seen? No. Strangers are in the jungle, but we can't find them and…" He paused, probably considering what information he should divulge. "Perhaps it would be best for you to talk to our clan elders. Are you alone?"

"No. My brother and some Sandseeds are traveling with me."

"In the trees?"

"On the ground." I told Chestnut about the attack and how I had been acting as a scout for our group.

Chestnut accompanied me to the Zaltana homestead. It contained a vast network of living, sleeping and cooking areas connected by bridges and suspended above the ground. Hidden by the thick jungle vegetation, the homestead was hard to find, but once inside the complex, I continued to be amazed the tree canopy could camouflage such a collection of rooms.

Built of wood, the floors of the buildings were anchored to wide branches. Ivy grew on the outside of all the walls to hide their shape. Almost all of the furniture was constructed of wood, and rope hammocks provided comfortable places to sleep. Handcrafts made of jungle items like seeds and sticks decorated the various rooms, including animal sculptures created by colored pebbles glued together.

The main throughway of the homestead tended to be common areas of each of the families within the clan. The living and sleeping quarters branched off from the public rooms.

Besides being extensive, the homestead was also well defended. The Zaltana magicians kept a vigilant watch for any strangers.

After our arrival, Chestnut hurried to find the clan elders and I scanned the path back to Moon Man. Once I was certain that the way was clear, I made contact with the Story Weaver's mind.

Come, I told him. *Come quickly.*

We are on the way, he replied.

I raced to my parents' suite. A few surprised glances and quizzical calls followed me as I dashed toward the Liana quarters, but I ignored them.

My mother, Perl, paced the living room. The air smelled like ginger and cinnamon, but her perfume distillery set up on the long table against the back wall appeared to be empty.

"Yelena!"

She flew into my arms. A few inches shorter than me, the slender woman clutched me as if to keep from falling.

"Mother. What's the matter?" I asked.

"Esau," she said, and cried.

I suppressed the urge to shake her as she sobbed in my arms. Instead, I waited for the flow of tears to subside before I pulled her away and looked into her light green eyes. "What about Father?"

"He's missing."

8

I RESISTED THE URGE to use magic to calm my mother. Many horrible scenarios played in my mind before she settled enough to tell me the details. My father had been expected back from an expedition yesterday and had failed to return.

"There was a clan meeting," Perl said between sobs. "A couple of scouts had gotten lost, and he went to find them."

"Lost scouts?"

She gave me a watery smile. "Some of the newer ones will lose their way. Esau always finds them. No one knows the jungle as well as he does."

"Maybe one of the scouts was hurt," I said, hoping to calm her and to stop myself from imagining Esau being a victim of the Kirakawa ritual. "Why was he expected yesterday?"

"Another clan meeting. The jungle creatures have been restless and disturbed and we can't pinpoint why. When the two scouts failed to return, the clan decided everyone should stay close to our homestead. Each night we gather in the common room to make sure everyone is safe. Esau was only supposed to be gone a few hours." Tears tracked down her cheeks.

Her face reflected the hours of worry and fear. Her long hair had more gray than black. I couldn't leave her alone, yet I needed more information.

"I have to talk with the clan elders," I said. "You can come along only if you promise not to get too upset."

She agreed, but uncertainty filled her eyes. Her hand went to her throat. Maybe taking her with me was a bad idea. Perhaps Nutty could stay with her?

Perl stiffened as if with a sudden realization. "Wait," she said before bolting toward the lift.

As I watched her pull the ropes and ascend to the second floor of the apartment, my heart filled with dread. Esau had invented that lift, using vines from the jungle and a pulley system. I wouldn't be able to forgive myself if anything happened to him.

Panic made me fidget, and just as I was about to call out to Perl to hurry, the lift moved. My mother had splashed water on her face and had tied her hair back. She also wore my fire amulet around her neck. I smiled.

"For strength," she said, and she met my gaze. This time only stubborn resolve radiated from her. "Let's go."

I thought about the fire amulet as we made our way to the homestead's meeting room. Winning an acrobatic contest during an Ixian fire festival, I had achieved a moment of pure joy in the midst of hell. Reyad—one of my captors, the first man I'd killed—had tried to keep me from participating, and I was severely punished for my disobedience, but I knew I would do it again. I now realized the stubborn streak from both my parents had kept me fighting despite Mogkan and Reyad's efforts to control me.

Our clan name might be Zaltana, but our family name was Liana, which meant vine in the old Illiais language. Those vines grew everywhere in the jungle, pulling down trees in their search for the sun. When cut and dried, the vines turned rock hard.

Looking at the firm set of my mother's shoulders, I knew she had reached the point where she would no longer bend to her emotions, but do what was needed to help find her husband.

The common room was the largest area of the homestead. Big enough to hold the entire clan, the round area had a stone fire pit at its center. The black ashy remains of the fire drifted in the sunlight, streaming from the smoke hole in the room's wooden ceiling. Benches made of branches and hardened vines ringed the pit. The scent of many perfumes lingered in the air and I remembered the first time I stood here.

The entire clan had filled the room then. Curious to see the lost child returned from—according to their viewpoint—the dead, they peered at me with a mixture of hope, joy and suspicion. My hopes for an uneventful reunion dissolved when my brother declared to all that I reeked of blood.

Chestnut interrupted my reminiscence by introducing me to the clan elders. "Oran Cinchona Zaltana and Violet Rambutan Zaltana."

They bowed in the formal Sitian greeting. Their dark faces creased with worry. These two dealt with the day-to-day problems of the clan when our clan leader, Bavol, was at the

Citadel. Missing scouts plus unexpected guests equaled big problems.

"Your friends have reached the palm ladder," Violet said. "When they climb up, they will be escorted here." A slight smile flickered across her face.

Relieved they had arrived safely, I projected my awareness to encourage Leif to hurry. When Leif opened his mind to me, his annoyance was clear.

You should have taken me with you to search for the Vermin, he said. Leif's muscles ached from the day-long march through the jungle. The trails tended to get overgrown quite fast in the steamy warmth, and Leif had had to cut a path for the others with his machete.

We can fight about it later, I said. *Right now I need you here.*

I can't leave Tauno.

Leif and Marrok had reached the tree canopy, but through Leif's eyes I saw Tauno frozen about halfway up the rope ladder, clutching the rungs with a death grip.

I moved my awareness to Tauno. Although he couldn't hear my words in his mind, I sent him calming emotions, reminding him how he had climbed down from rocks in the blackness of the cave. I chased his memory of that descent and realized why he hadn't been frightened then.

Close your eyes, I instructed.

He did. Tauno relaxed his hold and climbed the ladder.

I pulled away and reconnected to Leif. *Hurry.*

By the time Leif and the others joined us, I felt my desire for action pushing out, threatening to explode. I updated the clan elders on what I knew, but the only information that Oran and Violet added was the direction that the lost scouts had been assigned. South and east, and Esau had gone east first to find them.

"It has to be the Daviians," I said. "We have to rescue them before they can do any part of the Kirakawa ritual."

"Let's go." Leif held his machete tightly, a fierce countenance on his square face.

"You do not know for sure if the Vermin have your father," Moon Man said. "Or where they are. Or how many Warpers there are. Or how well defended they may be." The words tumbled out in a rush. Moon Man's eyebrows pinched together, reflecting his obvious discomfort with being surrounded by walls.

"All right, Mr. Logic. How do you propose we get this information?" I asked.

"Marrok and Tauno will search for trail signs and report back."

"Where?" I asked.

"To the east."

"And stumble into the same ambush as my father? They'll be caught and killed," I countered. "It's too risky to send people out there. The jungle is the perfect setting for ambushes. Unless—" A sudden idea circled in my mind. I thought it over, looking for any holes. If the Daviians hid behind a null shield, no magic could pierce it, but mundane physical things like sound and light would.

"Unless," Leif prompted.

"Unless we could get a bird's-eye view," I said.

"They probably have men stationed in the trees," Marrok said. "Isn't that how the scouts would have been captured?"

"Actually I was being literal. I could link with one of the birds in the jungle and see out through its eyes."

"You will not see much during the daytime," Moon Man said. "The Vermin will be well camouflaged. In the night, they will need a small fire and the moon to perform even the first level of the Kirakawa ritual."

A cold wave of dread washed over me. "The moon rose last night."

"Too soon. They need time to properly prepare themselves."

"For someone who claims the old rituals have been lost, you certainly know a lot about them," Marrok said. Accusation laced his voice.

"The specifics of the ritual have been forgotten, but some knowledge about them has been included in our teaching stories," Moon Man replied, meeting Marrok's stare. "It keeps us from making the same mistakes over and over and over again."

A warning to Marrok or just cryptic Story Weaver advice, I couldn't tell. Marrok rubbed his healed cheek. He tended to stroke the spot whenever he was upset or frightened. The wounds from Cahil's beating went deeper than shattered bone fragments. Broken trust was harder to fix than bones. I wondered if Marrok would change his opinion about Moon Man if he knew the Sandseed had helped repair his injuries.

"Can a bird see at night?" Leif asked, bringing our attention back to the problem at hand.

"There'll be light from the fire," Marrok said.

"But what about guards in the trees or outside the firelight?" Tauno asked. "We need to know how many Vermin are there."

I considered the difficulties and a solution flew into my mind. "Bats."

Tauno hunched over. "Where?"

"I'll link with the bats to find the Vermin. Their fire should attract insects the bats like to eat," I said.

"Can we afford to wait until dark?" Leif asked. "What if Yelena can't locate them with the bats? Then we will have wasted time that could have been spent searching for Father."

"Yelena will find them," my mother said. She had kept her promise and controlled her emotions during our discussion. Her confidence in me was heart-warming, but I still worried. Three lives were at stake.

"What happens when we find the Vermin?" Marrok asked.

"An army of Zaltanas could capture them," Leif said.

"That might or might not work," Moon Man said. "It will depend on how many Warpers they have with them."

"No. It's too risky." Oran Zaltana broke the silence he had held during our discussion. "I won't send clan members until we know what and who we're dealing with."

I glanced at the floor beneath the ceiling's smoke hole. The patch of sunlight had shifted. It would be dusk in a couple hours. "Let's find the Vermin first and determine their strength. Everyone else should eat and rest. It might be a long night."

When we filed out of the common room, Chestnut touched my arm. He had stood apart from our group as we talked. His dark brown eyes showed concern. "Esau is my favorite uncle. Let me know if I can help."

"I will." I followed Leif and Perl back to her apartment. She made us sit down on the couch Esau had built from vines. The leaves in the cushions crackled under my weight. Perl went into the kitchen and fetched a tray of food and tea. Our mother hovered over us until we ate. I pushed the fruit and cold meat past my numb lips and chewed without tasting.

Eventually fatigue from climbing through the jungle caught up to me and I dozed on the couch. Nightmares about serpents coiling around my body plagued my sleep as they hissed in my ear.

"—wake up. It's getting dark," Leif whispered.

I blinked in the gray light. Perl, curled in a ball, dozed on one of the armchairs. Moon Man stood near the door to the apartment.

I woke my mother. "Can you fetch the clan elders? We'll need to make plans once I've found Esau."

She hurried out the door.

"Where do you want to go?" Leif asked.

"Upstairs, to my old room," I said and headed for the lift.

Leif and Moon Man joined me in the closet-size lift. Two thick ropes went through holes in the ceiling and floor. Moon man bent over to fit. His breath came in uneven huffs and he muttered about Sandseeds, the plains and suffocating.

Leif and I pulled on the ropes and the lift began to move. We ascended to the upper level and walked down the hallway. My room was on the right. Pulling back the cotton curtain, I let Leif and Moon Man precede me into the small clutter-filled space.

A few years after my kidnapping, Esau had started using the area for storage. Fourteen years of collecting jungle samples had resulted in rows and rows of shelves filled with glass containers of every size and shape. The only places free of the assortment were a small bed and a wooden bureau.

Wanting to focus all my energy on linking with the bats, I stretched across the bed. "Try to keep all distractions away from me and be ready to help."

Leif and Moon Man signaled their understanding. Both had enough magical energy I could draw from if needed. I tried to keep the horrible thoughts about Esau's plight in the back of my mind as I projected my awareness toward the mouth of the cave. The bats would soon be leaving their roost in search for food.

My mind met the dark consciousness of the bats. They didn't perceive the world by sight, but by sensing objects and movement around them. Unable to direct them to where I wanted to go, I flew with them, my mental perception floating from one bat to another, trying to make sense of my location in the jungle. The flutter of wings and hum of insects cut through the silent night air.

Even though the bats had spread over many miles, they remained connected to each other, and I soon had a detailed mental image of the jungle. It was a bird's-eye view without colors—just shapes, sizes and movement. In my bat mind, the trees and rocks were not visual, but in scapes of sound.

The straight walls of the Zaltana homestead felt odd to the bats. They avoided the clan's dwellings, but I jumped over to the minds flying east of the homestead.

Frustrated because I couldn't affect their movements, I had to wait and watch until one bat found a small campfire. I channeled my awareness on the bat as it dived and flew through the hot rising air, snatching the insects that danced above the light.

Instinctively avoiding the creatures below, the bat stayed high in the air. I used the bat's senses to determine the number of Vermin. Three around the fire, two crouched in the trees and four stood guard outside the camp. A pair of tents were close to the fire. Three unmoving forms lay flat on the ground next to them. Alarmed, I focused my attention on them until I felt their chests rise and fall.

When I had the exact location of the Vermin's camp in my mind, I withdrew from the bat's consciousness.

"There are nine of them," I said to Leif and Moon Man. "I don't know how many are Warpers."

"We should have enough Zaltana magicians to overpower them," Leif said. "If we could surprise them, it would give us the advantage. Can you form a null shield?" Leif asked Moon Man.

"No. That is not one of my skills."

I sat up. A wave of dizziness crashed into me and I hunched over until the feeling passed. Linking with the bats had used my energy. Moon Man put a steadying hand on my elbow and his strength coursed through me.

I thought about what Leif said. If we attacked with a large group, the Vermin would know we were coming, and they would either flee and hide again, or fight back. Either way they would have time to kill their prisoners. The element of surprise was key, but how to achieve that?

"Could Tauno shoot the guards with Curare-laced arrows and immobilize them?" Leif asked. "Or could we blow treated darts through reed pipes?"

"Too many trees," Moon Man said.

"It would be hard in the dark," I agreed. "We could get close and jab them."

"But what about the guards in the trees? Getting close without alerting them is a difficult if not impossible maneuver," Leif said.

If I'd had the ability to control the bats, I could use them as a distraction. We needed something else to cause a commotion. I followed the logic and found an answer.

Leif, sensing my mood, smiled. "What are you scheming, little sister?"

WE DIDN'T HAVE MUCH TIME to waste. Leif, Moon Man and I rushed down to my parents' living area. Perl had returned with Oran and Violet.

"Did you find them?" Perl asked.

"They're about three miles southeast of us."

"We'll need some magicians and soldiers," Leif told Oran.

"How many are there, and what do the Vermin plan to do?" Oran asked me.

"Nine. And it doesn't matter what they plan. The Vermin have Esau and your scouts. We need to rescue them!"

Oran hemmed and hawed. "We should consult Councilman Bavol—"

"Bavol's at the Citadel. It will take weeks to get a reply." I suppressed the desire to wrap my hands around Oran's thin neck.

"We can't leave our homestead unprotected," Violet said. "We'll call a meeting and request a few volunteers."

Sitians! I thought in exasperation, couldn't do anything

without consulting a committee. "Fine. Call your meeting. Do whatever." I shooed Oran and Violet out the door.

"Yelena—" my mother began.

"You can scold me later. We're leaving now."

Leif and Moon Man looked at me as if waiting for orders. "Get Tauno and Marrok. I'll catch up to you at the base of the ladder."

"Where are you going?" Leif asked.

"To get our distraction."

They hurried from the room and I was about to follow when my mother grabbed my arm.

"Just a minute," she said. "There are only five of you. What are you planning? Tell me now or I'm coming along."

That Liana stubbornness radiated from her and I knew her threats weren't idle. I sketched a brief outline of my plan.

"That won't work without some help," she said.

"But I'm going to—"

"Need more incentive. I have just the thing. Go. I'll meet you at the base of the ladder." Perl rushed off.

After a few minutes of frantic searching, I found what I needed. By the time I slid down the ladder, the others were ready. Shafts of bright moonlight pierced the darkness of the jungle floor, giving just enough light to make out the shadowy shapes of the tree trunks.

I told Tauno and Marrok how to approach the Vermin camp and guards and instructed them on where to position themselves nearby. "No noise. Keep your distance. Wait for my signal before attacking."

"Signal?" Marrok asked. His face hardened into grim determination, but uncertainty lurked behind his eyes. Even though Cahil had issued orders to his men, Marrok had really been the one in charge.

"Something loud and obnoxious," I said.

Marrok frowned. "This isn't the time to joke."

"I wasn't joking."

After a mere moment's hesitation, Marrok and Tauno set off. Moon Man stared after them. "What about us?"

There was a faint rustling from above as someone took hold of the rope ladder. A few heartbeats later, Chestnut joined us on the jungle floor. He wore a dark-colored tunic and pants, and his drum was tied to his belt. The green paint and dye had been washed from his hair.

"I'm glad I could help," Chestnut said. "But you need to know I've never done this before."

"Done what?" Leif asked. "Yelena, what's going on?"

"I'm hoping Chestnut will be able to call a few necklace snakes to join the Vermin's party."

"Ah. Your distraction," Moon Man said.

"How close do you need to be?" I asked Chestnut.

"Probably within a mile, but it'll all depend on how many snakes are around." He hesitated. "I'm used to chasing them away, not calling them. What if it doesn't work?"

As if on cue, the rope ladder swung with the weight of another person. Perl descended. She moved as graceful as liquid, and I would have bet Nutty hadn't been the only Zaltana child to drive her parents crazy by learning to climb before she could walk.

"Here." My mother handed me ten grape-size capsules and several straight pins. "Just in case your first plan fails."

"What if the second plan fails?" Leif asked.

"Then we'll storm the camp and hope for the best. Come

on." I put the capsules in my pocket, put the pins through my shirt so they didn't stick me, adjusted my pack so its weight rested between my shoulder blades, and pulled my bow.

"Be careful," Perl said.

I hugged her before setting off. While I had told Marrok and Tauno to take a wider more circuitous path to the Vermin, I wanted to lead the three men straight toward them. Once again I made a light mental connection to the bats flying above us. Guided by the bats' shape map of the jungle, I moved with ease through the tight trail even though the tree canopy blocked the dim moonlight in places.

The jungle's night sounds echoed in the damp air. A howler bat cried in a loud staccato. Valmurs climbed and swung through the trees. The rustle and shake of branches and bushes hinted at the unseen activity of other night creatures.

About a mile from the Vermin camp, I halted. Chestnut leaned his forehead on a nearby tree and power brushed my skin.

"There is only one snake nearby," he said. "He is waiting for the men in the trees to stumble into his trap. Necklace snakes are not active hunters. They prefer to lie in wait, using the element of surprise." Chestnut looked at me. "And I don't want to teach them how to hunt."

"That is a good point," Moon Man said.

"Now what?" Leif asked.

"I'm thinking," I said.

"Think faster," Leif urged.

One snake wasn't enough. Time for Perl's suggestion. I handed everyone two capsules and a pin. "Get as close to the guards as you can. Poke a small hole in the capsule and squirt the liquid near them. Don't get it on you," I instructed.

"Why not?" Leif asked.

"You'll have a necklace snake trying to mate with you."

"Gee, Yelena. I'm so *glad* you're home," Leif grumbled. "It's good to know Mother is doing something useful with her time."

"I thought your mother made perfumes," Moon Man said.

"It all depends on how you look at it," Chestnut said. "To a male necklace snake, that stuff *is* a perfume."

"There are six guards. Moon Man, Leif and I will each spray two," I said. Taking off my pack, I stashed it behind a tree. "Chestnut, you stay back here. Can you keep the snakes from grabbing us when they come?"

"I'll try. They have an excellent sense of smell so get clear once you spray that stuff."

"What about the guards in the trees?" Leif asked.

"Aim high and be quiet about it."

Leif muttered to himself as the three of us fanned out to approach the Vermin guards. Chestnut stayed behind to communicate with the predators while we moved into position. Once our distraction arrived and the guards became busy dodging amorous snakes, Leif and Moon Man would find Marrok and Tauno and await my signal. I would spy on the Vermin in the camp.

I crept through the trees, seeking a sign of the guards. I disconnected with the bats and reached out with my mental awareness, searching for the Vermin.

Beyond the outer guards, I knew the camp held six people, three Daviians and three Zaltanas, yet I couldn't detect them, which meant someone had erected a null shield. At least one of the Vermin was a Warper and he could be performing one of the Kirakawa rites while we snuck around in the dark. It was then I realized the sounds from the jungle had ceased.

My heart drummed a faster beat as my stomach cramped with fear. A presence hovered above me and I connected with a man crouched in the lower branches of a tree. His mind was alert for signs of intruders, but he hadn't detected me. Poking a hole in one capsule, I sprayed the liquid along the tree's trunk, and then slipped away.

Five minutes later, I found my second guard. She failed to notice my approach and I squirted some of Perl's snake perfume on the bushes near her. I hoped she would rub against them at some point.

As I retreated, I tripped over a buttress root and fell. I turned over on my back in time to see her aim an arrow at me.

"Freeze," she shouted. "Hands up."

So much for being quiet. I raised my hands and cursed myself for not reestablishing my link with the bats. Through their eyes, I never would have tripped.

She called to another guard.

"Stand up slowly," she ordered. "Leave your weapon."

My bow rested on the ground within reach.

She stepped closer and peered at me in the semidarkness. The guard gasped and said, "Soulfinder."

I rolled as her weapon twanged and snatched my bow. The arrow stuck the dirt. I jumped to my feet, swinging my staff in a wide arc. The end of my weapon caught her behind her ankles. I yanked her feet out from under her. She went down with a loud oath. The black shape of her partner grew bigger as he ran toward us. Great.

The air filled with a strange rasp as if a person had pulled a rope from a wooden holder very fast. The noise grew louder and came from all directions. The three of us stopped. All thoughts of fighting banished as we searched for the source of the sound.

A necklace snake slithered past my legs. It aimed for the female guard and wrapped around her with amazing speed. All my preconceptions about a slow-moving creature dissipated.

The other guard looked at his partner and bolted. Another snake slid after him. The vibrations of the necklace snakes and Chestnut's drum thrummed in my chest.

I projected into Chestnut's mind for an update. He kept the creatures from going after us, but he didn't know how long he could maintain control.

Faster is better, he said.

Right. I switched my awareness to Moon Man. He and Leif had marked the other four guards. They waited with Marrok and Tauno for my signal.

Running toward the campfire, I avoided snakes, terrified guards and broke through the null shield. I stumbled for a moment as an array of thoughts and emotions washed over me. The air was charged with magic and fear. My panic pressed on my back, but I forced myself to slow down.

When I reached the edge of the Vermin camp, my blood turned to ice. Three men pulled out the stomach of one of the prone forms on the ground. The Vermin turned their attention to me, their surprise evident in their openmouthed gapes. I had moved without realizing it and stood in the middle of their camp, screaming at them to stop.

10

WE BLINKED AT EACH OTHER for a stunned moment. Blood and gore dripped from the Vermin's hands. The three men then returned to their macabre task, ignoring me. Astonished, I moved toward them, raising my bow to strike when a blistering force slammed into me from behind as if I'd been struck with a red-hot iron pan.

I hit the ground hard. My bow flew from my grasp. My breath whooshed out. Searing pain clung to my back; I rolled over, convinced my clothes were on fire. Gasping for air, I thrashed on the ground until I spotted what had attacked me. I froze in horror. The Vermin's campfire had grown to three times its previous size. A man stood in the midst of the roaring bonfire.

The man stepped from the burning wood. Scorched black from head to toe, small flames clung to him like feathers. He advanced toward me. I broke my paralysis and scrambled away from him. He stopped. A trail of fire linked him with the campfire.

"Did I surprise you, my little bat?" the man asked. "Counted nine when there really were ten. Hot little trick."

He knew my consciousness had flown with the bats. But *who* was he?

I scanned the surrounding jungle, looking for my backup. Leif and my friends were at the edge of the clearing. Their arms and hands were raised as if they protected their faces from a searing wind. Sweat and soot stained their clothes and they averted their gazes from the man.

"No help from them, my little bat. They will burn if they come any closer."

I tried to project into the flaming man's mind, but his mental defenses proved impenetrable, a Warper of incredible strength. Running out of options, I glanced behind me and caught sight of my bow.

The blazing Warper pointed and a line of fire appeared between me and my weapon. I jumped to my feet. The heat singed the hair in my nose. The moisture evaporated from my mouth. I tasted ashes. A wall of hot air pushed against me and the Warper was before me. Yet his connection with the burning wood remained.

"Fire is your downfall, little bat. Can not call it. Can not control it."

My body roasted as if I had been staked to a spit over a giant campfire. I cast my awareness into the jungle, hoping to find help. Nothing but the panicked thoughts of my friends and one curious necklace snake nearby.

Just when I thought I would faint, he extended his hands and a bubble of cool air caressed my skin. The break from the heat was an intoxicating relief. I swayed.

"Take my hands. I will not burn you. Travel with me through the fire."

"Why?"

"Because you belong to me."

"Not good enough. Many others have made that claim."

"I need you to complete my mission."

"Which is…?"

The flames on his shoulders pulsed in amusement. He laughed. "Nice try. Take my offer or I will burn you and your friends into a pile of ash."

"No."

Flaring brightly, the flames jumped in size before he shrugged. "No matter."

The cold air disappeared and I gasped. The heat's intensity robbed my lungs of air.

"I need only wait until you go to sleep, little bat. Then I will take you."

My throat strained as my vision scrambled. Sleep was a nice way of describing the process of suffocation. It was a strange notion, but it gave me an idea.

With my last bit of energy, I grabbed a capsule from my pocket and crushed it in my hand. The sticky liquid coated my palm, dripping down my arm. My legs buckled as I collapsed to my knees. The last thing I remembered before the world melted was a brown and green coil reaching for me.

I woke, shivering. Chestnut's concerned face peered at me. He waved a large leaf, fanning me with cool clean air. Exhaustion lined his brown eyes.

"I guess that's one necklace snake who'll go away hungry," Chestnut said.

"What do you mean?" I asked, wincing at the sharp pain in my throat. When I tried to sit, I realized we were on a tree branch.

Chestnut helped me. "If you died, I told the snake he could eat you." He smiled.

"I'm sorry to disappoint him."

"No matter. Perhaps we'll have some extra Vermin to feed him." His grin faded.

I jerked as my memory returned. "The Fire Warper! My father! The others! What—"

Chestnut raised his hand. "When the snake grabbed you and pulled you into the trees, he distracted the Warper long enough for Leif to break through the wall of heat. With Moon Man's help, Leif was able to quench the link between the main fire and the Warper." Chestnut glanced away. "The Warper disappeared." He shuddered. "The remaining Vermin ran off, with Moon Man, Tauno and Marrok chasing after them."

"And Leif?"

"Below with your father."

Before I could ask, Chestnut said, "He's fine. Although I fear Stono will not live to see the dawn."

Sudden purpose energized me. "Help me get down."

My limbs trembled as I slid and crashed through the lower branches. I hit the ground hard, but didn't stop until I stood next to Leif. He had Stono's head in his lap. My gaze shied away from the gruesome mess that used to be Stono's stomach. My father and the other scout lay on the ground next to them, unmoving— still paralyzed by the Curare. I couldn't see my friends.

"Where are the others?" I asked.

"They haven't returned," Chestnut said. He sank to the ground next to Leif and took Stono's left hand in his own.

"At least he isn't feeling any pain," Leif whispered. Streaks of soot and sweat lined Leif's face. Burn holes peppered his clothes. He reeked of smoke and body odor.

I knelt beside Leif. I put two fingers on Stono's neck and felt a tentative heartbeat. Stono groaned and his eyelids fluttered.

"He's not paralyzed like the others so the Kirakawa ritual could work," I said.

"Can you save him?" Leif asked.

Stono's wounds were fatal. I hadn't healed anyone with such extensive damage before. Tula's windpipe had been crushed when she was killed. I was able to repair the damage, but couldn't "wake" her without her soul. Why not? According to Roze's fire scenario, I had the power to create a soulless army.

"Yelena." Leif's impatience cut through my musings. "Can you save him?"

Would I be able to save myself once I assumed his injuries? I drew in a shaky breath. Only one way to find out.

Closing my eyes, I pulled power and wrapped thick strands of magic around my stomach. I reached for Stono and forced myself to examine the bloody distended mass, seeing his wounds through my magic. His wounds pulsed with an urgent red glow as I focused on them.

Without warning, Stono's heart stopped its labor and his soul rose from his body. Instinct drove my actions as I breathed in his soul from the air and tucked it into a safe corner of my mind. I ignored his confused thoughts, concentrating on his injuries. My stomach exploded with the pain of a million sharp knives digging deep into my guts. Clutching my abdomen, I curled into a ball. Blood coated my hands, arms, and pooled on the ground. The air filled with the hot stench of body fluids.

I struggled to push the pain away, but it clung to me, eating its way through my spine and toward my heart. Leif's voice battered at my ears. He wanted something. Annoyed by his persistence, I transferred my attention to him for a moment. His energy flooded my body. We stopped the advance of pain, but we couldn't conquer it. It was only a matter of time before our strength failed and we would lose the battle.

Moon Man's resigned voice sounded in my mind. *I can not leave you alone. What made you believe you could counter the power of the Kirakawa ritual on your own?*

I didn't—

Know? Think? Does it matter now?

Moon Man's blue energy added to Leif's and together the three of us banished the pain.

I reached for Stono and laid my hand on his smooth stomach. *Go back,* I instructed his soul. A tingling sting pulsed down my arm. When I felt his gasp for breath, I pulled my hand back.

Too exhausted to move, I fell asleep where I lay.

At one point a hand shook me into semiconsciousness.

"Theobroma?" Leif asked, his voice a distant call.

My tired thoughts slogged through a fog. "Pack," I muttered.

"Where?"

Leif shook me again. I batted at his arms, but he wouldn't stop.

"Where?"

"Backpack. In jungle. Snake."

"I'll go," Chestnut said.

His retreating footsteps lulled me back to sleep.

I woke choking on a foul-tasting liquid. Coughing, I sat up and spit.

"You still need to drink the rest," my father said.

He offered me a cup.

"What is it?" I clasped the mug. The green-colored contents smelled like swamp water.

"Soursop tea. Restores the body's strength. Now drink."

I grimaced and put the cup to my lips, but couldn't produce the nerve to consume it.

Esau sighed. Blood and dirt matted his shoulder-length gray hair. He looked older than his fifty years. Weariness pulled at his broad shoulders. "Yelena, I would like to get home. And your mother must be having fits by now."

Good point. Cringing at the rancid flavor, I gulped the tea. My raw throat burned as I swallowed the liquid, but, after a few moments, I felt more awake and energetic.

The sun loomed high in the sky and the clearing was empty. "Where is everyone?" I asked.

Esau grunted. "I'll tell you on the way home." He stood.

Spotting my backpack nearby, I checked through the contents before shouldering the pack. My bow rested on the ground next to a wide scorch mark. I hefted the weapon, running my hands along the ebony wood. It appeared to be unharmed. A nice surprise since, during the skirmish, I had thought the Fire Warper had reduced my bow to a pile of ash.

A hot flush of fear raced over my skin when I thought of the Fire Warper. I had never encountered magic like his. I had been completely unprepared to fight him, and I couldn't think of anyone in Sitia who could match his power. But what about in Ixia? My thoughts turned to Valek. Would his immunity to magic save him from the Fire Warper's flames? Or would he be consumed?

"Come on, Yelena," Esau said.

I shook off my morbid thoughts and followed my father from the clearing. He set a quick pace, and, once I caught up to him, I asked him what had happened after I had fallen asleep.

He huffed in amusement. "Passed out, you mean?"

"I had just saved Stono's life. And yours, too."

Stopping, Esau grabbed me in a tight hug. "I know. You did good."

He released me just as fast as he had seized me and continued through the jungle. I hurried after.

"The others?" I asked.

"You were asleep for a full day. We thought it best for Leif and Chestnut to take Stono and Barken back to the homestead. The Sandseeds and the other Ixian fellow never came back."

I stopped. "They could be in trouble."

"Two Sandseed warriors and a swordsman against three Daviians? I doubt it."

"How about against three Vermin with Curare?"

"Ah, hell!" Esau spit. "I wish I had never discovered that

foul substance!" He pounded his fists on his thighs. "I had hoped the supply they stole from the Sandseeds would be almost gone by now."

"You extracted the drug from a vine in the jungle?"

"Yes."

"So how do they know how to make more?" I wondered out loud.

"And where are they making it?" Esau glanced around. "Maybe in the jungle. I'm going to cut down every single Curare vine and burn it," Esau vowed.

I put a hand on my father's arm. "Remember why you searched for it. There're plenty of good uses. Our immediate concern should be for Moon Man and the others. I'm going to try to contact him."

Gathering power, I projected my mind into the surrounding jungle. My awareness touched a variety of life. Valmurs swung through the tree canopy, birds perched on branches, and other small creatures scurried through the underbrush. But I couldn't locate Moon Man's cool thoughts.

Did the Vermin have him hidden behind a null shield? Was he dead? I searched for Tauno and Marrok, also to no avail.

My father said, "Let's go home and figure out a way to find them. *All* of them, including the Curare-making Vermin."

He reminded me of the other Vermin guards we had sprayed with the snake perfume. "We can question the Daviian guards. Are they at our homestead?"

Esau tugged on his stained tunic as if deciding how to tell me something unpleasant. "When you were picked up by that snake, the creature wasn't happy to discover you weren't a female snake. So in order for Chestnut to keep you from being

devoured, he had to concentrate all his efforts on saving you."
He paused.

"And that means...?"

"He lost control of the other snakes."

"The guards are dead?"

"An unfortunate development, but there is an upside," Esau
said.

"Which is?"

"Now there are four very full necklace snakes who won't
be bothering the Zaltanas for a long while."

I washed as much dried blood and sticky gore from my body
as I could in the small stream flowing underneath my clan's
homestead. My mother would worry and fuss over my dishev-
eled appearance despite the fact I would be standing before her
safe and sound.

Climbing the ladder into the tree canopy, I mulled over
recent events. There might be a group of Daviian Vermin
working in the jungle, gathering vines and distilling Curare. I
had no idea where Ferde and Cahil had gone or where my
friends had disappeared to. And there was a Fire Warper on
the loose who could possibly jump out of any campfire in Sitia.
My life in Ixia as the Commander's food taster sounded like a
vacation in comparison.

Why had I wanted to leave Ixia? An order for my execution for being a magician had been one compelling reason to
escape to Sitia. That and wanting to meet my family, whom I
had no memories of until Moon Man unlocked them. Well,
I'd met my parents and the execution order had been revoked.
The thought of returning to Valek and Ixia tempted me.

I reached the top of the ladder and arrived into a small receiving room made of branches tied together. Esau hadn't waited. The Zaltana guard stationed there informed me my father would meet me in my parents' living quarters.

Walking toward their apartment, I marveled at the ingenuity and craftsmanship of the vast complex of living areas built above the jungle floor. The Zaltanas were resourceful and determined and stubborn. All traits I had been accused of possessing.

I wondered if those qualities would be enough to counter the Fire Warper. Did I have the experience or magical knowledge to find Moon Man, recapture Ferde and stop the Vermin from killing more people?

The daunting and overwhelming to-do list would not deter me from making the attempt or die trying. But how many would be hurt or killed in the process because of me?

II

I NEVER REACHED my parents' suite. My cousin Nutty intercepted me en route, relaying a message to go to the common room. She scrunched up her face and tsked over my ripped and stained clothes.

"I have a change in my pack," I told her.

"Let's see then." She held out her long thin arms, waiting.

Knowing it was useless to argue with her, I opened my bag and showed her the other set of skirt/pants and cotton top she had sewn for me. I thought a lifetime's worth of events had happened since then, but in reality it had only been two seasons.

Nutty examined the clothes with a dismayed purse to her full lips. "You'll need some new ones. I'll make them for you." With a slight nod of farewell, she hopped up into the tree branches with the grace and speed of a valmur, disdaining the practical rope bridge.

"Oh, snake spit," she called from above. "I'm supposed to fetch Uncle Esau and Aunt Perl." She changed directions and disappeared through the trees.

I reached the common room. Oran, Violet, Chestnut and the two scouts stood together. My strong relief over the absence of a fire in the central pit alarmed me. If I was afraid of a simple hearth fire, what would I do when faced with the Fire Warper again? I avoided thinking about that scenario and focused my attention on the matter at hand.

When he saw me, Stono sat down. His face drained of color, and I worried he would faint. He muttered a thank-you to the floor, evading my gaze. Oran and Violet continued to question Chestnut on the necklace snakes.

Chestnut stammered and fidgeted. "I wanted to help."

"You didn't have our permission," Oran said. "And now how many are dead?"

"Six," Chestnut said in a quiet voice.

"Good for you, Chessie," Stono said. "I wish you had killed them all. Pulled out their guts and strangled them with it!" Stono's eyes lit with murderous intensity.

The elders rounded on Stono. Shock mirrored on their faces.

Violet recovered first. "Stono, you've had a difficult time. Why don't you go and get some rest," she ordered.

He stood on trembling legs and shuffled a few steps, but paused next to me.

"I'll kill the snake that tried to eat you if you want," he whispered in my ear. "Let me know what I can kill for you."

I turned to protest, but he moved away.

"What did he say?" Oran asked.

What, indeed? An offer of revenge on a snake or something more disturbing. "He said he would like to help me."

"Not without *our* permission." Oran puffed up his chest with importance.

"You can't just use our clan members as your personal army. Taking Chestnut into an unknown, dangerous situation that could have killed him was wrong."

I had had enough of Oran Cinchona Zaltana. Stepping close to him, I said, "Could have, but didn't. If we had waited for *your* permission, you *would have* lost three clan members. And I wouldn't debate too long on how you're going to search for a possible nest of Vermin living in *your* jungle. If you wait too long, they're liable to multiply."

"What are you talking about?" Violet asked.

It was then that Esau and Perl joined us. Having heard my warning, Mother touched her throat, and my father's grim expression deepened.

"Father, could you inform the elders about the potential threat? I have other business to attend to," I said.

"Where are you going?" Perl asked.

"To find my friends."

I found Leif in our parents' quarters. He was sound asleep on the couch and it occurred to me that I didn't know if he had his own rooms within the Zaltana homestead. Esau had knocked down the wall to Leif's room to expand his work area. Unwilling to bother my brother, I tiptoed past him and went up to my room. Soon the sun would set and I wanted to fly with the bats.

Lying down on my narrow bed, I felt sleep pull at me. I resisted, thinking of Moon Man. He had helped me and Leif in healing Stono. Perhaps the effort had exhausted him and rendered him unable to respond to my search.

As the light dimmed, I drew magic from the power source

and projected my mind into the jungle. Finding the collective consciousness of the bats, I joined in their nightly hunt for food.

I floated from one bat to another, sensing the space below and around. On the lookout for any fires or signs of people, I coasted through the air, feeling the sun leave the sky. I wondered how the bats could know the size and shapes of their surroundings without seeing them. Was it a skill I could learn? My magic let me feel living beings, but I couldn't sense anything from the lifeless objects in my path.

The bats invaded every section of the Illiais Jungle. Nestled below the Daviian Plateau, the jungle wasn't large. Two days of hard walking would see a person from one end to the other. The Illiais Market marked the western border of the jungle. A few bats swooped close to the market campfires, but they avoided the gritty air and noisy crowds of people.

I pulled my awareness back. Having found no physical signs of Moon Man or the others in the jungle, I decided Leif and I would travel to the market tomorrow. The market was the rendezvous location we had set back on the plateau. If Moon Man followed the Vermin from the jungle, he would eventually look for us there. I hoped.

When I awoke the next morning, a group of people were in my parents' living area, all engaged in animated conversation.

"It's your turn. I delivered a wagonload of pummelo fruit last time," Nutty said to Chestnut. "See?" She held up her right hand. "I still have the blisters."

"I'm not stupid. They're from staying up all night finishing the clothes you owe Fern," Chestnut retorted. "It's your turn to go to the market."

"You can't go collecting every single Curare vine, Esau. It will take you seasons," Perl said. "And what about the Vermin? If they caught you again—" Perl's hand flew to her throat as if she tried to block the emotion welling from her heart.

"I'm not worried about that," Esau said. "I'm worried about what they can do with the Curare!"

"Curare can be countered with Theobroma," Leif said to Esau. "We just need to make sure everyone has enough with them."

"Is not my turn," Nutty said.

"Is too," Chestnut countered.

"Yelena!" Nutty cried, spotting me. "I've made another pair of skirt/pants for you." She held a light blue-and-yellow print.

"Thanks," I said. "You don't have to go to the market, Nutty. I'll deliver the clothes for you. And Leif, Theobroma is good at regaining movement, but it leaves you helpless against a magical attack. Father, can you find a way to get the Theobroma to work against Curare without the side effects? That would be more helpful than tearing down every vine. Besides, I couldn't find any signs the Vermin are collecting vines right now, but I think sending out well-armed scouts to search the jungle from time to time would be a good idea."

"Yelena's here," Leif said. "Problems solved," he teased.

"I'll have an easier time with the Theobroma than convincing Oran and Violet to send out reconnaissance teams," Esau said. "They want to huddle in our homestead and hide!"

"I'll handle Oran and Violet," Perl said.

Her face had set in a determined frown, which she then turned on me. "You're leaving us already?"

"We need to rendezvous with our horses and our other team members," I said.

"Are they at the market?" Leif asked with a hopeful note in his voice.

"Too many people for me to determine. In any case we need to look for signs of Ferde and Cahil." They could be anywhere by now and doing unspeakable things. I shuddered as the image of Stono's ruined stomach rose in my mind.

"Not without breakfast." Perl hurried toward the kitchen.

"I'll go get the dresses." Nutty bounded away.

"I'd better get my pack ready." Leif smiled. "Never a dull day with you, little sister."

"What do you need?" Esau asked me.

"I'm running out of Theobroma and Curare."

He went into the lift to ascend to the second floor. Chestnut looked around at the suddenly quiet room. He fidgeted, avoiding my gaze and I realized he wanted to talk about something other than whose turn it was to go to the market.

"Now's the time," I said. "Once everyone comes back…"

"I can't…" He moved his hands as if he wanted to pull his thoughts from the air. "I'm having trouble getting past…" Wrapping his arms around his body, Chestnut rocked with frustration. "How can you be so calm? Standing there, making plans, barking out orders. Six people have died. Stono came back from the dead and now he's different—"

"Different? How?"

"It's probably nothing. He's had a shock, but he's harsher

somehow." Chestnut shook his head. "That's not the point. Six people killed by necklace snakes. That's the point."

I understood his problem. "You've never lost anyone to a snake before?"

"No one. I know it's not a terrible death. At least they're dead before they get swallowed. I've always been kind of curious…" He cringed with guilt.

"Curious to see a snake devour its prey and you feel responsible for not stopping the snakes?"

"Yes." The word hissed out.

"Think of what would have happened if the snakes had released the Vermin."

"You and Stono would have died."

"I'm not happy about the death of six people either, but, considering the alternative, I can rationalize it in my mind." A shiver raced over my skin. As long as I didn't think about it too much. "You asked how I can be so calm. I don't have time not to be. I would like to grieve and worry and carry on, but that doesn't get results."

"And results are important. Right, Yelena?" Leif asked as he entered the room. "One of the foremost things the First Magician taught me when I arrived at the Keep was to leave all sentimentality behind. Roze believes she was given the gift of magic to use for a purpose and she can't let guilt and remorse keep her from achieving that purpose." Leif rubbed his chin as his face settled into a thoughtful expression. "You're a lot like her."

"I am not," I said.

"It was a compliment. You're both intelligent. You're doers. Natural leaders."

I disagreed. I didn't conduct myself like Roze. She was a tyrant who thought she knew everything and didn't stop to consider other options or other people's views. I wasn't like that. Was I?

"Although *she* has a bad temper," Leif said. "She was wrong about Ferde and Cahil's direction. She's not going to be happy about it."

"That I would agree with," I said.

"Agree with what?" Esau asked. His arms brimmed with containers.

Nutty arrived with her stack of clothes, then Perl returned with a tray full of fruit and tea. By the time we ate, the morning hours were gone.

"We better go. It'll be a hard push to get to the market before dark," Leif said.

"Yelena, you have to come back and have a proper visit," my mother instructed. "Perhaps when your life settles down." She thought for a moment, and added, "Perhaps you can make some time to visit. I don't see things settling down for you for a long while."

"Do you know this from your magic?" I asked.

"No, dear. From your history." A smile quirked her lips before Perl's stern mother expression returned long enough for her to lecture me on being careful.

With our backpacks loaded, Leif and I climbed down the ladder to the jungle floor. He set a quick pace and I hurried after him. When we stopped for a short rest, I tossed my heavy pack down and rubbed my sore back. Now I could sympathize with a pack horse.... Kiki!

"Leif, does this trail stay wide until the market?"

"As long as no trees have fallen over recently. The Zaltanas keep this pretty clear. Why?"

"The horses."

He smacked his forehead with a hand.

I reached out with my mind and searched for Kiki's thoughts.

She hid with Garnet and Rusalka in the forest west of the market.

Late, she said in my mind. *Dirty. Hungry.*

Come meet us on the jungle trail? We'll get to the market faster. Groomed faster.

She agreed. Leif and I continued to hike for a while in silence. The insects' droning grew louder as the sunlight began to wane.

"I keep forgetting you can communicate with horses," Leif said. "I think you might be the first one in Sitian history."

"Are you sure?"

"All the Keep's students had to learn about past magicians and their powers, but Master Bloodgood would know for sure."

Bain Bloodgood, Second Magician, was a walking, talking history book. My list of questions grew longer each day. I had so much to learn about magic and history. The sheer amount overwhelmed me at times, and reminded me how unprepared I was.

And how did I end up with these Soulfinder powers? Both my parents hadn't enough power to be invited to the Keep so I hadn't inherited them. Sheer dumb luck?

Leif interrupted my thoughts. "Do you know anyone else who can talk to horses?"

"The Stable Master has said he knows the horses' moods and

intentions, but he doesn't hear their words in his mind per se." And he had looked at me as if I had grown wings when I mentioned it to him.

"How about in Ixia?"

I considered. When the Commander had taken control of Ixia over sixteen years ago, he had ordered Valek, his chief of security, to assassinate all the magicians. Then, whenever an Ixian developed the ability to use magic—usually after puberty—Valek would assassinate the person if they hadn't already escaped to Sitia. No magicians in Ixia, but my thoughts did linger on Porter, the Commander's kennel master. He had an uncanny knack with the dogs, and he hadn't needed leashes or a whistle to get them to obey him.

"Perhaps one other," I said. "Though he would never admit to it—that would be a death sentence."

"Maybe we could help smuggle him to Sitia."

"I don't think he would want to come."

"Why not?" The idea shocked Leif.

"I'll explain later." I didn't have the energy to educate Leif about the Commander's politics. Raised in Sitia, Leif believed Ixia equaled a horrible place to live. That with Ixia's strict Code of Behavior, uniform requirement and having to obtain permits to marry or move to another house, the citizens had to be extremely unhappy. Ixia wasn't perfect, but there were benefits to living there. For me, Valek was one.

I missed seeing him every day, missed discussing poisons and fighting tactics and missed having a soul mate who knew what I needed before I did. I sighed. Better to have an immunity to magic like Valek than to be this feared Soulfinder. A Soulfinder, and completely useless against a Fire Warper.

The Commander's views on magic didn't seem so extreme now. Magic was messy. And what the Vermin had done to increase their powers remained more horrible than anything I had witnessed in Ixia.

"Leif, what about that Fire Warper?" I asked. Since the incident in the jungle, I hadn't had time to discuss it with him. "Have you seen a magician step from a fire before?"

"No. Roze Featherstone can make huge fires that'll consume whole buildings, but she'll burn if she gets too close to one. Since you've come home, I've been seeing all types of strange magic. You bring out the best and the worst in people," Leif tried to joke.

I failed to be amused. "The Vermin are using old magical rituals. Do you know anything about them?"

"The Sandseed Story Weavers' powers are legendary. They used to be called Efe Warriors. I had thought the stories of these Warriors were exaggerated." Leif paused for a moment. "Until now. Two thousand years ago, well before the Sitian clans united, the Efe Tribe dominated the others. Using blood magic, the Efes had no rivals. The other clans would give them whatever they wanted. Food, gold or sacrifices, hoping to placate them. A disagreement erupted between the Efe rulers and a civil war started. The ensuing battle flattened the Daviian Mountains."

"Mountains?"

"Now a plateau."

"Oh my."

"Right. After that a new leader named Guyan took control of the tribe's survivors. He declared he would plant the seeds for a new tribe in the sands that fell when the mountains were destroyed. That's how they got the name Sandseed and their magicians were then called Story Weavers."

The rumble of hooves interrupted Leif's tale. Kiki's face was a welcome sight, although her blue eyes looked tired and mud covered her copper-colored coat. Garnet and Rusalka hadn't fared any better.

Leif and I fed and watered the horses. I wanted to groom them and let them rest, but Leif insisted we get to the market first.

"Too many predators at night," Leif said. "The horses will attract every tree leopard in the jungle."

Market not far, Kiki said. *Jungle smells…odd.*

We mounted and galloped toward the market. Being with us, the horses didn't have to hide and we groomed them near the Zaltana campfire behind the market buildings as the sun began to set. Many clans had built permanent sites for their members to stay while trading or purchasing goods.

The Illiais Market did not close until late into the evening hours. An array of torches was lit to allow business to continue, although the commotion of customers bidding, arguing and shopping quieted in the evenings.

After the horses were settled, I strolled quickly through the collection of bamboo buildings topped with thatched roofs. Most of the owners had the bamboo shade walls down to block the cold night breeze. When I had been here before, it had been the beginning of the hot season, and the shades had been rolled up to help cool the workers.

Scanning the people at the market, I searched for Moon Man. I stopped a few customers and asked if anyone had seen my friends. One stand owner recalled spotting some men running through the market a few days ago, but he couldn't describe them.

My imagination kicked in and visions of Moon Man, Tauno and Marrok staked to the ground for the Kirakawa ritual filled my mind. Hidden behind a null shield, I wouldn't be able to find them, and every minute we delayed was another minute for Cahil and Ferde.

Focusing on the task at hand, I breathed in the market's smells to ease the tightness in my chest. The exotic spices offered by the Greenblade Clan mixed with the smell of roasting meat. My stomach growled with hunger. Before I could stop to eat, I delivered the package of clothes to Fern. The small woman huffed with relief.

"I thought Nutty wouldn't have them done in time," she exclaimed from behind a table piled with bolts of cloth.

"I thought you sold fabric," I said.

"I'm expanding my business. Nutty's getting quite the reputation."

"Is that good or bad?" I asked.

"Both. A few of the Greenblade women have gotten tired of their plain green tunics and leggings and wanted a more colorful wardrobe. They've been buying every single one of Nutty's shirts, dresses and skirt/pants. I supply the cloth and we split the profits. However, the clan elders are not too happy about the break with tradition."

As a forest-dwelling clan, the Greenblades usually wore the colors of the forest. I glanced around and, sure enough, spotted a few women wearing Nutty's bright cotton creations. I had assumed they were Zaltanas, but upon closer examination, I could see the lighter maple coloring of the Greenblade's skin.

In Ixia, I knew which Military District someone lived in by

the color of their uniform. Here, it was all a matter of knowing how each clan preferred to dress. Interesting.

"Yelena, do you need some new material?" Fern asked. She pulled out a bolt of fabric from under her table. "I just finished this beautiful green pattern. See?" She held it up to the torch-light. "Just a hint of gold woven through the fabric. Matches your eyes perfectly."

I laughed. "You're quite the saleswoman. But Nutty just made me another outfit."

Undaunted, Fern found another bolt. The rich gold color caught my attention as soon as she spread it out. "This would be for the shirt." She watched me for a moment. "Should I send this to Nutty for you?"

"You're evil," I said.

She grinned. "I'm only thinking about what's best for my customers."

"And your cash box."

A predatory smile flashed on her face. I paid her for the material and left before she could convince me I needed another set. I bought some Avibian honey for the Stable Master before buying some grilled beef to eat as I searched through the other market stands. Items displayed for sale or trade included handcrafts, clothing, fruit and baked goods.

I stopped for a minute to examine an intricate silver ring that held a black moonstone. Putting it down, I dismissed the thought of purchasing the ring. Only a few coins remained of the money I had earned as a Magician's Aide.

Besides, I already wore a butterfly pendant and snake bracelet. Both had been carved and gifted to me by Valek. I fingered the pendant on my chest, wondering about Valek.

Was he in his carving room, creating another animal statue? Perhaps he was discussing military tactics with Ari and Janco or dueling with Maren. She had taught me how to fight with a bow, and Maren's own skills had improved. Perhaps she was with Valek right now, working on some complicated project that required them to be together every day. Maybe Valek would forget about me. Be content to have Maren by his side.

No. I forced myself to ignore those thoughts. I had plenty to worry about without creating phantom worries. Determined, I headed back to our campsite. Perhaps another magical sweep of the area would reveal Moon Man and the others to me.

Leif and I waited another day for some sign of Moon Man. I prowled around the market, cursing under my breath. Each minute we delayed reduced the possibility of recapturing Cahil and Ferde. I scanned the forest with my magic, connecting with the woodland creatures. The area remained serene. Undisturbed.

That night we discussed our next move. Sitting by the fire, I stared at the flames. My bow was within reach, but I didn't believe the weapon would do much damage against the Fire Warper.

"We should go back to the Citadel," Leif said. "That makes the most sense."

"What about the Sandseeds? They left their clan unprotected in the plains. They might need help, and we should tell them about Moon Man and Tauno."

"Tell them what? That we lost them? I'd rather tell them Tauno is afraid of heights and Moon Man is claustrophobic."

And I would rather have them with us. Delaying the decision, I said, "Our direction of travel is the same for either the Citadel or the plains. Tomorrow we'll go north."

Leif agreed. He spread his bedroll by the fire and lay down. Using Kiki's saddle as a pillow, I put my cloak on and tried to get comfortable on the cold ground next to Leif.

"You should move closer to the fire. You'll freeze," Leif said.

"I'm fine."

He was quiet for a while. "Perhaps Moon Man and the others are lost."

"Doubtful. If they were lost in the jungle, I would have found them."

"Marrok's afraid of getting lost," Leif said in a soft voice. "And you're afraid of—"

"Leif, go to sleep. We have a long day tomorrow." I rolled over, turning my back to him. I didn't want him to put a name to my fear. Naming it made it true.

Cold and uncomfortable, I tossed and turned, trying to sleep. Disturbing dreams of fire and death invaded my mind. Flames would spark in a benevolent dream, here and there until they multiplied and consumed the picturesque scene, burning the images into a storm of black ash. I woke coughing on imaginary smoke, my body coated with sweat.

To avoid the nightmares, I watched the moon rise above the forest's trees. When Ferde had been on his soul-stealing rampage, the Master Magicians and I theorized the timing of his ritual murders were linked to the phases of the moon. We were wrong. He just needed enough time to torture his victims into submitting their wills to him so he could steal their souls when they died. The old Efe symbols and ritual he used to collect their souls would have made him the most powerful magician in Sitia if he been able to gather all twelve of them.

Valek and I had stopped him from absorbing Gelsi's soul and

completing the ritual, but now he was free to try again. And Cahil helped him. How could he? I couldn't really believe Cahil would get involved after witnessing what Ferde did to those girls. But he had assisted with Ferde's escape from the Keep's protective cells, and now traveled with him. Was he that greedy for power? He could no longer claim the Ixian throne. Did he want to rule Sitia instead?

I studied the moon. Waxing toward full, the bright disk lit the landscape. I wondered about the moon's power and why certain things like the Kirakawa ritual needed the moon's presence to work. I could feel the invisible layer of power blanketing the sky, but I felt nothing from the moon.

In a subtle flicker of the light, Moon Man coalesced out of a blue shaft of moonlight as if he had been summoned by my thoughts. He stood next to our fire without clothes or his weapon.

Are you a dream? I asked him.

Deep lines of exhaustion etched his face, but he managed a weary smile and said, *Perhaps I have always been a dream. What do you think?*

I think I'm too tired to discuss Story Weaver philosophy with you right now. And if you're not real, then, at least, make yourself useful and tell me where you really are!

I am here. Moon Man slumped to his knees.

12

I JUMPED TO MY FEET and ran to Moon Man's prone form by the campfire. Wrapping my cloak around Moon Man's muscular shoulders, I shared energy with him.

"Are you all right? What happened? Where are the others?" I asked.

"Everyone is fine. I will explain later." He pulled the edge of my cloak closer to his face.

"Will you? Or will you just spout some vague details in typical Story Weaver style?"

He answered with a soft snore.

I suppressed the desire to share more power with him and wake him. Sleep was the best way for Moon Man to recover his strength after using magic. Unfortunately, I couldn't sleep. I grabbed an extra blanket from Leif's saddlebags and spread it over Moon Man. My cloak didn't seem adequate protection for him against the chilly night air. Despite my reluctance, I added some logs and coaxed the fire into a warm blaze.

As I stared at the dancing flames, I wondered what other

surprises waited for me. The answers would be revealed in time, but my ability to deal with them remained uncertain.

Even with the loud calls of shoppers and stand owners from the bustling market, Moon Man didn't wake until the sun reached its apex. By the time the Story Weaver finished eating the meal Leif had thoughtfully prepared for him, my impatience had built up enough energy that I could probably scale a smooth tree without the aid of a rope.

"Tell us everything," I demanded before he could swallow his final bite.

He smiled at my agitation. Weariness still pulled at his features, but his eyes sparked with an amused glint.

"And don't try any of that cryptic Story Weaver mumbo jumbo or I'll…"

"What?" Moon Man asked.

"I'll hurt you. Bad. So talk."

Moon Man glanced at Leif.

My brother shrugged. "I've seen her swinging that stick around. Now, if you had your scimitar…"

"Too risky," Moon Man said. He saw the rising fury in my eyes and wisely began telling us what had happened.

"After you and Leif distracted the Fire Warper, we chased the Vermin through the jungle. And would have caught them if you had not needed my help." Moon Man aimed a pointed stare at me. "How is the scout?"

"Alive and well," I said.

"Back to his old self?"

I hesitated, but I wouldn't let Moon Man change the subject. "He's fine. Continue your story."

"Helping you drained all my energy and I needed to rest for a while," Moon Man said. "Marrok tracked the Vermin to the Illiais Market and then north to the city of Booruby. It is a thriving place and we lost the Vermin's trail. Too many people."

He shuddered. The motion reminded me of Leif's claim that Moon Man was claustrophobic. The city was the complete opposite of the wide open space of his home in the Avibian Plains. Located at the northern tip of the Cowan Clan's lands, Booruby's eastern side bordered the plains, and was too far for my magic to reach.

"Where are the others?" Leif asked.

"We rented a room at one of the inns. I left Tauno and Marrok there to hunt down any information about the Daviians while I rejoined you."

Leif looked around the campsite. "How, exactly, did you get here?"

Moon Man grinned. "A secret Story Weaver power."

"You used the moonlight," I said.

He beamed his approval. "I came through the shadow world. Moonlight reveals the world of shadows, allowing access."

"Is that where you showed me the story of my life?" I asked, remembering the dark plain that had transformed into visions of my childhood.

"Yes. It is a place where I unravel story threads to help others learn from their past as they weave their future."

"Is it a physical place?" I had been there twice. The second time Moon Man had brought Leif and me to untangle our knots of hostility and anger toward each other. Each time, though, I had felt intangible, as if my body had turned into smoke.

"It exists in the shadows of our world."

"Can anyone with magical powers get into the shadow world?"

"So far, only Story Weavers have the ability. But I am waiting to see if there is another who is brave enough to claim that gift." His eyes met mine, and I caught a glimpse of shadows. I looked away.

Breaking the silence, Leif said, "However you arrived, you still need to work on your transportation skills. Maybe next time you can bring some clothes along with you."

Leif and I bought Moon Man a tan-colored tunic and pants, and we purchased supplies for the trip. Packing the saddlebags, I readied the horses. Moon Man would ride Garnet until we reached Booruby.

We went north, taking a well-used path through the forest. I scanned our surroundings with my magic, but thought the odds of being ambushed remained low because of all the other caravans and travelers crowding the trail. Leif also used his magic to smell the intentions of the Vermin, but he couldn't discern anything.

Once we reached Booruby, we would find the others and decide our next move. I brooded over the fact we had lost the Vermin and worried about which direction Cahil and Ferde had gone. Back to the plains or plateau? Or engaging in another scheme to gain power?

Ferde had kidnapped Tula from her home in Booruby. His only victim found alive, Tula had been sent to the Magician's

Keep. I healed her body and found her soul only to lose both to Ferde. Guilt welled in my throat. His freedom ate at my heart.

I tightened my grip on the reins, causing Kiki to snort in agitation.

Sorry. I relaxed. *I was thinking about Ferde and Cahil.*

Peppermint Man like apple, Kiki said, referring to Cahil.

Why do you say that? I knew Kiki loved apples.

He black apple. No one wants.

I saw an image of rotting apples on the ground.

Bad. But good come.

Kiki showed how the seeds inside grew roots and became a tree after the apple decayed. *Are you saying a good thing might come from Peppermint Man? Or if he dies, it would be beneficial?*

Yes.

Cryptic horse advice? Well now I could die happy—I'd heard it all.

Two days later, we reached Booruby. Clusters of wooden and stone houses marked the outskirts of the city. The forest thinned. And the clear air fogged to a haze of smoke, coal dust and sawdust that hovered over the main street's buildings. The thick air assaulted us with the smells of garbage mixed with human waste. People bustled along the walkways and wagons full of goods choked the roads. Stores and stands had been wedged between factories and business offices.

Moon Man's alarmed face showed his discomfort as we maneuvered our horses through the crowded streets. He led us to the Three Ghosts Inn. The stone-faced building leaned its narrow four-story height against its neighbor. Through a tight alley, we led the horses to an empty stable just big enough to hold six horses.

The stalls were clean and had fresh straw and water. A stable boy soon joined us as we took off the horses' saddles. The quiet boy helped us groom and feed them. He shot me a shy smile when I tipped him.

We had passed a number of inns on our way into the city. "Why this inn?" I asked Moon Man as we carried our bags through the alley.

"I liked the name. Although…" He paused as if deep in thought.

"Although?" I prompted.

"I have not encountered the three ghosts. Perhaps you will have better luck."

I laughed. "You don't really believe in ghosts?"

Moon Man stopped and I bumped into him. He turned around, revealing his shocked expression. "How can *you* not? They are lost souls. You can help them find their way. Like you did for Reyad."

I put a hand out to steady myself. "Reyad was…" The man I had killed in Ixia. The reason I had been awaiting execution before Valek offered me the food taster's job. "How did you—"

"Story Weaver, remember? I know all the threads that are woven into your life."

"But I thought his ghost had been my imagination. A manifestation of my fears. Why haven't I seen any others? If I can help them, why aren't they all around me?"

"Perhaps they are and you do not wish to see them."

"This is weird," Leif said.

I agreed with him. My skin crawled with goose bumps, imagining being surrounded by invisible ghosts.

"I could teach—"

"Let's get inside." I cut off Moon Man's offer. Of all the things I wished he would teach me, seeing ghosts wasn't high on my list.

"Yes, let's. I'm hungry." Leif patted his stomach.

We entered into a common area. Wooden tables and long benches scarred with hard use lined the slender room. A fire crackled in the stone hearth, but the area was empty.

"Dinner's a few hours off," a woman said. She leaned from a doorway near the back wall. Spotting Moon Man, she smiled and walked toward us. "Mr. Moon! I'm so glad you're back. Your friends left this morning, but I suspect they'll be coming back for dinner. Mr. Tauno loves my vegetable stew."

The woman's steel-gray hair was pulled back into a bun. Small wisps of hair framed her oval face. Her fair skin caused me to wonder if she was a refugee from Ixia. When the Commander had launched his campaign to take over Ixia, many Ixians fled to Sitia before the Commander closed the border.

The innkeeper scanned Leif and me with bright intelligence in her sky-blue eyes. Her gaze lingered on my hands before returning to Moon Man.

"Will you be needing another room?" she asked.

"Yes. Mrs. Floranne, this is Yelena and Leif."

She wiped her hands on her apron before shaking our hands. "I'll be showing you to your rooms, then."

We followed her up the stairs. Stopping on the third floor, she led us down the slim hallway. She opened the second door on the left.

"This'll be Miss Yelena's room. Will Mr. Leif be staying with you, Mr. Moon, or do you need another room?"

Sweat beaded Moon Man's face and he glanced around the tight hallway as if seeking a way out.

"Leif can stay with me," I said, spotting two beds inside the tiny room.

Disapproval radiated from Mrs. Florannc's stiff demeanor, but before she could comment I added, "He's my brother."

Her face softened and she relaxed. "I'll be ringing the bell when dinner's ready. Don't be late." She left us alone.

Leif stifled a giggle. "Interesting place you found here, Mr. Moon."

"If Leif had been my lover instead of my brother, would she have let us stay together?"

"I do not know," Moon Man said.

"Perhaps the ghosts dislike improper behavior," Leif said, laughing.

Moon Man went to his room down the hall to check if Tauno or Marrok had left us a message. I mulled over Leif's comment as we put our few belongings on the beds.

"Is it considered improper if Valek and I...? You know."

"Yelena," Leif said with mock indignation. "Don't tell me you and Valek—"

"Just answer the question."

"Some clans like the Bloodgood Clan are very strict and require a couple to be married before living together. Others, like the Zaltanas, prefer a couple to marry, but don't get upset if they're not. Then there are the Sandseeds who don't even believe in marriage. They just do what they want." He spread his arms wide. "With their aversion to wearing clothes, I don't understand why the Sandseed Clan isn't overrun with children."

"We are careful with our seeds of life," Moon Man said from the doorway. "I did not find a note. Do you want to take a walk through the city? I need..." His gaze traveled around the room. "It is better for me outside."

Leif licked his lips. "I don't know. I don't want to miss dinner. That vegetable stew'll be smelling good."

"Do not worry. We will hear the bell. The entire city knows when the Three Ghosts Inn is having dinner."

We left the inn and wandered through the streets. I used my magic at different locations to find a sign of the Vermin, but there were just too many people around. Their thoughts and emotions crashed against me, and I blocked them out to avoid being overwhelmed. Leif, too, was inundated with smells. We searched the city and listened for any snippets of information.

A sparkle drew my gaze. Rows and rows of glass animals were displayed inside a store window. The beautiful jewel colors of the statues radiated as if a fire had been captured within their cores. They reminded me of Tula. She had sculpted animals with glass from her family's factory. Had she created these animals? Was this her family's store?

I peered through the window but couldn't see past the display. Should I go in and ask? Perhaps her family wouldn't want to see me again. Considering what had happened to Tula and her sister, Opal, I wouldn't blame them for hating me. After all, the only reason Opal had been kidnapped after Tula had died had been to exchange her life for mine. At the time, I had thought Ferde held Opal, but it had been Alea Daviian, seeking revenge for the death of her brother, Mogkan. Another man whose death I had been part of.

In Ixia, Mogkan had been power-hungry. He had taken control of not only Commander Ambrose's mind, but the minds of thirty innocent people. He deserved to die, but Alea had failed to see it my way, and now she was also dead. I sighed. I should stay far away from Opal and her family.

Death followed me. And perhaps ghosts as well? Was Alea or Mogkan's ghost haunting me? I held my hands out and turned in a circle, spinning my arms. Nothing.

Leif and Moon Man were engaged in a debate half a block away. I stepped toward them.

"Yelena!" a voice called from behind.

A woman carrying a small crate hustled along the sidewalk. A white kerchief covered her hair, and, even though soot smudged her face and hands, I recognized Opal's bright smile and I couldn't resist giving her a quick hug.

"What are you doing here?" she asked.

"I have some business." Before she could ask what kind, I hurried on. "Is this your family's store?" I pointed to the glass shop.

"Oh no. Our factory is on the east side of town, practically in the plains. We sell our glassware through a bunch of stores in Booruby. You have to come visit us!" She twisted her hands together. "That is, if you want to." She averted her face. "I mean after what I did…"

Opal yanked her focus from the ground and met mine with a sudden intensity. The shy, uncertain girl who had come to the Keep transformed in front of my eyes. "Let me make it up to you. You *will* come visit."

"You did nothing wrong," I said with conviction. "You have nothing to make up for."

"But I pricked you with Curare!"

"Alea forced you. And I must admit, that was a pretty good trick." I had thought once Opal was freed, the danger was gone. A near fatal mistake.

"But—"

"You can't let the past ruin your future. Let's call it even and start anew."

"Agreed. Can you come to dinner this evening?" she asked. Then her mouth dropped in shock and she stepped back.

Moon Man loomed behind me, blocking the sunlight.

"You'll not be missing dinner," Leif said, copying Mrs. Floranne's lilt.

Opal relaxed a bit when she saw Leif. "You can come too. And…your friend?"

I understood Opal's fear. At first glance, Moon Man resembled Ferde. But Opal had only gotten a brief glimpse of Ferde through her sister's memories so she could not really compare the two. I introduced her to the Story Weaver.

"I think I should wait for Tauno and Marrok to return," Moon Man said. "You and Leif go. I will see you later tonight."

Moon Man raised his eyebrows, giving me a signal. I opened my mind to him.

Perhaps her family will have some information about the Vermin. Ask them.

Yes, sir, I replied.

He flashed me a smile before he left. Opal hurried into the store to finish her deliveries. While Leif and I waited for her,

I returned to examining the glass animal statues in the window. Leif joined me.

"Look at how they glow!" he said. "Which one would you pick? The snake?"

"No. I've had my fill of snakes. I like the horse, but the eyes are the wrong color. They should be blue."

Leif laughed. "You're biased. I'd buy the tree leopard. The detail is amazing. I wonder how the artist is able to get the leopard's green and yellow pattern just right."

"The pattern is inside." Opal exited the store. "There's a thin layer of clear glass on the outside."

"Did Tula make these?" I asked.

Sadness welled in her eyes. She blinked back tears. "No. Tula's are too precious to sell."

"Opal, I'm—"

"Don't say it," she said. "Starting anew, remember?"

"Yes."

"Good. Let's go." Opal led the way.

I worried the girl's parents wouldn't be so forgiving, but they greeted us warmly. Their house and glass factory had been built on the edge of the city, surrounded on three sides by the Avibian Plains. The location explained why Ferde had chosen Tula. Keeping the kilns hot, Tula had been in the factory all night alone where no one could witness her abduction.

Opal guided us on a tour of her family's business and we met her remaining sister, Mara, and her younger brother, Ahir. The promised meal consisted of beef stew served in a bowl made of bread.

"Less to wash," Opal's mother, Vyncenza, said with a grin.

Leif sat next to Mara and flirted with her. He even joined

her in the kitchen to help clean up. I couldn't blame him, the beautiful loose curls of her golden-brown hair hung past her shoulders. Kindness radiated from big tawny eyes, and she listened to Leif's tales with rapt attention.

While the others cleared the table, Opal's father, Jaymes, regaled me with stories about his business and his family.

"...she wasn't paying attention and set fire to her mother's apron! It was another four seasons before we would let Tula handle a punty iron again." He laughed and launched into another one.

When he had run out of anecdotes, I asked him about news from Booruby.

"The Cowan elders are always arguing about how many trees to cut down, and now they want to start taxing the sand I import for my glassware." He tsked over the prospect. "Rumors about the other clans have always been good fodder for the gossips. This year's is about those Daviians. Everyone's worried about them, but the magicians have Tula's killer in jail and I'm sure the Sandseeds will take care of the rest. They always do."

I agreed, but my mind snagged on the fact that he still believed that Ferde was locked away. Not good. Why hadn't the Council informed the populace? Probably to avoid frightening them. Ferde was still weak, and they had hoped to recapture him by now. Should I tell Jaymes? He had two other daughters. The people should also be told about the Vermin's Kirakawa ritual. They could help find the Vermin and keep their families protected. But would they panic and hinder our efforts instead?

It was a difficult choice to make on my own and the

benefits of having a Council to vote on important issues became clearer to me. No one member could be held responsible for a bad judgment.

Delaying a decision, I asked him if his children still worked alone at night.

"No. No. I work the entire night shift. We've learned our lesson and won't be caught unaware again."

"Good. Keep vigilant. The Cowan Clan leaders are right to be worried about the Daviians."

Opal returned, giggling. Water splotched her long skirt and she tucked a few stray strands of damp hair back under her kerchief.

"Water fight," she said. And before her father could scold, she added, "Mama started it!"

He sighed but didn't appear to be too upset. Opal grabbed my hand, wanting to give me a tour of the house. The room she shared with her sister resided on the second floor of the stone house. The air smelled of honeysuckles. Hanging over the one empty bed was Tula's grief flag. The white silk banner had been part of her funeral ceremony. The Sitians believed that once raised, the flag released Tula's soul into the sky. Having freed Tula's soul from Ferde, I knew the Sitian custom just helped comfort the families.

"Why is the flag hung over her bed?" I asked.

"It's to keep her spirit from returning to earth," Opal answered. "All the things that she might want to come back for are under the flag. She can't see them there."

I looked under the banner and spotted a small shelf filled with glass animals. The figurines were lifelike and well-made but had not captured the inner fire like the ones I had seen earlier.

"Tula gifted a couple statues and sold many others, but those she kept for herself. I tried to copy her, but mine come out differently. I have only sold a few." She shrugged.

"You made the ones in the store window. Didn't you?"

"Yes." Again she made a dismissive shrug. "The store owner is a kind woman. She knew I was coming today and put them in the window. My animals are dull in comparison to Tula's."

"Opal, they're stunning. How did you get them to glow?"

She pressed her hands over her heart as if she couldn't believe what she heard. "You see the light?"

"Of course. Doesn't everyone?"

"No!" she cried. "Only I see it—and now you!" She twirled with delight.

"And Leif. He saw it also."

"Really? How odd. No one else in my family or my friends can see the inner light. They all think I'm daft, but they humor me anyway."

"How do you make them?"

She explained the process of glassblowing to me. More detail than I needed, but I understood the basics.

"Usually you shape animals from solid glass, but, when I try it, the animals resemble blobs. To make a tumbler or vase, you have to blow an air bubble into the glass. I can't do that either. I turn purple trying to get a starter bubble but have never accomplished it. However once I fail to make the bubble, I shape the piece so I don't waste the glass. That's when I get results. Not only does my animal look real, but a spark remains inside even when the piece has cooled."

I thought for a moment. "But eventually the middle would cool. What keeps it glowing?"

She threw her arms out in a frustrated gesture. "I don't know. I put my heart into these."

The answer popped into my mind. "Magic."

"No. Master Jewelrose has tested me. I didn't have enough power to stay at the Keep."

I smiled. "She should test you again." Dax's taunt about weird powers replayed in my mind. If Opal had been born a Zaltana, the test would have been different. "You have enough power to capture fire inside your statues."

"Why can't anyone else see it?"

"Perhaps a person has to have some magical ability to see the fire," I theorized. "If that's the case, you need to sell these at the Citadel's market where there are many magicians."

She pursed her lips in thought. "I obviously don't meet a lot of magicians. Can you take one of my statues along and test your theory?"

"On one condition."

"Anything!"

"That you let me pay for it so I can keep it."

"You don't have—"

I put my hand up, stopping her. "You said anything."

She laughed. "Okay, but I'll charge you the wholesale price. I know just the piece to give you, too. It's in the factory."

Opal dashed down the steps and flew out the door. The cold rush of night air reminded me that we needed to get back to the inn. I thanked Opal's parents for the meal. They told me Leif had gone with Mara to the factory.

I found Opal there. She handed me a package. Wrapped

with layers of cloth to protect the glass, the fist-size parcel fit neatly in my hand.

"Open it later," she said. "I had another one in mind for you, but this one…called. Crazy. I know."

"I've heard stranger things. I'll write you a letter when I get back to the Keep and let you know how the experiment went." I gently placed Opal's package in my backpack, slung the straps back over my shoulders then paid her for the statue. "Do you know where Leif is?" I asked.

She blushed. "I think he's sweet on Mara. They're in the back in the mixing room. She's *supposed* to be measuring sand."

I wove my way through the kilns, workbenches and barrels of supplies. The hot air baked into my skin. Light gray smoke rose from the burning coals and flowed through the chimneys to vent outside. Opal's family used a special white coal mined from the Emerald Mountains to heat their kilns. Cleaner than the black variety, the white coals burned hot enough to reach the two thousand degrees needed to melt the sand ingredients.

In the back room, a table filled with mixing bowls lined the far wall. Leif and Mara leaned over a deep bowl, but they were looking at each other instead of the concoction. The cloth masks used to prevent them from breathing in the fine particles hung around their necks.

I paused before interrupting them. Mara's hands were coated with sand, and granules peppered Leif's hair. He looked younger and his face shone with delight. It was a side of Leif I hadn't seen before, and I wondered if he had someone he cared about back at the Keep. I realized I knew nothing about certain parts of Leif's life.

Taking a few steps backward, I moved from their sight. I called Leif's name loud enough for them to hear me over the noise of the kilns. He now stood away from Mara when I came into view, the sand gone from his hair.

"It's getting late. We need to get back."

Leif nodded but didn't move. I understood the hint and left.

Outside the factory, a strong breeze hustled the clouds overhead. Shafts of moonlight poured from the sky between the breaks. When Leif joined me, we headed back to the inn. He was quiet.

"Do you want to talk about it?" I asked.

"No."

After several steps, he asked, "Did you learn anything about the Vermin from Jaymes?"

"The city is worried about them, but there is no information on where they might be if they're even here at all." I told him about Opal's glass animals, and he seemed intrigued by the magical element.

"Did you tell Mara about Ferde's escape?" I asked.

"No. I just told her to be extremely careful."

We walked for a while in silence. The air bit through my shirt and I wished I had my cloak. Booruby resided on the edge of the temperate zone with warm afternoons followed by cold nights.

"I like her," Leif said, breaking the quiet. "I haven't liked anyone before. Too busy and too worried about you to care for another. I couldn't keep you safe. I didn't lift a finger to help you. Finding you became more important than living my own life."

"Leif, you were eight years old and would have been killed if you had tried to stop Mogkan from kidnapping me. You did the right thing."

"Getting killed would have been easier. No guilt. No worries. No fear. Caring for someone is terrible and wonderful. I don't know if I have the strength to do it for another. How do you deal with it?"

"I focus on the wonderful parts and suffer through the terrible parts, knowing it will end eventually."

"Did you like Valek as soon as you saw him?"

"No. In the beginning our relationship was purely business." The first time I had met Valek he had offered me the choice of going to the noose or becoming the next food taster. My family knew I had been the Commander's food taster, but not why. Someday I would tell them about Reyad's torture.

"When did your feelings change?"

That was a harder question. "I guess the first time he saved my life." I told Leif about the Ixian fire festival and how Irys had hired four goons to kill me because my uncontrolled magic could flame out and ruin the power source.

"So the first time you met Master Jewelrose, she tried to kill you? And you told me before Valek had wanted to kill you twice. Gee, Yelena, you're not a people person, are you?"

"There were other circumstances," I said in my defense.

"It all sounds too complicated. I shouldn't get involved with Mara."

"That would be taking the easy road. Safe yet dull. Why do you like her?"

"She smells like the jungle on a perfect day. It's a light whiff of the Ylang-Ylang flower combined with the sweet aroma of living green and a touch of the nutty earthy essence. It's a scent you can wrap around yourself and feel at peace. Only those dry and sunny days will produce that smell, and they are as rare as a solid-white valmur." Leif took a deep breath. "She has a soothing, contented soul."

"Sounds like she might be worth the effort. There might be plenty of rainy days, but those perfect ones will make all the memories of rain disappear."

"Is this from experience?"

"Yes."

We reached the Three Ghosts Inn and entered the building. Moon Man and Tauno sat at one of the tables in the common area. Customers filled the room.

Tauno held a bloody cloth to his temple and his split lower lip bled.

"What happened?" I asked when we joined our friends. "Where's Marrok?"

Tauno's face was glum. He glanced at Moon Man as if seeking the Story Weaver's permission.

"We found the Vermin," Tauno said. He winced. "Or I should say they found us. A group of five soldiers with the Soulstealer and Cahil. They surrounded us, dragged us into a building and threatened to kill us. Cahil drew Marrok away and they had a private discussion. They laughed and left together, seeming the best of friends." Tauno put a hand to his ribs and cringed with pain. "The others descended on me and I have no memory except waking in the empty building."

"When did this happen?" I asked.

"This morning."

"I am glad he is alive, but I wonder why they did not kill him," Moon Man said.

Contemplating the situation, I said, "Taking a captive through crowded streets would be difficult. If they wait until nightfall to perform Kirakawa on him they risk being discovered."

"So why not just kill him?" Moon Man asked.

"Because they want us to know they have Marrok," Leif said.

"As a hostage?" Moon Man asked.

"No. Marrok left with Cahil. They're flaunting the fact that Marrok is now with them," I said. "And they know everything he knows. Including our present location."

13

"DO YOU THINK THEY WILL attack us here?" Leif asked.

I glanced at the fire warming the inn's common room. Would the Fire Warper risk being seen by the other guests?

"They could watch the building and follow us, waiting until we get to a secluded spot to attack," Moon Man said.

"That's a happy thought," Leif muttered.

I reached out to Kiki. She dozed in the stable but roused at my light mental contact. If Vermin skulked around the inn, she and the other horses would be upset.

Smell? I asked.

Night. Straw. Sweet hay, she said.

All good for now.

Kiki help? Watch. Listen. Smell for you.

What if you get tired?

Rusalka. Garnet. Take turns.

Good idea. I'll come and open the doors.

Lavender Lady stay. Kiki do.

I smiled, remembering how she had unlatched her stall door in the Keep's stable when Goel had attacked me. One of Cahil's men who held a grudge, Goel hadn't seen her. Probably hadn't known what hit him until he regained consciousness among the broken boards of the pasture's fence.

"…Yelena? Hello?" Leif poked my arm.

"I'm here."

"What are we going to do?" Leif asked me.

"It's too late to go anywhere else. Kiki and the horses will watch the outside of the building and alert me if anyone approaches."

"Ooh, guard horses. How quaint." Leif pointed to the hearth. "What if Mr. Fire Warper decides to jump out of the fire? I don't think Mrs. Floranne will be serving him a bowl of her stew."

"Can we douse the fire?" I asked.

"No," Leif said. "The inn will get too cold and Mrs. Floranne won't have hot coals for breakfast."

"Leif, do you always think with your stomach?" I asked.

"Is there any other way?"

I sighed. "We'll post a watch inside. Moon Man, how many entrances to this building?"

"Two. The main one leading to the street, and one in the back through the kitchen."

"How about upstairs? Is there another staircase in the kitchen?"

"Yes, but we can secure the door into our hallway."

"Good. We'll each take a two-hour watch. I need to rest after I heal Tauno's injuries so I won't take the first shift. Moon Man can start, followed by Leif, me and Tauno."

We left Moon Man in the common room. I helped Tauno to his room. Stiff and sore, he moved with care. When he was comfortable on the bed, I pulled a string of power and examined the damage. Aside from two broken ribs, his other wounds were minor. Staring at his injuries until they transferred to me, I hunched over with the pain and then pushed it away.

Tauno squeezed my hand in thanks before falling asleep. I trudged to my bed, not as exhausted as I had been in the past. Perhaps my healing skills improved with practice. Or had I grown used to relying on my magic?

"Yelena, wake up." Leif shook my shoulder.

I peered at him through heavy eyes. He placed the lantern on the table.

"You're the one who set the schedule. Come on." He pulled the blanket off me. "Most commanders don't take a turn guarding the troops. They get a good night's sleep so they can make the right decisions in the morning."

I sat on the edge of the bed, rubbing my eyes. "I'm not a commander and we're not a troop."

"I disagree. You've been leading the way. You're the one who knows what you're doing."

"I—"

Leif put his fingers on my lips. "Don't say it. I like—no—*need* to believe that you know what you're doing. Makes it so much easier to follow your instructions, especially when I'm acting as bait for a fifty-foot-long snake."

"Fine. I have things well in hand. I don't need much sleep because I have all the steps we need to take already planned out. Happy now?"

"Yes." Leif stretched out on his bed.

I picked up the lantern. "Sweet dreams."

"They will be now."

The hallway of the inn was dark and quiet. I checked the door leading to the kitchen stairs. It remained locked tight. Good. Descending into the common area, I thought about Leif's comments. I might be the one making the decisions, but I didn't believe I had enough knowledge to be a commander. Gut instinct still propelled my actions.

Valek had taught me about strategy and clandestine operations, and my Ixian friends, Ari and Janco, had taught me to fight. Late-night sessions with Janco were the reason I could pick locks. However, my magical training with Irys had been interrupted by Ferde's quest for power.

There could be a magical way to find Ferde and counter a Fire Warper, but since I hadn't read all those books about magic and history, and I hadn't explored my powers to find their limits, he was the test I hadn't studied for, the quiz I was bound to fail. Out of my depth.

The empty common room echoed with my footsteps. I made a circuit of the area to check for intruders before I set the lantern down and went outside to visit the horses. The cold air stabbed through my cloak.

Kiki stood in the alley next to the inn. Her dark coat blended with the shadows, but the white blaze down her face reflected the moonlight.

Smells? I asked, reaching up to scratch behind her ears.

Fresh. No bad.

Any trouble?

She snorted with amusement. *Two men. Woman.*

She replayed the memory of two men robbing a woman.

They had been so preoccupied with searching her packages they failed to notice Kiki's quiet approach. Quiet, because Kiki, like all the Sanseed horses, refused to wear metal horseshoes.

Kiki had spun and used her back legs with expert precision. The men landed half a block away, and the woman, after staring wide-eyed at Kiki, took off in the opposite direction. I wondered why the lady had been out so late.

She'll probably spread rumors about being rescued by a ghost horse, I said to Kiki. *Maybe they'll change the inn's name to Four Ghosts.*

I like ghosts. Quiet.

You see ghosts?

Yes.

Where?

Here. There. Places.

Here? I looked around. The empty street seemed deserted. *I don't see any.*

You will. She nuzzled my cloak, sniffing the pockets. *I like peppermints, too.*

I gave her the mints. *Care to elaborate on the ghost issue?*

No.

She retreated down the alley and I returned to the inn. The lantern's flame flickered as I made another sweep of the kitchen and rooms upstairs before settling down near the hearth. Embers glowed within the remains of the fire. Suppressing my apprehension, I added a few logs to coax the coals into a small fire to heat water for tea. Such a diminutive blaze shouldn't be big enough for the Fire Warper.

Perhaps the size of the fire equaled the size of the Fire Warper. The image of a foot-tall Fire Warper leaping from the hearth caused me to laugh, but knowing he needed only one flame to start a fire ruined my good humor.

Searching my pack for tea leaves, I found Opal's package. Curious to see which glass animal had called to her, I unwrapped the thick cloth. A charcoal-gray bat with green eyes came to life in my hands. I almost dropped the piece in surprise, but even with its wings outstretched the palm-size creature didn't take flight. Opal's magic—not life—glowed from the core of the bat. Closer examination revealed flecks of silver along the bat's body and wings.

An invigorating tingle swept up my arm. I mulled over the benefits of being a creature of the night. Could I locate Marrok or Cahil now while the city slept? Drawing power, I projected my mind and encountered a confusing array of dream images. Once again too many people for me to sort through. I pulled back.

The water bubbled. With reluctance, I returned the statue to my pack and found the tea. Over my steaming cup, I watched the miniature fire. I considered making an attempt to contact Bain Bloodgood. The Second Magician might have some advice on how I could find one soul among so many.

The Citadel was three days away by horseback. Too far for me to project in normal circumstances. Desperation increased my distance, but then I had no control of direction. Also, Bain would be asleep, his mental defenses impenetrable. I decided to wait until the morning to try.

The desire to sleep dragged at my body. I made several rounds of the room just to stay awake. When seated, my attention lingered on the fire's dancing flames. They pulsed in a rhythm that matched my heartbeat. The flames' movements appeared choreographed, as if they tried to communicate something to me. Something important.

I knelt near the fire. Fingers of orange and yellow beckoned. *Come*, they invited. *Join with us. Embrace the fire.*

I inched closer. Waves of heat caressed my face.

Come. We need to tell you…

What? I leaned in. Flames crackled, sap hissed and boiled and the harsh scent of burning hair billowed.

"Yelena!"

Moon Man's voice drenched me with cold reason. I scurried away from the hearth, stopping when I reached the far side of the room. Chills raced over my skin and I shivered.

"Thanks," I said to him.

"I thought something was not right." Moon Man descended the rest of the way down the stairs. "I woke feeling as if the threads of my blanket had ignited."

"It's a good thing you did."

"What happened?"

"I'm not sure." I wrapped my cloak tighter. "I thought I saw souls in the fire."

"Trapped?"

I barked out a laugh. If I had said that to anyone else, they would have believed I was a raving lunatic. Moon Man wanted details. Details I couldn't provide.

"I think they wanted me to join them."

He frowned and stared at the hearth. "You should not be left alone with a fire. I will finish Tauno's shift."

"Finish?" I glanced out the window. The curtain of darkness

had thinned. I had lost track of the time, and failed to wake Tauno for his turn. Not a good sign.

"Go get some sleep. We will need to make plans when you wake."

The deafening peal of Mrs. Floranne's bell jarred me from sleep. Leif sat on the edge of his bed with his head between his hands, blocking out the noise. With silence came relief and he dropped his arms.

"She'll be ringing that again if we don't get down to breakfast soon," Leif said.

All the motivation I needed. I kicked off my blanket and followed Leif from the room. We joined Moon Man and Tauno in the common area. The crowded inn buzzed with conversation. Mrs. Floranne poured tea while her staff served breakfast. The smell of sweet syrup wafted through the air.

The good night's sleep reflected in Tauno's face. The swelling was gone and the bruises faded from bright red to a light purple smudge. He moved without wincing in pain.

We ate our breakfast of honey, eggs and bread and discussed our next move.

"We should search the city," Leif said. "Quarter by quarter until we either find them or determine they're not here."

"It would take a long time." Moon Man spooned a glob of eggs onto a slice of bread.

"They are gone," Tauno said.

I stopped eating. "How do you know?"

"They mentioned leaving Booruby."

"Why didn't you tell us last night?" I stabbed my eggs with my fork.

"I was distracted by the pain and did not remember the comment until now."

"Would it have made a difference?" Leif asked.

I thought it over. Tauno had been in bad shape. But with no fatal injuries, I could have left him here and...what? Scanned the surrounding forest with my magic? I didn't know which direction they had gone and they had almost a full day of travel.

"Probably not," I sighed. "Tauno, do you remember anything else? Did they say where they were going?"

"The need to hurry was all I sensed. Perhaps that is why I was not killed. They did not have enough time."

"The best strategy would have been to keep us in the dark about Marrok, wondering if he is dead or alive and what he told them." I sipped my tea. "However, Cahil likes to feel superior and probably believes letting us know Marrok has betrayed us would make us doubt our instincts and slow us down."

Cahil had tried that tactic with me before. When he had thought I was a spy from Ixia, he had ambushed me in the forest. Then, he wanted me to believe Leif set me up to demoralize me. It hadn't worked. And it wouldn't work now.

If anything, I was more determined to find them. Even though we had lost their trail. My appetite gone, I pushed my plate away.

"What's next?" Leif asked.

The door to the common room banged open. Marrok stood in the threshold with a bloody sword in his hand.

The four of us jumped to our feet. Breakfast forgotten, we pulled our weapons as the conversation in the inn's common room dwindled into a deadly silence.

"Come on." Marrok gestured from the doorway with his sword. "Let's go before they catch up."

"Who?" I asked.

"Cahil and his…his…friends." Marrok spit the words out. "I escaped." Horror bleached his face, and blood dripped from a cut on his throat. "I've lost them, but they know we're here."

"How many?" I demanded.

Marrok straightened. "Seven."

"Armed?"

"Swords, scimitars and Curare."

"How soon?"

Marrok glanced over his shoulder and froze. He dropped his sword. It clattered on the stone floor. A big hand shoved him, pushing him to the ground.

Behind Marrok, Cahil, Ferde and five Vermin streamed into the common room.

14

WITH THEIR WEAPONS pointed toward us the Vermin and Cahil fanned out in front of the door. Two Vermin had scimitars, two had swords and one held a blowpipe to his lips.

"Everyone just stay calm," Cahil ordered. His long broadsword made an impressive threat. The people in the common room stayed in their seats. Mostly merchants and salesmen, there wasn't a soldier among them.

Marrok remained on the floor. A Vermin stood over him with the tip of his scimitar pointed at Marrok's throat.

I glanced at Tauno. "You said they were gone."

His face had paled and, although he held his weapon, he hadn't nocked an arrow. Moon Man eyed the Vermin as if judging the distance between their necks and his scimitar. Leif's machete glinted in the sunlight from the open doorway.

"Change of plans," Cahil said.

Cahil had let his blond hair grow past his shoulders and it was unbound. Besides that, he remained the same. Same gray traveling clothes, same black riding boots, same washed-out blue eyes and same hate-filled expression on his bearded face.

"My friend wanted to exchange Marrok for Yelena." Cahil inclined his head to Ferde.

I noted his use of the word *friend*. How could he call that creature his friend?

The Soulstealer's plain homespun tunic and pants hid most of the red tattoos covering his body. With a scimitar in one hand and a blowpipe in another, he looked at me with cold calculation. Despite his lean and powerful build, I sensed his magic remained weak. Yet a bite of fear nipped my stomach.

"I hope you have a few more Warpers with you," I said to Cahil. "The Soulstealer is no condition to fight three magicians."

"I may have failed in my power quest," Ferde said. "However, I now serve another who has learned blood magic."

The sound of roaring flames reached me before the heat. A quick look over my shoulder confirmed the blaze in the hearth had grown. Terror boiled in my throat, prompting me to act before the Fire Warper appeared.

Pulling power, I sent a thread to Moon Man. *Take out the man with the blowpipe. I'll take Ferde.* He agreed. *Leif,* I said, *attack the man over Marrok then keep Cahil busy.*

When? Leif asked.

"Now." I shouted and projected my awareness into Ferde's mind, bypassing his mental defenses and seizing control of his body. It was a self-defense move I had learned when Goel had captured me. Chained and left with no recourse except using my magic, I had sent my soul into Goel's body.

Once Ferde realized I had invaded, he concentrated all his energy on ejecting me. I ignored his efforts. He threatened to kill me the same way he had murdered his other victims.

Memories stabbed; sounds of their screams pounded; the smell of rancid blood pierced and visions of mutilations assaulted. His black desires of power and dominance through torture and rape revolted me.

To stop him, I harvested his soul and wrung it, exposing his deep fears and the events that had caused his addiction to power. The favorite uncle who had tied him down and sodomized him. The older sister who had tormented him. The father who had belittled him. The mother he had trusted and confided in. The mother who had sent him back to live with his uncle as punishment for lying.

A Story Weaver may have helped Ferde untie the knotted strands of his life, but I wrenched them apart, broke the threads. He became the helpless victim again. I examined his memory for every bit of detail, looking for information about the Daviian Vermin. When I finished, I peered through his eyes.

My body lay on the ground, comatose. Moon Man fought a Vermin. They maneuvered around a headless body. Cahil hacked at Leif, whose machete was no match against Cahil's longer sword. Leif would soon be forced to surrender. Tauno stood in the same spot as if rooted to the floor. Marrok had regained his feet and sparred with one of the Vermin near another body. The people in the inn had organized a bucket brigade to dump water on the fire.

Even though my time with Ferde felt like a lifetime, only seconds had passed. I raised the blowpipe in the Soulstealer's hand and aimed. First Cahil. Reloading, I shot each Vermin with a Curare-laced dart, ending the fight.

Water wasn't going to stop the Fire Warper, but with his cohorts neutralized, he conceded the fight. "Next time, my little bat." The fire died with a hiss and puff of oily smoke.

I returned to my body. My limbs felt as if they weighed a thousand pounds each. Leif helped me to stand on weak legs.

Mrs. Floranne came over. She clutched her apron between her hands and worried at the fabric. "What should we be doing?"

"Send someone to fetch the city guards. We'll need help transporting the prisoners to the Citadel," I said.

She sent the stable lad.

"Have they all been hit with Curare?" Leif pointed to the prone figures.

I looked at Ferde. He had collapsed in a heap on the floor. "All but one. I've examined his soul, and he won't be giving us any more trouble."

"For how long?"

"Forever."

"Do you think that was wise?" Moon Man asked. His scimitar dripped with blood and gore, and lacerations criss-crossed his chest. "You could have achieved the same result without damaging his mind."

"I—"

Leif jumped to my defense. "Hold on, Mr. Let's-extermi-nate-all-the-Vermin Man. Given the chance you would have decapitated him. Besides, he deserved it. And it doesn't matter anyway; Roze would have done the same thing to him once he arrived at the Citadel. Yelena just saved time."

Small darts of fear pricked my heart. Leif's words repeated

in my mind. *Roze would have done the same.* He was right. Numbness spread throughout my body. I hadn't even stopped to consider the implications before acting.

Don't get in my way; I'm the all-powerful Soulfinder. Disgust coursed through me. History books hadn't been kind to Soulfinders. The vision of Flame Me being burned at the stake rose in my mind. Perhaps the Councilors and Roze were right to fear me. After what I had just done to Ferde, I feared I might turn into a power-hungry despot.

"We need to leave as soon as possible," Moon Man said.

We had assembled in the inn's common room again. The city guards had taken Cahil and the others into custody yesterday. We had spent the day explaining to the city officials about Cahil's group; an afternoon's worth of discussion to convince them to send the prisoners to the Council. Leif and Marrok would accompany the city guards to the Citadel this morning. I intended to go with Moon Man and Tauno to the Sandseed homeland in the Avibian Plains.

"You're worried about your clan," I said.

"Yes. Also I think we need to learn more about the Kira-kawa, the Fire Warper and your abilities before we have another run-in with the Vermin."

"But your clan has forgotten the details. How are you going to learn more?" Leif asked.

"We can consult Gede. He is another Story Weaver, but he is also a descendant of Guyan and may have more information." Moon Man stole my ginger muffin and ate it.

Although I was curious to know more about how Guyan had reunited the Sandseeds after their civil war with the Efe

Warriors, Moon Man's comments reminded me I needed to try to contact Irys and let her know what had happened.

We finished breakfast and made arrangements to leave. Moon Man and Tauno would get the horses ready while Leif and I tried to communicate with Irys.

We returned to our room. I lay on my bed.

"Do you think you can reach her from this distance?" Leif asked.

"I hope to, but I may need a boost of energy."

Leif sat on the edge of my bed. Closing my eyes, I drew power to me and projected my awareness toward the Magician's Keep in the Citadel. I bypassed the chaotic jumble of minds in the city and reached for the wide-open fields marking the eastern border of the Greenblade Clan's lands. The few live-stock I encountered hunched against the damp wind.

Pushing past the barren farmland, I aimed for the white marble walls of the Citadel. But my mind stretched thin as if it had turned to taffy. Leif's warm hand encompassed mine and a surge of strength pushed my awareness further, but I couldn't reach those walls. The effort left me drained.

Leif gave my hand a squeeze before he stood. He searched through his pack and before I could ask, he handed me a yellow leaf rolled like a scroll.

"Eat it," he said. "It'll give you energy."

I sniffed. The leaf smelled like spearmint and rosemary. An odd combination. As I crunched the leaf, the bitter mint taste dominated and it shredded like paper in my mouth. "Yuck. What is it?"

"A baka leaf. One of Father's discoveries."

After a while, I felt better. We packed our bags and joined

Moon Man and Tauno in the stables. The four of us mounted. Leif and Marrok rode together on Rusalka and headed toward the city's garrison. Marrok would borrow one of the guard's horses for the trip to the Citadel.

The rest of us went east through Booruby's crowded streets. Tauno shared Kiki's saddle with me, and Moon Man rode Garnet.

When we reached the Avibian Plains, the horses broke into their gust-of-wind gait. We traveled until the sun set then halted to rest. Our stopping point was a bleak section of the plains. A few stalks of grass clung to the sand, and no trees or firewood were in sight. Tauno reconnoitered the area as soon as he dismounted.

Moon Man and I tended the horses. Once they were fed, watered and rubbed down, Moon Man removed the oil nuts Leif had given to him. One of my father's finds, the oil nuts would burn long enough to heat water for stew. The night air smelled damp, hinting at rain.

After arranging the fist-size lumps into a circle, he lit the nuts on fire by striking two stones together to make a spark. I guessed Story Weaver powers didn't include lighting fires. Interesting.

Tauno returned with a couple rabbits he had shot with his bow and arrow. He skinned the animals and added the meat to the stew.

After dinner I asked Moon Man about Guyan. "What happened between the Efe rulers?"

"Just over two thousand years ago, the Efe Tribe was a peaceful nomadic people, following the cattle and the weather." Moon Man reclined against Garnet's saddle, warming to his tale. "Before becoming an official member of the tribe, the young people would make a year-long pilgrimage and bring back a new tale for the tribe. It is said that Hersh was gone many years, and, when he returned, he brought back knowledge of blood magic.

"At first he taught a few Efe magicians, called Warriors, how to boost their powers. Little rites requiring a drop of their own blood. The extra power would dissipate when the task was completed. Then Hersh showed them how to mix their blood with ink and inject it into their skin. Now the power did not dissipate and they became stronger Warriors. Soon they discovered using another's blood was even more potent. And heart's blood, taken from the chambers of the heart was incredibly empowering."

Moon Man shifted his weight and stared into the black sky. "The problem with using blood magic is it becomes addictive. Even though the Efe Warriors were powerful, they wanted still more. They did not kill their own clan members, but sought victims from neighboring clans. No longer content to follow the cattle and forage for food, they stole what they needed from others.

"This abuse continued for a long time. And would have continued if an Efe named Guyan had not stopped the Warriors. He kept his magic pure. Sickened by the horrors he witnessed, Guyan organized a resistance. The details of the battle are lost to time, but the amount of magic pulled from the power blanket was enough to knock over the Daviian Mountains and shred the blanket of power. Guyan organized what was left of the clan, and established the role of Story Weavers, who helped mend the people and the power." Moon Man yawned.

I compared his story to what I had learned about Sitian history. "Can you really mend the power source? I read a history where a magician had bunched the power around himself, and it took two hundred years for it to smooth out."

"Guyan was the first Weaver," Tauno said. He hadn't moved a muscle during Moon Man's story. "Guyan's incredible powers could mend the power source, a skill not seen in another since."

Moon Man agreed. "The blanket is not perfect. There are holes, tears and thin patches. There might come a point in time where it will be worn away and magic will be a story of the past."

A loud pop sounded from the campfire. I jumped. The last of Leif's oil nuts sputtered and died, leaving the three of us in darkness. Tauno offered to take the first watch as Moon Man and I readied for bed.

I lay awake shivering in my cloak, thinking about the power source. Finding out about those holes called Voids had been a nasty surprise. Alea Daviian had dragged me into an area without power to torture and kill me. Being unable to access my magic, I had felt quite helpless. The fact I had been tied to a cart had reinforced my complete lack of control. Alea erred by not searching me for weapons, and I had used my switchblade to escape.

Alea had also wanted to collect my blood and I wondered if she'd planned to perform the Kirakawa ritual on me. I supposed I wouldn't ever know. I couldn't ask a dead woman. Or could I? An image of invisible spirits hovering over me filled my mind and I felt as if a layer of ice coated my skin.

The next morning we ate a cold breakfast of jerked beef and cheese. Moon Man estimated we would reach the Sandseeds' main camp by late afternoon.

"I tried to reach the elders," Moon Man said. "But there is a strong barrier of protective magic tenting the encampment. Either my people managed to fight off the Vermin and this new shield is a safeguard against another attack, or the Vermin have taken control and are defending themselves."

"Let's hope for the first one," I said.

We mounted and rode for most of the day, stopping only once to rest the horses. Before we reached the point where we would be visible to the Sandseeds' camp, we halted. Tauno would scout the camp and report back.

Taking off his bow and arrows, Tauno doused himself and his clothes with water then rolled in the sandy soil. Granules clung to his skin. He blended in so well with the surroundings, he soon vanished from our sight.

I paced and fretted while Moon Man appeared serene.

"Worrying can not change anything," he said to my unspoken question. "I would rather conserve energy for when we can do something."

"You're right, of course, but on occasion logic does *not* win against emotions."

He shrugged. I resisted thinking worrisome thoughts and focused instead on what I could do.

Smells? I asked Kiki.

Sweet. Home, she replied. *Itchy.*

Clumps of mud clung to her copper coat. I rummaged in my pack until I found the currycomb. I was still combing Kiki when Tauno returned.

"The camp is secure. If we leave now we can get there before dark," Tauno reported.

As we prepared to go, he told us what he had seen. "Everything looked normal. Yanna washed clothes and Jeyon skinned a hare. I crept closer and saw the elders arguing over the fire. The children at their lessons. The youths practicing with their wooden swords. Many heads drying in the sun."

"Heads?" I asked.

"Our enemies," Moon Man replied in a matter-of-fact tone as if decorating with decapitated heads was a normal occurrence.

"It is a good sign," Tauno said. "It means we have won the battle."

Yet Tauno didn't look happy. "Did you talk to anyone?" I asked.

"Yes. Jeyon signaled to me everything was fine. I did not want to waste the daylight finding out the details." He peered at the sky. "A hot meal by a warm fire will be most welcome."

I agreed. Tauno joined me on Kiki's back, and Moon Man mounted Garnet. In high spirits we joked and raced to the Sandseeds' camp.

The gray twilight waned as the white tents of the camp became visible. Many Sandseeds had gathered near the fire. A few stirred the contents of large cooking pots, and, by the heady aroma, I guessed venison stew bubbled inside. Yum. Others waved to us as we approached. We slowed the horses.

The air shimmered with the rising heat. I scanned the area with my magic, but felt only the strong protection Moon Man had mentioned. The magic didn't feel like an illusion, but my experience was limited.

When we crossed the magical barrier, I braced myself. Even Tauno gripped my waist tighter. But the scene didn't change. The Sandseeds stayed the same. Three men and two women came over to us as we stopped the horses while the rest resumed their evening's work.

The women's faces appeared to be strained with either worry or grief. There must have been Sandseed casualties. The Sandseed men grabbed the horses' bridles. An odd thing to do, considering they had trained the horses to keep still. Kiki reared. I held her mane as she jerked away from the Sandseeds' grasp.

Bad smell, she said.

Firelight flashed on steel. I turned in time to see a mass of well-armed Daviian Vermin erupting from the tents.

15

TAUNO'S BOWSTRING TWANGED and I yelled, "Go! Go! Go!" Kiki was free, but two Sandseeds held tight to Garnet's bridle. A quick glance to the side revealed ten feet separated us from the fastest Vermin.

I pulled my staff from my pack as Kiki turned. She used her rear legs to keep the Vermin occupied while I brought my bow down on the temple of a Sandseed holding Garnet. A pang of regret touched my heart as the man crumpled to the ground. He had probably been forced to ambush us. But I didn't let the feelings stop me from attacking the second man clutching Garnet.

"Go! Go! Go!" I yelled again.

Even with Moon Man's scimitar, Tauno's arrows and my bow, the Vermin outnumbered us. It was only a matter of time before they would overrun us. In a flurry of hooves and steel and shouts, the horses headed away from the Sandseed camp, breaking into their gust-of-wind gait.

We had ridden through most of the night to get as far away from the Vermin as possible. The horses slowed. Heads down, they panted. Their coats gleamed with sweat. Only a couple dark hours remained. Dismounting, we removed their saddles. While I walked the horses to cool them down, Moon Man and Tauno searched for wood and game.

No one said a word. The shock of the attack had yet to wear off and the vivid memory of it played over and over in my mind. The ramifications alone were too awful to consider right now.

We ate another rabbit stew in silence. I thought about our next move.

"The elders…" Moon Man's voice seemed loud in the thick night air.

"Are still alive," Tauno said. "For now."

"Would they kill them?" A shudder gripped my body at the thought of all those drying skulls.

"The trap was sprung. They have no need for them," Moon Man replied then seemed to reconsider his words. "They might keep them as slaves. The Vermin are lazy when it comes to domestic tasks."

"And they're just busy beavers when it comes to ritual killings and gaining power," I said. "Lucky us." The scene once again flashed in my mind. "Do you think some of your people escaped?"

"Perhaps. They would have left the plains, though." Moon Man considered. "The Sandseeds no longer control the protective magic over the Avibian Plains. To stay within its borders would be too dangerous for them. Right now, the Vermin are using the protection to keep their presence a secret, but now that we have fled, I believe they will use it to find us. Perhaps to attack us with magic."

"Then we shouldn't linger long. Is there any way to know if they find us?"

"We can create a barrier to alert us to an attack and maybe deflect an initial foray."

"We should saddle the horses in case we need to make a quick exit." I stood.

"That would be prudent." Moon Man helped me with the horses.

Kiki snorted in annoyance when I tightened her straps.

Tired, she said. *Don't need. Smell good.*

For now. If the smells turn bad, we can leave faster. I fed her some peppermints and scratched behind her large ears. She sighed and her eyes drifted shut.

After the horses were ready, the three of us sat in a circle around the fire.

"Maybe we should douse the flames." Worried that the Fire Warper would sense me through the blaze, I hadn't used my magic near a fire.

Moon Man dumped water onto it. Puffs of gray smoke rose into the air.

"Yelena, I want you to pull threads of magic and I will do the rest," Moon Man instructed.

Concentrating, I gathered strands of power. Moon Man plucked the strands from me and weaved them into a net around us. Tauno's pinched and sullen expression reflected his discomfort. As the only one without magic, he didn't have the ability to see the protection building around us.

When Moon Man finished, I disconnected from the power source, feeling drained of energy. The net pulsed with magic even though we no longer fueled it. I wondered why it still worked. In all my past efforts, the power dissipated as soon as I stopped using magic. Except for my mental connections with Kiki and Irys, every time I wanted to heal or project I had to consciously draw from the power source. Yet the Sand-seeds had their protection, and there were other lingering spells.

An image of the knife in Valek's suite came to mind. When Valek had assassinated the King of Ixia, the King cursed him, vowing his blood would stain Valek's hands forever. Since magic doesn't work on Valek, the curse transferred to the knife instead. The King's blood still clung to the blade and remained as wet and bright as the day the King had been killed.

I asked Moon Man how the protective net stayed active.

"Mostly we channel the magic through us. But there are times when you can loop the power back to the source. It can be very difficult to do, and, by having you draw the power, I could save my energy for knitting it together and redirecting it back to the source. Large-scale protection like the one covering the Avibian Plains and the Sandseeds…"

A hitch of emotion stopped his words. He closed his eyes and swallowed his grief before he continued. "Huge magical loops require an immense effort by many magicians, but can be effective for a long time. The protection we just created will last for a few hours before dissipating. Enough time to give the horses a chance to rest."

"And then what?" I asked, but he looked at me. Leif's comments about my role as commander flittered through my mind. I answered my own question. "We leave the plains. Head toward the Citadel and let the Council know what's been going on with the Vermin."

"Hopefully they will already know. The Sandseed survivors would have gone to the Citadel." Moon Man scowled. "If there were any."

Waiting for the horses to regain some of their strength proved to be difficult. Our protective net flashed whenever the Vermin's magic scanned the area. So far the net hid us from the Vermin, but each encounter weakened the fibers.

The desire to flee and the need to sleep battled within me. I wanted to stay awake in case the Vermin attacked, but I dozed off and on until the sky brightened with the rising sun.

The few hours before dawn had been enough time for the horses. We mounted and headed northwest, riding hard. During our rest breaks, Moon Man searched for any sign the Vermin's magic had found us. I projected my awareness to learn if they physically pursued us. In our haste, we left a physical trail even my untrained eyes could follow.

A couple hours short of the Avibian border, we stopped for a longer rest. Moon Man proclaimed the Vermin had lost us, and I couldn't sense anyone nearby.

Since we had been traveling together for fifteen days, we automatically attended our chosen tasks, even with the Daviian threat hanging over our heads.

By the time I had finished rubbing down the horses and seeing to their needs, I smelled rabbit stew cooking on the fire.

Tauno sat next to the pot. His shoulders hunched as if a great weight pressed down on him, and his attention remained fixed on the ground. He hadn't uttered more than a few words since yesterday. Perhaps he felt guilty and responsible for leading us into an ambush. I debated discussing it with him, but considered he might be more comfortable talking to Moon Man. I wondered if Moon Man was his Story Weaver. Every Sandseed had a Story Weaver to guide and advise them throughout their lives.

I glanced around, realizing Moon Man hadn't returned from collecting firewood even though a pile of branches rested near the cook fire.

"Tauno, where's Moon Man?" I asked.

Tauno didn't even lift his head when he said, "He was called to the shadow world."

"Called? Does that mean another Story Weaver survived the Vermin attack?"

"You will have to ask him."

"When will he be back?"

Tauno ignored the rest of my questions. Frustrated, I circled the area, searching for Moon Man, and found his clothes in a heap on the ground. I moved to return to the fire and bumped into him.

I jerked back in surprise. Moon Man seized my upper arms to keep me from falling.

"Where have you been?" I asked.

He peered at me with an alarming intensity. Blue fire flecked his brown eyes. I tried to move, but he wouldn't let go.

"They are dead," he said with a flat voice. "Story Weavers and Sandseeds gone. Their souls haunt the shadow world."

His grip on my arms tightened. "You're hurt—"

"You can help them."

"But I don't—"

"Selfish girl. You would rather lose your abilities than use them. And that is what will happen. You will become a slave to another."

His words slapped me in the face. "But I've been using them all along."

"Anyone can heal. You, though, hide from your real power and others suffer for it."

Stung and hurt, I tried to break loose, but his hold wouldn't release. In order not to injure him, I projected into Moon Man's mind. Thick ropes of gray power surrounded him. The shadow world still held his mind. My efforts to cut the ties failed.

"The shadow world calls."

Moon Man began to fade. My body became translucent. He planned to take me with him to a place where I feared I couldn't access my magic. Reaching into my pocket, I pulled my switchblade and triggered the blade. I slashed him across his stomach. Moon Man shuddered and let go. He collapsed to the ground, curling into a ball on his side.

I looked at Moon Man's still form. The gray power had vanished, but I wasn't sure of his mental state. Perhaps the shock and grief had been too much for him. Difficult to believe. He had been a calm and steady presence all along.

I knelt next to him. The blood from his wound soaked his shirt. Drawing power, I focused on his stomach. The cut pulsed with a red light and a line of pain formed on my own stomach. I huddled on the ground, concentrating on the injury. My magic repaired the damage.

When I finished, Moon Man grasped my hand. I tried to pull free, but he squeezed. My body jerked as the image of headless bodies slammed into my mind. They crowded close, enveloping me with the reek of dead flesh as they demanded revenge. Another jerk and the scene of a massacre flooded my senses. The burning stench of body fluids and death stung my nose as blood soaked into the sand. Mutilated bodies were strewn in a haphazard, irreverent manner and left for the vultures to find.

Moon Man sat, and I tried to break his hold. His gaze met mine.

"Is that what you saw in the shadow world?" I asked.

"Yes." Horror filled his eyes as the gruesome images replayed in his mind.

"Give the memories to me." I felt his reluctance. "I will not forget them."

"Will you help them?"

"Can't you?"

"I can only help the living."

"Are you going to tell me how or spout some cryptic bullshit?"

"You do not want to learn. You have refused to see what is all around you."

"You didn't answer my question."

Pain creased his face and the light in his eyes dulled. He would be unable to function with the dreadful knowledge of how his people suffered.

"Give them to me. I'll try to help them, but not right now." I mentally added soothing-the-dead-Sandseeds to the end of my long list of things to do. After I dealt with the Fire Warper, which should be a breeze. While I was lying to myself, I included flying and turning stones into gold to my list. Might as well think big.

Moon Man released the emotional turmoil of his visions. He wouldn't forget the images, but they would no longer strangle him. I gathered his grief and guilt and anguish to my soul. So much carnage and blood. All to boost the Vermin's power. So many dead. Too many. How to soothe those victims? Stopping the Vermin from increasing their strength might work. What if they tried again? Perhaps destroying the power blanket to keep everyone from using magic would work. A drastic and desperate measure that might not even be possible.

Letting go of my hand, Moon Man stood.

"What you said about my future. Is it true?" I asked.

"Yes. You will become a slave to another." The discussion over, Moon Man returned to the campfire.

We ate the stew in silence. Packing up, we mounted and spurred the horses toward the Avibian border. When we reached the road located between the plains and the fields of the Green-blade Clan's lands, we turned north toward the Citadel and slowed the horses to a walk. At this late hour, the road was empty.

Being out of the plains gave us at least an illusion of safety, but I wanted to ride a little farther before we stopped for the night.

The next three days dragged. With hardly a word spoken between the three of us, an awkward hush resulted as we traveled to the Citadel. Moon Man's comment about my future repeated in my mind, grating on my nerves like a high-pitched squeal. I wanted to know who would force me to be a slave and when, but I knew Moon Man would reply with a cryptic remark and I wouldn't be smart enough to figure it out. The air turned cold and damp as we went farther north, and one night sleet pelted us, making our ride miserable.

Seeing the welcome sight of the white marble walls of the city on the third day, I spurred Kiki into a gallop. Gone from the Keep for eighteen days, I missed Irys, my old mentor who answered my questions with a refreshing directness, and my friends at the Magician's Keep.

After crossing the south entrance gate of the outer wall, we walked the horses through the streets of the Citadel. Puddles of icy muck peppered the walkways. Citizens hurried through the intermittent rain, and the grayness cast a mournful facade over the expanse of marble buildings. The smell of wet wool clung to the air. We aimed for the Council Hall, which was located with the other government buildings in the southeast quadrant of the Citadel.

Home? Kiki looked with longing at the four towers of the Keep.

Soon, I said. *Rest here for now.* A stable for the Councilors had been erected behind the building. *At least you'll be out of the rain.* Once Kiki and Garnet were settled, we entered the hall.

A guard informed us a Council meeting had just finished and we should go in before the Councilors left for the day. Entering the Great Hall, I spotted Irys talking to Bain Bloodgood, Second Magician. Groups of Councilors and aides formed small knots and the noise of their discussions filled the room. By the harsh tones and strident voices, I sensed the discussion hadn't gone well and an undercurrent of fear trembled against my skin.

Moon Man and Tauno went directly to their Councilman, Harun Sandseed. I hung back, not wanting to interfere with the Sandseeds. Irys hurried toward me. She wore her stern Fourth Magician expression. She was worried. I scanned the clumps of Councilors with more care and I discovered the reason for her concern.

Cahil stood with Roze Featherstone and another Councilor. He laughed and talked as if he belonged there.

16

I MOVED TO CONFRONT Cahil. He should be in the dungeon for aiding and abetting a murderer, not standing in the middle of the Great Hall having a conversation with Roze. My alarm increased when I saw a few Vermin inside the Hall.

Irys had other plans. She grabbed my arm and pulled me aside. "Now is not the time," she said, appealing to me.

"What is going on?" I demanded.

Irys glanced around the room. A few Councilors stood close enough to overhear us, so she switched to our mental communication.

Cahil claims he's been on an undercover mission this whole time, she said. *He says that he didn't free Ferde.*

Why would anyone believe that? I asked.

Because Roze corroborated his story.

A lightning strike of shock ripped through my body. I hoped I misunderstood her. But her grim expression didn't change.

It gets worse, she said. *Cahil says he caught Marrok rescuing Ferde and, after interrogating him, Cahil discovered Ferde was on his way to rendezvous with others. Cahil followed the Soulstealer to discover what they plotted.*

That's ridiculous. We know Cahil beat Marrok to find out about his birth parents.

It's Cahil's word against Marrok's at this point because there is no evidence to say who freed Ferde. Especially since Ferde can't be questioned. Irys frowned. *We'll talk about your actions later, but whatever you learned from Ferde's mind can't be used as evidence.*

Why not?

Because you were emotionally involved with the Soulstealer and your impartiality is suspect. I know—she went on, sensing my protest—*it isn't right, but when the Council discovered what you had done to Ferde, it confirmed their fears about you being a Soulfinder and validated Roze's warnings.*

I sighed. It had confirmed my fears, too. *Where's Ferde now?*

In the Citadel's jail, waiting for the Council to decide what to do with him. Although I think executing him would be a kindness.

Her censure hurt and guilt welled. I forced my thoughts away from Ferde and concentrated on Cahil. There had to be a way to show the Council the truth about his involvement. *Where's Marrok? What has he said?*

Marrok is being held for questioning. He claims he didn't free Ferde. He had no motive. But Cahil says Marrok wanted to frame him for the escape so Marrok could lead Cahil's men. And also that Marrok lied to him, and Cahil really has royal blood.

My mind spun. Cahil had an answer for everything. *So why was Cahil traveling with Ferde?*

He says it was part of the undercover mission. Once he caught up with Ferde, he convinced Ferde he wanted to be a part of their plans.

While he traveled with the Daviians, Cahil says he recruited them to switch sides. She gestured to the Vermin in the room.

Did he mention the Vermin using blood magic and the Fire Warper?

No. He didn't, but Leif tried. Leif attempted to discredit Cahil and many of the Councilors thought he exaggerated about the Daviians. Unfortunately, Leif's reputation for seeing doom and gloom in everything worked against him.

Did Cahil say what the Vermin plan to do? Half of me didn't want to hear Irys's response. I steeled myself.

According to Cahil, the Daviians' leaders are in league with the Commander of Ixia. Together they plan to assassinate the Council and Master Magicians and, in the ensuing chaos, the Daviians will offer to help Sitia battle the Ixians. But there won't really be a war and the Daviians will eventually turn Sitian's government into a dictatorship.

Exactly what the Council feared since the Commander took over Ixia, and, combined with the resultant bad feelings from the Ixian Ambassador's visit, the Councilors were primed for Cahil's lies. So now it seemed Roze was right to warn the Council about the Commander. And I had no evidence to prove them wrong.

What about my training? I asked.

I didn't think Irys could look any more upset, but she managed to deepen her scowl. *The Council has given Roze permission to "assess" your involvement in these events and to determine what risk you pose to Sitia.*

I'm sure that would be impartial. Do I have any say in this?

No. But the other Masters will be there as witnesses. All except me. My objectivity is considered compromised by our friendship.

Moon Man and Tauno finished their conversation with Harun. They came toward us.

Did you hear about the Sandseed massacre? I asked Irys.

Yes. Horrible news, and it gave Cahil more proof of the Daviian threat. The Council is preparing the Sitian army for war.

I didn't even have to ask. Irys saw the question in my eyes.

War against the Daviians and against Ixia.

So much for my job as Liaison. War between Sitia and Ixia was the one thing I had hoped to avoid. There had to be more going on with the Daviian Vermin, though. I knew the Commander would never team up with them. They used blood magic, and he wouldn't condone the use of any magic. Besides, he could attack Sitia without the Vermin's help. Again, I had no proof.

Moon Man and Tauno joined us.

"There are about a dozen Sandseed survivors," Moon Man said. "They came to the Citadel and are staying here for now. Only one Story Weaver besides me survived. It is Gede, and he is the one we need to talk to about the Fire Warper."

Irys said, "Who—"

Moon Man kept talking. "You said Master Bloodgood has a few books about the Efe, right?"

"Yes," I said.

"We should examine them. Gede and I will come to the Keep tomorrow morning." Moon Man turned and walked away.

I watched his back, feeling uneasy. His whole attitude toward me had changed since he had tried to drag me into the shadow world. He acted as if he had given up on me.

"That was rather abrupt," Irys said.

"He's been through a lot."

"And so have you. Tell me about this Fire Warper. Leif had only sketchy details."

I reported all our adventures to her as we left the Council Hall and headed toward the Keep.

The next morning we assembled in Bain Bloodgood's study. Occupying the entire second floor of his tower, Bain's office was ringed with bookcases. They had been built around the long thin windows and every shelf overflowed with texts. A desk, a few wooden chairs and a ratty armchair looking as old as Bain resided in the center of the room. The sharp tang of ink permeated the air. Ink stained the desk's top and Bain's fingers. And the only space on the floor without a pile of books was a foot-wide path from the door to the desk.

The tension in the room pressed on my skin. Moon Man had folded his large frame into one of the chairs. He appeared uncomfortable and he glanced with longing outside. I shared his discomfort. The room felt crowded and tight even for me. Bain sat behind his desk, with Dax Greenblade standing next to him. Dax was Bain's apprentice and he had the unique talent of being able to read ancient languages. His help in finding Ferde and rescuing Gelsi had been vital.

Irys stared at the other Sandseed Story Weaver with ill-concealed dislike. Gede had arrived with Moon Man and he had pushed his way into the room as if he belonged there. He carried his bulk with authority and appeared to be taller than he was. It wasn't until he stood next to Irys that his true height was revealed. He matched Irys's five feet eight inches.

"Those books belong to me," Gede said.

Silence met his statement. Dax glanced at me. Incredulity flashed in his bottle-green eyes.

"My ancestor labored to banish all the knowledge about the blood magic, yet there they sit—" he gestured to the two open books on Bain's desk "—for anyone to pick up and read."

Irys said, "I doubt anyone but Master Bloodgood and Dax can read or understand the language—"

Gede cut her off. "It is all you need. One person to read it, to get ideas and to experiment with the knowledge. Blood magic is like no other—once you start you can not stop."

"It appears the Vermin have discovered the information without these books," I said.

"How do you know?" Gede asked. He peered at Dax with open suspicion. "Perhaps someone has been feeding them information."

I stepped in front of Gede before Dax could defend himself. "Not from here. Besides, having these books might prove to be an advantage. Your ancestor Guyan defeated the Efe and perhaps the books contain information about how to counter the Vermin's blood magic and to defeat the Fire Warper."

"All the more reason to give them to me," Gede said. "The Sandseeds will deduce a way to oppose the Daviians. After all, they are our problem."

"Not anymore. They've gone beyond your problem," Bain said. "We will keep the texts here. You're welcome to study them with us."

But Gede wouldn't back down on his claim and Bain refused to give in. Eventually Gede rose to leave. He paused before me and scanned me with cold calculation in his dark eyes.

"Did you know Guyan was a Soulfinder?" Gede asked me.

Surprised, I said, "No. I thought he was the first Story Weaver."

"He was both. You know nothing about Soulfinders." He

glared at Moon Man. "Your education is pathetic. I can teach you how to be a true Soulfinder."

My heart jumped in my chest. The prospect of learning more about Soulfinders both thrilled and terrified me.

Gede must have seen the indecision on my face. "You do not need these books to defeat the Fire Warper."

Too good to be true, I knew there had to be a catch. "I suppose you'll guide me with some cryptic nonsense."

"Bah!" Again Gede shot Moon Man an annoyed look. "There is no time for that. Interested?"

Logic warred with emotion. "Yes." Emotion won.

"Good. I am staying in the Citadel's guest quarters. Come at twilight. The moon should be up by then." Gede swept out of the room, with Moon Man trailing behind him.

Irys raised one slender eyebrow at me. "I don't—"

"Think it's the best decision." I finished for her. "Think I should rush into the situation and hope for the best."

She smoothed out the sleeves of her tunic, giving me a wry look. "No. I don't trust him."

I lingered outside Roze's tower, debating. This meeting with her, Bain and Zitora could be a trap. She could either trick me into confessing to conspiring against Sitia, or it could be my chance to redeem myself. Nice to have choices.

Bain opened the door and said, "Come in, child. It is cold outside."

Decision made, I followed Bain into Roze's home. A huge fire crackled and popped, spitting out sparks, which would have burned the threadbare carpet if Roze hadn't doused the errant embers with her magic. With the memory of her fire attack seared in my mind, I chose a hard wood chair as far from the hearth and from her as possible.

Spartan and bare, the room lacked the cozy comfort of Irys's living area and the scholarly smell of Bain's study. Zitora, Third Magician, perched on the edge of her seat, another straight-backed chair without cushions. She kept her gaze on her hands. They were laced together in her lap. Bain occupied the only comfortable seat. Overstuffed and worn thin, the chair's fabric was close to tearing, and by the annoyed frown on Roze's face whenever she glanced at Bain, I guessed he had taken her favorite spot.

"Let's get this over with," I said into the awkward silence.

"Nervous?" Roze asked.

"No. I have a meeting in an hour and I need to wash my hair." Roze drew a breath.

"Ladies, please. This is difficult enough as it is," Bain said. "Put your differences aside and let us assess the situation."

Roze kept her comment to herself. Impressive. She gave Bain a stiff nod. He smoothed the wrinkles in his robe before continuing. "Yelena, you have shredded Ferde's soul."

"I—"

"No commenting until I am finished."

The stern tone in Bain's voice raised the hair on my arms. He was the second most powerful magician in the room. "Yes, sir."

Satisfied, Bain resumed his lecture. "Your rash actions have set off a ripple of discontent within the Council. First you acted without their permission. Second, your ability to shred a soul alarmed the Councilors, including me. You have lost their trust, and therefore the information you uncovered through Ferde is invalid."

I tried to meet Zitora's gaze, but she averted her face.

"You are hereby ordered to stay out of Sitian affairs while we deal with this new Daviian threat. Roze has agreed to let you work with Gede to discover the extent of your powers and we will reassess how you can aid our efforts in the future." Bain gestured for me to comment.

Protests pushed in my throat, but I swallowed them down as I wrestled my thoughts into a logical response. This meeting was an ambush. They didn't want to question me, just dictate to me.

"What about Cahil? You can't believe him?" I appealed to Bain.

"There is no proof he lied. First Magician supports him."

"He's always been selfish," Roze said. "He wants only one thing. To aid the Daviians against Sitia runs counter to his desire. He needs our help to launch his campaign to claim Ixia. A country in the midst of a civil war wouldn't be able to aid him at all."

Roze's reasonable logic worried me more than her anger. "How about the Fire Warper?"

A bright fireball erupted from the fire, and hovered above us. I squinted into the harsh light. The heat of the flames fanned my face. Roze curled her fingers into a fist and the fire ball disappeared. Opening her hand, she gestured and snuffed out the hearth fire, casting us into cold semi-darkness.

"I'm First Magician for a reason, Yelena. My command of fire is my best ability. You need not fear the Fire Warper. *I'll* deal with him." Flames ignited. Once again heat and light emanated from the hearth.

I couldn't suppress my skepticism.

"Do you really think I would let the Daviians and this Fire Warper take control of Sitia? They wouldn't take proper care of my country. No. I will do all I can to keep them from power, including protecting you from the Fire Warper."

Now she was outright scaring me. "You want me dead."

"True. You're a threat to Sitia, but there is no proof. I can't obtain the Council's support to have you executed. But once I have evidence, you're mine."

This was more like the Roze I knew and hated. We glared at each other.

Bain cleared his throat. "Child, by listening to the Council and working with Gede Sandseed you will regain the Council's trust."

Learning about my powers was what I had desired all along. Ferde was no longer a threat and the Council knew about the Daviians. If they wished to believe Cahil, why should I care? The Commander's army would prevail against Cahil. I had sought to avoid a war, but I held no sway within the Council. Why couldn't I be selfish for once and stay out of politics while I explored my powers?

I agreed. But the slight rush of relief failed to ease the pang of doubt. Moon Man's comment about becoming a slave to another echoed in my mind.

I returned to my rooms in Irys's Keep tower. She had given me three of the ten floors to use. I trudged up the steps, anxious, worried and frustrated. Roze's boast she could handle the Fire Warper had better be true. Bain's Efe books described power symbols and blood rituals, but he had discovered nothing to counter them. And there was no mention of a Fire Warper.

Dax had translated the bulk of the books, but a few chapters remained. He planned to spend the afternoon working on them. My worry also stemmed from a comment Dax had made about Gelsi. Bain's other apprentice, Gelsi, had been Ferde's last victim, but I stopped him in time and revived her body and returned Gelsi's soul.

When I had inquired about her, Dax's vague response caused me to question him further.

"To tell the truth," Dax had replied, "she's different than before."

"Different how?" I had asked.

"She's harsher. Unhappy." He moved his arms in a gesture of futility. "She no longer enjoys life. She's more preoccupied with death. It's hard to explain. Master Bloodgood is working with her. We hope it's a condition she can work through and not—" Dax shrugged "—permanent. Maybe you can talk to her?"

I promised to visit her. Thinking back, I had returned two people's souls to bodies that had been dead. Gelsi and Stono. And both came back changed. Were their altered personalities due to something I did when I held their souls? My anxiety grew over what I might discover about my Soulfinder abilities with Gede.

Uneasiness soured my stomach, and I remembered the attack Roze had sent me where Flame Me made a soulless army. While it didn't apply to Gelsi and Stono, I recalled Stono's offer to kill for me.

With those morbid thoughts, I reached my rooms. Even though I had three levels, I only possessed enough furniture to occupy one. An armoire, a desk, a single bed and night table looked lonely in the round room. I would need to do some shopping when I had the time. Right now finding souls took priority over finding curtains. Then I could be Yelena, the all-powerful Curtainfinder. Able to decorate a room in one hour.

I laughed out loud.

"What's so funny?" a heart-melting voice asked from behind me.

Valek leaned in the doorway, his arms crossed over his chest as if he visited me every day. Dressed as one of the Keep's servants, he wore a gray tunic and pants.

"I was thinking about curtains." I moved toward him.

"Curtains are funny?"

"In comparison to all my other thoughts, yes, curtains can be amusing. But you, sir, are the best thing that's happened to me all day, all week and, now that I think about it, all season." Two steps and I was wrapped in his arms.

"That's the best welcome I've had all day."

I could only imagine what he had been up to. His ability to get into any building undetected made him the most feared man in Sitia. And his immunity to magic terrified the Master Magicians. He was Commander Ambrose's best weapon against them.

"Do I want to know why you're here?" I asked.

"No."

I sighed. "Should I know why you're here?"

"Yes. But not now." He leaned over and his lips met mine, and it no longer mattered why.

The late-afternoon sun woke me and reminded me about my meeting with Gede. I nudged Valek awake. We huddled under the blankets against the icy air.

Valek moved to get up. "I'll make a fire—"

"No!" I grabbed his arm, stopping him.

He peered at me with concern. I marveled at the rich sapphire color of his eyes and how they contrasted with his pale skin.

"You'll need to reapply your skin-darkening makeup," I said, brushing a black strand of hair away from his face.

He held my hand. "Nice try, but you *are* going to tell me why you don't want a fire."

"Only if you tell me why you're here." I countered.

"Agreed."

I filled him in on the series of events with Cahil, Ferde and the Fire Warper.

"It's ridiculous to think the Commander is working with these Vermin." Valek looked thoughtful. "So the Wannabe King has chosen to ignore the truth about his birth. You got to admit his ability to dupe the entire Council is impressive."

"Not the entire Council. Irys doesn't believe Cahil and I'm sure there are others." I waved my hand in a shooing motion. "Doesn't matter. It's not my concern. I've been told to be a good little student and mind my own business."

Valek snorted. "Like *you* would listen to them."

"I agreed."

He laughed long and hard. "You. Not. Get involved." Valek paused to catch his breath. "You've been in the midst of trouble ever since you became the Commander's food taster, love. You would never walk away."

I waited until he wiped the tears from his cheeks. "This is different. Then I didn't have a choice."

"Oh? And you have a choice now?"

"Yes. I'll let the Council deal with these Vermin and I'll stay out of trouble."

"But you know they can't counter them."

"They don't want my help."

Valek sobered and a hard edge glinted in his gaze. "What happens when the Vermin win?"

"I'll stay with you in Ixia."

"What about your parents? Leif? Moon Man? Irys? Do they come with you? And what happens when these Warpers with their incredible blood magic decide to follow you to Ixia? What choice will you have then?" He studied my face. "You can't let your fear of the Fire Warper stop you from—"

Annoyed, I snapped. "The Council has stopped me. They're the ones who are against me." Besides, I didn't want to think about my family—they were all grown people able to look after themselves. Then why did guilt tug at my heart and doubt squeeze my chest?

"You just said there're a few Councilors on your side. Once the Council hears Marrok's evidence tonight, they'll believe you about the Wannabe King."

"How did you know about Marrok?" Irys had just told me this morning. I had insisted on attending Marrok's questioning, but she said the session was closed, for Councilors only.

Amusement returned to Valek's face. "Servants. Their information network is far superior to a corps of trained spies." In an offhand way, he added, "I'll tell you about the session later tonight."

"You rat! It's a closed meeting. Only you would try to pull it off."

"You know me, love."

"I know. You crave a challenge and you're cocky."

He grinned. "I wouldn't call it cocky. A certain amount of

self-confidence is needed, especially for my line of work." He turned serious. "And for yours."

I ignored the implication. "Speaking of work, we made a deal. Why are you here?"

He stretched his arms over his head and yawned, pretending to consider my question.

"Valek," I warned, poking him in the ribs. "Tell me."

"The Commander sent me."

"Why?"

"To assassinate the Sitian Council."

17

I GAPED AT VALEK. Assassinating the Council would help the Vermin and support Cahil's claims. "You're not—"

"No. It's the wrong thing to do right now. The Commander based his decision on the state of Sitian affairs before these Vermin showed up. He allowed me a degree of flexibility on this mission. We need to find out what's going on. The Council meeting tonight might reveal crucial information."

"We?"

"Yes. *We.*"

I sighed. I was disobeying direct orders from the Master Magicians and the Council again, getting involved with Sitian affairs. Would I ever agree with their decisions or was I deep down an Ixian just pretending to be impartial? Perhaps my session with Gede would be useful. I needed guidance as well as information.

Valek and I agreed to meet back in my room later tonight. He left.

Apprehension swirled around me like a thick fog as I dressed and walked to the Citadel's guest quarters. The small clouds in the sky darkened as the light faded. The streets hummed with people finishing up their tasks for the day. Lamplighters began lighting the vast network of street lanterns. The main thoroughfares would be lit, but the back alleys would remain dark.

My concern grew as I passed a number of Vermin sauntering along the streets as if they owned the place. I avoided their gazes and wondered how the Council could be so swayed by Cahil's words. Perhaps a Warper had influenced them with magic, making them more agreeable.

The Citadel's guest quarters were located in a building behind the Council Hall and next to the stables. The two-story structure housed many apartments and I peered through the gloom, trying to determine which one Gede occupied. A shadow moved next to an entrance. Moon Man stepped from a pool of darkness.

"This way," he said.

No emotion showed on his face. Gone was his sense of mischievousness and the spark of amusement in his eyes. I missed them.

"Moon Man, I—"

"You must not keep Gede waiting," he said in a flat voice. "Your Story Weaver is ready for you."

He ushered me inside, closing and locking the door behind us. Heat pressed against my skin as if I stood in an oven. A roaring fire blazed in the hearth, illuminating the living area. All the furniture had been pushed against the walls. Gede sat cross-legged on a mat in front of the fire. A few Sandseeds sat in the cleared space in the center of the room.

"Come. Sit." Gede pointed to a mat in front of him.

I hesitated.

"You are the Soulfinder. You should not be afraid of fire. Sit or learn nothing."

Removing my cloak and pack, I placed them by the entrance. I longed to pull my bow from its holder but ignored the desire. Instead, I joined Gede on the floor. Sweat ran down his round face. His skin appeared black in the firelight. A trick of the light revealed an intricate tattoo design connecting the scars on his bare arms. But when I blinked, the design was gone.

"As a Soulfinder you can examine a soul, twist it, hold it and return it. You can send your soul to others. And you can project your soul to the other worlds, and return without any harm being done to your body," Gede instructed.

"The other worlds?"

"The fire world, the sky and the shadow world. You know about the shadow world from Moon Man. Moonlight is the gateway to the shadow world. The sky is the final resting place of our essence. The fire world is what some call the underworld. What it is supposed to be under, I have no idea. But that is where the Fire Warper lives. And where you must go."

"Why? Why must it be me?"

Gede's disappointment was evident by the sagging of his shoulders. "You are the Soulfinder. The Fire Warper's soul is there."

The heat from the room baked into my body. My shirt clung to my back. "How do I get there?"

"Through the fire."

When I didn't say anything, Gede continued. "Only you can go in and leave without being harmed. The Warpers have been feeding this creature with souls from the Kirakawa ritual. His strength grows."

The flames in the fire pulsed with an urgency. They swelled to man-size. I looked at Gede in alarm, but he appeared serene.

"He waits for you. Go to him," Gede said.

I stood. "No. I'm not ready. I don't even know how to fight him. With magic?"

Gede sneered with disdain. "You have no idea, do you? All the better."

Confused, I glanced between Gede and the fire, expecting the Fire Warper to step from the conflagration.

"He comes for you. If you will not go on your own, then I will provide an incentive." He snapped his fingers. "Moon Man, show your pupil what she needs to do."

Moon Man strode toward the blaze. The flames reached out to him. He extended his hands and the fingers of fire wrapped around his arms.

"No," I yelled. "Get back." I grabbed Moon Man's shoulders and pulled to no avail.

The tendrils of fire advanced and crawled over my hands. A burning excitement tingled and souls writhed in agony within the depths of the blaze. Caught between worlds. Hundreds of them. They dragged us toward them.

My first instinct had been to resist, but their need for freedom, for relief clawed at my body. I needed to help them. Leaning with Moon Man, I pushed forward. The fire burned on my skin, but the pain stayed bearable and a cooling relief lurked on the other side. If I could just get through.

A hand tugged on my shoulders. I tried to shake the person off. "It's okay. They need me."

An arm from outside the fire world circled my neck and

squeezed. My hands still clutched Moon Man's shoulders, trapped in the fire world. "No. Stop. I must…"

The souls ceased their pleading and flinched. "Wait." The word wheezed from my lips as I strained for air. But they hid and cowered. "I've come to help—"

"But who will help you, my little bat?" the Fire Warper asked.

I lost my grip on the Story Weaver. Without the breath to speak, I projected, *Do something!* into Moon Man's mind.

I can not. I have no power here.

The fire world blurred into a blob of orange and yellow. I plucked at the arm around my neck, but my hands weighed a hundred pounds. The blob transformed into black.

I woke. Lying on my back, I squinted and blinked until my eyes adjusted to the darkness. The cold air moved like silk over my hot body. My head throbbed and the skin on my hands and arms sizzled with pain. I drew a thread of magic and used it to soothe my head and heal the blisters.

"How about helping me," Leif said. He held out his arms. They had been scorched.

Leif sat next to me. We were in an alley in the Citadel. Concentrating, I pulled power and healed his burns. My energy sapped, I leaned back against a wall as a wave of dizziness made my head spin.

"What happened?" My voice croaked as pain ringed my neck.

"I had business in the Citadel tonight and thought I'd wait for you by the guest quarters. Out of nowhere Valek appeared." Leif paused, but when I failed to explain, he continued. "He muttered a comment about a Council meeting and asked where you were. By the firelight blazing through the windows, it wasn't hard to figure out. Valek picked the lock and we peeked in time to see you and Moon Man hug the fire."

He wiped soot from his face with a sleeve. "Valek attacked the Sandseeds inside and yelled for me to get you. Gede screamed for me to leave you alone, that you need to learn. Valek's scarier than Gede, so I listened to him, but I couldn't pull you away from the fire. I choked off your air until you passed out. Carried you out here."

I touched my neck. "Did you do the same for Moon Man?"

"He was too far in. I couldn't reach him." Leif's voice cracked with anguish. "Does the Fire Warper have him?"

"I don't know. It was strange. I'm not certain what just happened." My brain felt overcooked and logic stuck to the sides of my skull like a burnt crust. I needed another opinion. "Where's Valek?"

"Disappeared. But he left your cloak and pack. And orders." Leif smiled ruefully. "We are to leave the Citadel as soon as possible."

"Did he say why?"

"No. Just to meet him about two miles south of the Citadel."

I stood, wrapped my cloak around me and shouldered my pack. My legs protested the weight. "Let's get our horses and supplies from the Keep."

Leif shook his head. "He said not to return to the Keep for *any* reason."

I mulled over the implications. Valek had been in the closed Council session where they questioned Marrok. Evidence must have been gleaned, but obviously not in our favor. So much for my promise to visit Gelsi.

★ ★ ★

We fled the Citadel and camped in a farm field west of the main road. With no supplies, and me refusing to let Leif light a fire, a miserable night loomed. We huddled in the dark.

Leif muttered over Valek's reason for sending us here. I cursed my own stupidity; I didn't have to wait for Valek. I could contact Irys myself.

I asked Leif to keep watch.

"Better than freezing to death," he said.

Lying on the hard ground, I projected my thoughts. Irys's tower sparked with life. And instead of finding the Master Magician sleeping, she was bent over a handful of books in her study. Because of the bond we shared, her thoughts were open to me.

Irys, I said in her mind.

Yelena! Thank fate! Are you okay?

I'm fine.

Where are you?

I don't know if I should answer. What happened at the Council session?

A long pause. *Marrok confessed.*

To what? He didn't do anything.

To freeing Ferde and conspiring against Sitia.

Stunned, my mind blanked for a moment. *What…what was his motive?*

Just like Cahil said. Marrok wanted to get Cahil arrested and be in charge of Cahil's men. But…

Go on, I urged.

There's a new wrinkle. Marrok conspired to team up with Ferde and the Daviians to provoke a war with Ixia.

Why is that new? We already know the Daviians want war.

The new part is Marrok named accomplices. Another pause. *You and Leif.*

My body numbed. *Unbelievable. Someone must have forced Marrok to confess. It's all a lie. Did you feel any magic being used? How can the Council swallow that?* The thoughts tumbled one after another.

Unless you have some proof otherwise, the Council has signed an arrest warrant for you and Leif. They wish to capture you so you can be safely executed.

I almost laughed at the words *safely* and *executed* said together. The whole situation was ridiculous.

I'm not supposed to be telling you this either. I could be incarcerated in the Keep's dungeon if the Council finds out. Bain and I are already being watched for disagreeing with them. They've gone quite mad.

That's putting it mildly.

What are you going to do? Irys asked.

There has to be a reason the Council has gone mad. Discovering the reason should be next. Guess I really was going to stick my nose in Sitia's business. Nothing like having a warrant for your execution to get a girl motivated.

But all the clans will be alerted to your arrest warrant, and there's already talk of a reward. There's no safe place for you in Sitia.

I'll figure something out, and I think it's best if I don't contact you again for a while. You're already under suspicion. I don't want to compromise you any further.

Good point. Be very careful, Yelena.

I'll try. But you know me.

Yes, I do. So I'll say it again. Be very careful.

I pulled my awareness back, breaking our connection. Exhaustion dragged at my body and I would have drifted to sleep if Leif hadn't bumped my arm.

"Oh, no you don't, little sister. You were gone a long time. Tell me what's happening."

I filled Leif in on the details and managed to shock him into a rare silence.

"So what do we do now?" Leif finally whispered.

"We wait for Valek."

Valek arrived near dawn. He rode Kiki and had Rusalka in tow. The saddlebags bulged with supplies. Fatigue lined his face.

He peered at me. "You know?"

"Yes."

Valek dismounted. "Good. Saves time. The Citadel and Keep are crawling with soldiers looking for you."

"How did you get the horses out then? A secret spy maneuver?" Leif asked.

"No. A distraction at the Keep's gate, and I bribed the guards at the Citadel's south entrance."

Leif groaned. "Now they'll know where we are."

"I want them to think you went south. But you should get as far away from here as possible."

"And go where?" Leif asked.

"Ixia."

"Why would we do that?" Leif's jaw set into a stubborn line.

Danger flashed in Valek's eyes, but he bit back a sarcastic reply. "Things are happening too fast right now. We need to regroup and plan. We need reinforcements."

Valek made sense. Ixia was the only place where we would be safe.

"We should go now," I said.

"I'll meet you at the Commander's castle." Valek handed me Kiki's reins.

She nudged my arm, but I ignored her. "You're not coming with us?"

"No. I still have a few of my corps inside the Citadel. They need to be informed about what's happening. I'll join you at the castle afterward."

Before he could go, I pulled him aside. We embraced.

"Stay safe," I ordered.

He smiled. "I'm not the one getting pulled into fires, love."

"How did you know I was in trouble?"

"After I heard the Council agree to your execution, I had an odd notion the Council was the least of your worries."

"Thank you for saving me."

"You keep things interesting, love. It would be boring without you."

"Is that all I am to you? An amusement?"

"If only it was that simple."

"I guess I'm no longer retired." I managed a tired smile.

Valek kissed me goodbye. "Take a roundabout route to Ixia. The borders north of the Citadel will probably be watched."

"Yes, sir."

Valek left and the air turned cold. I shivered. Kiki nipped at my sleeve and I opened my mind to her.

I stay with Lavender Lady. Keep warm.

I'm glad you're here, I said. I checked my pockets for a treat. No luck.

Ghost put peppermints in bag.

I laughed. Kiki always knew where to find the mints. I marveled that Valek had taken the time to include treats in his packing. The horses' name for him was perfect, though. He appeared and disappeared as if he were a true ghost.

"Which way?" Leif asked.

Good question. Valek said to go around. The best direction would be to head northwest through the fields of the Stormdance Clan's lands. Then head north toward Ixia, skirting the Featherstone lands surrounding the Citadel. I outlined my plan to Leif.

"Lead on." Leif's resignation tainted his voice. "I've never been to Ixia."

Throughout the day, our passage through the fields hadn't drawn any notice, but we still felt exposed by the daylight. Leif and I decided to do the bulk of our traveling during the night. After a short break for dinner, we rode through the dark hours. Between galloping, walking and resting, the horses made progress toward our goal.

We found an apple orchard as the sun dawned. Kiki sniffed around the neat rows of trees, but they had been picked clean of apples. Nothing grew in this area during the cold season. Deciding to camp within the shelter of the orchard, we found a site hidden from the few surrounding farmsteads.

"Have we crossed into Stormdance lands?" I asked Leif as I pulled Kiki's saddle off her back.

"Not yet. See that ridge?" He pointed to the northwest.

"Yes."

"That's their border. Stormdance lands are mostly shale.

They have a few farms in the eastern portion of their territory, but the west side is just sheets of shale on top of rock. The storms blown in from the Jade Sea have carved fantastic sculptures along their coast, but no one lives there. They only go to the coast to dance." Leif sat down and assembled sticks for a fire.

I plopped next to him. Saddle sore and drained of energy, I delayed grooming the horses. "Why do they dance?"

"It's how they harness the power from the storms. They capture the storm's force in glass orbs. It's a dangerous dance, but the risk is worth it. If they're successful, they protect our land. Instead of being lashed with gale-force winds and soaked with heavy rains, Sitia receives a mild rain. The added benefit is the Stormdancers can use those orbs to fuel their factories."

I gestured for more information.

"Haven't you paid attention in class?"

"My lessons kept getting interrupted by mundane things like chasing after a Soulstealer. I'll try harder in the future to ignore such events."

"Boy, you're grumpy when you're tired." Leif started a small fire and poured water into his cooking pot. "This container was made by the Stormdance Clan. They smelt ore to manufacture different metal items, including Sitian coins. They also produce parchment and make ink from indigo plants they grow on their eastern farms."

I mulled over Leif's lecture. Buying goods at the market, I hadn't stopped to consider who might have made them. In Ixia, every Military District had a particular product or service contributing to the Territory which could be used for barter and trade. It appeared Sitia worked the same way, although the

Stormdancers were a new twist. I wondered if they could harness the power of the blizzards blowing down from the northern ice pack. Life in MD-1, MD-2 and MD-3 turned into a struggle for survival during the cold season.

Would Commander Ambrose consider lifting his ban on magicians to alleviate the storms? He had grown up in MD-3, working in the diamond mines so he was no stranger to the incapacitating snowstorms. Even Valek, who had lived in MD-1, had seen his father's leather business destroyed by the heavy snow.

I thought about the chain of events that had started with the collapse of Valek's father's roof. He didn't have enough money to replace his equipment, feed his family and pay taxes to the King. When Valek's father asked the soldiers, who had come to collect the taxes, for an extension, they had killed three of his four sons. That act sent Valek on a mission of revenge against a King who allowed his soldiers to murder innocent children. Becoming the best assassin in Ixia, Valek eventually joined forces with Ambrose. Together they had defeated the King and gained control of Ixia.

If the roof hadn't collapsed, I wondered if the King would still be in power or if Ambrose would have found another assassin to help him. Would I even be here?

I shied away from those thoughts and focused on our present situation. Leif and I needed to guard our small camp. He manned the first shift while I tried to sleep.

The fire had been doused as soon as our meal was cooked. The smoke drifted on the breeze. Dreams swirled in my mind like sparks rising from a hot fire. The dizzying images slowed for a moment, and each time I glimpsed a horror. Stono's twisted stomach transformed into a necklace snake. Blood rained in the Illiais Jungle. Severed heads floated over the sands of the plains. And fire danced on my skin. The hot prick of each flame both seared and excited me.

I jerked awake. My skin tingled. Afraid to go back to sleep, I sent Leif to bed.

Uneasy sleep came in fits during the next two days. We kept out of sight, used small fires to cook meals before we extinguished the flames, and shivered on the cold, hard ground. On the third day, we crossed into the Krystal Clan's lands and turned north for the Ixian border.

Located directly west of the Featherstone Clan and the Citadel, the rolling terrain of the Krystals' land was dotted with clumps of pine trees. Quarries stretched between the wooded areas. The Krystal Clan mined marble for buildings and exported the high-quality sand needed by the glassmakers in Booruby, leaving behind deep pits gouged into the ground.

We avoided the bustle of activity around the quarries and journeyed through the pine forests. Another day of travel would get us to the Ixian border. Our approach to the boundary needed to be considered with care. Sitian soldiers could be waiting to ambush us. And if we managed to get through, I would need to choose the right words when addressing the Ixian guards. Or risk being arrested by them.

In the end, all the planning, all the time and energy Leif and I had spent finding the perfect spot to cross the border without alerting the Sitians was for naught. Just as we made our way into the hundred-foot-wide swatch of cleared land that was the official neutral zone between Ixia and Sitia, two riders on horseback bolted from the pine forest and into the borderland.

Two things happened that made the riders' presence go from bad timing to a deadly coincidence. Their horses headed straight toward us, and a whole squad of Sitian solders erupted from the woods in armed pursuit.

18

ONLY ONE OPTION REMAINED. We spurred our horses toward the border, hoping the Ixian guards would listen to our story before killing us. The unwelcome riders drew up beside us as we entered Ixia's Snake Forest. They kept pace as we penetrated deep within the forest before stopping.

As expected, the Sitian soldiers hadn't followed us into Ixia.

"Stay where you are," a voice ordered from the woods. "You are surrounded."

I knew the Ixians would be quick to find us. Just not this quick. I had chosen midmorning to cross into Ixia to avoid the changing of the guards. At this time, there was only one team of soldiers on duty.

"Drop your weapons and dismount," the unseen guard said.

Topaz. Garnet, Kiki said. She whinnied a greeting.

Cahil's horse? I pulled my bow and rounded on the riders, ignoring the orders from the guards. Two men sat on Topaz and Moon Man rode Garnet. "What? How?"

With shaking hands, one of the riders on Topaz pulled

back his hood, revealing his pale face before collapsing. Tauno held him tight.

"Marrok! What—" An arrow struck a tree next to me.

"Drop your weapons and dismount. Or the next arrow goes into her heart!" the Ixian shouted.

I tossed my bow to the ground and gestured to the others to follow. Tauno slid off Topaz, lowered Marrok down, then removed his bow and arrows. Moon Man frowned but released his scimitar before getting off Garnet. Leif tossed his machete next to my staff.

"Step away from the weapons and raise your hands."

We did as instructed. I made sure to step closer to Marrok. An arrow had pierced his side.

The ring of Ixian soldiers closed in. I counted four men and two women. Armed with crossbows and swords, they advanced on us.

"Give me one good reason why I shouldn't send you back to the squad of southerners?" asked an Ixian captain.

His uniform was mostly black except for a row of yellow diamond shapes down his sleeves and pant legs. We had crossed into Ixia's MD-7.

"Because it wouldn't be diplomatic to turn away a Sitian delegation," I said.

The captain laughed. "Delegations come with *honor* guards not *fleeing* guards. Want to tell me another one?"

"I'm Liaison Yelena Zaltana. I'm here to speak with the Commander even though my visit is not sanctioned by the Sitian Council."

"Yelena? The ex-food taster who saved the Commander?" the captain asked.

"Yes."

"But you have magic. Why would you want to come back to Ixia? I could kill you now and be considered a hero."

"I see your reputation has preceded you," Leif said, grinning. I hoped his good humor was relief over seeing Moon Man alive and well and not over the death threat to me.

I frowned at him. Leif didn't understand just how precarious a situation we were in. The captain's boast had merit. I was quite sure the rumors about the order for my execution had traveled throughout Ixia, while the fact that the Commander had ripped up those orders when I agreed to be a Liaison probably had not.

Especially since everyone in Sitia and Ixia believed the Commander had stayed behind in Ixia when the Ixian delegation visited Sitia a couple months ago. The Commander had been disguised as Ambassador Signe, and *she* had no authority to cancel an execution order.

Because of the edict that magicians were not allowed in Ixia unless invited, and any Ixians discovered with magical powers were put to death, I had one volatile situation on my hands.

While killing us wouldn't be easy, the captain had what amounted to standing orders to execute us on the spot. If he succeeded, though, he would have to face Valek. I shied away from that line of thought.

Instead, I said, "The Commander has appointed me as a Liaison with the Council. I am a neutral third party so I would *not* come with an honor guard of Sitians. I come with friends. Those guards had been chasing him." I gestured to Marrok's prone form. "I *need* to discuss something important with the Commander right away."

The captain's crossbow wavered. He appeared to be considering my answer. I pulled a thread of magic and skimmed his mind, touching only on his surface thoughts and emotions.

His ambition warred with his intelligence. Tired of guarding the border, the captain wanted a promotion and reassignment. Killing these southern magicians would give him enough recognition to become a major. But what if Yelena told the truth? The Commander wouldn't be happy to have his Liaison killed. Still, bringing a magician close to the Commander would be dangerous. What if Yelena lied and planned to assassinate him?

I nudged his thoughts to trust us and to believe that if he led us to his commanding officer, he would be doing a commendable deed.

"You will accompany me and my squad," the captain said. "We will confiscate your weapons and horses, and you will obey all orders. Any trouble or signs of revolt and you will be incapacitated." He signaled for a few of his soldiers to approach us. "Search them. What about him?"

I looked at Marrok. "Let me attend to his wounds, Captain…"

"Nytik." Again the captain signaled to one of his soldiers. "Lieutenant, search him for weapons."

After the lieutenant secured Marrok's sword, he gave me permission to examine him. The arrow had pierced Marrok's right side, missing his ribs. There wasn't much blood and the arrow hadn't gone deep. Why was Marrok unconscious?

Accessing my magic, I scanned the rest of his body. He had been beaten. Two ribs and his collarbone were broken. A mass of bruises covered his body and his jawbone was cracked.

"Leif, I'm going to need some help." Healing the extensive

damage in Marrok's body would exhaust me and I needed to reserve some energy in case Captain Nytik changed his mind.

"A poultice?" Leif knelt next to me.

"No. His story threads are frayed." Moon Man placed his large hand on Marrok's forehead.

I glared at Moon Man. "Stay away from him. Leif, let's deal with the physical injuries first."

Moon Man retreated. Leif and I drew power from the source. With my brother's help, I assumed his injuries and repaired them. When Marrok woke, Leif gave him water and a sustaining tonic to revive him.

I questioned him on what had happened and why he was here, but Marrok just stared at me with a wild, unconnected look in his eyes. Worried about his mental state, I projected my awareness into his thoughts.

A cacophony of images flooded his mind. Memories and emotions and secret thoughts were exposed, unlocked and left to run amok, as if someone had taken a library full of books and torn and scattered them all around the room. The sheer amount of disarray overwhelmed Marrok. He could no longer bring two thoughts together to form a coherent sentence.

And there in the middle of the mess, gleefully shredding what remained of Marrok's mind, was Roze Featherstone, First Magician.

She turned to me. *There you are. I knew I'd find you in here if I looked hard enough. Now I can discover where you've been hiding.*

She advanced, but I held my position. *I'm not a memory, Roze. You won't be able to extract anything from me.*

I wouldn't be so sure. Too much confidence can be a weakness.

You tried twice before and failed. I'm feeling pretty certain about my prediction. Why did you destroy Marrok's mind?

She glanced around at the chaos. *He's a criminal. And you shouldn't be so shocked. It's no different than when you destroyed the Soulstealer's mind.*

I ignored the jab. *Marrok isn't a criminal and you know it. Did you force him to make a false confession?*

He was honest, unlike you. You've been lying to us and to yourself, thinking you can be a benefit to Sitia. Now the Council knows the danger and I have permission to eliminate the threat you pose.

Again I failed to be impressed with her boast. *How did Marrok and the others find us?*

Roze smiled. *You'll have to figure that out on your own.*

Are you trying to tell me I have a spy in my midst?

Dishonest people tend to find each other, Yelena. It's the price you pay for associating with the criminal element. Frankly, I was surprised the Council hadn't given me permission to neutralize you before. After all, how can they trust the heart mate of the most feared man in Sitia? Think about it. How could you be a Liaison when it's obvious where your loyalties lie? First sign of trouble and you're running for home. I will tell you one thing. You won't be safe in Ixia.

I didn't say anything, but she laughed. *I have found what I needed. Good luck trying to put the pieces of Marrok's mind back together.*

She faded from his consciousness. Standing in the middle of the destruction she had left behind, I knew restoring order would be an impossible task. I returned to my body. There was nothing I could do.

Roze had the Council's support against me. If I hadn't known any better, the web of lies Cahil spun made complete sense. Roze even made sense. If she was as dedicated to Sitia as she claimed, then her efforts to discredit me were valid. Why trust me? I'm a Soulfinder, the one type of magician with an evil history. It would take a major effort and physical evidence to counter Cahil now.

"Moon Man, how did you find us?" I asked.

"Logic. I knew you would go to Ixia and I knew you would not cross the Avibian Plains in order to go around Featherstone lands. So that left west. Tauno found your trail in the Krystal lands."

It was too much of a coincidence. "But Leif saw you disappear into the fire. And what about Marrok and the horses? How did you get them?" He had help and must have been sent by Cahil or Roze. Moon Man worked for them now.

"Gede pulled me from the fire. Marrok had been dumped in the infirmary and left unguarded. The horses came when we needed them."

It still sounded too easy. "Why did Gede insist I go into the fire?"

"You will have to ask him. He is your Story Weaver now. I can not guide you." His tone held sadness.

"Why did you go into the fire, Moon Man?" Leif asked.

"Gede is the only surviving leader of my clan. I follow his orders."

"Even when your life's at stake?"

"Yes. Loyalty to one's clan comes before personal safety."

"Like being bait for a necklace snake?" Leif gazed at me.

"Exactly," Moon Man said.

"Can your man walk?" Captain Nytik asked. He had been standing nearby, watching us with distaste creasing his forehead. "We need to get moving."

Marrok couldn't walk, but he could ride. Kiki and Topaz's heads were together. I connected to Topaz, and asked, *Go home? Miss Peppermint Man?*

No. Stay.

Why? Topaz had been with Cahil for a long time.

Bad smell. Blood.

I turned to the captain. "He'll sit on his horse."

With the lieutenant in the lead, Moon Man, Leif, Tauno and I followed. The captain and his remaining soldiers formed a rear guard. We traveled north through the Snake Forest. On a map, the forest resembled a thin rope of green that undulated along the entire east-west border from the Jade Sea to the Emerald Mountains. After a half day of travel, we arrived at a guard station and barracks.

Another round of explanations had to be endured before we could care for the horses and eat lunch. We sat in the middle of the guard house's dining area surrounded by fifty suspicious soldiers who shot us hard glances between bites of food. Moon Man guided Marrok with a gentle patience. Basic skills like eating and caring for himself would all have to be relearned.

During our cold meal of venison jerky and bread, I explained to my companions about Ixia's uniform system. "Everyone who lives in Ixia must wear a uniform. The standard colors for the shirts, pants and skirts are black and white, but each Military District has its own color. We're in MD-7, which is governed by General Rasmussen, who reports to the Commander. Rasmussen's color is yellow and you'll see a line of yellow diamond shapes somewhere on the uniforms." I gestured to the guards around us. Their uniforms matched the captain's, but the rank insignia on their collars were different.

"A cook's uniform is all white with diamonds printed side by side across the shirt. The color of the diamonds tells you which district the cook works in. Red is the Commander's color."

"Who's that?" Leif pointed to woman heading our way. She wore all black, but had two red diamonds stitched onto her collar. Her blond hair was pulled into a tidy bun. She held two bows in her hands.

"She's an adviser to the Commander." I stood and grinned.

She tossed me my bow. I caught it. The noise in the room ceased the instant it hit my hand.

"Okay, Puker, let's see if you've been practicing," she said with an exultant yet predatory glint in her eyes.

"*Adviser* Maren, didn't your mother teach you it's not nice to call people names?" I hefted my bow. "Especially not *armed* people."

She waved away my comment. "We'll deal with the niceties later. Stuck in this backwoods, I haven't had a decent bow fight in a long time. Come on!" She beckoned me to follow as she threaded her way through the dining room.

"Should we be worried?" Leif asked.

"She taught me all her tricks, but I've learned a few new ones since our last fight. This should be…interesting."

"Play nice," Leif said.

I navigated through the quiet room. It erupted with sound as soon as I left. A mass of soldiers followed me outside.

Maren stretched her muscles before picking up her bow. Tall and lean, she made a formidable opponent. She swung her six-foot staff with deft hands. At a slight disadvantage, my bow measured only five feet. I removed my cloak and rubbed my hands along the smooth wood of my weapon, setting my mind into the zone of concentration I used when fighting. Not quite magical in origin, this mental state kept my mind open to my opponent's intentions.

As soon as I was ready she attacked with two quick strikes toward my ribs. I blocked both, countering with a strike to her arms. The fight began in earnest.

The rhythmic crack of our weapons filled the air. I ducked a temple strike and thrust the end of my bow staff toward her stomach. She stepped back and attempted to trip me with her bow. I jumped and did a front kick in midair, hitting her shoulder. Maren retreated a few steps before coming at me with a series of jabs.

"Did you get tired of losing to Janco all the time and request a transfer?" I asked, knocking her bow aside and executing a flurry of temple strikes. Maren had been a captain in the Commander's Special Forces, along with my friends Ari and Janco.

"I was promoted," she said. She met my assault and feinted to the right.

Sensing her intentions, I ignored the feint and stopped the blow to my head just in time. "Promoted to adviser? Sounds shady. Bribe anyone I know?"

"Once I beat Valek, I could choose any job in Ixia."

I froze for a moment in surprise and she hit my upper arm, knocking me over. I rolled, avoiding her jabs, but she pressed her advantage. Two moves later, she sat on my chest and pressed her bow to my neck. The crowd of soldiers cheered.

"Concede?"

"Yes."

She grinned and pulled me to my feet. "Rematch?"

"Give me a minute." I brushed the dirt from my clothes.

"What's with the skirt?"

"It's not a skirt. See?" Pulling the fabric apart, I revealed the pants.

She snorted with amusement. "We need to get you back into uniform, Yelena."

Her use of my proper name meant that I had at least impressed her with my fighting skills. Which reminded me of her comment that had thrown me off guard. "What's all this about *you* beating Valek? You're adequate with a bow, but, come on, Valek?"

Valek had issued a challenge to everyone in Ixia. Beat him in a fight with the weapon of your choice and win the right to become his second in command. Many soldiers had tried and failed to win the right.

"Adequate?" She laughed. "I guess *when* I beat you again, you'll up it to decent."

"That's *if* you beat me, and you haven't answered my question."

"I had help. Happy now? Valek never said we had to beat him one on one. Three of us got together and we won the right to pick any position in Ixia. I chose to become an adviser for the Commander. I'm in MD-7 on a temporary assignment to deal with some—" she glanced at the soldiers "—issues."

Three against one was still good odds for Valek. I wondered who the other two were, and the answer came to me. "Please don't tell me Ari and Janco were your partners."

Her chagrined expression confirmed my guess.

"Janco was insufferably smug before. There'll be no living with him," I said.

"Valek's challenge has been modified. Since Janco and Ari have been promoted to Valek's seconds, if other soldiers want to claim the second positions they must beat Ari and Janco, but no more than six can attack at one time. Valek's seconds should be able to handle three each. If a soldier wishes to fight Valek alone, he must beat one of us to have the chance."

"Having Janco in charge when Valek's away is a scary state of affairs."

"Not as scary as when you're begging for mercy." Maren swung her bow.

I blocked and countered. Soon we were engaged in another brisk fight. But this time I stayed focused. I swept her feet out from under her and stepped on her bow before she could roll away. I won the match and received a few cheers from my brother, who had joined the audience. Moon Man and the others stood apart. He watched me with no expression on his face.

"Tie breaker?" Maren didn't wait for an answer. Round three began.

We fought until we reached an impasse.

Leif's voice interrupted us before we started another match. "As much as I enjoy watching my sister get beaten, we really need to talk to the Commander. You're wasting time."

Maren studied Leif with a dubious expression. "I don't see a family resemblance."

I introduced my brother to Maren. "Although I hate to admit it, Leif's right. We need to go."

Maren shook her head. "General Rasmussen wants to talk with you first. These soldiers have orders to keep you here until he gives you permission to leave."

"But I've explained—"

"Everything but exactly what you need to discuss with the Commander."

"That's classified."

"That's what I was afraid of." Maren leaned on her bow. "The general has become…cautious in his advancing years. *He* won't let you leave unless you tell him the reason you came to Ixia."

From her choice of words, I could tell there was more to the story. She worked for the Commander but was helping the general, and probably reporting every bit of information to Valek.

"We'll talk to the general then," I agreed.

"Great. I'll schedule an audience with him tomorrow."

"Tomorrow? We have pressing business."

"I'm sorry. The general retires early. He'll see no one tonight."

Leif opened his mouth to protest. I touched his arm, stopping him. Maren and I had dueled the afternoon away, and I suspected she had a good reason for it.

"All right. We'll wait until tomorrow. How long will it take us to get to the manor? Perhaps it would be best to leave tonight?"

"No. It would be *best* to leave in the morning. It's a half-day's ride." Maren led us to a brick cottage with a stable nearby. "You can stay in our guest quarters. This location is a popular spot for travelers from MD-6 to stop."

The castle complex was located in the southern end of MD-6. Two-and-a-half days' ride directly north of Sitia's Citadel. I found it interesting the two centers of political power remained physically close while their governing styles were worlds apart.

We entered the cottage. Although the furnishings in the

main room were sparse, it looked comfortable enough. Guards stationed themselves outside, but one lieutenant followed us in.

"Beds! They have beds with feather mattresses," Leif called from a bedroom.

"There is wood in the back, and you can dine with the soldiers for your evening meal. I'll let the general know when you're arriving." Maren left with the Lieutenant close on her heels, but two guards remained positioned by the front door.

A quick peek out the side and back windows revealed the presence of more guards. We were surrounded. I thought about Maren's comments. A few of the things she said didn't add up. I wondered what she planned to do. All I knew were my plans, and they didn't include visiting the general.

I joined my traveling companions in the bedroom. Moon Man sat next to Marrok, who lay on his back, staring at the ceiling. Tauno perched on the edge of a chair.

Leif had stretched out across one of the beds. A sigh of contentment escaped his lips. "I haven't slept in a bed since… since…I can't even remember!"

"Don't get too comfortable," I said.

He groaned. "Now what?"

I put a finger over my lips then pointed to my forehead. *Too many ears around*, I said in his mind.

What's going on? he asked.

We are not going to waste time with the general, Moon Man said.

I scowled at him in surprise, forgetting that he could link his mind to ours.

Since you have chosen Gede as your guide, I had to channel through Leif.

I ignored Leif's confusion. *Unchannel then. This is a private conversation.*

Moon Man remained quiet for a while. *I will withdraw.*

Care to tell me what that was about? Leif asked.

I filled him in on my conversation with Roze. *Moon Man's a spy.*

No way. You can't believe that.

Are you saying Roze is lying?

No. I'm saying maybe you're overreacting. Moon Man admitted Gede is his boss. Their clan was decimated by the Vermin so Gede and Roze want the same thing. Gede probably sent Moon Man to keep an eye on you.

And that's different than spying how?

He's probably here to protect you. To keep you safe until your name can be cleared.

It would be nice just to ask him, but I'm sure he has a vague non-answer already prepared.

That's harsh, Yelena. He has witnessed the massacre of his clan. Although, I do wish for the old Moon Man back, Leif said. *I'll take his teasing, cryptic advice and mysterious arrivals over his somber demeanor any day.*

My brother put another pillow under his head. *Looks like we'll be in Ixia for a while. Leif Liana Ixia has a nice ring to it. If they don't execute me for being a magician, perhaps I can find a job at an Ixian apothecary. Do they have uniforms for an apothecarist?*

We're going back to Sitia.

To certain death? No thank you. Perhaps the Commander will need one of my tisanes?

We need to talk to the Commander and rendezvous with Valek. I hoped.

Surrounded by guards. Remember?

That's right. We're outnumbered. It's a shame we don't have magic to help us. A mage could put the guards to sleep. Or better yet we could use Curare. Too bad I don't have any blowpipes in my backpack.

Sarcasm is an ugly trait, little sister. You should avoid it.

And you give up too easy. And trust too easy, but I wouldn't say it to him.

I blame the feather mattress. It has sucked all my motivation. If there is a comfortable bed in my apartment above my apothecary shop, I will be quite content living in Ixia.

Leif. I warned.

All right. All right. I'll make you a few blowpipes just in case we can't put everyone to sleep. He grumbled to himself as he rolled out of bed and went over to his pack.

I debated what I should tell Tauno and Moon Man. As long as we didn't have a fire, I could warn them about my plans. And I wanted them with me so I could keep an eye on them.

"We should go to bed early tonight," I said to them. "To *rest* for *tomorrow.*"

They appeared to understand my hint. Once the Ixian soldiers had gone to bed, we would make our escape.

I planned to be at the Commander's castle before the MD-7 guards realized we had gone. Approaching the main gate of the castle complex without an Ixian guide would create instant suspicion, but that was a problem I would deal with when it arose.

After having dinner with the soldiers, I eyed our new set of guards with care, trying to size them up. I knew Tauno and Moon Man wouldn't pass for Ixian, so either Leif or I would have to wear a uniform and pose as a soldier until we reached the Commander. Ideally, I should disguise myself, but at five feet four inches tall, I doubted I would find a uniform that fit.

Not bothering to build a fire, we retired early. I slept for a few hours. The luxury of being in an actual bed made it difficult to rouse. But I forced myself to get up and woke the others, gesturing for quiet.

Leif didn't have the skills to put our guards to sleep, but he could complement my energy. I held his hand and projected my awareness to the circle of soldiers. Three men and one woman stood watch. Reaching farther, I connected to the horses in the stable.

Ready? I asked Kiki.

Yes.

The two stable lads slept on bales of hay, content to have horses in their stables. To them the musky smell of horse, manure and straw equaled a feather bed.

I swept the barracks with my mind, seeking trouble. At two hours past midnight, the garrison was calm. Since I couldn't put the entire garrison into a deep sleep, I hoped we were far enough away not to wake them. I returned to the sleeping lads and sent them into a heavy slumber.

The guards who ringed our quarters proved resistant to my mental suggestion. Their Ixian training fought my magic and I feared I would have to resort to using the Curare. Before I broke the connection, one of the guards jerked in surprise as a sharp point jabbed his neck. His vision spun as the drug entered his blood. I pulled away before the man passed out.

Leif released my hand.

"Time to go," I said, moving fast. We had help and my heart soared. One person always knew when I needed him. I threw open the door, expecting Valek, but found Maren instead. She dragged one of the guards into the guest quarters, and was soon followed by three others who each carried in a prone form, dumping them onto the floor.

Her companions wore MD-7 uniforms.

"Guess we had the same idea. My men will pose as your guards while we head toward the castle," she explained.

"Will they be out long?" I poked one of the men on the floor with the toe of my boot.

"A good six hours. I used Valek's sleeping potion on them." She smiled with a mischievous glint in her gray eyes.

"*Adviser* Maren, you aren't doing a little moonlighting with Valek's corps now, are you?" I tsked with mock concern. "How did you know when to strike?"

Maren gave me an odd look. "When the horses left the stable, I thought you might be ready to go."

"Are you coming with us? Can you ride?"

"Yes. I have a horse nearby. I need to return to the general's manor house before you're discovered missing. I'll take you to MD-6's border and introduce you to the soldiers at the way station there. They will take you to the Commander's castle. Your weapons are outside. Let's go."

Leif, Moon Man, Tauno and I carried our saddles until we were far enough away to risk the noise. Moon Man and Marrok rode on Topaz. Marrok still couldn't speak, but he mounted when Moon Man asked him to.

Maren proved to be an adept rider and we covered the distance to MD-6 in record time. Before she alerted the way-station guards, I asked her, "What will happen when General Rasmussen finds out we escaped?"

"Once you're with the Commander, he can't admit to trying to delay you, because he'll have to answer why. He'll probably have his people keep the whole incident quiet. Valek will most likely let him believe he got away with it. Until Valek needs something from him." Another predatory grin spread on her face.

Our transfer to MD-6 and into the hands of General Hazel's soldiers proceeded with quick efficiency. The new guide wore a captain's uniform with blue diamonds instead of Captain Nytik's yellow.

In fact, the whole trip to the Commander's castle went smoothly. Admitted into his complex without any trouble, I should have savored those few quiet hours. Because after we met with Commander Ambrose, nothing went right.

19

AFTER OUR ARRIVAL at the castle complex, we waited in the outer courtyard. We received many curious glances from the castle's denizens, and I knew the servants would soon be gossiping and laying bets about who we were and why we had come. They probably didn't recognize me without my food taster's uniform on.

Grooms from the stable appeared to take the horses. I wanted to stay with Kiki, but we were instructed to enter the castle to await a meeting with the Commander.

My companions exclaimed over the odd-shaped structure. With its multiple levels of unusual geometric shapes, the castle resembled a child's toy. Balanced on the rectangular base, the other floors of the castle were a combination of squares, triangles and even cylinders built on top of one another in a haphazard fashion. On some levels all three shapes could be found. The windows of the building also reflected the architect's fondness for geometry, including octagons and ovals.

It had been a year since I last saw the castle. Once part of my everyday routine, I had grown used to its strange style. Now, the sight of the structure jolted me and unease fluttered through my body.

The four towers at the corners gave the viewer some sense of symmetry. They rose a few stories higher than the main building and colored glass decorated their windows. I paused. The Magician's Keep also had four towers in the corners and I wondered about the similarity.

A servant led us to an austere waiting room with minimal comforts. Served refreshments, I automatically tested the drink for poisons, surprising Leif when I gargled the juice. He had been staring at the blank walls, probably wondering where all the legendary paintings and gilded mirrors had gone to. I assumed the Commander had destroyed all the treasures from the King's era, but, remembering a comment Cahil had made to me about the amount of money needed to support Ixia, I wondered if Commander Ambrose had traded them for services instead.

"Did you live here?" Leif asked.

I nodded. "For two years." One of them in the dungeon. Not many people in Sitia knew about Reyad. I preferred to keep the details of that time to myself. However, most Ixians were aware I killed Reyad.

"Where did you stay?"

"I had a room in Valek's suite."

Leif shot me an incredulous look. "Boy, you worked fast."

"And you assume too much." One day I would tell Leif and my parents about my ordeal, but not today.

Leif grew thoughtful. Tauno napped in one of the wooden chairs. I marveled at how the Sandseed could wedge himself into a small space and still look comfortable. During our time together, he had adapted to being within walls.

Moon Man, on the other hand, fidgeted in his chair. I couldn't determine if his discomfort grew from being in a confined space or from my hostility. He claimed I had a new Story Weaver. It was an easy way for him to avoid telling me the truth.

Knowing we were headed toward Ixia, Cahil must have planned Marrok's escape. The Sitian guards who chased them were probably part of the ruse, too.

I longed to pace the room. The wait stretched as long as a necklace snake. There was nothing to avert me from my list of worries. Valek remained near the top. Where was he? By this time, he should be back in Ixia. Thoughts circled in my mind. To distract myself, I sat in one of the hard chairs near the only window. Outside, a portion of the barracks and practice yard where the Commander's soldiers lived and trained was visible, reminding me of Ari and Janco, my soldier friends who, according to Maren, were now Valek's seconds in command.

I stood, desiring action. Perhaps I should just go to the Commander's office. I knew how to get there, and I hated this unsettled sensation sloshing in the pit of my stomach. Why was I so on edge?

Understanding crashed through me and I needed to sit down again. Inside these walls I had always been a prisoner. Either by the bars of the dungeon or by the belief I had ingested a poison called Butterfly's Dust, knowing I couldn't get far without the daily antidote keeping me alive. And all the logic in the world couldn't convince my body I was free.

Finally, an adviser arrived to lead us though the main corridors of the castle. Leif gasped in surprise when we entered the main hall. Greeted by the sight of the silk and gold tapestries hanging in tatters, I sympathized with my brother's reaction. Black paint stained the once famous quilts that had symbolized each province during the King's era. They now represented the takeover. The old provinces had been torn apart and borders redrawn into eight neat Military Districts.

Commander Ambrose's disdain for opulence, excess and greed was evident in every part of the stone building. Stripped of the trappings of royalty, the castle had been robbed of its soul, and reassigned as a basic utilitarian structure.

The transformation of the throne room was another example of his disregard. Instead of lavish decorations and thick carpets, the room buzzed with the activity of numerous advisers and military officers from every Military District in Ixia, with no sign of a dais or throne in sight. With desks wedged in tight together, getting the five of us through the room turned into an exercise in agility as we threaded our way toward the back.

The Commander's office matched the rest of the castle. Stark, neat and organized, the room lacked personality but reflected its occupant perfectly.

Wearing a tailored black uniform with real diamonds glittering from his collar, Commander Ambrose stood when we entered. I studied his clean-shaven face as I introduced him to my companions, detecting only a faint resemblance to Ambassador Signe. As if they were truly cousins instead of the same person.

The power of his gaze, though, remained the same. My heart flipped in my chest when he focused his gold-colored eyes on me.

"This is an unexpected visit, Liaison Yelena. I trust you have a good reason for bypassing standard protocol," he said, raising a single slender eyebrow.

"An excellent reason, sir. I believe Sitia will try to mount an offensive against you."

The Commander glanced at my companions as he considered my words. More gray had infiltrated his black hair, which had been cropped so short it looked as if Kiki had grazed on it.

Walking to his office's door, the Commander called to one of his men.

"Adviser Reydon, please escort our guests to the dining hall for lunch and then to the guest suite." He turned to the others. "The Liaison will dine with me and meet up with you later."

Leif looked to me for guidance. I opened my mind to him.

Do you want us to stay? he asked.

I don't think you have a choice.

He isn't my Commander. I don't have to listen to him.

A childish, stubborn remark. Perhaps Leif felt left out. *Be a good guest and do as he says. I'll let you know what happens.*

You sure you don't need backup? This guy creeps me out.

Leif, I warned.

He left the office with obvious reluctance, shooting me an annoyed frown before following the adviser.

When the room emptied, the Commander gestured for me to sit in the chair in front of his desk. Unnerved, I perched on the edge.

He served me a cup of tea before settling behind his desk. I sipped the drink with care, testing for poisons. In command of a powerful military and with eight ambitious generals to oversee, the Commander needed a food taster on his staff.

"Why have you come?" he asked.

"I told you. Sitia plans—"

He stopped me with a dismissive wave. "You know that's old news. Why are you *really* here?"

"To ask you to delay a first strike."

"Why?"

I paused, gathering my thoughts. Only logic would persuade the Commander. "The Sitian Council has had a dramatic change of opinion from wanting to trade and communicate with you to being terrified of you."

"Yes. They're very unstable."

"But not *that* unstable. They're being influenced."

"With magic?" The Commander said the word as if it pained him.

General Brazell and Mogkan—my kidnappers had used magic and Theobroma on him to gain control of his mind despite his ban on magicians. Though his firm censure softened, the Commander still viewed magicians as untrust-worthy. Consenting to let me act as Liaison for Ixia had been his first and only concession.

Valek had theorized the Commander feared magicians, but I believed it had more to do with what the Commander referred to as his mutation. Born with a female body, he believed his soul was a man's and he worried a magician would expose him. But from my interaction with him when he had been disguised as the female Ambassador Signe, I had sensed the presence of two souls within his body.

Standing in front of him, I suppressed the desire to project into his mind, avoiding even a surface sweep. It would be a serious breach of protocol. Besides, it felt wrong.

"Magic could be a factor, but there could be another reason or even a person influencing them. At this point I don't know, but I want to find out. If you kill them all, you might not solve the problem and those who replace them will be worse," I said.

"Sounds rather vague. Perhaps you have more information on this?" The Commander flourished a scroll then handed it to me.

I unrolled the parchment. Each word I read increased my concern and outrage.

"And if you notice—" he leaned over and tapped the bottom "—it's signed by all the Councilors, but it's lacking two Master Magicians' signatures. Curious."

Curious wouldn't be the word I would use. *Disastrous* sounded more fitting. I worried about Irys and Bain. If the Council tried to coerce their signatures, what had happened to them by refusing? I focused on the paper in my hand. Fretting wouldn't help Irys and Bain.

In short, the letter warned the Commander about my renegade status and suggested my treasonous companions and I be killed on sight. Probably the reason Roze had been confident I wouldn't be safe in Ixia.

"They seek to undermine your credibility all the while planning to attack me. Do they think I'm a simpleton?" He relaxed back in his chair and sighed. "Explain to me exactly what's going on."

"If I knew exactly, then I wouldn't have sounded so vague." My turn to sigh. I wiped a hand over my face, thinking how best to tell the Commander about Cahil. Did I mention the Fire Warper or not? I had no idea what role he played in all this. Exactly the problem.

So I explained about Ferde's escape with Cahil's help and how Cahil had turned it all around to implicate Marrok, Leif and me.

"Sounds like assassinating the Council would be a good deed for Sitia," the Commander said.

"That would give Cahil and his cohorts evidence they were right to suspect you. Sitia would rally behind them in support. Valek agrees with me. He hasn't targeted the Council yet. He's on his way here."

If the Commander was surprised, he didn't show it. "So you already delayed my preemptive strike. Yet you have no proof."

"None. That's why I wanted you to wait before launching another attack. We need more information. Valek and I—"

The office door opened. Star came into the room, carrying a tray of food. The Commander's food taster froze in shock when she recognized me. My own pulse skipped when I saw my old uniform being worn by her. And not just any woman, but the former Captain Star, who had been the leader of a successful black market and racketeering ring before Valek uncovered her operation.

Star stared daggers at me. Her goon's unsuccessful attempt on my life had led to her capture. Already warned about Valek's setup, Star could have disappeared into her own underground network. Instead, she had let petty vengeance rule her and now she tasted food for the Commander.

"At least you survived the training," I said to her.

She looked away. The long red curls of her hair had been tied into a sloppy knot, and her prominent nose led the way as she walked. Putting the tray onto the Commander's desk, she performed a fast taste and left. Even though two lunches had been set on the tray, she tested only the one.

I eyed my food. Star seemed surprised at my presence, but that could have been an act. She could still be nursing her desire for revenge. The Commander handed me a plate. Not to appear rude, I took a tentative bite of the meat pie, chewing slowly and rolling the food around my tongue. The beef was flavored with rosemary and ginger and lacked poisons. At least, I couldn't taste the poisons I remembered. I lost my appetite when I remembered Moon Man's comment about learning by doing and how easy it was to forget dictated information.

We talked about minor things while eating. When I complimented his new chef on the lemon-wedge dessert, he told me Sammy now held the position.

"Rand's fetch boy?" I asked. He was thirteen years old.

"He worked with Rand for four years and it became evident only he knew all the ingredients in Rand's secret recipes."

"But he's so young." The kitchen during meal times had been a cacophony of ordered chaos guided by Rand's firm hand.

"I gave him a week to prove he could do it. He's still there."

I had forgotten age didn't matter to the Commander. He could have forced Sammy to divulge the recipes, but he respected ability over experience or gender. My young friend, Fisk the beggar boy turned entrepreneur, would have flourished in Ixia.

When we finished lunch, the Commander moved the tray aside and repositioned his snow cat statue. Glints of silver sparked from the black stone. The single piece of decoration in the room, the cat was one of Valek's carvings. Killing a snow cat was considered impossible. The citizens of Ixia avoided the lethal creatures living on the northern ice pack. The cat's pre-ternatural ability to escape death made it feared.

Commander Ambrose was the only person to successfully hunt and kill one, and in doing so, he proved to himself that despite his mutation he could infiltrate a man's world just as he had lived among the snow cat's world. He believed his female body had just been a disguise for his soul. Only the Commander and I knew about his hunt and dual personalities. He had sworn me to secrecy when I had rescued him from Mogkan's mind control.

"Before Star came in with lunch you mentioned getting more information about the Sitian Council. Now that you're a wanted criminal, how do you plan to achieve that?" the Commander asked.

"I had hoped to infiltrate the Citadel and talk to one of the Councilors. But I fear the Master Magician's magic would discover me, so now I want to borrow Valek and a few of his men. They could assist us in contacting the Councilor."

"Which one?"

"Bavol Cacao Zaltana, my clan's Councilman. He has been my strongest supporter and if you see by his signature…" I picked the Sitian letter up and pointed to his name. "He didn't include his family name, Cacao, in his signature, so it's not an official inscription. I believe it's a message to me that he can be approached."

The Commander stared across the room as if considering my words. After a while, he brought his attention back to me. "You want me to risk my chief of security to help you gain information. All the while I'm to do nothing and hope the Sitians don't attack before you discover what's going on?"

"Yes." Although, the way the Commander said it made the situation sound terrible. There was no sense sugarcoating it. And the last thing I wanted was to put Valek or anyone else at risk. But it had to be done.

The Commander rested his chin on his folded hands. "The information isn't worth the risk. I could wait to see what develops with the Council and then decide how to handle it."

"But—"

A warning flashed in his eyes. "Yelena, why would you care what happens to the Council? They have turned their backs on you. You can't go back to Sitia. You would provide the most help here with me as my adviser."

An unexpected offer. I considered. "What about my companions?"

"Magicians?" A small crease of distaste pinched his forehead. "Two."

"They could be part of your staff if you want. But they can *not* use their magic against any Ixians without *my* permission."

"What about *my* magic? Would you place the same restrictions on me?"

The Commander's gaze didn't waver. "No. I trust you."

I froze for a moment in shock. His trust was an honor, and, considering the recent reaction from the Sitian Council about me, the temptation to become his adviser warred with my emotions. It would probably be easier to stay and help defeat Cahil from this side of the border.

"Don't answer right away. Talk to your companions. I should have news from Valek soon. We'll meet again then. In the meantime, do you need anything?"

I thought about our dwindling supplies. If we left, we would need more provisions. "Could you exchange Sitian coins for Ixian?" I rummaged in my pack, placing various loose objects on his desk to get them out of my way.

"Give them to Adviser Watts. You remember my accountant?"

"Yes." The covering on Opal's bat had come undone and was all over the bottom of my pack. I removed the glass animal and freed it from the wrapping. The Commander gasped.

His focus was riveted on the statue in my hand; his fingers poised as if to snatch the bat.

"May I see?" he asked.

"Sure."

With a snap of motion, he plucked the statue from my palm. He spun the bat, examining it from every possible angle. "Who made this?"

"My friend, Opal. She's a glass artist in Sitia."

"It glows like there is molten fire on the inside. How did she make it?"

Trying to comprehend his words, I stared. He saw the inner glow. Impossible. Only magicians could see the light.

The Commander had magical powers.

20

THE GLASS BAT GLOWED for the Commander. I had
theorized only magicians could see the inner light. But I could
be wrong. Maybe I hadn't tested the bat on enough people. If
the Commander had magical power, his magic would have
raged uncontrolled and flamed out by now, killing him. The
Masters in Sitia would have felt him long ago. Irys would have
sensed it when she stood next to him.

Shaking those ridiculous thoughts out of my mind, I
answered the Commander's questions about glassmaking.

"But what causes it to glow?"

I knew if I said *magic*, he would drop it as if burned. Instead,
I told him the internal workings were a family secret.

He passed the glass bat to me. "Extraordinary. Next time
you see your friend, please ask her to make one for me."

I found the coins I had been searching for, and repacked my
bag. Only when I had slung my pack onto my shoulders did
I realize I forgot to rewrap the bat.

The Commander picked up the coins, walked to his office

door and opened it. Summoning Adviser Watts, he asked him to exchange my money and to show me to the guest area.

Dismissed, I followed Watts into the throne room, holding the bat in my hand. The adviser noticed the creature when handing me the Ixian coins.

"Sitian art?" he asked.

I nodded.

"Not a bad likeness, but rather dull. I thought the Sitians had more imagination than that."

I mulled over the Commander and Adviser Watts's comments as I followed Watts through the castle. Still unable to bend my mind around the Commander's ability to see the glow, I had to postpone further ruminations when I entered the guest suite.

Leif peppered me with a million questions the moment I stepped through the door. The guest quarters were rather lavish by Ixian standards. The main room contained a comfortable sofa and soft chairs as well as a number of desks and tables. A faint odor of disinfectant scented the air. Four bedrooms branched off from the living area, two on each side. Sunlight streamed in through the circle of windows in the back wall, warming the empty room.

I stopped Leif's questions with a look. "Where are the others?"

He pointed to the second door on the right. "They're all resting. Moon Man and Marrok are in the big room next to Tauno's."

Double doors marked the entrance to Moon Man's room.

"Which one is mine?"

"Second door on the left, next to me."

I went into my room. Leif trailed along like a lost puppy. A simple layout of a bed, armoire, desk and night table all made of oak decorated the small interior. The bedding looked fresh and inviting. I stroked the soft quilt. The air smelled of pine. The lack of dust made me remember Valek's housekeeper, Margg. She had plagued my existence when I first became the food taster, refusing to clean my room and writing nasty messages in the dust. I hoped I wouldn't run into her during this trip.

Leif's questions began again, and I filled him in on what had happened in the Commander's office, neglecting to mention his ability to see the bat's glow. I wasn't convinced that the Commander had magic, and certainly wouldn't try to persuade Leif or anyone else.

"Black and red really aren't my colors. Which Military District has green? Maybe I can open my shop there," Leif said.

Leif's joke wasn't as funny now. "MD-5 is green and black. General Brazell used to govern the district, but now he's in the Commander's dungeon." I wonder who was promoted.

"What are we going to do next?"

"I don't know."

Leif pretended to be shocked. "But you're our fearless leader. You have it all planned out. Right?"

I shrugged. "I'm going to take a long hot bath. How's that?"

"Sounds good. Can I come?"

"As long as you promise not to spend all day in there." I gathered some clean clothes.

"Why would I?"

"You thought the feather mattress was a luxury. Wait until you see the Commander's baths."

★ ★ ★

The hot water soaked my aches away.

Leif joined me in the corridor with a contented smile on his face. "I won't have any trouble adjusting to life in Ixia. Those pools and the overhead duct, pouring water...amazing. Does every town have a similar bathhouse?"

"No. Only the Commander's castle has such luxury. It's a holdover from the King's regime. The Commander usually disdains the extravagance, yet it remains."

During my soak, I had thought long and hard about our situation and the Commander's offer. The temptation to stay tried to overpower my logic, but I knew we needed to return to Sitia. The Sandseed clan had already been destroyed by the Vermin, and Cahil and the Fire Warper remained a problem.

How I would deal with them continued to be a mystery. Not being able to trust Moon Man, Tauno or Marrok, left Valek, Leif and me against the Daviians, the Fire Warper, Cahil and his army.

And what would happen if I revealed Cahil's involvement with the Vermin? The Council trusted him. I would need to convince them of his deceit. I would need hard evidence to gain their trust. Evidence I lacked.

In fact, the more I thought about the whole situation, the less confident I felt about my ability to find a solution.

When Leif and I returned to the guest suite, Moon Man and Tauno waited for us in the living room.

"How's Marrok?" I asked Moon Man.

"Better."

"Can he talk?"

"Not yet."

"Soon?"

"Perhaps."

I stared at him. He answered in typical Story Weaver fashion. Refraining from shaking information out of him, I asked, "Have you learned anything while working with Marrok?"

"I have seen bits and pieces. Marrok's feelings of betrayal are making it difficult for me to get through to him. He does not trust me." Moon Man's eyes met mine and I could see his unspoken words.

"Trust has to go both ways."

"It is not a lack of trust which causes me to keep my silence. It is a lack of acceptance on your part."

"And you're afraid of what you might discover once you accept your role in all this, aren't you?" Leif asked me.

A knock at the door saved me from having to reply to Leif's question. One of the housekeeping maids handed me a message from the Commander. We were invited to dine with him in his war room.

"You don't have an answer for me. Do you have an answer for the Commander? Are you going to stay and be his adviser?" Leif asked when the maid left.

"Actually Leif, I don't have any answers. I've no idea what I'm doing or going to do." I went into my room and shut the door.

The Commander's war room was located in one of the four towers of the castle. With long stained-glass windows reflecting the lantern light, the circular chamber reminded me of the inside of a kaleidoscope.

Our conversation followed mundane topics while we ate

spiced chicken and vegetable soup. Leif wolfed his food with obvious relish, but I took my time, sampling all the dishes with care. A few guards stood near the Commander. Star hovered close by, ready to taste the Commander's food whenever a new course was served. Moon Man and Tauno remained quiet during dinner.

We discussed the new general in MD-5. Colonel Ute from MD-3 had been promoted and transferred. The Commander thought it best an officer from outside the district be in charge. In other words, a loyal person who had not been tainted by General Brazell's attempt to become the new leader of Ixia.

When the subject turned to General Kitvivan's worry over the upcoming blizzard season, I told the Commander about the Stormdance Clan and how they handled the storms from the sea.

"Magicians could harness the power of the blizzard," I said, "saving the people in MD-1 from the killing winds. Then you could use the power for General Dinno's sawmills in MD-8." Dinno used the wind to fuel his mills, and calm days hurt production.

"No. The matter of magicians and magic in Ixia will *not* be discussed," the Commander said.

His stern tone had once intimidated me, but not this time. "You want me to be your adviser, yet you won't consider using magic for the good of your people. I'm a magician. How can I be an effective adviser to you?"

"You can advise me on how to counter the magicians in Sitia. I'm not interested in what magic can do for Ixia." He made a cutting motion with his hand. End of discussion.

I wouldn't let the subject drop. "What happens when one

of your generals becomes ill or injured and I can save their life with my magic?"

"You don't. If they die, I'll promote another colonel."

I considered his answer with mixed feelings. I knew his firm style of governing was inflexible. The Code of Behavior's strict list of proper Ixian conduct left no room for debate. However, I hoped once he saw the benefits of magic to his people, he might relax his views.

As if reading my mind, the Commander said, "Magic corrupts. I've seen it before with the King's magicians. They start out wanting to help and performing great deeds, but soon the power consumes them and they hunger for more despite the cost. Consider what has occurred to Moon Man's clan. Frankly, I'm surprised something like that hasn't happened sooner."

"My clan will repopulate," Moon Man said. "I have no doubt."

"And I have no doubt if these Vermin of Sitia are conquered, it's only a matter of time before another magician wishes to take over the current government. The talent to control another's mind and body is intoxicating and addicting. Better to ban magic and eliminate magicians altogether."

I wondered if the Commander's views would change if he knew he might possess the skill to access magic. My thoughts returned to Opal's bat and his ability to see the glow, mulling over the implications.

"Better to kill people the old-fashioned way," Leif said, his voice indignant. "You're saying that taking over a government with poisons, knives and swords is *much* better than using magic. Frankly, I see no difference."

"Magic forces a person to do things they don't want to. It controls their will." The Commander leaned forward; his eyes lit with an intense passion.

Leif quailed under the Commander's scrutiny, but he continued with his debate. "And your Code of Behavior doesn't force people to do things they don't want? Everyone in Ixia *wants* to wear uniforms? They *want* to obtain permission to marry or move to another district?"

"Small inconveniences to live in an area where there is no hunger and no corruption. To know exactly where your place is in society and what is expected from you. Being rewarded for your abilities and efforts instead of getting privileges because of who you were born to or what gender you are."

"But the reward for having magical abilities is death," Leif said. "I'm sure the families of those potential magicians don't feel the loss of their loved one as inconvenient. Why not send them to Sitia instead?"

"Send them so they could be used against me?" The Commander's voice reflected his incredulity. "That would be poor military strategy."

Leif remained quiet.

"No government is perfect," the Commander said, relaxing back into his chair. "The loss of a few personal freedoms has been embraced by most of Ixia, especially those who suffered under the King's corruption. However, I know the younger generation is feeling restless and I will have to address that issue fairly soon." He stared at Leif as if contemplating the future. "Yelena, I see your intelligence is a family trait. I hope you both decide to stay."

A determined line formed along my brother's jaw. Leif

could be stubborn and perhaps he viewed changing the Commander's mind about magicians as a challenge.

A messenger arrived and handed a scroll to the Commander. After reading the message, he stood. "Please enjoy the rest of your dinner. I have some matters to attend to." He left, taking his guards and Star with him.

Before Star followed him, she flashed me a calculating look.

The Commander's opinions about magic and magicians replayed in my mind as we returned to the guest suite. Although I agreed with Leif that Ixians with magical powers should not be killed, I also felt magic corrupted. Even Roze, the most powerful magician in Sitia, had been affected. To fear my potential as a Soulfinder was one thing, to support Cahil was another.

When we arrived at our quarters, I pulled Leif into my room.

"What's the matter?" he asked.

"I want to contact Irys. See what's going on in the Citadel."

"What I want to know is what's going on with *you?*"

"What do you mean?"

"Since crossing the border, you have changed, treating Moon Man like a traitor and not trusting anyone. If you decide to stay as the Commander's adviser, *you'll* be a traitor to Sitia. What happened to Liaison Yelena? The neutral third party?"

"To be a Liaison, I need to have support of *both* parties. Are you going to help me contact Irys or lecture me?"

Leif grumbled and pouted but agreed to share his energy. I lay on the bed and drew power, projecting my awareness south to the Keep. Bypassing the busy thoughts of the Citadel's inhabitants, I searched the campus for Irys. I couldn't find her within her tower, but I sensed a faint echo as if the scent of her soul remained behind after she had left the room. Odd.

I moved on to the Keep's other towers, hoping Irys was visiting with another Master. Zitora's thoughts were walled off from intruders. Bain's tower had that same odd feeling as Irys's, and the cold barrier of Roze's mind slammed into me. I bounced off and retreated, but an icy wind sucked me back toward her. This time her barrier was down, and cold fingers clamped around my awareness, pulling me into her mind.

Searching for someone? Roze asked.

I refused to answer.

You make it so easy, Yelena. Roze laughed. *I knew you would contact Irys. You won't be able to talk to her, I'm afraid. The Council decided Masters Irys and Bain were engaged in treasonous activities. They're currently in the Keep's cells.*

21

HOW DID YOU MANAGE to frame two Master Magicians, Roze? I said, suppressing my shock and outrage.

They refused to sign the letter to the Commander, and they have been stalwart defenders of you and your brother. She said the word *brother* with heated contempt. *They doubted Cahil's word. Cahil, who single-handedly increased the strength of our army with Daviian Warriors.*

Those Warriors are not there to help you. They're there to use you.

I'm not going to take advice from you. Roze tightened her grip on my consciousness. *A simpleton who's about to lose her mind.*

She peeled the layers of my consciousness away with a knife made of ice. Cold stabbed deep into the core of my thoughts, attempting to expose what I kept hidden.

Thinking of becoming an adviser to the Commander, what a laugh. After I'm done with you, you won't be able to advise a baby on how to suck its thumb.

Unable to pull away, I panicked. Leif's energy poured into me, but I still couldn't break free. Flayed by her arctic magic, I remained helpless.

Valek was in Sitia to assassinate the Council. Hmm...most interesting, she said.

Desperate and knowing I couldn't sever her hold, I reached closer to her, searching for a part of her I could control. Her soul. I tugged at the ghostlike force, smelling its rotten stench, and feeling it fray as if her soul was splitting into multiple personalities.

Roze jolted in horror and expelled me from her grip. As I escaped, her words reached me.

Try to rescue Irys and Bain. Come to the Citadel. We're ready for you. Roze yanked a defensive wall between us, breaking our link.

I returned to my body, feeling exhausted and weak.

Leif loomed over me. "What happened? I lost you."

"I got caught by Roze..." My thoughts returned to what she had said about Irys and Bain.

"And?"

"And, I broke free before she could dissect *all* my thoughts."

"What did she find out?"

I told him she knew about the Commander's offer and about Valek being in Sitia.

He creased his thick eyebrows as he considered. "Knowing about Valek could be a good thing. The Council can take measures to protect themselves in case Valek comes back."

"*If* Roze warns them. Their deaths may be exactly what she wants."

"No. Roze wants what is best for Sitia. She's a strong-willed person and many Councilors are swayed by her arguments, but I don't believe she would use murder or magic to get her way."

I shook my head. After the attack, I knew she would resort

to both to get what she wants. "You were her student. Of course you still hold charitable thoughts for her."

"I know her better than you." Leif's voice huffed with anger. "I've worked for her and with her for nine years. Her methods can be harsh, but her concern is *always* for Sitia. She has *always* supported Cahil's desire to become King of Ixia. In her mind, your Soulfinder abilities are a threat to Sitia. And I'm starting to agree with her." Leif stormed from the room.

I wondered what had really upset Leif. In my opinion, Roze was a murderer. She didn't kill the body, but she destroyed minds without any remorse. Look at Marrok. But then again I had done the same thing with Ferde. At least, I admitted to being a killer. Was I any better? No.

My mind sorted through all the information from Roze. Rescuing Irys and Bain became a priority. I needed eyes and ears inside the Citadel's walls, and a way to get messages inside the Keep. All without being seen or without risking anyone else. Magic was no longer an option. If I projected my awareness near the Keep, Roze would catch me again. Mundane methods remained my only recourse.

A plan formed, making my heart buzz with the possibilities. If I hadn't been so drained of energy, I would have started preparations that night. Instead, I mapped out the steps I needed to take to return to Sitia.

I hovered at the entrance to Dilana's workroom. The Commander's seamstress sat in a pool of early-morning sunlight, humming to herself as her deft fingers repaired a pair of pants. Her soft curls glowed like fresh honey. I hesitated, not wanting to disturb her.

My need for information, though, spurred me into the room. She glanced up in surprise and my heart stopped. I braced myself for her reaction, guessing hate and anger ranked at the top of her list.

"Yelena!" She jumped to her feet. "I heard you were back." She pulled me into a warm hug then released me for inspection. "You're still too thin. And what's this you're wearing? The material is far too light for Ixia's weather. Let me get you some proper clothes and something to eat. I have a fresh loaf of cinnamon bread." She moved away.

"Dilana, wait." I grabbed her arm. "I ate breakfast and I'm not cold. Sit down. I want to talk to you."

Her baby doll's beauty hadn't dimmed with time or grief, but I could see a touch of sadness in her eyes despite her smile.

"It's so good to see you again." She rubbed a hand along my arm. "Look at how tan your skin is! Tell me what you've been doing in Sitia besides sunning yourself."

I laughed at the fantasy of me lounging in the sun, but sobered. She wanted to avoid the subject. Avoid the reason I thought she might hate me. But I couldn't go on without saying anything. "Dilana, I'm sorry about Rand."

She waved the comment away. "No need. The big oaf got himself mixed up with Star and her nefarious deeds. Not your fault."

"But he wasn't her target. I was and—"

"He saved you. The dumb ox died a hero." She blinked back tears threatening to spill over her long eyelashes. "It's a good thing we didn't get married or I'd be a widow. No one wants to be a widow at twenty-five." She took a deep breath. "Let me get you a slice of bread."

Dilana left before I could stop her. When she returned with a plate, she had regained her composure. I asked her about the latest gossip.

"Can you believe Ari and Janco are working with Valek? They were in here last month trying on their new uniforms and preening in front of the mirrors."

"Do you know where they are?" I asked.

"Some mission with Valek. I had to make a sneak suit for each of them. I used up all my black fabric to cover Ari's muscles. Can you imagine that big lunk sneaking around?"

I couldn't. Ari didn't strike me as the assassin type. He was more of a one-on-one fighter. Same with Janco. He wouldn't feel right killing someone without a fair fight. So why *were* they with Valek?

Dilana continued to chat. When the subject returned to uniforms, I asked her about getting an adviser's uniform. "The Commander has asked me to stay and I feel like I stand out in these Sitian clothes." Not an outright lie, yet a pang of guilt twinged in my chest.

"Even though coral is a beautiful color on you, you'll be warmer in a uniform." Dilana bustled over to her piles of clothes. She picked out a black shirt and pants. Handing them to me, she shooed me behind the changing screen. "Try them on."

I fingered the two red diamonds stitched on the shirt's collar. The last time I had stood here, I had been exchanging my red prison gown for the food taster's uniform. When I pulled my shirt off, I saw my snake bracelet. Round and round, it hugged my arm. I suppressed the sudden laughter bubbling in my throat. I've come full circle, but this time I put on an adviser's uniform. It fit better than my food taster uniform, molding to my body like a second skin. The Commander wanted me to help him, while the Council wanted me dead. About a year ago, the opposite had been true. This time I allowed the hollow snort of laughter to escape my lips.

"Something wrong?" Dilana asked.

I stepped out. "The pants are a little big."

She grabbed the waistband and pinched the material together, marking it with chalk. "I'll have these fixed by lunch."

I changed, thanked her and headed out to visit Kiki and the horses. The Commander's stables were located next to the kennels. The animals shared a training ring and there was a pasture for the horses along the castle's walls.

Kiki dozed in her immaculate stall. I checked on the other horses. Their coats gleamed in the sunlight. They seemed content and well cared for. I complimented the stable boys and girls, who nodded and resumed their work. Their demeanor reminded me of adults and I wondered if they had any fun.

On my way back to the castle, I spotted Porter, the Commander's Kennel Master. His dogs never wore leashes and their obedience to him was uncanny. I paused and watched him work with a litter of puppies. He had hidden treats in the training yard and taught the pups how to find them. Being puppies, they frequently forgot what they were supposed to do, but once Porter caught the attention of a dog, he touched its nose and said, "Go find."

Energized with its mission, the puppy scented the air and made a beeline for a treat. Impressive. Porter noticed me watching and gave me a curt nod. He had been good friends with Rand, and I recalled a conversation I had had with Rand about Porter.

Rand hadn't believed the rumors about Porter's magical connection with the dogs. Since there was no proof, Rand stayed true to their friendship when everyone else avoided contact with the Kennel Master. As long as Porter continued to be useful and did not draw attention to himself, his job for the Commander was secure.

I wondered about the magic, though. If he had magic and could use it without getting caught, then there might be others in Ixia doing the same thing. Porter had worked for the King many years before the Commander's takeover, giving him plenty of time to learn how to use and hide his power. Perhaps communicating with the dogs was all he could do.

One way to find out. I pulled a thread of power and made a mental connection with one of the puppies. Her energy and enthusiasm jumped from one smell to another. When I tried to communicate with her, she either ignored me or didn't hear me. Her nose filled with the scent of soft laced with a sharp hint of squish, and she dug into the ground seeking a worm. When a voice of warmth and caring called, she left her task and ran toward Porter.

He gave all the puppies a rawhide stick to chew and filled the row of bowls with water. I moved my awareness to him, sensing his surface thoughts. They were focused on the tasks for the day, yet uneasiness lingered. *Why was she here? What does she want?*

To help Ixia, I said in his mind.

He jerked as if bitten in the leg and glared at me.

You hear me, don't you? The rumors are true.

He strode toward me. I checked the empty yard. Although I knew how to defend myself, his tall muscular frame reminded me that, despite the gray hair, Porter remained a formidable opponent. He stopped mere inches from me.

"You're here to help Ixia?" Porter growled. If he had hackles they would have been raised. "You can help by leaving us alone."

He didn't mean him and the dogs. I caught a brief image of other Ixians.

"There must be something I can do?"

"Like you did for Rand? No, thank you. All you'll do is get us killed." He turned away, but his words, *or enslaved*, reached me.

A cold splash of fear drenched me. Was there someone in Ixia using magicians against their will? Why was I surprised? Magic and corruption went hand in hand. Would it corrupt me as well? I'd been using my magic without stopping to think about the consequences. Connecting with Porter could get him killed, and I did it just to satisfy my own curiosity. If I was so blasé about using magic now, how would I view it in the future? Would I crave it like an addiction? I began to think it would be better not to use magic at all.

Before I could return to the castle, I heard Kiki's whinny. I hurried back to the stables, but Kiki had already opened the door and met me in the walkway.

Foot hurt, she said.

She followed me to the training yard and bent her front right hoof back for me to inspect the underside. A rock was lodged in her frog.

When did this happen?

Night. Didn't hurt then.

Out in the sunlight, she didn't appear to be as well groomed as I had thought.

She snorted. *Lavender Lady take care.*

You wouldn't stand for the stable boy?

Too rough. Wait for you.

You're spoiled rotten.

I left Kiki in the yard, and fetched my pick and brushes.

She lifted her leg and I dislodged the stone then pulled the shedding blade through her copper hair. After a while, I removed my cloak. When I finished, clumps of horse hair clung to my sweaty clothes.

You're beautiful and I need a bath, I said to her. *Pasture or stall?*

Stall. Nap time.

And what about your snooze before I groomed you?

Pre-nap.

Ah, the life of a horse. I made sure her bucket held fresh water. On my way out, I bumped into Porter.

"You're good with that horse," he said.

I waited, sensing he had more to say.

"Maybe you *can* help us." He scanned the area. A few lads worked nearby. He lowered his voice. "There's a meeting tonight in Castletown. Forty-three Peach Lane rear door. Come during dinner. Don't let anyone know where you're going."

22

HE STRODE AWAY. TONIGHT I had planned to be on my way to Sitia. A visit to Porter would delay me, but it seemed too important to ignore.

After my jaunt to the stables, I arrived back at the doors of the guest suite at the same time as a messenger. The Commander wanted us to meet him in the war room this afternoon. Inside, Tauno paced the living area like a trapped animal, prowling next to the windows.

"Why don't you go outside?" I suggested to him. "The soldiers run laps around the castle complex for exercise. You can join them if you want."

He stopped in surprise. "I can leave this room without being escorted by an adviser?"

"The advisers are a courtesy provided by the Commander to help you find your way around the castle. If you go out on your own, you'll get some suspicious looks, but as long as you stick to common areas, no one will bother you. Just make sure you're back for the meeting." I told them about the message.

Moon Man sat next to Marrok on the couch. Marrok stared at us with an intense expression as if he tried to decipher our conversation.

"Interesting how you see the advisers as a courtesy, while Tauno sees them as guards," Moon Man said.

I ignored the Story Weaver's comment and gave Tauno directions to find his way outside. Even with my assurances, he still pulled the door open as if he expected to be accosted.

"Has Marrok said anything yet?" I asked.

"No, but he is understanding more and more. Unlike you."

I scowled. "What is that supposed to mean?"

Moon Man refused to answer. My plan to leave my companions in Ixia so I could travel faster through Sitia became more appealing as time went on. The Commander would keep an eye on them and I wouldn't have to worry about being betrayed.

I looked around the room. "Where's Leif?"

"In his room," Moon Man said.

Judging by the monosyllable response through Leif's door, I guessed he was still upset with me. I told him about the meeting then retired to my room.

A quiet group followed me to the Commander's war room. Tauno had returned, seeming more settled since he had burned off some of his energy. Moon Man's calm demeanor returned, and Leif frowned at the world at large and me in particular. My brother knew how to pout.

The Commander had a surprise waiting for us. Valek, Ari and Janco sat around the circular table. My emotions flipped to joy at seeing them.

"Valek was just informing me on the state of affairs in Sitia," the Commander said. "Continue."

"I found the situation to be rather ah...unique." Valek leaned back in his chair. He scanned my companions with a thoughtful purse of his lips. The sharp features of his angular face would soften only when he smiled.

"Unique is putting it mildly," Janco said. He rubbed the scar where the bottom half of his right ear used to be. A sure sign of his worry.

"Try alarming," Ari added.

Panic began to simmer under my heart. Ari tended to counter Janco's exaggerations with cool logic. His steadying presence helped keep Janco in check. Opposite in appearance, Janco's wiry build reflected his quick wit and lightning-fast fighting style, while Ari's strength could outmuscle most others.

"Alarming would work," Valek agreed. "Taking out the Council wouldn't result in better leaders. In fact, it would have inflamed the citizens to all-out war. And they have some new players who could potentially tip the battle in their favor."

"Players? Try creepy men. Scary magicians. Evil demons." Janco shuddered.

Valek shot Janco a warning look. "I need to obtain more information before I can assess the true nature of the threat and determine the best way to counter it."

"Why have you returned?" the Commander asked.

Another glance from Valek, but this time he aimed it at me. "I require more help. Things were getting a little too hot even for me."

So much for my plans to travel to Sitia alone.

The room fell quiet as Commander Ambrose considered. "What do you need?"

"A few more men, Yelena and her brother."

I had suspected Valek would want me. By Leif's grunt of shock, I knew his surprise matched my own when hearing his name.

"She hasn't agreed to be an adviser yet so I can't order her to assist you," the Commander said.

"Then I will have to ask." Valek looked at us.

"Yes," I said the same time Leif said no.

"I'm a Sitian, remember? I can't aid Ixia in overthrowing Sitia," Leif said.

"I don't want to take control of Sitia," the Commander said. "I just don't want them to invade us and I will take preventative measures to stop them."

"By helping us, you will also help your country," Valek said.

"We can do it on our own. We don't need you or Yelena." Leif turned to me. "You could never have been a true Liaison, little sister. Ever since we've been in Ixia, you have revealed your true loyalties."

Outraged, I asked, "Is that what you believe?"

"Look at the evidence. At the first sign of trouble, you run for Ixia. We could have returned to the Citadel, and explained everything to the Council."

His accusations stabbed me as if he held a knife.

"The Council will not believe us. I told you what Irys said."

"But what if you lied? You know I don't have the power of mental communication on my own. You don't trust us so why should we trust you?"

First the Council had turned on me and now my brother.

"Believe what you want, then. Valek, can we do without him?"

"We can."

The Commander stared at Valek. "You *will* tell me your plans before you disappear again."

"Yes, sir."

"Good. You're all dismissed." The Commander stood.

"What about us?" Leif gestured to Moon Man and Tauno. "Can we return to Sitia?"

"Consider yourselves a guest of Ixia until this unfortunate incident is resolved," Valek said.

"What if we no longer wish to be guests?" Moon Man asked.

"Then you will be our first prisoners of war and your accommodations will not be so luxurious. It's your choice." The Commander left.

Leif glared at me and I wanted to laugh. His current reaction mirrored the first encounter I had had with him after fourteen years of being apart. Another full circle. I felt dizzy. Perhaps this was a sign I should stay in this spot to avoid having to exert time and effort to go around again.

Valek turned to Ari and made a slight movement with his hand.

Ari nodded and stood; his blond curls bounced with the motion. "We will be happy to escort you to your quarters."

A gamut of emotions flowed over my former companions' faces as they followed Ari from the room. Leif barely contained his fury, Tauno looked worried and Moon Man appeared thoughtful.

Janco brought up the rear of the procession. He flashed me an inviting smirk. "Training yard, four o'clock."

"You need more lessons?"

"You wish."

My smile faded when the door closed. Valek remained on the far side of the table, his face serious. I felt awkward and uncertain.

"Is it that bad?" I asked.

"It's a situation I've never encountered before. I'm worried."

"About Ixia?"

"About you, love."

"Me?"

"I've always been amazed at how you can draw unwanted attention and ire from powerful people. This time, though, you managed to get a whole country upset. If I was the Commander, I would wait out the political strife in Sitia and then offer you to the victors in trade for Ixia being left alone."

"Good thing you're not the Commander."

"Yes. And we should leave Ixia before the Commander figures it out. What were you planning?"

I tried to look innocent. "Me? You're the one with the plan."

"And the adviser uniform you had Dilana size for you? You weren't thinking of sneaking off to Sitia without me, were you?"

Another betrayal. "Did she tell you?"

"I had ripped a hole in my favorite pants. When I dropped them off, she asked me to deliver your uniform and gifted me with a leer. I would guess the servants were already betting how soon one of them would spot us together." He sighed. "If only intelligence information worked through my corps as efficiently as gossip flowed through the servants, then my problems would be minimal."

In one fluid motion, Valek stood. He walked over to me, his smooth stride graceful as a panther. Powerful energy coiled in his body. He leaned on my chair's arms, bringing his face inches from mine. His black hair hung to his shoulders; his expression was lethal. "I'll ask you again. Your plans include me, correct?"

I slumped deeper into my chair.

"Yelena?" His voice warned.

"You said you had never encountered this situation before. It's an unknown. I don't want to risk…"

"What?"

"Risk losing you. With your immunity I can't heal you!"

"I'm willing to take the chance."

"But I'm not willing to let you."

"Sorry, love, that's not your decision. It's mine."

I grumbled. Events had spiraled out of my control. Again. I just spun in circles and never gained any ground.

"Okay, I promise not to go to Sitia without you." Which didn't include my meeting tonight with Porter.

"Thank you." Valek brushed his lips on my cheek. A tingle sizzled up my spine.

"What about your plan?" I tried to stay on topic, but I lost my motivation once Valek's musky smell enveloped me.

"This *is* my plan."

He moved closer and kissed me. Warmth spread throughout my body. The panic clutching my throat eased. I pushed away my worries and focused on Valek, wrapping my arms around him. But the feel of his muscles through his shirt wasn't enough. I yanked at it, wanting to touch his skin, wanting to wear his skin.

He pulled away, straightening. "In the war room, love? What if someone comes in?"

I stood and removed his shirt. "Then they'll have a good story to tell."

"Good?" He adopted the pretense of being offended.

"Prove me wrong."

His eyes lit with the challenge.

Valek and I ended up underneath the war room's round table. Lying together, I felt safe for the first time in weeks. We discussed the events in Sitia.

"I could hardly move within the Citadel," Valek said. "The air was so thick with magic I felt like I swam in syrup."

"But you weren't detected."

Valek's immunity to magic remained a powerful weapon. Without it, I couldn't have defeated Ferde.

"No. Although it was only a matter of time. With that many—what do you call them?—Warpers, my presence would have eventually caused a noticeable dead zone."

I considered how fast things had changed in the Citadel. Twenty-two days ago Moon Man had speculated the Daviians had eight Warpers, but once he realized they were performing Kirakawa we knew the actual number of Warpers could be much higher, depending on how many victims they had used. And how far along in the ritual they were. Plus only a victim with magical powers could make a Warper.

If they had been preparing for this offensive for a while, then who were the victims? They wouldn't have used clan members and the Sandseed Clan would have noticed if a couple of their Story Weavers went missing. So would the other clans. Unable to deduce an answer, I put the question to Valek.

"They're probably targeting the homeless. Who would miss a few beggars in a big city? No one."

"What about the need for magicians?"

"The first year after a magician reaches adolescence is a difficult and vulnerable year. Half the people don't even realize they can access the power source, and the other half don't have a clue how to use it. The Warpers could be hunting the streets, looking for someone in that precarious situation."

My conviction to stop using it became stronger the more I learned about magic and how others exploited it.

Valek and I mapped our return to Sitia and planned how to contact Bavol Zaltana.

"I'll leave Ari and Janco here. They won't be happy, but security around the Citadel is too tight and we're better off just going ourselves. Two of my corps have already been caught inside." Valek sat up with reluctance. "I have some business to attend to. I'll meet you in my suite later tonight and we can finalize our time schedule. I'll have your belongings delivered there."

I should retrieve my pack, but realized I had no desire to see Leif or the others. But I remembered something. "Why did you want Leif to come with us?"

He shook his head. "You wouldn't have agreed anyway."

"To what?"

"To letting Leif get caught and using your mental connection to him to find out what's going on in the Keep. But now you're mad at him—"

"No. He would be killed. I'm not *that* angry with him." Besides, if I used my magic anywhere near the Citadel, all the preparation in the world wouldn't be able to help me.

"She's quick and fast, but she can't get past," Janco sang as he blocked my rib strikes.

"You need to work on your rhymes. Either that, or I'm

getting better." I faked a temple strike and swept his feet out from under him. Before I could press my advantage, he rolled away and regained his feet.

"You hesitated," Ari said from the sidelines. "Too busy talking."

I renewed my attack and Janco countered with ease. We fought in the soldier's training yard, which had been filled with the sounds of practice until Janco and I started this match. We had attracted quite a crowd.

"Can't talk and fight. So much for being polite." Janco spun his bow. His weapon blurred.

I backed up and blocked the flurry of hits, keeping pace with his attack until he changed the rhythm. I missed a connection. The air exploded out of my lungs as Janco landed a solid blow to my solar plexus. I bent over, coughing and gasping for breath.

"Funny," Janco said. He smoothed his goatee with a hand. "You're usually not this easy to beat. Have I succeeded in hiding my thoughts?"

Once I regained my composure and straightened, he smiled sweetly at me. The last time we had fought in Sitia, he had found out about my zone of concentration, a semimagical state allowing me to notice my opponent's intentions when I sparred with them. This time I had tried to fight him without setting my mind into that zone.

"No. You're still self-centered and overly cocky," I said.

"They're fighting words."

"Do you need more time to rest? Now you're management, you probably need to expend extra energy moving that paunch."

He swept his bow toward my legs in response and we engaged in another match. I lost again, but kept challenging him until we were both sweat soaked and exhausted.

"Your fighting improved as the matches went on," Ari said. "But it wasn't your best." He looked at me as if waiting for an explanation.

I shrugged. "I was trying something different."

"It's not working. Better go back to your old style."

"I like her new style." Janco piped in. "It's good for my ego."

Ari frowned and crossed his massive arms over his chest.

"Life or death, Ari, and I'd go back to using all my tricks. Don't worry."

He seemed mollified, and I hadn't lied. When push came to shove, I knew I would fall back on using my magic. Another problem. Magic made me lazy and when I encountered a bad situation, I reached for it without thought. I needed to improve my other skills, because magic wouldn't help me against the Fire Warper.

I changed the subject and asked my friends about their new jobs. Janco regaled me with the story of their battle against Valek. Every time Ari shook his head, I knew Janco had exaggerated a detail.

"What is it like being second in command of Ixia's intelligence network?" I asked.

"I don't like all this sneaking around," Ari said. "There's a lot more going on in Ixia than I thought. And there's so much to do. Valek is the king of delegating."

"I'm getting to use my lock-picking skills." Janco grinned. Pure mischievousness danced in his eyes. "And the information we've discovered. Did you know General Dinno has—"

"Janco," Ari warned. "We enjoy the work. It's just not what we had expected."

"Nothing is," I said.

My bones ached with fatigue. I waved goodbye to Ari and Janco and headed toward the baths. Before joining my friends in the training yard, I had retrieved my pack and stashed it in the changing room. After a long soak, I dried and dressed in my adviser's uniform in preparation for the meeting with Porter. I rationalized I would draw less attention wearing a uniform than my Sitian clothes.

I cut a hole in the pant's pocket and strapped my switchblade to my right thigh. Not wanting to show up armed with my bow, I felt it prudent to have a knife on me just in case. Braiding my hair into one long braid, I let it hang between my shoulder blades.

Although my stomach grumbled with hunger, Porter had instructed me to come during dinner. His timing made sense, as most of the castle's inhabitants would be busy either serving dinner or eating it. And Castletown should be relatively quiet.

I stopped beside the pasture on my way out, checking to see if anyone followed me. A few servants hustled between buildings, but no one paid me any attention. The cold hung in the air as if waiting for a breeze. I fed Kiki and the other horses some apples.

Smells? I asked Kiki.

Big snow.

When?

Half moon.

Three days. Valek and I would need to leave sooner than planned.

Kiki come?

Of course, and Garnet, too.

She sighed with contentment as I scratched behind her ears. When I felt certain no one watched me, I headed toward the south gate. I joined in with a group of town residents returning home for dinner. With my Ixian wool cloak covering my adviser's uniform, I blended right in. My group hurried over the grass field surrounding the walls. The Commander had ordered all buildings within a quarter mile of the castle be destroyed when he had gained power. He also renamed Jewelstown, named in honor of the former Queen Jewel to the rather unoriginal Castletown.

Once we reached the edge of town, the group dispersed as the others headed for their homes. The symmetry of the town with its neat rows of wooden buildings conflicted with the asymmetrical style of the castle complex. The logical array of businesses interspersed among residences made navigating the town easier. Each district had a name matching the merchandise sold there. Peach Alley would be located in the Garden District.

A few townspeople bustled about, all intent on some errand. I walked as if I had a purpose so I didn't attract unwanted attention from the town's guards, who watched the streets.

The colors of the buildings thinned toward gray as the sun set. My perceptions shifted, and I felt as if I had entered into a colorless shadow world. The buildings transformed into a watery representation of a town populated with ghosts.

I stumbled over some unseen curb and snapped back to the real world. Dismissing the strange spell, I rationalized hunger as the culprit. I picked up my pace, determined to find the right address before the lamplighters came out. Peach Lane seemed devoid of life, and only when I went around to the back alley did I see signs of habitation.

A glow of firelight came from number forty-three. Keeping to the shadows, I approached the back door. I pulled a thread of magic and scanned the area. Inside the house I felt Porter waiting with two young girls. They were nervous about being found, but I didn't sense any duplicity.

I paused as the realization of how much I depended on my magic dawned on me. Not only with searching for attackers, but with Kiki, too. Could I completely stop using my magic? It would be much harder than I thought.

The door opened right after my light tap, as if Porter had been hovering near it. He pulled me into the room and closed it behind me.

"Did anyone see you?" he asked.

"No." I looked around the room. Small and tidy, the sitting area had a couch, a chair and three dogs getting nervous attention from the girls. The girls perched on the edge of the couch with their backs straight. They wore students' uniforms, which consisted of a simple jumper made of red linen. White-faced, their gazes jumped between Porter and me.

"You said I could help you?" I asked.

"We're taking a big chance trusting you." Porter picked up a half-chewed roll of rawhide from the floor. He clutched the dog's treat in his hands as he stared at me. "You must promise not to tell Valek or anyone else about all this."

"I can't promise until I hear what 'all this' is."

The rawhide popped and cracked in Porter's hands. He glanced at the girls and sighed. His wide shoulders drooped with the release of his tension, and he gestured to the empty chair. "Have a seat. This is going to take a while."

As soon as I sat down, one of the dogs came over and put

his head in my lap. Peering at me from between his gray shaggy hairs, he pleaded for attention. I stroked his smooth head and scratched behind his ears. The dog's tail thumped on the floor. The smell of wet dog and wood smoke mixed into a stuffy odor.

Porter tapped the roll on his leg as he talked. "I've set up a network of people throughout Ixia to help me in smuggling children out of the country."

I leaned forward in alarm, thinking about Mogkan's kidnapping ring and how he had taken children from Sitia to Ixia to abuse them for his own purposes. "Children?"

"They seem like children to me." Porter gave the two girls a grandfatherly smile. "Adolescents who have just discovered their magical powers." He pointed to the couch. "Young people like Liv and Kieran. I've been helping them to escape to Sitia before their powers are known to others. But I believe something has gone wrong."

"What?" I prompted when Porter appeared to be lost in his own thoughts.

"I was in MD-7 last month. General Rasmussen has a nice wolfhound I wanted to breed with my bitch. While there, one of my contacts who works in the general's stables told me the last person I sent through the network never arrived. And two others he had sent on never made it to the border contact. They have all disappeared."

My stomach twisted around my heart. "Do you think Valek has killed them?"

"I don't know and I can't risk asking around. If my network has been compromised then I won't be able to send Liv and Kieran. Eventually they'll get reported."

I hadn't thought it possible, but the girls' faces turned whiter. Considering Porter's story, I said, "Tell me how your network operates."

"I have four contacts from here to the border. A few people know about my underground efforts and they'll send their son or daughter to me as an apprentice. The Commander gives me complete management of his kennel and no one pays too much attention to my students. They come and go as part of their animal husbandry training. It's risky, being this close to Valek, but then I usually know where he is and can send my charges when he's gone on business." Porter paced. "It's too risky to have a guide with them, so I instruct the person how to find the first contact and then he sends them on until they get to the border contact, who takes them into Sitia. They have transfer papers with them if they're stopped by the guards. If they had gotten caught, I would have been arrested by now." His erratic movements showed his frustration.

"How can I help?"

He stopped. "I wanted you to go along with Liv, and maybe find out what's happening to my charges. With that adviser's uniform you can go anywhere in Ixia without permission."

"No. Too dangerous for Liv. The best thing to do would be for me to disguise myself as a student and go through your network alone."

Porter's eyebrows spiked up in surprise. "You would do that for us?"

"Yes. Unfortunately though, it will have to wait."

The ability to connect with the power source began at the onset of puberty. A person typically had a year before anyone else noticed and reported them, and another three to four years to learn how to harness their power. A fledgling magician's power, when uncontrolled, could flame out and warp the blanket of power that covers the world, causing trouble for magicians everywhere. And the stronger the magician, the bigger the flameout. One-trick power similar to Opal's ability to capture magic in molten glass tended to be unconscious and didn't require formal training.

"How long do the girls have?" I asked.

"A year at most for Liv. Kieran is younger so she could last up to two years, but I'd rather they both be gone as soon as possible. I can hide them here if we're desperate. I've had some refugees who didn't have time to work in the kennel," Porter said.

"Give me a couple months. Sitia's not the best place to be sending anyone right now. Once I settle another matter, I'll come back and help you. For now, I can teach the girls how to tame their powers enough so they don't give themselves away."

Relief shone on Liv and Kieran's young faces. I worked with them for the next hour. Irys would be proud over how much I remembered from her guidance. A finger of dread stabbed my guts with the thought of Irys. I hoped she was still alive.

After my session, the girls left Porter's together while I waited for them to be well away before I left. The need to begin my journey back to Sitia pressed on my mind as I worried about Irys and Bain locked in the Keep's cells.

I made a quick sweep of the area outside Porter's door with my magic. The activity around the houses seemed muted as everyone finished their daily tasks. No one lurked in the alley.

With a wave goodbye, I exited Porter's. I stood outside and

let my eyes adjust to the darkness. When the shadows grew less black, I strode toward the street.

About halfway there I felt a presence behind me. I spun, grabbing for my switchblade. Something jabbed me in the neck and I saw Star lower a thin pipe.

I yanked the dart out of my throat. "How?"

"Some great magician you are," Star said. "Missing my own tiny talent."

My world spun and I stumbled. Star caught me, but I had no energy to fight her off. "What?"

She cradled me in her arms. "Valek's goo-goo juice. Relax, Yelena. Star's going to take *good* care of you."

My last coherent thought focused on how her sinister expression didn't match her soothing words.

23

THE WORLD STIRRED. MY thoughts scattered and failed to connect. Warm hands guided me. Whenever the hands pulled away, the ground swelled and I tumbled off my feet.

I thought about the lack of fear for only a moment before the air spun around my head. Lying down felt best. I sensed movement and smelled horses.

Inside my chicken crate, I wondered what I was supposed to be doing. Important things? My mind chased the thought until the sunlight lit the dust motes. I studied the flecks floating above me. The flecks transformed into daggers. I wanted to knock them away. My hands stayed glued to my back. A leather strap lodged in my teeth. The problem disappeared with the sun.

Time ebbed and flowed. My crate opened. It closed. Faces peered. Mouths talked. Words chimed in my ears. Some like *eat, drink* and *sleep* I understood. Others resembled a baby's babble. Goo-goo. Goo-goo. A prick on my arm or neck or back. The air filled with colors. My crate bobbed on an invisible sea.

A small lucid part of me wanted action. Freedom. Majority ruled and I let the world slide by me content in my crate. My crate. My crate. I giggled.

The fire woke me. A finger of flame poked. I jerked away, no longer inside my crate. My thoughts congealed into a coherent whole. The air became invisible, revealing my surroundings. I braced for another prick. When none came I focused. The booted feet of a couple guards stood near me. I lay on my side in front of a campfire. Darkness pressed against the firelight, and my hands were tied behind my back.

Actual conversation reached my ears. The baby babble was gone. But for how long? I coaxed my mind to think, but my thoughts remained sluggish.

A man's voice. "Should not do this," he said. "She should stay under until we reach our destination. Jal is the only one strong enough to counter her power."

A familiar voice said, "I made a promise to her. I want her to know who has her, and what we plan to do to her."

Footsteps approached and I tried to put a name to the familiar voice. My mind churned as if mired in river mud.

"Take the gag off," Familiar Voice said from behind me.

One of the guards removed the leather strap. A mixture of pain and relief flowed into my cracked lips. I licked them, tasting blood. Other aches and cramps woke. Only the sight of a pair of black riding boots covered with dust could distract me from my medley of aches.

My gaze followed the boots up to jodhpurs that disappeared under a gray riding cloak. I squinted in the firelight, hoping the person in front of me was an illusion.

The cocky smirk caused my heart to stutter. And when he

kicked me in the ribs, I knew all hopes for a pleasant reunion were gone. I coughed and wheezed as the pain shot through my body.

"That's for hitting me with Curare!" He kicked me again. "And that's just because I can."

His words sounded thin and distant, reaching me through my efforts to reclaim my breath. He loomed over me. When the sharp pain dulled to a loud throb, I struggled to a sitting position. I glanced around. Four guards stood a few feet away and I counted three Daviian Vermin nearby, but I couldn't tell if they were Warpers or not.

"Cahil," I said between gasps. "You're still...scared. Of me."

He laughed. The washed-out blue of his eyes sparked with amusement.

"Yelena, you're the one who should be scared." He crouched down.

We were face-to-face. He held a dart between us. A drop of clear liquid hung from the end. Fear coiled in my stomach as I smelled the sweet odor. Curare. I tried not to let my terror show on my face.

"*I* allowed you this brief moment of lucidity. Listen closely. Remember what I said to you the last time we were together?"

"When you wanted to exchange me for Marrok?"

"No. When I promised to find a person who could defeat you and Valek. I've met with success. In fact, you have already had an encounter with my champion."

"Ferde?" I played the simpleton to prolong the conversation, hoping my slow mind would produce a plan for escape.

"Act the fool, but I know better. My champion makes you sweat with fear *and* desire. The Fire Warper has been called to this world with one mission. To capture you. And you're powerless against him." Pure satisfaction shone on Cahil's face. "I will deliver you to Jal and the Fire Warper. Jal will perform the Kirakawa ritual's binding ceremony on you, taking your powers as the Fire Warper claims your soul."

My mind buzzed with the need to stop him yet produced nothing intelligent. I couldn't even connect with the power source. "And what do you get, Cahil?"

"I get to witness your death and watch your heart mate suffer before he meets the same end."

"But Jal gains power. Do you really believe Jal will let you rule? And what about the Fire Warper? Do you think he'll be content to go back after his task is complete?"

"He has come asking for you. Once he has you, he'll go back. Then Jal rules Sitia, and I rule Ixia."

I saw a faint trace of uncertainty in Cahil's eyes. My mind pulled free from the mire of the goo-goo juice and I made a connection. "Before you said you called him. Now you say he has come. Which one is it?"

"It doesn't matter."

"Yes it does. If you called him, you have control over him."

He shrugged. "Jal will deal with him. As long as I have Ixia. I don't care."

"You should care. The need for power is addicting. Ask your Daviian friends about the history of the Sandseed Clan and the Daviian Mountains. Then you'll realize Jal won't be content with just ruling Sitia. Once your usefulness is gone, you will be too."

"You're just trying to trick me. I know better than to listen to you."

He tried to stab the dart into my throat. I fell back and pulled power as Cahil pinned me with his weight. With no time to think, I focused the magic on my neck as he jabbed the dart into my skin. Closing my eyes, I treated the area as I would an injury. In my mind's eye, I saw the Curare as a pulsing red light, spreading through my throat. I used power to push the liquid back through the tiny hole in my skin. It trickled down the side of my neck.

My gaze met Cahil's when I opened my eyes. He stared at me with a mixture of triumph and hatred.

Hoping he hadn't seen the drug run out, I said, "Pay close attention, Cahil. You'll see the truth." I acted as if I had been paralyzed, unfocusing my eyes and letting my body go slack.

He grunted and stood. "I've seen the truth. That's why I want you dead."

The Vermin joined him next to the fire, and I watched them from the corner of my eye.

"I felt magic. Brief. Did she use her power on you?" one of the Vermin asked Cahil.

"No. I got her in time."

They discussed their plans for leaving in the morning.

When the others moved to set up camp, Cahil said, "I should kill her now."

Alarmed replies told him it would be imprudent. For the first time ever, I agreed with the Vermin.

"Jal needs her and we do not wish to infuriate the Fire Warper," another said.

"Why should *I* care about infuriating the Fire Warper?" Cahil asked. "*I'm* in charge. He should answer to *me*. He should worry about infuriating *me*, especially after the fiasco in the jungle."

Soothing words were muttered.

"Put her back in the box," Cahil finally said. "Secure it, just in case we encounter trouble."

Two of the Vermin lifted me. I concentrated on being a dead weight. My hands were tied and I couldn't use magic without alerting them. I knew one of the three was a Warper but was unsure about the other two. At this point I needed more information. I decided to wait for a better opportunity and hoped I would get one.

The Vermin climbed onto a cart, dropped me into a crate and shut the lid. In the darkness the sound of metal latches being closed grated on my skin. I bit down on a cry of dismay when the snap of three locks sounded. The coffin-shaped crate seemed to press into me, and I drew in a couple of calming breaths. My gaze found the small slit between the boards, allowing air to come in. And light. The faint flicker of firelight seeped through the cracks.

I wiggled into a more comfortable position. My mind raced over my limited options. Magic remained my only weapon. The desire to project my awareness and scan my surroundings pulled at me, but I knew if they discovered I wasn't drugged, all possibility of escape would be gone. Would the Warper feel my power while he slept? Could I put the Vermin and Cahil into a deep sleep? I would still be locked in a box, but I could call someone to break me out.

Who? Only a fellow magician could hear my mental call, and I had no idea where I was. If I was lucky enough to find a local citizen, perhaps I could discover my location.

Unable to plan a course of action, I marveled over my ability to push the drug out of my body. Had I known I possessed that skill, I wouldn't be in this situation. And my problems with Curare, sleeping potion and goo-goo juice were solved. Although it was hard to celebrate when locked in a box.

Ever since I went to Sitia, all I wanted was to learn about magic, to discover the extent of my powers and be reacquainted with my family. Events conspired against me and I had hardly had time to catch my breath, let alone spend time exploring my magic.

Pushing the Curare out of my body was a new wrinkle. My abilities only affected living things, since my magic didn't move the drug; it must have made the muscles in my body do the work.

Desperation and raw instinct had gotten me this far. I hoped it would carry me through, and as much as I disliked using it, magic was unavoidable. If I was lucky enough to survive this, I planned to retire as a Soulfinder and limit my magic to only communicating with Kiki. I wondered if she knew I'd been taken. Did Valek know? And what about Star's role in all this?

Too many questions without answers swirled in my mind. Eventually, my thoughts bounced back to the need to do something soon, because I sensed being delivered to the Fire Warper would be the ultimate end.

"Let's get moving. If we push, we can reach the Avibian border by sundown."

Cahil's voice woke me from a light doze. A few disorienting seconds passed before I remembered my predicament and his words sank in. Shock followed understanding. We were in Sitia. I must have been under the influence of the goo-goo juice for days. Where was Valek? So much for my promise not to go to Sitia without him.

"Should we check on her?" a voice with an Ixian accent asked.

"No. She's under Curare now. She can't do anything besides breathe until the potion wears off," Cahil answered. "Finish feeding the girls. We'll let the juice wear off before we prepare them for the ritual."

The girls? I peered through one of the slits in my crate. Another crate lay beside mine. My stomach turned to ice. How many and could I help them? I suppressed a hollow laugh. Here I was trying to save others while locked in a box.

Two lids slammed then the crate lurched forward. The sound of trotting horses added to the rumble of the wagon. We were on our way.

My body went through a gamut of emotions as the day passed. Sometimes terrified, sometimes hopeful and sometimes bored, I even listed an inventory of woes. Thirsty, hungry, aching ribs, numb hands, sore muscles and a burning cramp between my shoulder blades. With the noise of our travel masking my movements, I attempted to alleviate some of my misery. I squirmed and wiggled until I managed to squeeze my body and legs through my arms. The benefits of keeping limber and being small became apparent as I succeeded in bringing my tied hands to the front of my body. I almost groaned aloud when cool relief spread over my back.

Having my hands in front allowed me to explore. I patted my right thigh, checking for my switchblade. No luck. Even the holder had been removed. I stared at the knots on the leather straps binding my hands and pulled at them with my teeth. I untied a few before the wagon stopped, but I decided to keep working, risking discovery.

"We'll camp here," Cahil said. "When you're done setting

up, let the girls out. They should be lucid by now and you can get them ready for the Kirakawa tomorrow."

"What about the Soulfinder?" one of the Vermin asked.

"Drakke will give her another dose tonight. Too much Curare could stop her heart," Cahil replied.

I listened to the sounds of the men in the camp as I continued to gnaw and pull at my bindings. The smell of roasting meat stole into my crate. My stomach grumbled with alarming loudness. After a while, two crates were opened and two scared voices asked questions. By the brief flash of a red jumper through the slits in my box, I guessed the girls were the students from Ixia. Liv and Kieran. My heart went out to them.

Again I wondered how the Vermin and Cahil had managed to smuggle us all out of Ixia. Perhaps the Vermin had posed as traders taking a wagonload of goods across the border.

I caught glimpses of the camp. A tent had been erected and I counted four guards and three Vermin. Some of the guards I recognized as Cahil's men, while two looked unfamiliar. All were armed with swords or scimitars. I searched for some sign of my backpack. The limited view hindered me, although I guessed my pack would be found with Cahil.

The daylight faded, and I renewed my efforts on the leather strips around my wrists. Each shrill scream from one of the girls spurred me on. I ignored the pain, the smell of fear and the metallic taste of blood as I yanked at the knots. Cahil had mentioned a ritual tomorrow. Tonight would be my only chance to escape.

The last knot proved impossible to untie, but my spit had soaked the leather enough to give a little when I moved. I pulled my hand through the last loop, scraping off a layer of skin in the process. Panting with relief, I relaxed and waited for my crate to open.

My plan was simple, with as much chance for failure as for success. Time moved at a glacial pace. Years crept by. When the rasp and click of the lock finally sounded, I laced my hands behind my back and froze.

A soft yellow glow of firelight reflected off the Vermin who opened my crate. He lifted the lid up with one hand and reached toward me with the other. He held a tiny dart between his finger and thumb.

I moved.

Grabbing his hand in both of mine, I yanked him toward me, unbalancing him. He grunted with surprise. His weight came forward. I bent his hand back and shoved the dart into the Vermin's shoulder. Letting go of his hand, I covered his mouth to stifle his yell.

Mere seconds later the Curare paralyzed his muscles. The lid rested on his back and his body leaned on my chest. Knowing I probably had seconds before someone discovered us, I pulled the rest of him inside my box. An awkward, difficult maneuver to do while trying to keep the lid from slamming down.

Once the Vermin joined me, I wriggled from under his body and lifted the lid to peek out. The guards remained by the fire, but the other two Vermin were out of sight. The two girls had been stripped and tied down by the fire. Bloody cuts lined their arms and legs. There was nothing I could do for them right now. One problem at a time.

I slid down to the end of my crate and considered my options. Try to sneak out of the box and slip into the night or just shove the lid up and make a run for it?

What I really needed was a distraction, but that involved magic. By the time they figured out the magic came from me, I would be gone. I hoped.

A flicker of black above the campfire gave me an idea. Pulling a strand of power as thin as a spider's silk, I projected my mind toward the bat. He flew through the hot, insect-filled air rising from the flames. I tapped into the collective consciousness of his fellow bats and sent them all an image. An image of insects covering the men below. Large juicy crawling things. Easy picking for a mass of hungry bats.

Black shapes swooped down from the sky. The guards yelled and swung their arms around. Cahil and the Warper exited the tent to investigate. The Warper yelled about magic, but his words were cut off as the bats attacked.

I pushed the lid wide and hopped out. After a quick glance to make sure no one had noticed me, I stepped off the wagon and bolted for the darkness, keeping the wagon between me and the campfire.

I encountered the third Vermin who had been tending the horses. Prepared for my approach, he had pulled his scimitar. With a gesture of his weapon magic slammed through my mental defenses and my body froze. Another Warper. I cursed as he called for his companions. Then I realized he didn't have control of my mind. I projected to the two horses.

Tired, sore and unsettled by the smell of blood, the horses welcomed my contact. I appealed to them for help.

Bad men want to hurt me, I said in their minds.

Kick?

Please.

The one horse backed up. With a blur of motion, the

Warper went flying. As soon as the man's head slammed into the ground, he lost consciousness, releasing his magical hold on me.

Thank you. I ran.

Kick others?

Sounds of pursuit drew closer. The bats had lost their insect image when I switched my efforts to the horses.

If you can, I said, increasing my speed. Shouts of surprise reached my ears. I glanced over my shoulder. Four figures still chased me. The terrain remained flat and featureless, as if part of the Avibian Plains. A black bulge in the distance looked promising. Perhaps it was a cluster of trees.

The men gained on me. My hopes to reach cover faded with every step.

I pulled power and planned to baffle my pursuers' minds, betting my life on the pure conjecture that I possessed the ability to project confusing images into four minds in rapid succession.

A figure on horseback approached from the left, aiming for me. I caught a glint of moonlight off a sword. My options dwindled to either bewildering the men or stopping the horse.

My chances of success went from doubtful to none when a cold sting pricked my back.

24

I DIVED TO THE GROUND, rolling into a ball. The power I had drawn to confuse my pursuers I now applied to the area turning numb on my back. In my mind, I saw the Curare spreading through my muscles, seeking my bloodstream. I swept at it, using my magic like a broom and guiding the substance to the hole. A warm wetness spread on my shirt.

The effort left me weak, and I debated the merits of pretending to be paralyzed. The ground vibrated with the drumming of hooves. The animal cut between the guards and me. An unexpected sound of steel hitting steel rang in the cool night air. I crouched.

The horse made a quick turn and came back. Recognition shot through me. I knew that gait. I jumped to my feet.

"Yelena!" Valek threw me my bow.

I caught it in midair. Kiki spun and Valek slid off her back. The rapid clash of blades followed as Valek engaged four men in a sword fight. I hurried to join him before the remaining

Vermin and Cahil caught up. Four against one was pushing it for Valek. He would be outnumbered against six.

With the occasional kick from Kiki, Valek and I fought side by side. Cahil and the Warper hung back. I strengthened my mental defenses, sensing the Warper would try a magical attack.

Once Valek cut a guard's arm in half, we pressed our advantage. As the man fell to the ground yelling with pain, Cahil ordered the remaining men to disengage. They stepped back. Valek shot me a questioning look.

"The girls are still at the camp," I said.

He nodded and we stalked the retreating men.

The Warper threw his arms up and yelled, "Inflame."

Power pressed on my skin. With a whoosh of hot air, the guard on the ground burst into flames. Valek and I jumped away. The man screamed and writhed. He stilled as the intense heat consumed him. Acrid puffs of charred flesh reached us, and I covered my nose.

"Come! Find your soul mate!" The Warper's voice cut through the roaring fire.

A man's form coalesced from the pulsing flames.

"What's going on?" Valek asked.

"Let's go." I scrambled onto Kiki's back, Valek right behind me. Kiki took off.

"What about the girls?"

Guilt stabbed my heart. "Later."

I let Kiki decide our direction. Eventually we came to a farmhouse, modest in size and surrounded by precise flower beds. Kiki stopped at the stable and Valek slid off.

Where are we? I asked Kiki.

Ghost's house. Good hay. Nice lad.

I eyed the wooden structure with sudden distrust. *Ghosts are here?*

Kiki snorted and nudged Valek. *Ghost.*

Moon Man had explained to me Valek's immunity to magic made him appear as a ghost to magical creatures.

I looked at him. "Summer home? Isn't it a little dangerous?"

He smiled. "Safe house for my corps. A base of operations."

"How convenient."

The stable was empty. Valek helped me remove Kiki's saddle and groom her, delaying the inevitable conversation.

I sagged with fatigue, but needed to know what he had been doing while I was in my box. "How did you find me? And your timing was impeccable as always."

Valek pulled me into his arms. I molded to him, seeking warmth and comfort. My body shook with a delayed reaction. The horror of the Warper setting his own man on fire replayed in my mind.

"You're welcome, love. I had wanted to sneak in and unlock you tonight, but you had other plans. I should have been more prepared, but when I saw him poke you last night, I thought for sure you would be out of it." He pulled me away. "Let's go inside. I need a drink."

The interior of the farmhouse lacked the homey warmth of its exterior. Spartan and utilitarian, Valek's operatives obviously didn't entertain guests here. Valek lit a few lanterns, but I refused to let him build a fire. We huddled together on the couch, sipping brandy.

"General Kitvivan's white brandy?" I asked.

"You remembered!" Valek seemed surprised.

"There are tastes and smells that call certain memories.

White brandy reminds me of the Commander's brandy meeting."

"Ah, yes. And after having to taste all those brandies for the Commander, you drunkenly tried to seduce me."

"And you refused." I couldn't pinpoint a specific time or event when Valek's feelings for me had changed. He had shocked me with his declaration of love in Brazell's dungeon.

"I wanted to accept. But I didn't know if your desire was from your heart or from the brandy. You might have regretted it later."

The image of Valek wearing his dress uniform recreated the desire to seduce him again, but we had much to discuss.

"Enough small talk. Tell me everything," I ordered.

He sighed. "You're not going to like it."

"Compared to what I've just been through these last—what? Three days? I don't even know. It can't be that bad."

"I knew you were swimming in some very dangerous waters," he said, "but I hadn't known they extended so deep."

"Valek, get to the point."

He fidgeted. Fear brushed my heart. Something horrible had happened. I had never seen him fidget before. He stood and started prowling the room. His liquid movements were soundless.

"Five days ago you were taken—"

"Five days!" So much could have happened in that time. My thoughts went to Irys and Bain. They could be dead.

Valek put up his hand to forestall my questions. "Let me finish first. You were kidnapped by Star, and the reason she was able to smuggle you so far south, was because…I let her." He paused to let his words sink in.

I stared at him in astonishment. "You set me up?"

"Yes and no."

"You need to do better than that."

"I knew Star would want to exact some type of revenge on you. She has kept in contact with the underground network, and I allowed her because then I could learn who the new players were. With the Code of Behavior, there will always be a black market for illegal goods and forged papers. I like to keep tabs on the network to make sure things don't go too far, like when Star hired assassins to ruin the Sitian trade treaty. And when—"

"Get to the point."

"Star knew you would be at Porter's safe house—"

"Porter set me up?"

"I don't think so. Are you going to let me tell you or not?" He put his hands on his hips in annoyance.

I gestured for him to go on.

"I've known about Porter's rescue operation for a couple years and have allowed it to continue. However, recently, his charges have been disappearing and I've been wondering why. But that wasn't the reason I watched the house. I had followed Star and three of her men there, and was shocked to see you walk blindly into her trap. Didn't you even see her?"

"She used a subtle kind of magic."

"I haven't felt her, and I've been working with her for a while."

I thought back to the night I had been captured. The only odd event had been when my perception had altered for a moment before returning to normal. Perhaps she had affected my vision somehow. "You didn't pick up on my magic, either. And it flared out of control a couple times within the castle."

"I will keep it in mind," Valek said with an icy tone. "Star's motives for ambushing you, I understood. The surprise arrived when she and her friends also targeted the girls. I needed to know where they were taking you."

I mulled over his explanation. "You could have helped me that night, but instead decided to wait?"

"A calculated risk. I wanted to discover the extent of her operation and why she kidnapped the girls. I had no idea you would end up across the border and in the Wannabe King's hands."

Valek knelt in front of me, and would have taken my hands in his had I not kept my arms crossed. Anger simmered deep within me. I had lost five days. Five days for the Fire Warper to grow stronger.

"This wouldn't have happened at all if you told me about your meeting with Porter," he said.

"A *calculated* risk. Like it or not, I'm a magician, and if there's a way to help my colleagues I'm going to try. I wasn't going to tell the Commander's magician killer about it." Still, a small, guilt-inducing thought about killing magicians being preferable to using them to increase the Fire Warper's power pulsed in my mind.

Valek sank back onto his heels. His expression hardened into his metal mask. "Magician killer? Is that what you think of me?"

"That *is* one of your duties for the Commander. I know how you operate. You like to stalk your prey before you pounce. Allowing Porter's network to continue is part of your modus operandi."

His expression turned flat and emotionless; my anger had ruled my tongue. My fury, though, remained.

I changed the subject. "How did Star get us into Sitia?"

As if reporting to the Commander, Valek said, "Put you into crates, stacked boxes of goods on top, and dressed as traders. They had the proper papers. The border guards did a cursory check and off you went." He paused as extreme irritation flashed through his eyes. "The border guards will be taken to task and retrained."

Valek stood. "I was going to suggest we get a few hours' sleep and try to rescue those girls. But since *I'm* the magician killer, I guess I won't concern myself about their fate." He left the room.

25

THE LIFE DRAINED from the room after Valek's de-
parture. I blamed fatigue for my harsh words, but knew it was
wrong. I had lost control of events the moment we crossed into
Ixia. But the real truth was I had never had control. From the
instant the Fire Warper stepped from the fire in the jungle, I'd
been ruled by fear. Which had kept me alive, so far, but it had
certainly made a mess of things. Valek was just the latest in a
long list.

I sighed. There was a good reason for the fear. The Fire
Warper's power surpassed my own, and I didn't think a
bucket of water would douse him. Curling up on the couch,
I made plans to free those girls. I couldn't counter the
Warper, but at least I could try to stop the Vermin from
gaining more power.

But what about the next shipment of young magicians from
Ixia? From what Valek told me, I guessed Star had tapped into
Porter's network, kidnapping his charges and selling those ado-
lescents for the Vermin to use in the Kirakawa ritual.

After a few hours of restless sleep, I went to the stables. Kiki dozed in her stall, but she woke to my call.

Do you have enough energy for a trip? I asked.

Yes. Where?

Back to where you found me.

Bad smell.

Yes, but I need to go back and pick up their scent. They've probably moved into the plains by now.

We go fast.

That's what I'm counting on. Not bothering to saddle her, I hopped onto her back. All I had was my bow. I glanced at the farmhouse. If I had apologized to Valek, he would have come with me, but I wasn't ready to admit I needed to apologize. At least he would be safe for tonight.

We were soon near the border of the Avibian Plains. Evidence of the Vermin's campsite littered the ground, and from the number of items left behind, it appeared Cahil had left in a hurry. Only a few hours of darkness remained.

Kiki, which way? I asked.

She headed south, and I let her choose her speed. She trotted until we reached the plains, then broke into her gust-of-wind gait. The air sped past my ears as the ground blurred. She didn't maintain the pace for long, slowing when the smell of wood smoke and horses strengthened.

The Vermin's magic waited on the plains. Unlike the Sand-seeds' net of protection, the Daviians preferred to lay traps, which would spring on the unsuspecting victim. Kiki sensed these hot spots and avoided them.

A faint glow of firelight shone through Kiki's eyes. We stopped and I was considering my next move when Kiki reared and danced to the side. The sizzling odor of blood burned in Kiki's nose. She would have bolted, but I steadied her with a soothing hand while my mind turned numb with shock.

They hadn't waited for the next moon. Guilt slammed into me. I hunched over Kiki's back, rocking with anger and frustration.

Girls hurt? Kiki asked.

Yes.

Go. Stop.

What? But she didn't wait. She galloped toward the camp.

Kiki!

Help. Fix. She ran through the camp. Rearing and jumping as if crazed with fear.

Her sudden arrival surprised everyone. The guards scattered and dodged her flailing hooves and my bow. Kiki knocked down Cahil's tent, kicked the wagon over and sent the horses running.

I froze in horror when I spotted the two Warpers stooped over the still forms of Liv and Kieran. Blood coated the Warpers' arms up to their elbows. They each cradled a fist-size lump of meat in their hands, lovingly stroking the object. I gasped with recognition. They each held a human heart. Liv and Kieran's hearts.

Kiki knocked me to my senses when she dumped me onto the ground. I gained my feet, ready for an attack, but the Warpers remained engrossed in their ritual.

Help, Kiki ordered as she made another loop of the camp.

I glanced at the fire. No Fire Warper yet. I mentally kicked myself for even worrying about him, and drew a thick strand of power. The Vermin defensive magic tried to clamp down on my connection, but I had pulled such a fat rope it failed to cut even a thread.

I launched my awareness at the Warpers. A fog of magic surrounded them. Instinctively, I knew in order for them to consume and maintain the power, they had to milk the blood from the hearts and inject it into their skin.

The Kirakawa ritual had its own power and I couldn't interfere with the Warpers. Their black lust for magic sickened me and for a moment my vision filled with blood.

But a movement from the corner of my eye caught my attention. Liv's ghost stood next to her dead body and she gestured to me, thumping her heart with a fist. I squinted at the apparition. Her ghost or her soul? When I understood her motions, I cursed myself for my stupidity.

I couldn't affect the ritual, but there was one thing only I could do. Concentrating on the girls' hearts, I reached for their souls. The ritual had trapped them within its chambers. I inhaled their essence, leaving behind dead flesh. The Warpers wouldn't gain any power tonight.

Kiki slowed near me. I grabbed her mane and hauled myself onto her back. Within two strides she moved into her special gait.

When we reached the edge of the plains, I asked Kiki to stop so I could release the girls' souls. The sun began to rise, casting long shadows on the ground. I wished I had known the girls better so I could make Sitian grief flags for them. The occasion called for the fanfare of raising their flags to memorialize the girls' short lives.

Without silk or a flagpole, I settled for expressing my deep regret for not saving them. They felt content and relieved to be free. But what else could they say while I held their souls?

A vile thought occurred to me. I wondered if my powers

were enhanced while they remained with me. Could I counter the Fire Warper if I increased my strength? Shuddering in revulsion for just thinking about it, I released their souls to the sky. They rushed from me. A lingering tingle of joy vibrated inside me before my body sagged with fatigue.

I arrived at Valek's safe house without any memories of the trip. Kiki headed for the stable and I summoned enough energy to give her a good rubdown. The stack of hay bales outside her stall appeared to be too inviting for me to pass. I lay down on top of them and fell asleep.

An army of flaming soldiers chased me. My legs refused to run any faster as the burning men advanced. Leif rushed to my aid but, as soon as he drew near me, he burst into flames. Only Valek remained. He stood amid the conflagration, untouched by the searing heat. A block of ice, he seemed indifferent to my plight.

"Sorry, love." He shrugged. "Can't help you."

"Why?"

"You won't let me."

The fire soldiers closed in until a circle of fire surrounded me. Tongues of flames licked at my clothes then grabbed the fabric.

"Yelena!"

Bright yellow and orange danced along my cloak. Their movements held my attention in a bizarre fascination as they consumed my clothes.

"Yelena!"

Cold water splashed on me, followed by a drenching deluge. Steam hissed. I yelled and woke, choking on the water. Valek stood next to me. He held an empty bucket.

"What?" I sat up. My clothes and hair were soaking wet. "What was that for?"

"You were having a nightmare."

"And shaking me awake seemed too tame?" He was still angry.

Valek didn't answer. Instead, he pulled me to my feet and pointed to the figure-shaped scorch mark on the topmost hay bale. The place where I had slept.

"You were too hot to touch," he said in a deadpan.

I shivered. If Valek hadn't been here, what would have happened?

"I take it your rescue attempt last night has angered some powerful people? I saw you and Kiki create chaos in the camp, ruining my plans yet again. What else did you do?"

Valek hadn't gone to bed. He had left to help the girls. Kiki and I could have gone with him. Together we might have reached the camp in time to save Liv and Kieran. Guilt balled in my chest, souring my mood. I hadn't managed to do anything right. I didn't find Cahil and Ferde in time. The Sandseed Clan was gone. Irys and Bain were locked up. I had upset my friends and my brother. And Valek.

He stared at me with his flat expression, giving nothing away. An invisible wall grew between us. Mine or his? I told him about the girls' souls and how I had removed the power from the ritual.

"I should have let you kill Cahil," I said.

If the change in subject surprised him, he didn't allow it to show on his face. "Why?"

"It would have prevented all this."

"I think not. Cahil's involvement is recent. These Vermin

are prepared. They've been planning this move for a while. Cahil wants you dead and wants his throne. I believe the whole Kirakawa ritual sickens him."

"He helped with the kidnapping."

"Because he wanted you. He wasn't at the camp last night. He's probably heading to the Citadel."

"How do you know?"

Valek gave me a tight, joyless smile. "When you stormed the camp, I stole into the tent, intending to put the Wannabe King out of my misery. I had a few seconds to determine he was gone before the tent collapsed on me."

I suppressed a chuckle. From the annoyed frown, I knew Valek wouldn't appreciate it.

"But I found that." He gestured to the floor. My backpack rested against Kiki's stall door.

A happy cry escaped my lips and I knelt down to check the contents. Before I dug into the pack, I looked up to thank Valek, but he was gone. I considered finding him to explain, but I wasn't ready to breach the wall surrounding me. Inside my little cocoon, I could pretend the Fire Warper's threat to the people I loved didn't exist.

My pack still held my switchblade, my Sitian clothes, my lock picks, vials of Curare, lumps of Theobroma, jerky, tea and Opal's glass bat. The glow from the statue seemed brighter.

The intricate swirls of liquid fire drew my gaze. I marveled at Opal's talent. The whirlpool of light in the core of the bat transformed into a snake. The roar of a kiln beat at my ears. Hands wielded a pair of metal tweezers to shape the thin glass body before it cooled. The thoughts of the glassmaker reached me. Opal's thoughts.

She dripped water on a groove in the glass near the end of the pole. The snake cracked off. Using thick mittens, she picked up the piece and put it into another oven to cool slowly. This one was not as hot as the first.

Opal, can you hear me? I asked.

No response.

When my awareness returned to the bat in my hand, I knew I had reached Booruby with my mind without expending a lot of energy. Booruby! A six-day ride south of here. I hadn't been able to reach Bain from Booruby and I had been closer. What would happen if Irys held the snake? Would we be able to communicate over vast distances without sapping our strength? My mind raced with the implications.

The cold air intruded on my excitement. My wet hair felt icy in the breeze, and I remembered Kiki mentioning snow. We were north of the Avibian Plains, but I had no idea if the farmhouse resided in the Moon Clan's lands or Featherstone's. Either way, by the time the storm reached us, it would turn to rain and sleet. And by looking at the gray wall of clouds advancing from the west, it wouldn't be long before the storm hit.

I shouldered my pack and went inside. Valek had lit a small fire in the living room. His soft tread padded on the floor above me. Probably planning to sleep after being up all night.

Hesitating on the threshold of the room, I debated. My cloak was soaked. I needed the fire to dry it and I wanted to warm myself.

In the end, I changed into Sitian clothes, hung my cloak by the hearth and filled a pot for tea. I heated the water, but avoided looking directly into the fire. Feeling uneasy, I chewed a piece of jerky and drank the tea as far away from the flames as I could get. Unable to stay in the room any longer, I wanted to run upstairs to Valek. Instead, I grabbed a blanket off the couch and ran to the stables, joining Kiki.

She snorted in amusement when I made a bed of straw in her stall. I filled two buckets with water and put them next to me.

If I start to smoke, pour these on me, I said to her. *I don't want to set fire to the barn.*

Soon after I laid down, an odd melody of sleet drummed on the slate roof. The whistle of wind through the rafters augmented the beat. Lulled to sleep by the storm's music, I slept without dreams.

The arrival of a strange horse woke me and Kiki the next morning. At least I hoped the weak storm light meant the beginning and not the end of the day.

Valek led in a black horse with white socks. With its long legs and sleek body, the animal was built like a racehorse. Pulling a thread of power, I linked my mind with the new arrival.

He felt uncomfortable in this new barn. Strange smells. Strange horse. He missed his stall and friends.

Smells here are good, I said in his mind. *You'll make new friends. What's your name?*

Onyx.

I introduced him to Kiki.

Valek tied Onyx to a hitch. "We need to leave for the Citadel." He saddled Onyx. "This weather is good cover."

My heart twisted with pain. He had gotten his own horse so he didn't have to sit with me on Kiki. "How far?"

"Two days. I have another safe house about a mile north of the Citadel. We can set up operations there."

We worked in complete and utter silence.

The next two days felt more like ten. With the nasty weather, Valek's cold shoulder and my anxiety to hurry, I would have preferred spending the time in the Commander's dungeon.

Our arrival at the safe house seemed a relief until the necessity of planning our actions made our strained relationship almost unbearable. I remained stubborn, believing the distance between us would make it easier for me to make life-threatening decisions.

After we settled into the cottage, I headed for the Citadel. The weather again promised rain, lending a bleakness to the landscape. Bare trees and brown hills seemed muted and barren of life. I knew if I swept the area with my magic, I would feel the small stirrings of creatures, waiting for the warmth. But the risk of using magic this close to the Keep was too high.

Disguised as a Featherstone clanswoman, I wore a long-sleeved linen dress underneath a plain sand-colored cloak. Although I left my bow behind, I had access to my switchblade. My hair was pulled into a stylish knot favored by the Featherstones and held in place by my lock picks.

Valek had styled my hair. He worked in a cold and efficient manner, making it easier for me not to grasp his hands and pull him close. His deft fingers twisted the strands of my hair expertly, and a strange vision of fire melting his arms to stumps rose in my mind.

I banished the image and put my hood over my head. The

north gate of the Citadel wasn't as busy as I had hoped. In fact, once inside, only a few people walked the streets. They hunched over their packages and stared at the ground. The weather could be a factor, but the rain had ceased. The streets should be teeming with citizens hurrying to the market before the next squall.

Even the beggars were few and far between. Most of them wore expressions of worry as they glanced around, and none approached me.

The Citadel's white marble walls looked dingy and dull. The green veins resembled streaks of dirt and the whole town felt as if a layer of grime coated it. The grunge had built up in the cracks, and soaked into the foundations. The shine was gone from the town. And it wasn't due to the weather.

I missed a step when the first Daviian Vermin came into my sight. But soon they were everywhere. Hunching over, I mimicked the citizens' posture, searching for an alley or side street free of Vermin. Blood throbbed in my ears. The Vermin's gazes burned into my soul. When I entered a shortcut to the market, my legs wobbled with relief. But I kept out of view until I had studied the center square, watching the people scurrying around the market's stands. The sense of fear even diluted the usual heady smell of spices and roasting meat.

The concentration of citizens meant more Vermin. I waited until I spotted my target and then joined the shoppers. When I drew beside a young boy of ten, I had to suppress a smile as I listened to him barter with the stand owner.

"Four coppers, take it or leave it," Fisk said, sounding like an adult.

"I can't feed my family for that!" the owner countered. "Since you're my friend, I'll take seven coppers."

"Belladoora is selling them for four."

"But look at this quality. Hand embroidered by my own wife. Look at the detail!" He held up the fabric.

"Five, and not a copper more."

"Six, and that's final."

"Good day, sir." Fisk walked away.

"Wait," the stand owner called. "Five then. But you're stealing the bread out of my children's mouths." He grumbled some more while wrapping the fabric in paper, but he smiled when the boy paid him the money.

I followed Fisk to his client. The woman paid him six coppers and he handed her the package.

"Excuse me, boy," I said. "I'm in need of your services."

"What can I do for you?" he asked. Then his eyes flew wide with shock before worry touched them. He glanced around with small furtive movements. "Follow me."

He led me to a tight alley and into a dark dwelling. I stood in the blackness while Fisk lit a few lanterns. Thick curtains hung over the windows and only a few chairs decorated the barren room.

"This is where we meet," Fisk said.

"We?"

He smiled. "The Helpers Guild members. We plan our day, divide up the money, and exchange gossip about our clients."

"That's wonderful." Pride at what Fisk had accomplished filled my heart. The grubby beggar boy I had met on my first Citadel visit had transformed into a productive member of his family.

Fisk's own pride showed in his light brown eyes. "It's all because of you, my first client!"

Instead of begging for money, now Fisk and the other beggar children helped shoppers find good deals, carried packages and would do just about anything for a small fee.

His grin dropped from his face. "Lovely Yelena, you shouldn't be here. There's a reward for your capture."

"How much?"

"Five golds!"

"Is that all? I thought it would be more like ten or fifteen," I teased.

"Five is a lot of money. So much I wouldn't trust my own cousin not to turn you in. It's dangerous for you here. For everyone."

"What's been going on?"

"These new Daviian Clan members. They have taken over. At first it was just a couple of them, but now the streets are filled. Ugly rumors about their involvement with the Sandseed genocide has everyone frightened. People living in the Citadel have been questioned, and certain beggars have disappeared. Whispers about how the Council members have lost control have spread, yet they are preparing for a war."

Fisk shook his head. He had wisdom beyond his years. I mourned the loss of his childhood. Being a child of beggars had robbed him of fun, wonder and the ability to make mistakes without fatal consequences.

"How about the Keep?" I asked.

"Locked down. No one enters or leaves except under the Daviians' armed escort."

The state of affairs was worse than I had anticipated. "I need you to get a message to one of the Councilors for me."

"Which one?"

"My kinsman, Bavol Zaltana. But I don't want you to write anything down. It must be a verbal message. Can you do it?"

Fisk frowned, considering. "It will be difficult. The Councilors all have an escort while out in the Citadel, but perhaps I could set up a distraction..." He rubbed his hands along his arms as he contemplated the task. "I can try. No promises. If it gets too hot, I'm out of there. And it's—"

"Going to cost me. And you must not repeat the message to anyone."

"Agreed."

We shook hands on the deal. I told Fisk my message. He left to recruit a couple helpers. I returned to the market to purchase a few items and to eat, killing time without appearing to be.

My gaze kept returning to the Keep's towers. Located within the Citadel's marble walls, the Magician's Keep occupied the northeastern section. Unable to suppress my desire to see the pink-pillared entrance gates, my path led to the Keep.

Instead of appearing warm and inviting, the cold stone seemed impenetrable and daunting. I longed to make contact with my friends and colleagues inside. Where were Dax and Gelsi? Had they been allowed to continue their studies? I felt blind and cut off, frustrated and lost. As if I had been exiled and would never see them again.

Daviian guards stood next to the Keep's guards. Feeling too exposed, I returned to Fisk's meeting room to await the boy's return. Time crept along in mind-numbing increments. A small tan spider built its elaborate web in the corner of the room. To help the spider, I hunted for an insect to place on the sticky strands.

Fisk arrived as I stood on a chair, attempting to nab a moth. He puffed out his chest and declared the mission a success. "Councilor Zaltana said he would meet with you tonight in his home." Fisk deflated a bit with his next remark. "He warned his residence is guarded by a Warper. What's a Warper?"

"A Daviian magician." I considered the complication. "What time?"

"Anytime, but if you're out on the streets after midnight, the guards will arrest you. I would suggest after the evening meal. There is usually a flurry of activity as the shops close and everyone heads home." Fisk sighed. "It used to be a good time to beg. People would feel guilty passing by a child without a home when they had a warm comfortable bed waiting for them."

"Used to be, Fisk. That's in the past. I bet you have a nice home, now."

His posture straightened. "The best! Which reminds me. You had better leave before my helpers come back. We meet in the morning and again in the late afternoon."

I paid Fisk, thanking him for the help. "If you ever get caught, don't hesitate to tell them about me. I don't want you to be hurt because of me."

Fisk gave me a confused frown. "But you could be taken and killed by the Daviians."

"Better me than you."

"No. Things are bad and getting worse. If you're killed, I have a horrible feeling life wouldn't be worth living."

* * *

Fisk's dire comments followed me as I traveled through the Citadel. Keeping to the back alleys, I hid behind buildings until the streets filled with residents hurrying home, just as Fisk had predicted. I joined the flow, blending in as the sky grew dark and the lamplighters began their evening chore. When I passed Bavol's dwelling, I slowed long enough to determine his house was empty.

I made another loop around the street to make sure, then slipped behind the building. Using my picks, I unlocked the back door and startled a woman.

"Oh my!" She dropped a rake. It clattered on the edge of the stone heath, and the fire she had been stirring to life dimmed.

"I didn't mean to startle you," I said, thinking fast. "I have an urgent appointment with Councilman Zaltana."

"I don't remember him telling me about a guest. And certainly no guest would come creeping in the back door!" She swept up the iron rake and hefted it in her big hands. She wore a type of loose tunic the Zaltanas preferred, but it was hard to see in the semidarkness.

I chanced it. "We just set the meeting today. It's regarding *clan* business."

"Oh my." She bent and raked at the coals. When a flame ignited, she used it to light a lantern. She peered at me through the glow. "Goodness, child. Come in then. Shut the door. This is all highly unusual, but I don't know why I'm surprised. These are unusual times."

The woman bustled and fussed about the kitchen, claiming the Councilman would soon be home and would want his supper. I helped her by lighting the lanterns in the dining room and living room. Bavol's home was decorated with jungle art and valmur statues. A pang of homesickness struck me.

When I heard someone at the front door, I hid in the kitchen.

"His guard dog doesn't come in the house," the woman said. "The Councilman won't allow it. The day that dog is allowed in will be the end of the Sitian Council."

But would the Warper use his magic to scan the interior? Would I feel the power? I hovered by the back door just in case.

The woman said, "Call me Petal, child," and invited me to join them for supper. She shooed away any protests about my limited time. "Nonsense, child. Let me tell the Councilman you're here."

"Ah, Petal," I said, stopping her. "Perhaps it would be best if you just asked him to come in here? Dogs have very acute hearing."

She tapped a finger to her forehead and then pointed to me before leaving. Bavol came into the kitchen with Petal on his heels. He greeted me with a tired smile.

"Smart to come before me," he said in a soft voice. He rubbed at the dark smudges under his eyes. Worry lines etched his face and he stood as if he strained under a heavy weight. "If you're discovered..." He sank down to perch on an edge of a stool. "You can't stay long. If they hear or see anything out of the ordinary, the Warper will barge in and I *will* tell him every-thing."

His matter-of-fact statement about his response to the Warper sent a ripple of fear through my body. What were the Warpers doing to gain information and cooperation?

"I'll be quick then. Why did the Council allow the Daviians to come?"

Alarm flashed on Bavol's face and he clamped his hands together in his lap. "Petal, could you please get me a glass of whiskey?"

She eyed him with annoyance. Even though she stirred her stew pot on the other side of the kitchen, she had been leaning toward us, trying to listen to our conversation.

With a huff of indignation, Petal left the kitchen.

Bavol closed his eyes for a moment and grimaced. But when he focused on me, his old confident self returned.

"We should have let them die," he said.

26

"LET WHO DIE?" I ASKED, but Bavol ignored me.

"At first the Daviians required minor things from us to keep them alive. A vote one way or another. The requests became more frequent and alarming. Visitors grew in numbers and the next thing we knew we had agreed to everything."

"Keep who alive?"

"We made a mistake, but you're here now. Perhaps it's not too late."

"Bavol, I don't—"

"The Daviians have our children."

I stared at him for a moment in stunned silence. "How?"

Bavol shrugged. "Does it matter how? Our families live with our clans most of the year. We're not home to protect them."

"Who do they have?"

"My daughter, Jenniqilla. She disappeared from the Illiais Market. I've been instructed not to tell anyone. But from the other Councilors' faces I knew the Daviians had gotten to everyone. Eventually, we talked about it amongst ourselves. All the Councilors with children had one taken. For the others, the Daviians kidnapped Councilor Greenblade's husband, and Councilor Stormdance's wife."

"Where are they keeping them?"

"If I knew I wouldn't be here talking to you," he snapped.

"Sorry." I considered the implications. Petal returned with two glasses of whiskey and handed one to me. She went back to stirring her pots.

"When?" I asked, thinking about Valek's comment that the Vermin had been planning this before Cahil had gotten involved.

"Fourteen days ago," Bavol whispered.

I thought back. Fourteen days seemed like fourteen years when I sifted through everything that had happened. The Vermin had grabbed the Councilors' families right after I fled the Citadel. It wasn't Roze influencing the Council after all.

"Do the Master Magicians know?"

"Master Bloodgood and Master Jewelrose suspected when we wrote the letter to the Commander. Master Featherstone interpreted their refusal as an act of treason. And the Daviians forced us to agree with her and sign their arrest warrant and help incarcerate them in the Keep. They cooperated," Bavol added when he saw my concern. "It's a shame Master Cowan is still too young to exert much influence on Master Featherstone."

"Do you think Roze is working with the Daviians?"

"No. She would be horrified to know they are making the decisions. We are voting with her, so she is content and the Daviians are offering her support in her campaign against the Commander."

"Couldn't she learn of your dilemma from your thoughts?"

Bavol's gaze snapped to me. "That would be a serious breach

of the Magician's Ethical Code. Master Featherstone would never resort to invading our private thoughts."

I had a difficult time believing in Roze's high moral standards, but I possessed no evidence to the contrary.

"Should I set an extra place for dinner?" Petal asked.

Bavol and I both shook our heads no. His anxious expression reminded me I needed to leave soon. She tsked and carried a stack of plates from the kitchen.

Finding and rescuing the Council's family members became a priority. There was one way I could discover where they were being held, but I would have to use magic.

"Bavol, I may be able to find your daughter through you. But I can't do it in the Citadel. Is there any chance you can leave?"

"No. My guard is with me always."

"Could you slip out the back door?"

"I have to make contact with my guard every hour. It is the only way he will give me any privacy."

"What about when you're sleeping?"

"He sits in the living room. Petal doesn't know about it, since she retires so early and sleeps like a log. I haven't been able to sleep since Jenniqilla's capture. I'm up before the sun and can send him back outside."

"It will have to be during the night, then. I'll make arrangements. Just don't be surprised if you have company in your bedroom tomorrow evening. And leave the back window open."

"That's Petal's room," he said.

"Perhaps you can make sure she remains asleep?"

He sighed. "I long for the simpler days. Never again will I complain about Councilor Sandseed's stubbornness or Councilor Jewelrose's petty problems."

"Dinner's ready," Petal called.

"You should go," he said.

"Do you know any way I could get into the Keep?"

"The emergency tunnel. But I don't know if it has collapsed or been sealed up. The magicians dug it when they first constructed their Keep, during the clan wars long ago. I hadn't known it existed until recently. Second Magician mentioned it to me a few days before they arrested him and Fourth Magician."

"Are Bain and Irys still being held in the Keep's cells?"

"As far as I know."

"Did Bain tell you where the tunnel is located?"

"He said something about the east side of the Keep, and about how it was big enough for a horse." Bavol stood. "We have lingered too long. I expect to hear from you again. Stay safe." He went into the dining room.

I waited a moment, then opened the back door. Peeking out, I scanned the dark alley. It appeared to be deserted, but without my magic, I couldn't be sure. I risked it and left Bavol's. The Citadel's quiet streets alarmed me. Only a few people walked on the roads, and most of them were Vermin. Even the taverns remained dark and desolate.

My chances of getting through the north gate undetected didn't seem likely. I considered going to one of the inns, but the Vermin could have people there watching for strangers. The longer I stayed on the street increased the danger of being caught.

In desperation, I found a house with an outside staircase reaching the ground of a narrow alley. Climbing up to the top of the steps without making too much noise, I stood on the handrail and reached for the edge of the roof. I discovered a problem with marble buildings as I tried to use the wall to push myself onto the roof. My foot slipped and I just managed to regain my balance and avoid plummeting four stories to the ground.

In the end, I employed my acrobatic training and made a leap of faith onto the roof. Good thing these same marble walls were thick enough to mask the sound of my thud.

I lay on the flat roof, gasping, glad Valek hadn't been here to see my awkward ascent. His ability to scale the Commander's castle walls was now more impressive. I wondered if he would be worried when I failed to come back. Perhaps it was for the best that I had stayed too long with Bavol. Multiple trips through the gate would arouse suspicion.

The night air turned cold. I huddled in my cloak and slept. Dreams of fire haunted me. No matter where I ran to or where I hid, the flames always found me. Always.

I woke sweat soaked in the morning light, achy and feverish. The prospect of climbing down from the roof unseen and finding Fisk was as appealing as taking a cold bath. At least descending proved easier than ascending the roof. I made it down the stairs and into the alley without incident. Although the thumping in my head failed to stop.

Bleary-eyed and tired, I searched for Fisk at the market. Remembering his meeting room, I hid nearby and waited for him.

The group of children who left the building caused me to smile. So intent on their day's work, they moved with purpose and carried themselves with a businesslike air. After they disappeared from sight, Fisk appeared beside me.

"Did something happen?" he asked.

"Nothing bad. I have another job for you." I told him what

I needed and he thought he could help me. "I don't want anyone to get into trouble, though."

"Don't worry, you picked a good night."

"Why is it good?"

"It's Midseason's Night. We celebrate the midpoint of the cold season. Gives everyone something to look forward to." Fisk grinned. "Doesn't Ixia have something similar?"

"Yes. They hold an annual Ice Festival. People display their handcrafts and get together to exchange ideas. I just hadn't realized we were this far into the season."

"The celebration's bound to be quieter this year, but there should be enough activity to hide ours." This time Fisk's smile held a hint of mischievousness, reminding me of Janco.

I'd bet Janco had been pure trouble as a kid. At least I hadn't upset him and Ari before leaving Ixia. Then again, since I hadn't brought them along, they could be annoyed with me, too.

We made plans for the evening and Fisk told me of a place where I could stay to wait for the night. After he left, I walked over to the Council Hall. I made a loop around it while trying not to appear as if I held any special interest in the square structure. The activity on the wide steps leading to the first floor was busy. The Councilors' offices, the great hall, record room, library and Citadel's jail all resided inside. My interest lay in the record room. Information from all the clans had been stored there, and I wanted to find any mention about the magician's emergency tunnel within the records. Or perhaps the library would have some reference to the Keep's layout?

Bain's private stash of books most likely contained the information I needed. The irony of my situation was not lost on me. The Second Magician had told Bavol about the tunnel's existence because he knew Bavol would be the first person I would contact. What Bavol had thought was an interesting tidbit of information turned out to be a message for me.

The lack of details remained a problem. East side of the Keep and big enough for a horse didn't give me much to go on.

The flow of people in and out of the Council Hall stayed steady. However, a few Vermin hung about and I decided not to risk my life for research.

When I headed back toward the market, a strange feeling touched my back as if a thousand little spiders crawled up my spine in unison. Turning a corner, I glanced to the side. A male Daviian walked a small distance behind me. He wore red pantaloons and a brown hooded short cape. When I rounded another corner, he remained on my tail.

His scimitar glinted in the sunlight. I entered the market. Pausing at a vegetable stand, I hoped the Vermin would pass me, but he leaned on a lamppost. Small darts of panic began to pierce my heart. If the Daviian was a Warper, I wouldn't be able to lose him.

Joining with a group of women, I stayed with them as they shopped. The man kept pace with us. I needed a distraction and fast.

One of the women in the group paid for a beaded necklace. She had been rather loud and full of opinions as we went from stand to stand, and she made her annoyance over my unwanted presence clear to me.

When the stand owner handed her the wrapped package, I leaned over and whispered to her, "He sold that very same necklace to my friend for two silvers last week."

The woman had just paid four silvers. As predicted, she loudly demanded the same price and the confused seller tried to reason with her. The ensuing argument drew a considerable crowd and I squeezed between them, hoping to lose the Daviian.

No luck. He caught sight of me and followed. A few shoppers temporarily blocked his way, and I ducked under one of the market stands.

Not the best decision, but I had run out of options. I hunched under the table. A purple cloth had been draped over it and the material hung to the ground. A few bolts of fabric and a box of buttons had been stored underneath.

I wondered when it would be safe to leave. Popping up just as the Vermin walked by wouldn't be ideal, so I squirmed into a more comfortable position to wait.

The purple fabric pulled aside. I froze.

A man's face peered through the opening. "Your friend's gone. It's safe to come out."

He backed away when I started to move. "Thanks," I said, brushing the dirt off my cloak.

"Attracting *their* attention is never a good thing," the man said. His round face held a serious expression. "People tend to disappear around here. Especially those with five golds on their head."

I calmed my furious heartbeat. The stand owner knew I hid under his table and he hadn't reported me. At least not yet. Perhaps he wished to strike a bargain? Something like six golds to keep quiet.

"Don't worry. You're a friend to Fisk and his guild. And just the fact the Daviians would be willing to pay five golds for your capture means you, of all people, scare them. I hope for the sake of my family the reason you scare them is because you can do something to bring our normal lives back."

"I scare them," I agreed, thinking about the Sitian Council and how terrified they had been over me being a Soulfinder. "But I don't know if I can restore your old way of life. I'm only one person."

"You have Fisk's help."

"Until my money runs out."

"True. That little scamp, forcing me to make an honest living!" The man paused and considered. "Aren't there any others to help you?"

"Would you help me?"

He blinked in surprise. "How?"

"Not all these Vermin are Warpers. They carry scimitars and spears, but look around you—they are outnumbered."

"But their Warpers have powerful magic."

"You don't have any magicians? No one has escaped from the Keep? No one has come from the other clans?"

His eyes lit with understanding. "But they're scattered around the Citadel. They hide in fear."

"A concerned citizen needs to convince them to act despite their fear, to organize them and, when the time is right, to lead them."

"You can do that. You're the Soulfinder."

I shook my head. "My presence would jeopardize the efforts. I'm needed elsewhere. If you're determined, you will find the right person."

The man smoothed out the fabric on his table. He appeared deep in thought. "Merchants come and go from the Citadel all the time…caravans of goods…"

"Just be very careful." I started to walk away.

"Wait. How will we know when the time is right?"

"I have a bad feeling that you won't be able to miss it."

After the day settled into night, I met up with Fisk and his uncle. People walked the streets in good humor despite their Vermin watchers and the late hour. While Fisk went to prepare for later, I led his uncle onto the roof.

Once we ascended, we traveled over the roofs of the Citadel to Bavol's dwelling. If they weren't out celebrating, the other residents had already gone to bed. I pulled the rope Fisk had bought for me from my pack, and secured it around the chimney before tossing the end over the side.

The glow from the lamplights didn't reach the back alley, so I hoped Bavol had remembered to open the back window. Clutching the rope, I shimmied down the side of the house and was relieved to find the window open. I climbed into Petal's room with the utmost care. Inside the room, I stilled and listened to her breathing, steady with the occasional snore. I yanked on the rope, then held it stable while Uncle slid down. He joined me in the room with a thump. We both froze until Petal resumed her even breathing.

Bavol, awake and ready, waited for us in his room. Uncle slipped into bed, pulling the blankets up to his neck and the Councilor came with me to the back window. Living in the jungle canopy all his life, Bavol had no trouble ascending the rope. I followed.

Traveling over the rooftops proved to be ideal. Eventually, we climbed down to the ground. When we came within sight of the north gate, we found a place to hide. No traffic.

I worried, and the longer the gate remained empty the greater my fear.

As I tried to decide if we should risk crossing through, a group of obviously inebriated men and women approached. With loud voices, a few of the group decided they wanted to go outside the Citadel, and a discussion ensued, leading to a fight.

When the guards became entangled in the brawl, Bavol and I slipped through the gate unnoticed. Once out of sight of the guardhouse, we ran. Our time was limited.

We reached Valek's cottage and I hoped we would be far enough away from the Citadel and the Warpers.

Kiki whinnied in her stall and I opened my mind to her.

Lavender Lady safe, she said with contentment. *Ghost upset.*

I'll talk later. No time right now. I hustled Bavol into the cottage. Valek sat on the couch, his expression set into cold fury.

I ignored his anger. He of all people should know the nature of this operation lent itself to unforeseen circumstances. However, I knew why Bavol's face blanched when he spotted Valek on the couch.

"You set me up," he said, taking a step back.

"Relax, Bavol. If Valek was going to assassinate the Council, you would be dead by now. He's helping me."

Valek snorted. "I am? Funny how I forgot. Or is it because someone forgot about me?" Sarcasm spiked each word.

Again, I ignored his fury and filled him in on what Bavol had told me. His face lost some of his ire as he considered the new information.

"Bavol, sit down. Close your eyes. Think of your daughter," I ordered.

When he settled on the couch, I reached for power. Touching the source caused a sudden rush of relief. I hadn't used magic in two days and reconnecting felt like being wrapped tight in my mother's arms.

I projected my awareness to Bavol. His loving thoughts dwelled on his little girl. She appeared to be around eight years old. Strands of gold streaked her long brown hair and a spattering of freckles dotted her warm maple-colored cheeks. A beautiful child, she twirled with delight after being presented with a piece of sap candy.

Through Bavol, I reached toward Jenniqilla. Within the memory, her happiness over the candy matched her joy over spending time with her father. I pushed past the memory and tried to find the girl.

She missed her father with a painful desperation. Cold and hungry, she wanted her father and mother more than food or heat. She rocked back and forth, trying to soothe the child in her arms. The two-year-old boy's crying had set off a chain reaction among the children in the room. A woman paced with a year-old baby girl and the man tried to cajole another two-year-old.

The gloomy light in the wooden room came from small cracks between the gray boards. The area contained no furniture and only two slop pots had been placed behind a ripped screen. From the harsh acidic smell, the pots hadn't been emptied in a while. A coating of grime clung to Jenniqilla's skin and she promised herself she would never fuss at her mother about bathing again. An icy chill seeped into her legs and back from the dirt floor.

Jenniqilla, I said in her mind. *Where are you?*

She glanced around, wondering if someone had called her name. Seeing no one, she continued to sing to Leevi.

I'm your cousin, Yelena. I need to know where you are so I can help you and the others.

She remembered how her second cousin was taken long ago, but had returned. *If she got away, than I can, too,* she thought.

Jenniqilla was too young to access the power source. She couldn't communicate with me directly, but she felt the intentions of my power. She remembered her kidnapping. Somehow, she had lost sight of her mother at the market. As she wandered around, searching for Mama a man dressed in the loose tunic of the Sandseed clan picked her up. Before she could yell, he clamped a sweet-smelling rag over her mouth and nose.

Jenniqilla woke inside a box and cried for Mama. A man banged on the wood and threatened to kill her if she didn't shut up. She felt movement and when the box stopped and opened, the same Sandseed man pulled her out and brought her to an old dilapidated barn smelling of rot. Within the barn was another structure. This one smelled like sawed wood and had shiny locks on the door.

When they shoved her through the door, dark shapes moved in the corners. Distraught and confused, she cried. A woman materialized from one of those black forms and took Jenniqilla into her arms. After she had quieted, the woman, Gale Stormdance, explained to her why they all were there.

Ask Gale where you are, I encouraged Jenniqilla.

But Gale wasn't sure. "I think somewhere in Bloodgood's lands," she said. Her face grew thoughtful, and I projected myself toward her and encountered a magical defensive barrier.

She stared at Jenniqilla in shock but lowered her defenses tentatively.

I'm here to help, I said to Gale, explaining who I was and how I had found her.

Thank goodness, she said. *I've been hoping a Keep magician would look for us. Why did it take so long?*

I updated her on what I knew, then asked her again about her whereabouts.

I only had a brief glimpse. I sensed her frustration.

Visualize the area around the barn for me.

Forest-covered hills loomed behind the barn and a large stone farmhouse was located to the right. Something odd had caught her eye on the left. A glint of sunlight off a crimson-colored pond. The shape, though, had been stranger than the color. Her mind sifted through all the panic and fear of being hauled out of a crate and taken inside to find the required image.

A diamond, she exclaimed. *The pond is shaped like a diamond.*

It was a start. I thanked her for her help and promised to find them.

I pulled away from Gale, away from Jenniqilla and back to Bavol. A thin filament looped around my mind as I returned to Bavol. As if another power had caught me in a parasitic embrace.

Through Bavol's confused mind, I returned to my body. Valek had disappeared and the smell of smoke burned my nose. I rushed to the window.

The stable was on fire.

27

"Kiki!" I screamed, running. The image of her trapped in her stall and engulfed by flames filled my vision.

A voice yelled my name.

A black horse stood in the pasture.

A Daviian Warper coaxed the blaze higher. Brighter. Hotter. It didn't matter.

The parasite in my mind had gained control.

I ran straight into the stable, diving into the fire.

The heat burned my face and seared the inside of my nose. Flames danced with delight on my cloak, eating the fibers in gleeful disregard. The soles of my boots melted. The smoke robbed air from my lungs. My throat closed.

Hot knives of pain stabbed into my skin. Layers burned off in sheets of torment. The sound of boiling blood sizzled in my ears.

Pleasure followed pain and the colors of my world turned from white-hot and blinding yellow into bloodred and ice-black.

I marveled at my surroundings. Lit with a soft gray light, the flat world extended for miles in every direction. With reluctance, I glanced at my body, expecting to see a burnt corpse, but was surprised to find no damage. A weightless feeling tingled, and my arms and legs were slightly transparent.

A ghost perhaps? Was I in the shadow world? Then where were the others? All the Sandseeds who waited for me. Perhaps they had been a figment of Moon Man's imagination.

A soft laugh sounded beside me.

"You don't see them because you have chosen *not* to see them," a voice said.

A voice I feared more than anything. The Fire Warper stood next to me. He had lost his cloak of flames and appeared as an ordinary man. Broad shouldered with short dark hair, he stood as tall as Moon Man. His skin gleamed as if carved from coal.

He raised his arm to me. "Go ahead, touch it. It's not hard."

I hesitated. "You read my mind?"

He laughed again. "No. I read the question in your eyes. Despite your fear, you're curious. An admirable trait."

The Fire Warper stroked my arm with his fingertips. I jerked away.

"So afraid of being burned. I knew I needed a big fire to attract my little bat. It wasn't that bad, was it?"

"Bad enough." Caught here with him, my fear turned to resignation.

He seemed delighted with my response. Gesturing around, he said, "So what do you think of my fire world? Rather dull?"

"Yes. I thought it would be…" I scanned the featureless plain, with black ground and crimson sky.

"Hotter? Filled with burning souls? That you would be welcomed by your old tormentor, Reyad, for an eternity of rape and torture?"

"Filled with souls," I agreed. Drawn into the fire before, I had seen others.

"That's because you were with Moon Man. He has *chosen* to see those unfortunate souls. They've all lived colorful stories of life. You block them from your mind. Unwilling to see and unwilling for Moon Man to show you."

"I saw them in the shadow world, and relieved him of those painful images," I protested.

"Really? Do they haunt your dreams? Are you working with Moon Man to soothe them?" He paused and, when I didn't answer, he smiled. "Of course not! You have locked them away just like you have pushed Moon Man and your brother out of your life. Soon Valek will follow."

"At least they'll be safe."

"No one is safe."

Tired of his wordplay, I asked him what he wanted.

The amusement dropped from his face in an instant. "The sky."

I stared at him.

"I rule the fire world. I now have control over the shadow world, thanks to those Daviian magicians. And even though the shadow world is a borderland between fire and sky, I still can't access the sky."

"Why?"

"Because once I rule the sky, I can return to the living world."

Horror rolled through me. "What's in the sky?"

"The source of all magic."

I didn't quite understand. All magicians had access to the power source. Would he block others from using it?

"You know so little of magic," he said. His expression was incredulous.

I peered at him. His face had changed from smooth to covered with burn scars. His skin rippled as if melting.

"Why do you need me?"

"You're the only one who can get me into the sky."

"And why would I do that?"

"Because this is what I'll do to your family and friends."

He touched my arm. Burning pain seared up my shoulder and encompassed my head. My eyes turned hot and dry. The other occupants of the fire world became visible through a shimmering veil of heat.

Souls writhed in pain, dancing as if flames clinging to a log. Twisting and contorting, their misery pulsed off them in waves. The force of their emotions slammed into me. I stepped back into the Fire Warper's embrace.

He pointed to the different souls. "A few belong here, like Hetoo and Makko. Others were sent by the Daviians to feed me. Increased my power so much I can travel into the shadow world and steal more souls." He dragged me through the sea of suffering. "Your brother would add nicely to my collection. His magic is strong. Moon Man." He savored the Story Weaver's name. "Would bring me a cooling blue power. Combined, your mother and father would give me a boost. But I'll let them *all* live if you help me."

"If I help you, you'll be able to rule the living world, so how does that save them?"

"I'll show them special favor."

I knew they wouldn't agree. Yet spending eternal life in complete misery wasn't an attractive alternative.

The Fire Warper released me. The souls faded from sight and the dull plain reappeared.

"Much better, isn't it?" he asked.

"Yes."

"This could be your eternity. It's not very interesting, but it is safe. However…"

I leaned forward.

"You could live in the sky. It's peaceful and filled with contentment and joy."

"Until you join them."

"I only need to use them for a while. Once I've returned to the living, I will let you preside over their happiness."

An appealing prospect, except he had changed his story and I knew then I couldn't trust anything he said or promised. Being dead hadn't released me from my responsibilities at all. Perhaps if I went into the sky, I could tap into the power source and stop him.

"What would I have to do?" I asked.

"You need to find a soul on its way to the sky and follow it."

"What about you?"

"I'll be with you."

I looked at him in confusion.

"When you go to the sky, you'll be able to explore all aspects of magic. But to get there, you need to draw a soul to you. You know how to do that. Once you have the soul, step into the fire. Come to me and together we will go to the sky," he explained.

"But I'm dead already. Why can't I take one of the souls that doesn't belong here?"

He shook his head. "You must come under your own volition. You're not dead. I pulled you from the flames before they could consume your body. Besides, all these souls belong here. They don't deserve to be in the sky."

Another contradiction. I didn't know what to believe. And his motives were unclear, so I asked him, "Why do you want to go back to the living world?"

His burned face creased with anger. Fire erupted on his shoulders. "He sent me here to spend an eternity in misery. But *his* descendant released me, fed me power in exchange for knowledge and obedience. My master is strong, but not that strong. I have exceeded my savior's power. Now I want to regain my life that had been stolen from me."

"Who sent you here?"

"An Efe traitor named Guyan. Now do we have an agreement? If not, then you will remain here." He shrugged as if my decision didn't concern him too much.

Guyan's name was familiar to me. He was Gede's ancestor. So my new Story Weaver was in league with the Fire Warper. Perhaps Gede was also their leader Jal. I would have to remember that tidbit the next time I had a lesson scheduled with Gede. I choked out a laugh. At this point, there would be no future sessions for me.

I scanned the flat plain, peering into the red-tinged light. A gray shape swooped from the air. It dived and danced over a figure. I moved closer. The shape was a bat. But there weren't any insects or sources of heat to warrant its actions. Yet it picked and yanked at the figure. Another torture on the poor soul?

"What do you see, Yelena?" the Fire Warper asked. "Your future?"

"Perhaps." I turned away.

"Will you come back?"

"Yes."

He held out his hand. I grasped it. My world melted in a blaze of heat and cooled just as quickly in a swirl of ash and smoke. I lay among the ruins of the stable. Charred beams rested in crooked angles, twisted pieces of blackened metal littered the floor, and the scorched smell of burnt leather hung in the air.

I stumbled from the still-warm pile of wood. Singed holes peppered my clothes and soot streaked my skin. My cloak was gone. The hair on my arms had been burned away. I reached for my head, stopping when I encountered half-burnt stubble instead of hair.

My ruined boots crunched on the remains of the stable and shuffled through ash-filled puddles as I walked out, seeking Kiki. No response to either my mental or physical calls.

A loud bang sounded behind me and I turned to see Valek standing in the doorway of the cottage.

I laughed at his expression of complete and utter surprise. Then my legs turned to liquid as I realized what I would really lose when I kept my promise to the Fire Warper. My efforts were so focused on trying to protect him—protect everyone— I hadn't considered the cost of keeping them safe. I fell.

He was beside me in an instant. Caressing my face with a feather-light touch, he looked uncertain.

"Are you real?" he asked. "Or just some cruel joke?"

"I'm real. A real simpleton, Valek. I should never have said…I should never have done…" I drew in a deep breath. "Forgive me, please?"

"Would you promise never to do it again?" he asked.

"Sorry, I can't."

"Then you certainly are real. A real pain in the ass, but that's who I fell in love with." He pulled me close.

I clung to him with my ear pressed against his chest. The beat of his heart, steady and solid, comforted me. His soul, nestled within its chambers, was unreachable with my magic, but he had given it to me freely.

"Why were you so determined to push me away, love?"

"Fear."

"You've faced fear before. What's different?"

Good question. The answer horrified me. All this time I believed I wanted to protect my friends and family from the Fire Warper. "I'm afraid of my magic." The words tumbled from my mouth, breaking through the invisible barrier I had built between us. "If I harvested enough souls, I know I would possess ample power to defeat *all* the Warpers, including the Fire Warper. That's tempting. Tempting enough to want to protect *you* from *me*."

Valek pulled back and tilted my head so he could meet my gaze. "But all you need to do is ask. We wouldn't hesitate to give you our souls to defeat the Warpers."

"No. There has to be another way."

"And that would be…?"

"When I figure it out, you'll be the first to know." Before he could comment, I added, "You never answered me. Am I forgiven?"

He sighed dramatically. "You're forgiven. Now come inside, you reek of smoke."

Valek helped me to my feet. I swayed on unsteady legs for a moment. "Where's Kiki?"

"Once you disappeared into the stable, she ran off and hasn't come back."

I wanted to find her and reassure her, but my body lacked the energy.

We walked to the cottage. The bright light of midday burned in the sky. I could no longer think of the sky without remembering my deal with the Fire Warper. Unease wrapped around chest.

"Where's Bavol?" I asked to distract myself.

"The Daviian Warper captured him while I tried to douse the fire. Will they kill him?"

"No. They need him and all the Councilors for a while to keep up the pretense that the Council and Master Magicians are in charge."

"How long will it last?"

"Not very."

"Will they come after us here?"

The Fire Warper had gotten what he wanted. "No. But we need to retake control."

"We, love? I thought you could handle this by yourself."

Dealing with the Fire Warper was my task, but, for the rest, I required assistance. "I was wrong."

Valek heated water and filled the cast-iron tub. He removed my pile of burnt clothes. By the time I finished bathing, he had brought me a clean outfit.

"What's this?" He held Opal's glass bat.

I told him about my visit with Opal. "As a fellow artist, what do you think of the construction?"

Valek examined the statue, turning it this way and that. "It's an accurate reproduction. The coloring matches one of the smaller jungle bat species. It's sticky with magic. I feel it, but can't see it. Can you?"

"The inside glows as if molten fire has been captured by ice."

"That would be something to see, then."

Thinking about what the Fire Warper had done to show me his world, I touched Valek's shoulder and opened myself to him, letting him see the bat through me.

"Ahh...spectacular. Can everyone see this?"

"Only magicians." And the Commander, I thought.

"Good. That lays *that* debate to rest. I am *not* a magician."

"Then what are you? You're not a regular person either." Valek pretended to be mortified.

"Come on," I said. "Your skills as a fighter have an almost magical air. Your ability to move without sound and blend in with shadows and people seem extraordinary. You can communicate with me over vast distances, but I can't contact you."

"An anti-magician?"

"I suppose, but I'd bet Bain could find it in one of his books." I told Valek about the tunnel and about the Councilors' families, describing the pond to him.

He considered. "That sounds like Diamond Lake in the Jewelrose lands. It's near the Bloodgood border. The Jewelrose Clan had built a series of lakes that resemble shapes of jewels and the water reflects the colors."

"Why red?"

"Because the Jewelrose Clan is famous for cutting rubies into diamond shapes. The Commander even has a six-carat ruby on a ring, but he had stopped wearing it after the takeover. I wonder..." Again, Valek's gaze grew distant.

"What?"

He looked at me as if deciding whether to tell me something important. "Have you shown your bat to the Commander?"

"Yes."

"And?"

I hesitated. I had promised the Commander to keep what he called "his mutation" a secret. Would telling Valek about the bat break that confidence?

"I know about the Commander, love. How could you believe that I spent the last twenty-one years with him and *not* know?"

"I..."

"After all." Valek made a scary face. "I am the anti-magician!"

I laughed. "Why didn't you tell me?"

"For the same reason you didn't." He wrapped my bat and placed it back into my pack.

"The Commander saw the glow. I think his body contains two souls, but I have no idea how or why it's magical. And if he does have magic, why didn't he flame out after puberty?"

"Two? Ambrose's mother died during his birth and there was some confusion. The midwife insisted a boy had been born, but later his father held a baby girl. They searched for evidence of a second child but found nothing. They chalked it up to the midwife being upset about losing her patient. Ambrose used to blame this invisible twin whenever he was in trouble, which from his stories was quite often. His family indulged him when he began wearing boy's clothes and calling himself Ambrose. It seemed mild in comparison to a few of his other antics."

"Was his mother a magician?"

"She was considered to be a healer, but I don't know if she healed with magic or with mundane remedies."

Valek drained the tub while I attempted to do something with my ruined hair. Some sections remained long, while others had been burnt to stubble.

"Let me, love." Valek removed the brush from my hands. He rummaged around the bath area until he found his razor. "Sorry, nothing else will work."

"How did you get so good with hair?"

"Spent a season working undercover as Queen Jewel's personal groomer. She had beautiful, thick hair."

"Wait, I thought all the Queen's servants had to be women."

"Good thing no one thought to look up my skirt." Valek grinned with impish delight as he cut my hair. Large chunks floated to the ground. I stared at them, trying to convince myself losing my hair didn't matter. Especially not when I considered I wouldn't need it in the fire world.

After he finished, Valek said, "This will help with your disguise."

"My disguise?"

"Everyone's looking for you. If I disguise you as a man, you'll be much harder to find. Although…" He studied my face. "I'll use a little makeup. Being a man won't draw unwanted attention unless they notice you don't have any eyebrows."

I touched the ridge above my eyes with my fingertips, feeling smooth skin. I wondered if they would grow back. Again, I dismissed the notion. It wouldn't matter in the end.

"What should we do first? Try to find the tunnel to the

Keep, if it even exists. Or go and rescue the Councilors' families?" I asked.

"We should—" Valek sniffed the air as if he smelled a dangerous scent. "Someone's coming."

28

HE SIGNALED ME TO WAIT and left without a
sound. I grabbed my switchblade and crept through the living
room. A murmur of voices filtered in from the kitchen. The
door flew open as soon as I reached it. I brandished my knife
at the hulking figure in the doorway.

"What happened to your hair?" Ari demanded. "Are you
all right?"

Janco followed him in. "Look what happens when you
sneak off without us!"

"I'd hardly call being captured and taken to Sitia inside a box
sneaking off," I said.

Janco cocked his head this way and that. "Aha! You look
just like a prickle bush in MD-4. If we buried you up to your
neck, we could—"

"Janco." Ari growled.

"If you gentlemen are finished, I'd like to know why you
disobeyed my orders," Valek said.

Janco smiled one of his predatory grins as if he had anticipated this question and already composed an answer. "We did *not* disobey any of your orders. You said to keep an eye on Yelena's brother, the scary-looking big guy and the others. So we did."

Valek crossed his arms and waited.

"But you didn't specify what we should do if our charges came to Sitia," Ari said.

"How could they possibly escape the castle and get through the borders?" The expression on Valek's face showed his extreme annoyance.

Glee lit Janco's eyes. "That's a very good question. Ari, please tell our industrious leader how the Sitians escaped."

Ari shot his partner a nasty look, which didn't affect Janco's mood in the least. "They had some help," Ari said.

Again, Valek said nothing.

Ari began to fidget, and I covered my mouth to keep from laughing. The big man resembled a ten-year-old boy who knew he was about to get into a lot of trouble. "We helped them."

"*We?*" Janco asked.

"I did." Ari sounded miserable. "Happy now?"

"Yes." Janco rubbed his hands together. "This is going to be good. Go on, Ari. Tell him why—although, I think they magiked him." He waggled his fingers.

"They didn't use magic. They used common sense and logic." Valek raised an eyebrow.

"There're strange things going on here," Ari said. "If *we* don't put it right, then it'll spread like a disease and kill us all."

"Who told you this?" I asked.

"Moon Man."

"Where are they now?" Valek asked.

"Camped about a mile north of here," Ari said.

The drumming of horses reached us before Valek could comment. Through the window, I saw Kiki followed by Topaz, Garnet and Rusalka.

"How did they find us?" Icy daggers hung from Valek's voice.

Janco seemed surprised. "They didn't know where we were going. I told them to wait for us."

"Isn't it frustrating when no one obeys your orders?" Valek asked.

We went outside. Tauno rode on Kiki and she came straight to me. She bumped my chest with her nose. I opened my mind to her.

Don't go into fire again, she said.

I didn't reply. Instead, I scratched behind her ears as Tauno slid off her back. He greeted me with a cold look and returned to the others. Leif, Moon Man and Marrok lingered near their horses while they talked to Ari and Janco.

From Leif's various frowns and Tauno's scorn, I knew they remained angry with me. I couldn't blame them—I had acted badly. Liveliness lit Marrok's face and I hoped Moon Man had been able to weave his mind back into a coherent whole.

Everyone went inside, but I stayed behind, taking care of the horses as best as I could with half-burnt brushes and scorched hay. Part of the pasture's fence had caught fire and collapsed. I stared at the gap, knowing the well-bred Sandseed horses didn't need a fence and Onyx and Topaz would stay with them. However, I attempted to fix the broken section. And kept at it while the sun set and the night air turned frosty. Kept working even when the horses decided it was too cold in the open and left the pasture to find warmth under a copse of trees nearby.

Valek arrived. I pounded on a post with a heavy rock. He halted my swing and removed the rock from my hand.

"Come inside, love. We have plans to discuss."

Reluctance pulled at my feet as if I walked through thick, sticky mud.

The living-room conversation died the moment I entered. Moon Man looked at me with sadness in his eyes and I wondered if he knew about my deal with the Fire Warper or if he was disappointed by my actions.

A fire had been lit. I sat down next to it, warming my frozen and bleeding fingers, no longer afraid of the flames. The trapped souls within the fire twisted. Their pain and presence were clear and I wondered how I had been able to ignore them before.

I averted my gaze. Everyone stared at me. Ari and Janco had gained their feet and held their bodies as if ready to spring into action.

"Did I pass your test?" I asked. "By not diving into the flames."

"That's not it," Janco said. "You have a rather ugly bat clinging to your arm."

Sure enough, a hand-size bat peered at me from my upper left arm. His eyes glowed with intelligence; his claws dug into my sleeve. I offered a perch and he transferred his weight to the edge of my right hand. Carrying him outside, my efforts to release him failed. He didn't want to leave. Settling on my shoulder, he seemed content so I returned inside.

No one commented on my new friend. In fact, Leif regarded the bat with an intensely thoughtful expression.

The others waited. A moment passed until I realized they waited for me to begin. To make the decisions. To set events into motion. Even after leaving them as prisoners of the Commander, they still looked to me. And this time, instead of backing down and pushing them away, I accepted the responsibility. Accepted the fact that they might be hurt or killed, and understood my life would be given in exchange for keeping the Fire Warper from returning.

"Leif," I said.

He jumped as if bitten.

"I want you and Moon Man to get into the Council Hall's library and find everything you can about a tunnel into the Keep." I explained Bain's comments. "Moon Man can disguise himself as a Vermin and hopefully you won't be caught. Do not use magic at all from now on. It will only draw them to you."

Moon Man and Leif nodded.

"Marrok?"

"Yes, sir."

"Are you able to fight?"

"Ready, willing and *able*, sir."

I paused, swallowing a sudden knot in my throat. By their determined expressions, I knew they were *all* willing. At least Valek's smug smile was better than hearing him say, *I told you so*.

"Good. Marrok and Tauno will accompany Valek and me. We'll go south to rescue the hostages."

Ari cleared his throat as if he wanted to protest.

"I haven't forgotten about you two. I need you to go into the Citadel and help organize the resistance."

"Resistance?" Valek asked. "I hadn't heard."

"I put an idea into a merchant's head, and, I think if Ari and Janco disguised themselves as traders, they could move about the Citadel. Ari will have to dye his hair. Oh, and find a boy named Fisk. Tell him you're my friend and he'll help you make contacts."

"And when and where, Oh mighty Yelena, do we resist?" Janco asked.

"At the Keep's gates. As for when, I don't know, but something will happen and you'll know."

Janco and Ari exchanged a look. "Gotta love the confidence," Janco said.

"And when do we start, love?"

"Everyone get a good night's sleep and we'll begin preparations in the morning. We'll leave early. Do you have enough disguises for four of us or do we need to get supplies? Money?"

Valek smiled. "You mean raid some laundry lines? Steal a couple purses? No. My safe houses are well stocked with all types of items."

Leif was the only one to be alarmed by his statement.

The room erupted with the noise of multiple conversations. Plans were made and actions decided. Tauno's unhappiness at being separated from Moon Man became apparent. He asked why we wanted him. I explained about needing a good scout.

"What about Marrok?" he asked.

"We need him just in case they've moved the captives. He can track them to the new location." Also I wanted to talk to Marrok and find out why he had accused Leif and me of helping Ferde escape.

The next morning, my group saddled the horses. Since we wouldn't be crossing the Avibian Plains, Valek rode Onyx,

Tauno sat on Garnet and Marrok rode Topaz. Valek had used his skills to transform us into members of the Krystal Clan. We wore the light gray tunics and dark woolen leggings that the clan preferred, which matched the short hooded capes and black knee-high boots.

Before we left, Leif handed me a bunch of his herbs. "Since you can't use your magic, you might want to have them. There are directions on how to use each one inside the packet."

"Leif, I'm—"

"I know. Truthfully, I didn't like the distrustful and mean person you became in Ixia. The fire brought my real sister back. So be careful, as I'd like to keep her around for a while."

"You take care, too. Don't get caught. I wouldn't want to tell Mother about it. She wouldn't be pleased."

Leif looked at Ari and Janco. They fought over who would drive the wagon and who would guard. "Do they always argue?"

I laughed. "It's part of their appeal."

Leif sighed. "I'm amazed we made it to Sitia without being discovered." He paused and considered. "I think I'm actually going to miss them."

"I always do."

We set a time and place for everyone to rendezvous, knowing the cottage would no longer be safe. I said goodbye to Leif and the others and we headed west, hoping to reach the Krystal Clan's border by nightfall. We would follow the border south to the Stormdance lands. Then cross through Stormdance and Bloodgood before reaching Jewelrose's border.

Should anyone stop us on the road, we concocted a cover story. We were delivering samples of quartz to the Jewelrose

Clan. Irys's clan cut and polished gems and stones of all types. They designed and produced almost all the jewelry in Sitia.

Disguised as a man, I used the name Ellion, and asked everyone to call me by that name.

The day turned warm in the bright sunshine and we set a quick pace. Valek hoped the temperate weather would draw people onto the roads.

"Why?" Tauno asked.

"Then we will be one of many instead of the only ones," Valek explained. They rode together and talked about how best to find the barn that held the Councilors' family members.

Kiki stayed beside Topaz. She had missed his company and I wondered if Cahil mourned the loss of his horse. They had been together since Cahil was young. My eyes rested on Garnet. I cringed when I imagined facing the Stable Master's wrath. Garnet had been with us so long and I had lost the Avibian honey I had bought to appease the Stable Master. He would make me clean tack and scrub stalls for weeks. I snorted with amusement. I had found one positive thing about spending eternity with the Fire Warper: no mucking out.

And no bat. My new friend hung from the edge of my hood. His weight rested comfortably in the small of my back. He seemed content to sleep away the daylight hours with me.

Marrok remained quiet throughout the day, but I wanted to know what had happened to him at the Citadel.

"Cahil tricked me," he said when I asked. "I fell for his lies about remaining with Ferde to discover the extent of the Daviians' operations. Applauded his plan to lure Ferde back to the Citadel. Commiserated over your ill-timed interference.

He convinced me to confess and name you and Leif as accomplices. It would help him persuade the Council to attack Ixia. He promised…" Marrok paused, rubbing a hand along his right cheek. "After I confessed, he turned on me. A mistake I paid for…" He shuddered. "Am still paying for."

"Betrayals are brutal," I agreed.

Marrok looked at me in surprise. "Don't you think leaving us in Ixia was a betrayal?"

"No. That wasn't my intention. I wanted to protect you and was honest with all of you from the start. I just wasn't honest with myself. A mistake."

"You're still paying for?" Marrok smiled. The gesture smoothed out the lines of worry and time on his rugged face, erasing years from his age.

"Yes. It's the problem with mistakes, they tend to linger. But once we're done with the Vermin and Cahil, I will have paid for all my mistakes. In full."

Marrok gave me a questioning glance, but I didn't want to elaborate. Instead, I asked, "Do you remember your rescue from the Citadel?"

He grinned ruefully. "Sorry, no. At the time, I was in no condition to think. Moon Man is a wonder. I owe him my life." He glanced around then lowered his voice. "Being here without him, I feel…fragile. And that's hard for an old soldier to admit."

We rode the rest of the way in silence. Around midnight we set up camp. Funny how we automatically attended to the chores without discussion. Tauno hunted for rabbits and I cared for the horses. Valek searched for firewood and Marrok prepared the meal.

"I'm used to soldiers' rations on the road, so don't expect this to taste like Leif's," Marrok said as he dished out his version of rabbit stew.

The stew tasted a little bland but filled our stomachs. After dinner, we arranged our sleeping mats and set a watch schedule. I shared a blanket with Valek, wanting to be near him. I clutched him tight.

"What's the matter, love," he whispered in my ear. "You're rarely this quiet."

"Just worried about the Councilors' families."

"I think we have things well in hand. Between my sleeping potion for the guards, your Curare for the Warpers and the element of surprise, we should rescue them in no time."

"But what if one of the captives is sick? Or dying? If I use my magic, I risk letting the Vermin know where I am and what I've been doing."

"Then you'll have to decide what is more important—one person's life or the success of the mission for Sitia's future. It's pointless to worry. Instead, use your energy to decide how you would react to each contingency you can imagine. It's more prudent to prepare for all possibilities than fret."

He was right. Eventually, I slept.

Shadows haunted my sleep. They roamed the shadow world, lost and afraid. Whenever the bright heat would appear, they hid and waited for the hot hunter to dissipate. Each time, the hunter captured more of them in his net of fire. They didn't understand why he came and they knew nothing about the bridge to the sky. They clung to this world, desiring revenge and justice. The shadows needed a guide to convince them to let go and to show them the way.

★ ★ ★

"Ellion...Ellion...Yelena! Wake up."

I pushed the arm away, wanting to roll over. "Tired," I mumbled.

"Yes, we *all* are. But it's your turn," Valek said.

I blinked. My eyelids would not stay open.

"There's a pot of tea on the fire." When I failed to move, Valek pushed me off the mat and curled in my place under the covers. "Ahh. Still warm."

"You're evil," I said, but he feigned sleep.

We had been on the road for the past four days, riding every minute we could to turn a seven-day journey into five days. And since Tauno had left before dinner to scout the area ahead, we had one less to guard the camp.

My bat swooped over the rising heat of the fire. He'd been staying with me during the day and hunting food at night. I longed to fly with him, soaring over the ground.

Tauno returned the next morning to report no signs of activity along our path to the Jewelrose border. "There is a good site to camp about two miles south of the border," he said. "I will join you there." He left.

I wondered what had kept him awake. Unlike Tauno, I had had a few hours' sleep last night. Perhaps I shouldn't complain anymore.

We packed and followed Tauno's trail. Another uneventful day and we found the camp location without any problems. Tauno reappeared with dinner hanging from his belt.

"I discovered the location of the barn," he said, while butchering the rabbits. "It is four miles west of here in a little hollow."

Valek quizzed him for the details. "We'll have to strike in the dark," he said. "We'll go after midnight, leave the horses in the trees and then attack."

Tauno agreed. He cubed the meat and dropped it into the pot. "I will sleep, then."

While Marrok stirred the stew, Valek prepped the reed pipes and I saddled the horses. Garnet sighed when I cinched his straps tight.

"It's not far," I said aloud. "Then you can rest."

I joined Marrok and Valek where they sat by the fire. They ate their stew and I filled a bowl for me. The broth tasted better; there was a hint of spice.

"This is good," I said to Marrok. "I think you're getting the hang of it. What did you add?"

"A new ingredient. Can you tell what it is?"

When I sampled another spoonful, I rolled the liquid around my mouth before swallowing. The aftertaste reminded me of Rand's favorite cookie recipe. "Ginger?"

Valek dropped his stew. He jumped to his feet but stumbled. A look of horror creased his forehead. "Butter root!"

"Poison?"

"No." He sank to his knees. "Sleeping draft."

29

VALEK COLLAPSED ONTO the ground. But just before he closed his eyes, he winked at me. I glanced around. Marrok hunched over his bowl, appearing to be asleep. A bone-deep fatigue spread throughout my body, but I remained awake. Perhaps I hadn't swallowed enough butter root.

Not wanting to be caught "aware," I pulled my switchblade and hid the weapon in the palm of my hand with my thumb resting on the button. Slumping over, I let my upper body fall to the side. The stew spilled off my lap and onto the ground, soaking into my pants. Great.

I feigned sleep. My muscles stiffened and the cold seeped into my skin. Trying not to shiver, I strained to hear any noise to give me a hint of what was going on.

The horses whinnied in alarm and I opened my mind to Kiki for the first time in days, hoping the tiny use of my magic wouldn't alert anyone.

Bad smell, she said. *Quiet Man tied reins.*

Quiet Man?

She huffed and showed me an image of Tauno.

Why would he do that?

Ask Garnet.

Where did you go today, Garnet? I asked.

See people. Smell fear.

I cut off the connection when voices approached.

"So easy! All the talk about the Soulfinder and the Ghost Warrior and look at them! Sleeping like babies," a male voice said.

"Trust is a powerful ally. Right, Tauno?" a female voice asked. She had the same lilt as a Sandseed.

Was Tauno in league with them? Or had they captured him today and forced him to help them?

"Yes. And trust is blind. No one suspected me even after the ambush in the plains." He laughed. "Trust is for stupid people. Even the Sandseed Elders had no idea. My ability to find the Daviian camps amazed them."

They chuckled, enjoying themselves. Anger seethed in my blood. Tauno could *trust* I would make him regret his actions.

As they decided what to do, I counted four distinct voices. Two men and one woman plus the traitor Tauno. They planned to use Marrok to appease the Council, and bring me to their leader, Jal.

"Kill the Ghost Warrior," one of the Vermin ordered. "Make sure you cut his throat and collect his blood. It will be just revenge for Alea and her brother."

I waited. Arms wrapped around my chest and another set around my ankles. They lifted me off the ground.

"Now!" Valek yelled.

I triggered my switchblade and yanked my knees toward my

chest, pulling the surprised Vermin holding my feet into my knife. Hot blood gushed onto my hands. I wrenched the blade out of his stomach before the other Vermin dropped me onto the ground. I scrambled to my feet as he pulled his scimitar.

Switchblade against scimitar. Bad odds. And I had used the Curare on my weapon on the first man. This wouldn't be a long fight. I glanced at Valek. He fought Tauno and the woman. His sword against their spears. Better odds. I hoped I could last long enough for Valek to help me.

"Drop your weapon," the Vermin ordered me.

When I didn't obey, the man swung and I dodged to the side. He lunged. I backed away. He swiped at my neck. I ducked. He hacked and I danced.

Winded with the effort, the Vermin said, "You will not be harmed if you surrender."

After another attack, I realized what he was doing. "You're not allowed to kill me," I said. "Jal wants me alive so he can feed me to his pet Fire Warper!"

My smugness infuriated him. He increased the pace of his swings. Bad decision.

"I can still hurt you. Bleed you. Torture you."

His blade sliced through my cape. I stepped back as blood welled from the slash along my arm. Really bad decision. He advanced. I retreated. His scimitar found more open areas and soon my arms and legs were crisscrossed with bleeding cuts. I felt light-headed and my feet moved with an unusual slowness. My energy drained at an alarming rate.

My bat appeared. He flew at the Vermin, diving and pulling his hair. The Vermin flailed his arms, giving me an opening, but my switchblade felt so heavy and my body reacted too slowly. The Vermin must be a strong Warper. He had weakened my mental defenses without my notice.

The Warper stared at the bat and the poor creature crashed to the ground.

"Is that all you have?" he asked. "What about your great soul magic? I think the Fire Warper will be disappointed." He shrugged. "Orders are orders."

He swung his weapon. My arms moved, but couldn't block the hilt of his scimitar from striking my temple.

My vision blurred as I crumpled to the ground. The world spun. I rolled away from the Warper. When I reached Kiki's hooves, I let the blackness claim me.

A hammer pounded on the side of my skull. Wake up, it pounded. Open your eyes. More hammering. I refused. The next time, a dull throb intruded on my oblivion. Come on, it pulsed. Open your eyes. Please.

I woke, feeling like a cutting board. My arms and legs burned with pain and my head hurt. Valek hunched over me, pouring water on my cuts, inflaming them.

"Ow! Stop that," I said.

"Finally," he said. But he didn't stop. He dabbed at them, cleaning the lacerations, and sat back on his heels. "That'll have to do for now. Come on. We need to go."

When I failed to move, he pulled me into a sitting position. A wave of nausea swelled.

"Here." He thrust red leaves into my hands. "I found them in your saddlebags. The note said to eat them for head pain."

I chewed one. My stomach settled, but my sight remained blurry. I peered into the semidarkness, assuming the fuzzy white blob in the sky meant the moon had risen. Had I slept all day? Valek's words finally sank in.

"Go where?" I asked.

Valek yanked me to my feet. "We need to find the barn."

My thoughts still moved as if coated with sap. "Barn?"

Valek shook the rest of the canteen's water onto my shorn head. A jolt went through me when the cold breeze hit my wet skull.

"When the Vermin don't come back with us, the others will know something has happened and will either kill their hostages or move to another location." Valek ennunciated each word as if speaking to a simpleton. "Here." He handed me a set of clothes. "Hurry."

I changed. The carnage around our campsite made me sick and I sucked on another red leaf. Valek had killed the woman and Tauno. Traitor! Marrok remained where he had fallen asleep. And the Warper lay on his side. His head looked misshapen, as if kicked by a horse.

Kiki? I asked.

Bad man. No one hurt Lavender Lady.

Thanks.

Peppermints?

When we're done. And apples, too!

I wore my coral-colored shirt and matching skirt/pants. They reflected the moonlight. No hope for me to blend in. Valek dressed in the Warper's clothes and he applied makeup to match the Warper's skin tone. Fear twirled up my spine as I figured out what he planned. At least, I wasn't going to be bait for a necklace snake. This time.

We untied the other horses. The smell of blood made them skittish, and they were happy to leave despite being tired. Valek and I rode Kiki and Onyx while leading the others. We traveled the four miles to the barn in silence. Approaching the edge of the woods with care, I strained to see a sign of the Vermin hideout. An eerie red glow shimmered above Diamond Lake. The small structure looked deserted, but after a moment, the figures guarding the doors became visible.

"Which horse?" I asked.

"Onyx. Kiki is too well-known."

I dismounted and told the horses to stay in the woods until I called.

"Take off your cape," Valek said. "Lie in front of me." He took his foot from the stirrup.

I pulled myself up and lay across the saddle. He handed me my switchblade. The weapon had been cleaned and the blade was retracted.

"It's been primed with Curare." Valek grabbed the reins with his left hand and held a scimitar in his right.

"Pretend to be unconscious," he ordered as he clicked at Onyx.

We entered the open area, hopefully appearing as the Warper coming back with his prize.

Feigning to be a dead weight, I bounced on Onyx's saddle. The motion made me nauseous. A whoop of joy cut through the air as we neared. I prepared for Valek's signal.

"Where are the others?" a male voice asked.

"They're coming," Valek said in a rough tone.

"Finally! We have her!" another man said as he tugged my legs. "Help me."

Valek slid off on the opposite side of the saddle, keeping Onyx between him and the Vermin.

Another person joined in pulling me off. "We'll keep her

asleep until she reaches Jal. Get the wagon, you'll leave tonight," the man ordered. He cradled me in his arms.

"Where is Jal?" Valek asked.

The man froze and I risked a peek. The tip of Valek's
scimitar touched the Vermin's neck. Although armed with his
own scimitar and a spear strapped to his back, the Vermin's
hands held me.

"At the Magician's Keep. Go ahead and find Jal. Just make
sure to take *her* with you." The man tossed me at Valek and
yelled for help.

At that close distance, even Valek couldn't dodge out of the
way. I hit him in the chest. We tumbled to the ground, but I
kept going until I cleared his body. Jumping to my feet, I spun
in time to see Valek rolling away to avoid being sliced by the
Vermin's blade.

Four more Vermin with weapons drawn ran toward us.

I triggered my switchblade and threw it at the Vermin attacking Valek. He grunted when the blade nicked his shoulder,
but he didn't stop. However, the Curare on my blade spread
throughout his body and paralyzed his muscles. I grabbed the
man's spear. Valek regained his feet and his weapon.

A mere second later, the others reached us.

Events blurred into one long fight. I used the spear's length
to my advantage, keeping the scimitars from reaching me.
After a fake to the midsection, I swept my opponent's feet out
from under him. I didn't hesitate to plunge the tip of the spear
into his neck. His soul rose from his body and hovered above
it. Should I help his soul?

Before I could decide, another man approached. But he
stopped and I felt strands of magic tug at my spear. A Warper

who could move objects. The spear flew from my grasp, turned and pointed straight at me.

"Jal wants me alive." I reminded him.

He advanced. "Why not use your power to stop me? Afraid the Fire Warper will tell Jal what you're doing?"

"Give the man a prize. Your intellect is truly amazing."

The spear's tip came closer and poked me in the hollow of my throat. "Surrender or I'll skewer her," the Warper called to Valek.

Valek disengaged, his gaze questioning.

"He won't do it," I said to Valek.

"You are right. How about surrender or I will set the barn on fire?" The Warper pointed to the building. "Do you want to be responsible for the deaths of ten children?"

30

"NO! DON'T," I YELLED. "Let the children go and I'll come with you."

"I know you will," the Warper said. "I am more concerned about the Ghost Warrior." He looked at Valek. "Put your weapon down."

Valek placed his scimitar on the ground, but as he straightened, he flicked his hand twice. A small dart pricked the Warper's neck. The man jerked in surprise.

"Move," Valek ordered.

I twisted, avoiding the spear's thrust, but I wasn't fast enough to stop the sharp edge from cutting a gash across my neck. A line of stinging pain registered in my mind. It was forgotten as soon as I saw the Warper turn. Fire erupted under the barn's door. He collapsed beside his colleague, finally overcome by Valek's sleeping potion.

Smoke reached my nose, igniting memories of dread and fear.

"Valek, go!" I waved him on and whistled for the horses. They came and I raced toward the barn. *Kiki help!* I said.

Valek had gotten the burning door opened, but flames crept toward the roof. Topaz and Onyx shied away from the acrid smoke, but Kiki and Garnet braved the heat.

"Tell them to move to the left side," I yelled to Valek over the roar.

He sprinted through the opening and I led Kiki and Garnet to the right side. I waited for two horrible seconds then banged on the barn's wall.

Kiki. Garnet. Kick. I dived to the side. The animals aimed their back hooves and punched a hole in the wall with their powerful legs.

When the opening was big enough for the adults, I stopped the horses. Pulling a few splintered boards clear, I looked inside and called to the captives. Even with the bright firelight, the room was obscured by smoke. But a person grabbed my hand. I pulled coughing children through the hole, counting them as they came out.

The smoke thickened and the inferno advanced.

When Councilor Greenblade's husband crawled out with a small child clinging to his back and a baby clutched to his chest, my count totaled ten children and one adult.

"Where's Gale?" I asked.

Hacking with the effort to expel the smoke from his lungs, he pointed through the opening. "Collapsed." He wheezed for air. "Couldn't take…them all."

I moved to go in, but he pulled me back.

"Roof." He coughed.

We shooed the children away from the barn mere moments before the roof buckled with a shower of sparks and an explosion of sound.

I counted children again. Ten. One adult. No Gale. No Valek. He was still in the barn!

Horror and anguish twisted around my throat and shredded my heart. I bolted toward the blazing building. The heat rolled off the structure, pushing me back. Roof beams had fallen on top of the Vermin. The flames lapped at their bodies and sucked their souls into the inferno.

A porthole into the fire world opened in front of me. I could have grabbed one of the Vermin's souls and returned to the Fire Warper. But I wasn't ready. I had a few more things to accomplish and a few goodbyes to make before I embraced the fire.

Then I would crave the fire. Living in this world without Valek held no appeal for me.

The blaze raged all night. By morning it settled into a large smoldering heap. Still too hot for me to search among the ruins for some sign of Valek or Gale. Instead, I led the children over to Diamond Lake to get cleaned up and tried to ignore the grief burning inside me.

Councilor Greenblade's husband, Kell, helped feed the children and tend their wounds. Kiki and Garnet drank from the lake, and I washed the soot from their coats. The water was clear. The red color came from the bottom of the lake as if someone had painted the rocks and gravel. Perhaps they had. After all, it was a man-made lake.

When everyone's needs were met, we headed back to the campsite. We found Marrok engaged in the grim task of burying bodies.

"Guess I slept through the battle," he said. "Did we win?" He inclined his head to Tauno. "Or lose?"

"Both," I said. My anguish over Valek threatened to push from my throat. I bit down hard on my lip, tasting blood.

"Care to explain?"

I filled him in on what had happened. He accepted Tauno's betrayal with a cynical snort and a wry twist of the lips that reflected his black thoughts about trust.

After I finished, he said, "At least your little friend is all right."

"Friend?"

He pointed to a nearby tree. "I thought he was dead, but when I went to pick him up he flew off. Scared the heck out of me."

I went over. My bat hung upside down on a low branch. The creature opened an eye halfway then closed it again, contented. Somehow I had created an emotional link with the bat that was similar to my link with Kiki.

Contemplation about my affinity for animals would have to wait, though. More pressing matters needed to be addressed— finding Valek's body, for one. But I said, "We have to find a safe place for the Councilors' family members."

Bavol Zaltana's daughter, Jenniqilla, pulled at my cape. "I want to go home," she said. Although happy to be free, sadness touched her eyes and weariness lined her young face.

I crouched down next to her. "I know, but I need you to pretend you're still a hostage for just a little while longer. It's really important. Can you help us out?"

Determination filled her eyes, reminding me of Fisk. I assigned all the older children small jobs, and they moved about with a renewed sense of purpose.

"What about me?" Kell Greenblade asked.

The Greenblade lands were east of Bloodgood's. "Do you know anyplace where we can hide all of you?"

He gazed off into the distance. Tall and wiry, he resembled my friend, Dax, another member of his clan. I hoped Dax and Gelsi were all right, and the thought of them being the next victims of the Kirakawa ritual made me restless to get moving.

Kell sensed my mood. His attention focused on me. "My sister has a farm outside of Booruby that could hold all of us."

"In the Cowan Clan's lands?"

"Yes." He tsked. "She married a flatlander, but he's a good man and will help us."

I looked at the ragtag group of children. Booruby was farther east than I had wanted to travel and it would be a slow trip.

Kiki nickered at me. *Get wagon*, she said.

The wagon was burned in the fire.

I felt her huff of impatience. *Horses run off. Take wagon.*

Where are they?

Stuck. Come. Kiki flicked her tail.

Marrok came with me. We mounted Kiki and she went southwest through a small wood.

What about Onyx and Topaz? I asked her.

I felt her sorrow. *Can't smell.*

We reached the wagon. When the fire had erupted, the panicked horses had bolted through the woods until the cart wedged between two trees. The animals had calmed, but their raised heads and alert ears meant they felt unsafe.

The wagon had been filled with empty coffin-shaped crates, but we found a toolbox underneath the floor. Getting the wagon free was difficult and time-consuming.

While fixing the broken wheel, Marrok lost his patience and

shooed me away. "You're rushing and making it worse. Go take a walk, Yelena. This is a one-person job anyway."

When I hesitated, he added, "Go look for him or you won't find peace. And we won't either."

Being busy had been good. Walking through the quiet forest, there was nothing to distract me from my flaming thoughts. No respite from the wrenching pain deep inside me. It felt as if I had swallowed a red-hot coal.

The barn's ashy remains drifted in the air. Only a few beams at the edge of the structure retained their shape. Everything else had been reduced to gray and white cinders. Smoke curled from a few hot spots, but otherwise a pine-scented breeze blew the acrid fumes away.

The crunch of my boots on the residue echoed a lonely and final sound in my ears. All hope disappeared when I found Valek's knives. Blackened and misshapen, the blades were half-melted. I collapsed to my hands and knees and sobbed, turning the ash under me into slurry. Gasping, ribs aching and throat raw, I tried to expel the smoldering sadness within, only stopping when all moisture was gone from my body. I sat back on my heels and wiped my face, smearing soot and tears.

Once my breathing returned to normal, I scooped up a handful of the ash near Valek's weapons and let the wind scatter them. Soon, love. I'll join you soon. The knowledge of our reunion in the other world was my only comfort.

Eventually I returned to Marrok. He had fixed the wheel. After looking at my face, he squeezed my shoulder. I had washed off the dirt, but I knew my eyes were red and puffy from crying.

Marrok steered the wagon, but finding a road around the wood used up our remaining daylight.

By the time we returned to the camp, Kell had settled the children next to the fire. I wanted to wake everyone and get moving, but Kell convinced me the children would be upset by being roused and hidden in those crates at night. After recalling my own horrible experience with the boxes, I agreed.

If Valek hadn't shot the Warper, I would have been shoved inside one of those crates. The Councilors' families would still be hostages, but Valek and Gale would still be alive.

I stared at the sleeping children. Jenniqilla had a protective arm over Leevi and the baby curled next to him, sucking on his thumb even while asleep. In that state, they embodied innocence and peace and joy and love. Valek had known the risk when he went into the barn and he hadn't hesitated. I would have done the same. Eleven living beings for one unselfish act. Pretty good odds.

Even with the wagon, the trip to Booruby lasted four days. Four days of worry, frustration, hunger, sleepless nights and noise. By the time we arrived, I had a new appreciation for parents, and was as glad to see Kell's sister as she was to see us. She wrapped Kell in a tight embrace for many heartbeats. I bit my lip and turned away. My empty arms ached.

Located about two miles south of Booruby, the farmstead appeared to be isolated from its neighbors, but her husband was quick to usher us inside. The children were fed their first hot meal in weeks. Marrok and I made plans to return to the rendezvous location to join the others. I kept my mind focused on action; otherwise, I knew I would surrender to the grief consuming me from the inside out.

We would risk crossing through the western edge of the

Avibian Plains. Garnet and Kiki's gust-of-wind gait would make up for the time lost traveling to Booruby.

Before leaving, Kell asked me, "How will I know when it's safe for the children to return home?"

I considered. "If everything works out, you will receive a message."

"And if it doesn't work out?"

Emotion choked his words, reminding me that his wife was one of the Councilors. If I failed, she would be among the first of many casualties.

"If you don't hear anything after fourteen days, that means the Daviians are in charge. Send the children to their homes and hope."

"Hope for what?"

"Hope a person in the future will be strong enough to rebel against the Daviian Vermin. And win."

Kell looked doubtful. "We have four Master Magicians and a Soulfinder, yet they still managed to take control."

"It has happened before. One person *can* bring peace to Sitia."

I didn't add that the man had leveled the Daviian Mountains in the process. But it did lead me to wonder if the Sandseeds' legendary warrior had had help. My mind reviewed Moon Man's story about the origins of the Sandseed Clan and I remembered the warrior's name was Guyan. Guyan had imprisoned the Fire Warper, and his descendant, Gede, had freed him. A complete circle.

Marrok and I said goodbye to Kell and the children. We traveled northwest, planning to skirt Booruby on our way to the plains. My little bat hung from Kiki's mane and didn't appear to be bothered by the jostling motion.

Our plans changed when I spotted Opal's family's glass factory in the distance and I had a sudden idea.

Before I could fully explore my intentions, we stopped outside their gate. Marrok accepted our detour without concern.

"Should I wait here?" he asked.

"Yes. I won't be long." I left Kiki with him.

As I approached the door to their house, Opal came out of the factory. She hesitated, but drew nearer, eyeing Marrok and me with suspicion.

"Can I help you, sir?" she asked me.

I had forgotten all about my hair. At least I knew my disguise worked. I smiled for the first time in days.

She squinted at me. "Yelena?" Then she glanced around in concern. "Come inside! There's a price on your head!" She ushered me into the house.

"Thank goodness you're okay." Opal squeezed me in a quick hug. "What happened to your hair?"

"It's a long long story. Is your family around?"

"No. They went into town. Father received a shipment of sand that was full of rocks so he went to complain and Mother—"

"Opal, I need more of your glass animals."

"Really? Did you sell the bat?"

"No. However, I discovered I can use your animals to communicate with other magicians far away without using my own magic. I'd like to buy as many as I can."

"Wow! I never knew."

"How many do you have?"

"Six. They're in the factory."

She set a quick pace as we crossed the yard and entered the factory. The heat from the kilns sucked all the moisture from my mouth. I followed her through the thick air and roar of the fires. Lined up on a table by the back wall were half a dozen glass animals. They all glowed with an inner fire.

Opal wrapped the animals and I counted out coins. Another idea flashed in my mind when she handed me the package.

"Can you show me how you make these?" I asked.

"It takes a lot of practice to learn."

I shook my head. "I just want to watch you make one."

She agreed. Picking up a five-foot-long hollow steel pipe, she opened the small door to the kiln. Bright orange light and intense heat emanated from the doorway, but, undaunted, she dipped the end of the pipe into a large ceramic pot inside the kiln that was filled with molten glass. Turning the pipe, she gathered a taffylike slug and pulled it out, closing the door with her hip. The slug pulsed with a red-hot light as if alive.

"You have to keep the blowpipe spinning or the glass will sag," Opal said over the noise. She rolled the slug over a metal table to move the glass off the end of the pipe and shaped it so the pipe looked as if it had a clear ball attached to its end.

Her motions quick, Opal then rested the pipe on the edge of the table and blew into the other end. Magic brushed my arm as her cheeks puffed. The glass on the opposite end didn't inflate with air. Instead, a thread of magic was trapped within its core.

"It's supposed to expand, but mine never does," she said as she went back to the kiln and gathered another slug overtop the first. She took the pipe to a bench designed to hold it and other metal tools needed to shape the glass. Buckets of water sat within easy reach.

Opal grabbed a pair of steel tweezers and pinched and squeezed the slug with her right hand while rolling the pipe with her left hand the whole time. "You have to move quickly because it cools fast."

Within seconds the ball transformed into a cat sitting on its back legs. She stood and put the cat back into the kiln, but this time she just spun the pipe above the pot. "You have to keep plenty of heat in the glass or you can't work with it."

Sitting back on her bench, Opal exchanged her tweezers for another set. These were bigger and as long as her forearm. "Jacks, a great all-purpose tool. I'm putting in a jack line so I can crack the piece off the pipe."

When the groove was to her liking, she took the tweezers in hand again and dipped them into the bucket of water. She dribbled a few drops into the jack line. "You have to be careful not to get water onto your piece. So you move from the pipe down." The glass hissed and a spiderweb of cracks spread over the glass on the pipe.

She carried the pipe to another oven close to the kilns. Shelves of trays had been stacked inside and Opal banged the end of the tweezers on her pipe. The cat fell onto the tray. She closed the door.

"If the glass cools too fast, it'll crack. This is an annealing oven." Opal pointed to the tracks underneath the oven. "To slowly cool the piece, the oven is pulled away from the kiln over the next twelve hours."

"Why do you blow into the pipe if the glass doesn't expand for you?" I asked.

"It's a step I have to do." She made a vague motion with her arms as if casting about for the right words. "When Mara does it, she makes beautiful vases and bottles. Mine always ends up looking like an animal and if I don't blow into the pipe it doesn't look like anything at all."

She cleaned up her work area, taking the tools from the water and drying them before replacing them. The bench needed to be ready for the next project, and working with glass didn't give you time to search for tools.

"I love creating things. There's nothing like it," she said, more to herself than to me. "Working the glass. Turning fire into ice."

I thanked Opal for her demonstration and rejoined Marrok. He leaned against Garnet.

"I think your definition of 'won't be long' doesn't match mine," he said by way of a greeting. "Did you encounter another change in plans?"

"Yes. You might as well get used to them."

"Yes, sir!" He grinned.

"Sarcasm? You've been hanging around with Leif too long. What happened to the tough old soldier who mindlessly follows orders?"

His demeanor sobered. "He lost his mind. And when he found it again, his priorities had all been rearranged."

"For the better?"

"Only time will tell."

We mounted and headed to the western edge of the Avibian Plains. Once in the plains, Kiki and Garnet broke into their gust-of-wind gaits and flowed over many miles. We camped outside the plains at night. I hoped our passage wouldn't attract any unwanted attention. My thoughts lingered on Opal's glassmaking skills. Better than giving in to the deep despair that threatened to overwhelm me whenever I thought of Valek.

Our journey to the rendezvous location lasted three days. During that time, Marrok had spotted signs of a large army that had crossed from the Avibian Plains and turned north toward the Citadel. At night, the glow of many fires lit the distant sky and wood smoke tainted the air.

We had agreed to meet Moon Man and the others in Owl's Hill, a small town within the Featherstone lands. According to Leif, the Cloverleaf Inn's owner could be trusted not to report us. "He owes me one," had been Leif's explanation.

Owl's Hill was located on a small rise about three miles northeast of the Citadel. The four towers of the Magician's Keep were visible from the road into town. A bright orange radiance shone from within the Keep's walls. The Fire Warper's home fire?

Still disguised as Krystal Clan traders, Marrok and I entered the town. Situated near the main crossroads, the Cloverleaf Inn's common room bustled with activity, but the stable was only half full. The stable lad suggested we arrive early for dinner as the inn was a popular stop for caravans.

"One less night of road rations," the boy said as he helped me rub down Kiki. "And the merchants prefer camping near here instead of overnighting in the Citadel."

"Why is that?" I asked.

"The rumors have been wild, so I don't know what to believe. But the merchants who do come back say everyone is afraid of these new Daviians and they say the Daviians have convinced the Council to prepare for a war."

"With Ixia?"

"Don't know. They've drafted every able-bodied person. Benn said the Daviians are in league with Ixia, and once a person's drafted they hypnotize him. They plan to use them in the army to turn Sitia into another Ixian Military District. MD-9!"

The boy regaled me with even wilder speculation. I knew the Commander wasn't in league with the Daviians, but the possibility of using the Sitian army against Sitia sounded like a Vermin tactic.

When we finished with the horses, I entered the inn. Marrok had already paid for two rooms for the night.

"We're running out of money," he said.

"Are the others here?" I asked.

"Ari and Janco are in the dining room. Leif and Moon Man haven't arrived yet."

That worried me. It had been thirteen days since we had left to rescue the hostages. Plenty of time for them to discover anything about the Keep's emergency tunnel.

In the back corner of the inn's common room, Ari and Janco held court. Drinking from tankards of ale, they were surrounded by a group of merchants. Serious expressions gripped all their faces and they peered at us with suspicion.

Marrok and I picked a table on the far side of the room. Eventually, the knot of people disbanded and Ari and Janco joined us. Ari had dyed his hair black and both of them had darkened their skin.

"Janco, do I see freckles?" I asked, failing to suppress a snicker.

"Don't laugh. It's this southern sun. It's the middle of the cold season and it's sunny! Bah." He looked at me. "Although, I'd rather have freckles than be bald!"

I put my hand to my hair. "It's growing."

"Enough," Ari said, and the mood around our table immediately dampened. "Were you successful?"

The question stabbed into me as if his words were flaming daggers. I struggled to collect my thoughts; to shoo my emotions away from the black, burning grief that refused to die down. Marrok saw my inability to answer and he told them about Tauno, the rescue and about Valek. To see my pain and shock reflected in my friends' eyes became unbearable. I excused myself and went outside.

Taking deep breaths of the cool night air, I wandered through the town. A few people walked along the dirt streets, carrying lanterns. I felt a tug on my cape as my bat landed on my arm. He stared at me with a sense of purpose in his eyes then flew off to the left. He returned, swooping around my head and again flew to the left. Getting the hint, I followed him until we reached a dilapidated building.

The bat settled on the roof as if waiting. I pulled the warped door open with trepidation, but the interior held a collection of discarded barrels and broken wagon wheels. When I turned to leave, I stepped on a wooden ball. A child's toy. I picked it up and examined it. My bat wanted me to find or see something in here.

I squashed my growing frustration and concentrated on using my other senses. Closing my eyes, I inhaled. The musty smell of decay dominated, but I detected a faint whiff of lemons. I followed the clean and pure scent—not easy as I tripped and banged my shins on the clutter—until I stood in the back corner. There a tingle danced on my skin, raising the hair on my arms. Instinctively I whispered, "Reveal yourself," and opened my eyes.

Gray light bloomed before me and transformed into a young boy. He sat on one of the barrels.

A ghost. A lost soul.

"Where is my mother?" he asked with a thin, tentative voice. "She was sick, too. She went away and never came back even when I cried for her."

I moved closer to the boy. The light from him illuminated the room. The rusted remains of a bed frame and other items indicated the area had been used as the child's bedroom long ago.

My bat fluttered in and circled above the boy's head. I waved it away and muttered, "Yes, yes, I know. I get it."

With a squeal sounding like an exasperated *finally,* he flew out.

I asked the child questions about his mother and family. Just as I suspected, they had lived and died here many years ago.

"I know where they are," I said. "I can take you to them."

The boy smiled. When I held out my hand, he grabbed it. I gathered him to me, inhaling his soul before sending it to the sky.

The true job of a Soulfinder.

Not to save souls and return them to their bodies, but to guide them to where they belonged. My true purposed flared to life finally. Stono and Gelsi should have both been released to the sky. Their personalities changed because they were unhappy at being denied peace.

Death was not the end. And I knew Valek waited for me, but he wouldn't want to see me until I finished finding all the lost and misplaced souls and sent them to their proper destinations.

There hadn't been a Soulfinder in over a hundred and

twenty-five years. Why wasn't Sitia filled with lost souls? Perhaps they were rare.

Renewed determination to find a way to defeat the Fire Warper spread throughout my body. I left the building and stopped. Five souls hovered in different locations along the street. The leathery flap of wings announced my bat's arrival. He settled on my shoulder.

"Did you call them?" I asked the bat. "Or did I?" I guess I should have been more specific when I called to the boy. Either that, or now I'd learned a trick I couldn't shut off.

I gathered and released souls as I headed back to the Cloverleaf Inn. Most went to the sky. One dripped with hate and when he sank into the ground, I worried I might have increased the Fire Warper's powers.

Before I could enter the inn, the clatter of hooves sounded behind me. I spun in time to see Leif stop Rusalka. His panic reached me before his words.

"Moon Man," he gasped. "Moon Man's been captured!"

31

BACK IN THE INN'S common room, the five of us sorted through all the details we had. Moon Man had been captured that afternoon.

"We found no references to the tunnel in the Council Hall's library," Leif said. "We were meeting with an old magician who was hiding from the Vermin. Another had told us he had information on the construction of the Keep, but when we talked to the magician he only had vague details. He knew how to create a null shield and he taught me how to make one. I shouldn't have tried it. The magic called the Warpers and we were attacked as we left his house."

"How did you get away?" Janco asked.

Leif threw his hands up. "One minute we're surrounded by Vermins, the next a group of brawling merchants and screaming children practically rolled over everyone. It was mass confusion. A man grabbed my hand and pulled me out. I hid until dark. One of the children from the Helping Guild told me Moon Man hadn't escaped."

"The Vermin will know we're here," Ari said. "We need to leave now. There's a caravan camping about two miles north of here. We can stay with them."

"Which way is the caravan going?" I asked Ari.

"They have a delivery in the Citadel tomorrow, and then they're going south to the Greenblade lands. Why?"

"Oh no!" Leif said. "She's got that look in her eyes. What are you scheming, little sister?"

"We have to get inside the Keep."

"Impossible. There's a bubble of protective magic around it. We couldn't find the entrance to the tunnel. A few Warpers have gained master-level power. You're powerful, but nowhere near their level. You'll be caught in an instant." Leif crossed his arms as if his statement ended the discussion.

"That's a great idea," I said.

"What?

I ignored Leif's confusion. "Ari, how ready are the people in the Citadel to revolt?"

"They're organized, have some weapons and a few magicians. What I would really like to do is run a few training sessions, but that's not going to happen. They're as ready as they're going to get."

"Would the caravan be willing to lend us one of their wagons?" I asked.

"Something could be arranged."

Comprehension dawned in Janco's face. "If we get you inside, can we keep the five golds?"

"Only if you get us back out again," I said.

"I don't like the odds," Janco said. He brightened. "Gotta love the underdog, though."

"There are *no* odds. It's suicide," Leif said.

"Look at it this way, Leif. It'll put an end to our arguing," I said.

"How?"

"We die, you're right. You don't die, I'm right."

"I feel *so* much better now."

Janco tsked. "Sarcasm is detrimental to the team spirit."

Ari frowned at me. "Don't you mean, *we* don't die, Yelena?"

I didn't answer. Valek waited on the other side. My reward.

We packed our supplies and headed out. The merchants of the caravan agreed to include us in their group and we spent most of the night preparing our wagon. When we finished with the cart's alterations, we stood around it, discussing the plan for the next day.

"Marrok, you'll ride Garnet. Janco can take Kiki, and Ari, you'll drive the wagon. No matter what happens, Ari, make sure we get to the Keep's gate," I ordered.

"Yes, sir."

"What about me and you?" Leif asked.

I grimaced. "We're the cargo." The last thing I wanted to do was get inside one of those crates again, but there was no other way. "Ari is going to use me to get us inside. He'll demand his five golds for bringing me to the Vermin."

"I never thought I'd miss my days as necklace snake bait," Leif said.

"What happens once we're inside?" Ari asked.

"That will be the signal for the Citadel's citizens to riot, which should keep a bunch of the Vermin and Warpers busy."

"But what about all those powerful Warpers?" Leif asked.

"Can you make a null shield?"

He hesitated. "Yes."

"When the riot starts, all the magicians will come to the Keep's gate and help you build and maintain a null shield," I said.

"But it won't last long."

"I just need a little time."

"Time for what?"

"To get to the Fire Warper."

Leif stared at me. "You can fight him?"

"No."

"Tell me again why this isn't a suicide mission."

"I think I can stop him and keep him in the fire world. And in doing so, I think I might be able to pull some of the Warpers' powers from them. If Bain and Irys are still alive, and if you round up as many magicians as you can, then you should be able to counter the Warpers."

"That's a lot of 'ifs' and 'thinks,'" Janco said.

"And there's no 'when,'" Ari said.

"When?" Leif asked.

"When she returns. There's a when, isn't there, Yelena?" Ari asked.

"The only way to keep him in the fire world is if I stay, too." The words tasted like ash in my mouth. Thinking about an event was completely different than stating it aloud. Once said, it was final. But Valek would be there and I *would* find him. No "if," "think" or "when" about it.

"There has to be another way," Leif said. "You always manage to produce ingenious plots."

"Not this time."

Everyone remained quiet.

I was about to suggest we all get a little sleep when Leif asked, "What if we can't counter the Warpers?"

"Then you'd better have a person who's unaffected by magic on your side," a voice said from beyond the wagon.

We all looked at one another. The same question perched on everyone's lips. A ghost voice?

"Although this time I would appreciate it if you didn't leave me behind." Valek stepped into view. He appeared to be solid. His angular face held annoyed amusement. The faint moonlight glinted off his bald head. He wore the brown tunic and pants of a Bloodgood clansman.

Disbelief followed surprise; I reached out to touch him. He pulled me close and my world filled with the sight, smell and feel of Valek.

Seconds, minutes, days, seasons could have passed and I wouldn't have noticed or cared. I clung to him as if my feet dangled over a precipice. His heart beat in my ear. His blood flowed in my veins. I molded my body to his solid flesh, wanting to fuse with him and let nothing—not even air— come between us.

Relief and joy frolicked in my heart, extinguishing the smoldering grief until I remembered my promise to the Fire Warper.

Blazing sadness ignited, flooding my senses. My reward for babysitting the Fire Warper would have to wait. Better to have him here.

I gathered my resolve and calmed myself. The others moved away, leaving Valek and me alone. His lips found mine. Our souls twined. The gaping emptiness inside me filled.

He pulled away, breathless. "Easy, love." His panting turned into a coughing fit.

"How did you survive the fire?" I asked. "The roof collapsed and you didn't…"

"Two things happened at once. At least, I think they did." He gave me an ironic smile. "I was carrying Gale when the roof fell. The force of it sent us through the floor and into a small root cellar." Valek rubbed his ribs and grimaced.

"You're hurt and I can't heal you!" A nasty gash snaked along the side of his skull.

"Just bruised." He ran a hand gently over his head. "A beam knocked me out and I would have probably died from the smoke and heat, but Gale kept us in a pocket of cool air. She had been hit by a piece of the barn's wall when it shattered. But she came to and used her magic. She conjured a cushion of air around us to keep the burning debris from filling our hole."

"Why didn't I see you the next morning? Why didn't you call out?"

"The roof had tented around us, and there was nothing you could do to help until the fire died." His hand went to his ribs again. "I didn't have enough air to yell and Gale needed all her strength to keep us alive."

"Why couldn't she blow the fire out? Or save the children?"

"Her powers are limited. It's all part of her weather dancing thing." He gestured past the wagon. "You can ask her. I've brought her along." When he saw my questioning look, he added, "We're going to need all the help we can get."

I looked on the other side of the wagon. Gale held Onyx's and Topaz's reins. Kiki had already found them and nuzzled Topaz. Garnet stood nearby. Gale's unease about being surrounded by horses was reflected in the queasy look on her face.

"Did you learn anything else?" I asked Valek.

"Yes. Finding clothes when you're half naked is harder than you think. And scared horses can travel pretty far in the wrong direction before you find them." He studied the group of horses. "Onyx and Topaz are fast, but there's nothing like a Sandseed horse when you're in a hurry. And despite your detour to Booruby, love, I had a hard time catching up."

"You could have found a way to tell me you were all right. I've spent the last week in utter misery."

"Now you know how I felt when you jumped into the stable fire. And you know how I'll feel if you don't come back from fighting the Fire Warper."

I opened my mouth then closed it. "You were eavesdropping."

"I had hoped to hear everyone discussing how much they missed my altruistic qualities, my legendary skills as a fighter and as a lover." He leered. "Instead, you're making plans for tomorrow. Interesting how life goes on in spite of itself."

Valek sobered and stared at me with a fiery intensity. "With all that planning, love, I'm sure you can figure a way to return."

"I'm not smart enough." My frustration wrapped around my chest and squeezed until I wanted to scream aloud. "I don't know enough about magic! I don't think anyone does. We're all just bumbling along, using it and abusing it."

"Do you truly believe that?"

"Yes. Although I'll admit to being a hypocrite. First sign of trouble and I fall back on using magic." My ability to guide souls hadn't taxed my energy like using magic. I didn't draw from the power source. It was a natural effort just like inhaling and exhaling. "When I think about magic, all I see is the harm it has done to this world."

"Then you're not looking in the right places."

And this from someone who was immune to magic's effects. I'd seen firsthand the Kirakawa ritual, the blood magic, the corruption of power, the Sandseed massacre and the tormented souls. It had to stop.

Valek studied my expression. "Think about what you said to the Commander about magic."

"I tend to agree with the Commander about how magic corrupts."

"Then why did you mention to the Commander how magic could harness the power of a blizzard and save his people instead of discussing the possibility of using power as a weapon? If magic corrupts, then why hasn't it corrupted you? Or Irys? Moon Man? Leif?"

"We haven't let it corrupt us."

"Right! You have the choice."

"But it's a very tempting choice. Power is addictive. It's only a matter of time."

"Oh yes. Sitia has been battling Warpers for ages. Though you wouldn't know it from all the peace and prosperity hanging around." Sarcasm dripped from Valek's words. "Let's see, how long ago did the magicians use blood magic? I think Moon Man told me two thousand years. Then you're right! It's only a matter of time. A matter of two thousand years. I'll take those odds any day."

"I never realized how annoying you can be."

"You know I'm right."

"I could prove you wrong. I can be corrupt." It was my turn to leer.

Valek looked over at Janco and the others. They milled

about a small fire, trying to appear nonchalant, but I knew they listened to every word.

"Not in front of the children, love. But I'll hold you to that."

The night disappeared in a hurry. We finished prepping the wagon and updating our plans to include Valek and Gale.

The others had taken Valek's return in stride, although Janco made a comment about Valek's lack of hair. "You ever notice how couples start to look alike?" he asked.

In a deadpan, Valek replied, "Yes. In fact, I was just thinking how much you and Topaz resemble each other. It's uncanny."

Ari chuckled at Janco's chagrined expression before saying, "The caravan is leaving soon. What part of the line do we want to be in?"

"Near the back, but not the last wagon," Valek instructed. "When we're out of sight of the gatehouse, head to the Keep."

"Yes, sir." Ari snapped to attention.

I stared at our small group. Marrok eyed Valek with dislike, but he had assumed the posture of a soldier waiting for orders. Leif chewed on his lip, a nervous habit. Gale's face was bleached with fear, but she set her mouth into a determined frown. She told me her power was weak compared to a Stormdancer, but she could agitate the wind and kick up enough dust to impair the Daviians' vision.

"We don't know what we'll encounter inside the Keep. Listen for instructions and follow orders even if they don't make sense," Valek ordered.

"Yes, sir," everyone said in unison, including Gale.

Before we could get into position, I handed three of Opal's glass animals to Leif and the other three to Gale.

"What are these for?" Leif asked.

"Keep one each, but give the rest to Moon Man, Irys, Bain and Dax if they're still alive." I swallowed the sudden lump in my throat. "I think I can use the animals to communicate with you when I'm in the fire world."

Leif peered at me with sad eyes, but I turned away before he could say anything. "Come on, you first." I gestured to the cart.

Leif, Gale and Valek hid in the three boxes at the bottom of the wagon. We put another empty crate and some genuine goods on top of them. Then I lay down inside the top crate.

When Marrok closed the lid, my heart slammed in my chest in a sudden panic. My throat closed when the rugs were piled on top. The wagon lurched. I wanted out. I felt trapped. The others could get out of their boxes through the hidden panels we had installed on the wagon's floor. I could not. This wasn't going to work. The Vermin would figure it out before we could reach the Keep. And then what would happen?

I drew in a few steadying breaths. We would be captured. I would be fed to the Fire Warper just like I wanted. All we would lose was the element of surprise. While helpful, I believed even with it the chances of the others living through the encounter were little to none.

My morose line of thought was not helping my state of mind. So I focused instead on the motion of the wagon. It had been a long and emotionally exhausting night. I fell asleep during the trip to the Citadel.

The sound of an unfamiliar voice roused me from sleep. We had stopped, and I gathered by the voices we were at the Citadel's north gate. The voices came closer and a person banged on my box. I jumped, clamping my lips against a shout.

"What's in this one?" a man asked.

"The finest silk sheets woven by the Moon Clan, sir," the merchant replied. "Perhaps you care to purchase a set? Just feel the fabric and you'll know your wife will be most anxious to try them out."

The man laughed. "I'll not be spending a month's pay for a night with my wife. That's why I married her."

Their laughter trailed away as the guard questioned the merchant on his reasons for entering the Citadel. After what seemed like hours, the wagon began to move. Ari picked up the pace and I guessed we had broken off from the caravan.

When the sounds from the market reached me, the wagon slowed. Ari called out to the stand owners, giving them the sign to prepare to revolt. A network of messengers would fan out to spread the news, then remain in place to deliver the signal for action.

The fighting would erupt when our wagon went inside the Keep. The cart turned around a corner. It stopped with a jerk.

Ari cursed and the jangle of many horses surrounded us. A familiar voice called out, "Oh no. This will not do."

Cahil.

32

CAHIL AND HIS MEN had found us. Trapped inside my crate, I could do nothing but wait for the inevitable. I hoped Valek and the others hiding in the wagon would be able to sneak away.

"I assume you have Yelena hidden somewhere in your wagon?" Cahil asked.

"Have who, sir?" Ari asked, playing innocent. "All I have is goods for the market."

"For the market? The market you just rode through without stopping to unload? I don't think so. Despite your disguises and weak attempts to explain your presence, I know who you are and why you're here. In fact, I was sent by Jal to come and escort you to the Keep."

I heard a creak as Ari shifted his weight and I detected a faint rustling from below me. Probably Valek opening his escape panel.

"Relax," Cahil said. "I'm not here to capture you. I'm here to join you. And I hope for the sake of all our lives you have a decent plan."

I had to let Cahil's words sink in. Had he just said he wanted to join us?

"A plan, sir?" Ari asked.

Cahil snorted with exasperation. "Yelena! Leif!" he called. "Come out and tell your big northern friend I'm telling the truth. Look for yourselves. My men have not drawn their—"

A surprised yelp followed a thud. Then Ari moved off the wagon and the rugs on top of my crate scraped away. The lid lifted. I had my switchblade in hand, but Ari's amused face greeted me. He helped me stand. Valek had a knife to Cahil's throat. He and Cahil were on the ground. Cahil's men remained on their mounts. The men appeared tense and alert but hadn't drawn any weapons. Leif and Janco joined Ari and all three pulled their blades. Marrok stayed on Garnet.

"Tell me why I shouldn't cut your throat?" Valek asked Cahil.

"You won't get into the Keep without me," he said. He kept still and held his hands up and away from his body.

"Why this sudden change of heart?" I asked.

Cahil's gaze met mine. Hatred still radiated from his eyes but the pain of betrayal tainted them. "You were right." He said each word as if it hurt him. "They're using me and…"

"And what?" I prompted.

"The rituals and killings have gotten out of hand. I can't be a part of it anymore." He looked at Marrok. "I wasn't raised to be a killer. I was raised to be a leader. I'll earn my throne the old-fashioned way."

Although the expression on Marrok's face never changed, his body relaxed.

"How do we know you're telling the truth?" Ari asked.

"Yelena knows through her magic."

I shook my head. "I can't use it. It will alert Jal and risk the mission."

"She already knows you're here. You have thwarted her a number of times, although it will be more difficult now, as she has gained an incredible amount of power through the Kirakawa ritual."

"She?" Valek and I asked in unison.

"We thought Jal was Gede," I said.

Cahil blinked at us for a moment. "You didn't know? What else don't you know? You *were* planning an attack at the Keep, right? I thought you had it all figured out."

"You thought wrong," I said, annoyed. "We had to guess about the state of affairs inside the Keep."

"Then here's a way for me to prove my loyalty. I'll tell you what's been going on and will help you get inside. Agreed?"

Valek and I exchanged a glance.

"Do I still get to kill him?" Valek asked.

"At the first sign of betrayal, yes," I said.

"What about after this is all over?"

"Then it's your call."

Cahil stared at us. "Hold on. I'm risking my life to help you. I'd like some guarantees."

"We've come to a point where there are no guarantees. For any of us," I said.

"That's not very encouraging," Cahil said.

"It's not supposed to be. You should know what happens when you play with fire, Cahil. Eventually, you'll get burned. Now, tell us what you know," I ordered.

Valek removed his knife from Cahil's throat and stepped

back. Cahil scanned the area. We had attracted quite the crowd, but I saw to my relief that there were no Vermin among them. Then it hit me—why not? I asked Cahil.

He gave me a sardonic smile. "They're all at the Keep. Roze plans a massive Kirakawa ritual using all the magicians she has captured to empower all her favorite Warpers in one sweep. And you're to be the coup de grâce."

My blood turned to ice. "Roze?"

A superior expression settled on Cahil's face. "Yes, Roze Featherstone, First Magician also known as Jalila Daviian, First Warper and founder of the Daviian Clan."

All color drained from Leif's face. "But how? Why?"

"I had no idea until Ferde was caught. She asked me to rescue him in exchange for the Council's support to invade Ixia," Cahil said. "I thought it was an undercover mission to learn who else was behind his bid for power. Though, when I discovered the truth about her and the other Warpers, I must admit it didn't bother me at the time. She promised to attack Ixia and make me king."

"How many Warpers are inside and who are the victims for the ritual?" I asked.

"Six very powerful Warpers, including Roze and Gede. They have been very careful about who they allow to increase their powers, keeping crucial information about the Kirakawa ritual to a select few. There are fifty Vermin soldiers and ten medium-powered Warpers. Two of those Warpers are scheduled to be given master-level powers during the massive ritual. The victims for this ritual will be the three other Masters, who are incarcerated in the Keep's cells, Moon Man and the Councilors."

"What about the students?"

"The older apprentices have been put in the cells. The younger ones obey out of fear."

"How does Roze plan to control the Master Magicians?"

"She has the power, but I think she does plan to prick them with Curare to save her energy. Once they are tied down, a dose of Theobroma will weaken their defenses."

"They seem to have an unlimited supply of Curare," I mused out loud.

"Gede Daviian has provided the drug for them. He also helped recruit dissatisfied Sandseeds to the Daviian Clan. And having a pet Fire Warper has made him the Daviians' most valued member."

I mulled over the information. "How do you plan to get us inside?"

"As my prisoner. She knows I went to find you. I'll bring you to her and since my feelings for you haven't changed, I won't have to act like I hate you. Sensing nothing wrong, Roze will probably order me to take the rest—" Cahil pointed to Ari and Janco "—to the cells."

"Why would I cooperate with you?"

"Because I'll have Leif, and I'll make a bargain to keep him safe in exchange for your cooperation."

My mind raced through the options and possibilities. For the first time, I felt hopeful about my friends' survival. "Cahil, when you take the others to the cells, can you free everyone inside?"

"As long as Roze is occupied."

Valek smiled. "What's the plan, love?"

We approached the Keep's gate at a slow walk. I sat in front of Cahil on his horse. Ari and Marrok sat on the wagon with their hands tied behind their backs. Valek and Janco hid in the bottom crates, and Leif sat on Kiki with one of Cahil's men sitting behind him armed with a knife.

I didn't have to pretend to be scared and concerned for my friends. We were waved through the gate without hesitation. Ari had informed the Citadel's citizens to wait ten minutes before storming the entrance to the Keep. Ten minutes for Cahil and the rest to free the prisoners and for me to jump into the fire. I hoped it was enough time.

The wagon bypassed the Keep's administration building to where the apprentice barracks formed a ring around an open area. A few students hurried past, keeping their gazes on the ground as they carried out their tasks.

The grassy glen had been transformed. I stared at the wasteland in shock. The bonfire was expected, but the grass around the fire had been covered with sand. Brownish-red stains soaked the sand and stakes had been driven into it.

It was the killing ground for the Kirakawa ritual. And the next victim had already been tied down and prepped.

Bloody cuts crisscrossed his abdomen, legs and arms. Although in pain, Moon Man still managed to smile. "Now we can start the party," he said.

Roze frowned at him and he writhed in agony. She stood next to Moon Man. Gede was beside her. Other Warpers ringed the fire pit, watching with predatory eyes.

"I see you finally managed to get something right, Cahil," she said. "Bring her here."

Cahil slid off the saddle and grabbed me around the waist. He knew he didn't need to help me down, so he must have a reason. I let him yank me from the saddle, and drop me on the ground.

"Where do you want to go?" he asked in a tight whisper as he jerked me to my feet.

"As close to the fire as I can."

"Really?"

"Yes." Although my heart beat a different answer. No! it pounded. Let's go! Run!

He clamped his hand around my arm and pulled me to Roze. We stopped a few feet from the fire. The heat pulsed in waves. Sweat dripped down my back.

Roze gestured to a couple of Warpers. "There are two hiding in the boxes. Take them."

The Warpers and a few soldiers advanced on the wagon. After some banging and cursing, Janco and Gale were hauled out.

"There are three compartments, but one is empty," a Warper called.

Roze looked at me with a question in her eyes.

"For me. So I could get inside the Citadel." The truth. I kept my mind on the task at hand and didn't allow it to wonder about Valek.

"At this distance, Yelena, do you realize your mental defenses are nothing but a thin shell? I will see your lies before you can form them in your mind. Remember that."

I nodded and strengthened my barrier.

She laughed and ordered the soldiers to take the others to the cells. "I'll deal with them later." Once the cart was out of sight, she peered at me and Cahil.

"Your capture was too easy," she said. "You must think I'm a simpleton, but no matter, I've only to expand a sliver of power to find out what you're planning." Her strong magic invaded my mind.

I kept my thoughts on saving Moon Man, Leif and the others as I mentally dodged her onslaught. It failed to work. To distract her, I asked, "Why?"

"Nice try." Her magic crashed through my defenses, and seized my body. "You are in my power now. Sitia is saved."

"Saved from me?" At least I could still talk. In fact, even with her incredible strength, she could only control either my mind or my body. Not both.

"Saved from you. The Commander. Valek. Our way of life is secured."

"By killing Sitians? Using blood magic?"

"Small price to pay for our continued prosperity. I could not let the Commander invade us. The Council failed to see the problem. I created the Daviians as a backup—a hidden weapon for when we needed them. It worked. The Council eventually agreed with me." Smug satisfaction shone in her eyes.

Through our mental link, I sensed she didn't understand the whole truth or she chose to ignore it. "The Daviians forced the Council to agree with you. They had their children."

Extreme annoyance creased Roze's forehead. She shot Gede a venom-laced look. He wisely remained quiet, but his muscles tensed.

"Are you sure you have control of the Daviians?" I asked.

"Of course. And once we choose a new Council we will attack Ixia and free them. They will welcome our way of life." She smiled.

"So you saved Sitia? Tell me, how is sacrificing the Council different than Valek assassinating them?"

Roze frowned and a wave of pain pulsed through my body. My thoughts scattered as an unrelenting torment twisted my muscles. When I regained my senses, I was lying in the sand, looking up at her.

"Isn't *choosing* new Councilors the same as *appointing* generals?" I asked.

Another jolt of pain sizzled along my spine. I arched my back and screamed. Sweat poured from my head and soaked my clothes. My heart pumped as if it ran for its life. I gasped for breath.

"Would you care to ask anything else?" Danger glinted in her eyes.

"Yes. How are your actions different than the Commander's?"

She paused, and I pressed my advantage. "You want to protect Sitia from the Commander, but in the process you turned into him."

Her mouth opened to protest, but I interrupted. "You're worried the Commander would invade Sitia and turn your clans into Military Districts. But you're planning to attack Ixia and turn his Military Districts into clans. How is that different? Tell me!"

She blustered and shook her head. "I'm…he's…" Then she laughed. "Why should I listen to you? You're a Soulfinder. You want to control Sitia. Of course you would try to sway me with your lies."

Gede relaxed and chuckled with Roze. "She will twist your words. You should kill her now."

Roze drew a breath.

"Wait for the ritual! I have something you want," I said.

"What could you have that I can not take from you?"

"According to the ritual, a willing victim releases more power than a resisting one."

"And you will submit to me in exchange for what?"

"For all my friends' lives."

"No. Only one. You choose."

"Moon Man, then." I hoped the others managed to escape.

She released her hold on me. I stood, but she pointed. "Lie in the sand," she ordered.

"Can I ask another question first?"

"One."

"What happens to the Fire Warper after this ritual?"

"Once you're dead, our deal is complete. We have promised him your power and fed him in exchange for knowledge about the blood magic. He will then have enough power to rule the underworld."

A shout reached us and I felt a magical onslaught.

Roze turned to the commotion and gestured to her Warpers. "Take care of them." Unconcerned, she said to me, "You know they will not get close to us. My Warpers and I have enough power to stop them."

"Yes, I know."

"But I don't think you believe it. Watch what I can do. This used to drain me of energy. Now it takes only a thought." Her gaze went to Moon Man's.

His face paled and his body jerked once then stilled. The shine in his eyes dulled as his soul left his body.

33

I DIVED OVER HIS PRONE form and inhaled his soul before crashing to the sand.

Gede gasped. "He was for the ritual."

Roze laughed and said, "Don't worry. She'll now give me two sources of power when I cut her heart out."

"We made a deal, Roze. My cooperation for Moon Man." I brushed the sand off my clothes.

"And you won't cooperate when I press a knife to Leif's throat?" she asked. By the expression on my face, she knew I would. "You're too soft, Soulfinder. You could have raised a soulless army. They would have been undefeatable. Magic doesn't work on them. Only fire."

Another cry split the air, but this time from the opposite direction. A Vermin raced toward us.

"Now what?" Roze asked him.

"The Keep's gates are under attack," he said, panting.

She glanced at the Warpers fighting with the Keep's magicians. A vision of the battle formed in my mind. The ferocity of the combat dwindled. The confusing array of magical images was gone and Gale's whirling dust devils had died. People fell to the ground after being hit with Curare-laced darts. Leif, Ari and Bain lay paralyzed. Janco fought a soldier, keeping the man between him and the blowpipes. His movements slowed as another Warper focused his magic on him.

Roze's Warpers had gained the upper hand; it was only a matter of time.

"There is nobody left to rescue you," Roze said.

Her comments hit home when she called a few Warpers away from the battle to deal with the revolt at the gates.

But there was one person I didn't see and that gave me some hope. "Roze, you haven't figured everything out."

She looked dubious. "What have I missed? Valek? Oh, I know he's here. Magic might not affect him, but Curare will do the trick."

"No. The Fire Warper."

"What about him?"

"You haven't taken into account that he might have different plans than you."

"Don't be ridiculous. Gede and I feed him. We give him his power. Who else would help him?"

"I would."

I ran toward the fire. Roze's yell sounded faint over the roar of the blaze. The heat encompassed me in a loving embrace. Burning pain transformed into pinpricks of pleasure. But this time the world didn't settle into the smooth plain of black. Souls filled my world, writhing and crying with misery. The air stank of decay and infection.

Help! Help! they cried.

The Fire Warper ordered them to be quiet and pushed them away from me. "She is here for me," he said. "She will not help you."

He studied me. "You have brought me a treat. No only a soul for the sky, but Moon Man's bright power will increase my strength."

Moon Man stood next to me. He peered about the fire world with mild interest.

"I'm sorry you're here," I said. "I didn't plan for it to be you."

"Why not? I am your guide, Yelena. In life and in death. That never changes."

"But you said Gede was my new Story Weaver."

"You were looking for an easy road. Which Gede provided. You could have reclaimed me as your Story Weaver at any time."

"How?"

"You just needed to ask. Or rather begged for my return— much better for my ego."

The Fire Warper stepped between us. "How sweet. Now take me to the sky," he demanded.

"No," I said.

"You cannot refuse me. We made a deal."

"I promised to come back. I didn't promise to take you into the sky."

"Then you and Moon Man will stay here in misery and I will use your power to reach the sky." He advanced and grabbed my arms.

My skin boiled as searing daggers of pain spread throughout my body. I screamed, but he didn't have the ability to take what he wanted. I had to give it to him.

He tried another tactic. Waving with an arm, a window opened and I could see Roze and her Warpers. Leif, Bain, Ari, Janco, Gale, Cahil and Marrok all were staked in the sand.

"They lost. There are a few more left, but when they are captured, the fun begins. However, if you lead me to the sky, I will stop Roze and release all your friends and family."

I looked at Moon Man.

"If you do not help the Fire Warper," Moon Man said, "we are stuck here and Roze will send each of them to suffer in this world with us."

This was the one scenario I had hoped to avoid. "Are you saying that's what I should do?"

"No. I am merely pointing out the consequences."

"Then what should I do?"

"Your decision to make. You are the Soulfinder. Find your soul."

I wanted to strangle him, but he was already dead. "Do you think you could give me a straight answer one time?" I demanded.

"Yes, I could."

I gazed out as frustration and futility twisted tightly around me. Sensing I was conflicted, the Fire Warper let the souls draw near to me so I could see the fate of my friends. Their cries grew shrill in my ears and the heat baked my skin, making it difficult to concentrate. The fetid odor assaulted my senses.

"Watch," he said, and pointed to the scene beyond the fire. "Roze has ensnared Irys in a cocoon of magic. She will force her to lie upon the sand and be tied down."

Sure enough Irys walked toward Roze. She knelt before her. Irys's eyes glanced to the side before the other Warpers secured her in the sand. I followed her gaze and spotted Valek.

He fought four Warpers with swords, but I knew they threw every ounce of magic at him. And by Roze's intent gaze, she aimed all her power against him. Even though the magic didn't work, he still felt the presence and it slowed his movements. A soldier waited nearby with a blowpipe, seeking the first opportunity to hit Valek with a dart.

"And Valek will be next," the Fire Warper said. "What do you want to do? Watch your friends and lover die or guide me to the sky?"

I held out my hand to Moon Man and to the Fire Warper. "Come," I said.

34

A TRIUMPHANT GRIN SPREAD on the Fire Warper's face. Moon Man remained unflappable. He held my hand. Even though it appeared to be made of smoke, his hand felt solid in mine. Moon Man looked at me. The oval shape of his eyes matched Roze's. Why hadn't I noticed the resemblance before?

Roze's comments replayed in my mind. Could I reanimate Moon Man's body after I took him to the sky? According to Roze, soulless bodies were unaffected by magic. Could I create a small force to help Irys and Valek?

My bat flew around my head. Odd. How could he be here?

Moon Man sighed. I missed the point. It didn't matter how the bat had gotten here, but why was he here at all. Bats. Opal's glass bat. I reached for my pocket, but the answer halted the motion. Opal's sister. Tula!

When Ferde had stolen Tula's soul and strangled her, I had used my magic to breathe for Tula, but as soon as I had stopped, she had stopped.

I didn't possess the power to raise a soulless army.

The magician born one-hundred-and-fifty years ago wasn't a Soulfinder, but a Soulstealer.

I was a true Soulfinder. And I knew what my job entailed. The Fire Warper grew impatient with my delay and reached for my free hand; I yanked it away. My bat cried out with joy and disappeared.

I sought Roze with my mind, seeing her soul and the souls of all her victims trapped within her. Their blood had been injected into her skin to bind them to her. I pushed at the blood, sweeping and forcing it through her pores, pulling the souls free, sending them to the sky.

She yelped and rolled up her sleeve. Black liquid oozed from her arms, dripping onto the sand. The putrid smell of rancid blood surrounded her like a fog. Each one I removed weakened Roze until only her own power remained.

Then I projected my mind to Gede and did the same to him. One by one I plucked souls from the Warpers, weakening them.

The Fire Warper cried an oath and lunged for me. Moon Man intercepted and fought him so I could return my attention to the Keep.

Roze's magical hold on Irys had slipped when I extracted her power. Freed from the magic, Irys used her own skills to draw a knife close to her and cut the rope. Once loose, she ran to a few others who had not been pricked with Curare but who, like her, had been captured by magic.

Gale and Marrok joined her and they attacked Roze. Valek's opponents had been distracted by the scene around them, giving Valek the opportunity to dispatch them. The man with the blowpipe ran off. Valek turned his full attention to Roze.

Satisfied all was well with my friends, I focused on the Fire Warper. He held Moon Man in a tight grip, compressing Moon Man's soul to bind him to the fire world.

"Stop," I said. "You'll gain no more power today." I pulled at Moon Man with my magic and he popped from the Fire Warper's grasp. "I find souls and ensure they arrive at the proper destination. He doesn't belong here. But you do."

I moved past him. He tried to stop me, but he was a soul just like all the others and I controlled him. Moving through the fire world, I found those who didn't belong and released them to the sky. The Fire Warper screamed at me with each one, but I ignored him. A long time passed as I freed them all, but my energy increased with every rescue.

"Why aren't I tired?" I asked Moon Man.

He smiled. "Think about what you have learned today."

I glanced around. The Fire Warper's power had diminished with each freed soul. Perhaps stealing his power had increased my own?

"No." Moon Man looked a little exasperated, as if he couldn't believe how slow I was. I did take some pleasure from his expression. To alter his calm demeanor required much effort on my part.

The Fire Warper glowered at me. "It is only a matter of time before I regain my strength," he said. "There is always someone who desires more power and I will be waiting for them."

"Not if I can help it," I said.

"Then you will have to spend eternity with me to prevent it. The knowledge is out there now. Another fool will figure out how to contact me through the flames."

He had a point. But I was the Soulfinder. In order to do

my job, I would have to stay in the underworld and send the souls to their proper places. Thinking about my job, I remembered a promise to Moon Man.

"Can you guide me to the shadow world?" I asked him.

"No. But you can lead me."

"And you call yourself a guide?"

He smiled serenely.

"I hate you." I clasped Moon Man's hand.

I thought of the shadow world with its gray plain and sky. The red glow faded and soon the featureless expanse spread in front of us.

"This is only the corridor between worlds, Yelena. Look deeper to see the real shadow world."

Another cryptic instruction. For all my abilities, I still couldn't get Moon Man to give me a straight answer. I pushed away my frustration and focused on who I was trying to find. The Sandseeds who had been killed by the Vermin in the Avibian Plains.

The flat area began to undulate and transform into the plains. Small outcroppings of rocks grew and the smooth gray ground sprouted grass and a few bushes. A cluster of canvas tents popped up and circled a fire pit. The scene before me resembled a Sandseed camp. Yet there was no color. Only black and white and every shade of gray.

Sandseeds huddled together in this camp on the altered Avibian Plain, living in the shadow cast by the real world. They clung to their memories of life, not realizing peace awaited them in the sky.

I walked among them and talked to them. Their numbers grew and I had to stop myself from reliving the horror of the

Vermin's attack and massacre. I made promises to watch over the living Sandseeds who had hidden during the attack. Days and weeks could have passed while I convinced them to move on. I had no concept of time.

Again, as I sent each one into the sky, my strength grew. "There are many more souls clinging to the shadow world," I said to Moon Man, thinking about all the towns and cities in Sitia and Ixia. "Let me return you to your body and you can tell the others my fate."

"I can not return," he said. "My body has died, unlike yours. And even if you heal me, I would be unhappy and would wish for death."

"Like Stono and Gelsi?"

"Yes. Eventually both will find their way back to where they belong."

"Then I will send you to the sky. You deserve to be there."

"Not until you understand."

"I do understand. I'm doing my job. I've resigned myself to living here to keep Sitia and Ixia safe from more Warpers!" I clamped my hands together to keep them from wrapping around Mr. I-know-everything-and-you-don't Man's thick neck.

"Have you truly resigned yourself?" he asked.

"I…" I huffed in frustration. I would rather be back with Valek, Kiki, my parents, Leif, Irys, Ari, Janco and my other friends. I had learned my true job, but there were still many aspects of my magic and others' magic to explore. I thought about Opal's unique ability. Then I remembered my glass bat.

Had it survived the fire? I felt inside my pockets. Odd how my clothing had survived the flames. My fingers touched a smooth lump. I pulled the animal from my cape. The inner core glowed with magic. Staring at the light, I saw Leif's sad face. He peered at me in sorrow, then disbelief when I smiled at him.

"Hello from the underworld," I said.

"Yelena! What the…? Where are…? Come back!"

"I can't. Tell me what has happened?"

He gave me a quick sketch of how the battle had played out after I jumped into the fire. Most of the Warpers were dead, only Roze, Gede and four others remained alive. They were in the Keep's cells, awaiting trial.

"They will be hanged for treason and murder," Leif said. He grew somber. "We buried Moon Man last week."

"Last week? But—"

"You've been gone for weeks. We keep the fire burning, hoping you'll return. Also Valek will not let us quench it. He's been helping the Councilors and Master Magicians recover from their ordeal and to smooth out relations with the Commander via Ambassador Signe. Valek went from the scourge of Sitia to the hero of Sitia." Leif smiled sardonically.

Valek. The one person I wouldn't mind spending eternity with.

Leif continued, "And the rest of us are coping with the aftermath. Many students were killed by the Vermin. We're still sorting out who is left. Your friend Dax is okay, but Gelsi died resisting a Warper."

Moon Man was right, Gelsi found her way back. I hoped Stono wouldn't suffer too much before his soul found the sky.

He paused. "The Sitian army's hunting down the remaining Vermin who escaped. The Sandseeds have moved back to the plains to repopulate." Leif sighed. "You're missed by every-one. Why can't you come back?"

"Someone needs to keep the Fire Warper from regaining power."

Leif frowned as he thought, then looked hopeful. "Bain has burned those old Efe texts to stop someone from learning about the blood magic."

"But there are others who know how to perform the ritual, and, even though you will execute them, they will be here in the fire world and able to communicate to someone who is determined to seek them out."

"You're a Soulfinder, can't you send them somewhere out of reach?" Leif asked.

"They don't deserve to be in the sky."

"Why not?" Moon Man said.

My mind thought over what I knew of the sky, which was very little. "I think they would taint it. It's pure and their vile deeds would soil it."

"Finally. What is the sky?"

What indeed? When I sent souls there, I felt refreshed, en-ergetic even though I used power, which usually caused me fatigue. I added souls to the sky. Adding to the power blanket surrounding the world.

The source of magic!

The world's soul.

Moon Man beamed at me. "Now you can send me there! And then you can return to your life."

He chuckled at my dubious expression. "You will find a way, Yelena. You always do."

"Last piece of cryptic advice?"

"Consider it my farewell gift."

I hesitated for a moment. Once Moon Man was gone I would be all alone.

"All the more reason not to stay," Moon Man said.

"There's one thing I won't miss."

"And that is?"

"You reading my mind all the time and making me figure things out for myself."

"All part of being your Story Weaver. It does not stop, you know. You will hear my voice in your mind from time to time, giving you my unique advice."

I groaned. "And I thought living in the underworld for eternity was bad!"

Before sending him to the sky, I stared at him, trying to hold his features, including his sardonic grin, in my mind. When he disappeared, his absence felt like an icy coating on my skin. I realized I still held Opal's bat, but my connection to Leif was broken.

I wandered through the shadow world and found lost souls. Every so often I checked in the fire world to make sure the Fire Warper remained as he should be. He cursed, taunted and tried to cajole me, depending on his mood.

Irys, Leif and Bain all talked to me through the glass animals. They were the only ones who had the ability to use them. Through them I knew Roze, Gede and the other Warpers would be hanged soon. I prepared to receive them in the fire world.

In the meantime, I stared at my bat, trying and failing to connect to Valek. My desire to talk to him, to hold him, clawed at my body. Frustration at my inability to communicate with him caused a window to open to the real world, and

I could view events around my fire. I laughed at my intense feelings of ownership. My fire. But I sobered. I knew after they hanged Roze and the others, my fire would be doused and my window closed for good.

The Council planned to hang Roze and her accomplices on gallows built in the bloodstained sand then burn their bodies in my fire. An insult given only to traitors.

The sand would be cleaned up and perhaps the gardeners would plant grass in the space. Or some trees. Flowers. A memorial? Perhaps a structure similar to one of the Citadel's jade statues or fountains. To remember me and Moon Man.

Now I was being maudlin and dramatic. Next thing I knew, I'd be designing the memorial, sketching its dimensions in the sand. I wondered about what they would do with all the sand. Send it to Booruby to be melted into glass? So Opal could turn fire into ice?

I froze in shock as a wild idea formed in my head. Thinking it through, I found many holes and reasons for it not to work. But success or not, at least I could say I tried. And the effort alone would keep Moon Man from nagging me for a while.

35

CALLING TO LEIF through my bat, I hoped there would be enough time. He seemed eager to help and rushed off to make the arrangements.

Events had to happen in a particular order for this to work. I returned to the fire world. The Fire Warper would be our first test subject. Watching out my window, I waited for Leif to return. I didn't like being in the fire world. The shrill noise drilled through my skull and the putrid smell permeated the air. I preferred the quiet dullness of the shadow world.

The Fire Warper enjoyed my anxiety. "Look at how you long to return. Your suffering is my only pleasure. And I will enjoy keeping you here. Already I sense an unhappy boy who seeks revenge on his tormentors. If his desire grows, I'll be able to talk to him. Unless you prevent it."

Doubt flared about what I planned. Was I being selfish? Could I still rescue souls lost in the shadow world? Yet I had done it before with the ghosts in Owl's Hill. Suppressing all my fears, I ignored the Fire Warper's comments.

What seemed like a couple of weeks to me, but could have been a month or more, passed. By my brief glimpses into the Keep, the cold season had ended and the warming season was in full swing. I received updates from Leif, but now that I had a chance to escape, my impatience grew.

Finally, all the elements were in place. The gallows were built and the needed equipment brought in. My incredible relief at seeing Opal surprised me. Her mouth was pressed in pure determination as she readied her tools.

Another worry crossed my mind. Within the underworld, I hadn't felt cold, hot, hunger or thirst. But if I stepped back through the fire, would it burn me? I would find out soon enough. The Fire Warper hovered near me, his amusement plain.

Opal grasped a long metal pipe and poked it into the kiln. I wondered where they had gotten the glassmaking supplies. She turned the pipe and drew it out. And proceeded to create a glass animal.

When she moved to blow into the pipe, I inhaled the Fire Warper's soul. He yelped in surprise and seared my skin as I sent him through Opal and into the glass. He screamed in panic and resisted. But I controlled him. He was a soul after all.

Opal jerked as if burned, but returned to her task, making the ugliest, squattest looking pig I ever saw.

Placing the animal into the annealing oven, the wait began. Had our experiment worked? If the Fire Warper was truly trapped within the glass, then we could encase all the Warpers who knew how to perform blood magic, preventing them from passing the information along. And I could go home.

Twelve of the longest hours passed before Opal withdrew

the pig and held the statue up for all to see. It was then I noticed just how many people had come to watch. I expected Leif, the Master Magicians and Councilors, but it appeared that Fisk and the entire Helping Guild members were there. My mother and father lingered at the edges. Perl's hand was clamped to her throat in dismay, but she looked as determined as Opal.

Cahil and a regiment of soldiers, including Marrok stood at attention. Ari and Janco waited with Leif. Janco scowled, showing his extreme dislike of magic.

Valek glowed with his own inner fire. For him, I would risk the flames' heat.

I turned my attention to Opal's creation. It pulsed with a muddy red light. The Fire Warper was locked inside.

The audience cheered. Opal placed the pig in the sand, and gathered another blob of molten glass, preparing for the next soul.

Roze, under the control of three Master Magicians, was forced to mount the gallows' steps. The noose was tightened around her neck and the executioner stepped back. Her face contorted with rage and she shouted.

Time froze for a moment and I felt what it would have been like to stand there terrified, waiting for the floor to open and my life to end with a quick snap of my neck. If I had chosen the noose instead of becoming the Commander's food taster two years ago, I wondered if any of this would have happened.

Roze fell in slow motion. Her body jerked at the end of the rope. Her soul flew. I captured it.

Her hateful thoughts filled my mind. *Guardian of the underworld suits you, Yelena. You belong here. You don't really believe you can go back? You'll be feared by all and become an outcast in record time.*

If I was a Soulstealer, I would agree with you, I said. *You don't scare me, Roze. You never did and that bothered you more than me being a Soulfinder.*

Opal blew. I sent Roze on her final journey. Then Gede. Then the other four Warpers. Seven in all, including the Fire Warper.

When all the Warpers had been encased in glass, Opal sank to the ground in exhaustion. Now I could leave. I glanced around, trying to determine whether I missed anything, whether a soul who could do harm remained. Roze's words had a bit of truth to them. Regardless of my explanations, Sitians would be frightened of me and the Council's suspicion and unease would linger for a long time.

I welcomed the difficulties. All part of living, and I planned to enjoy every minute.

As I walked through my window to the Keep, sounds reached me first. The roar of the fire. Leif calling my name. Then scalding heat sucked my breath away. Bright yellow and orange stabbed at my eyes. My cape caught fire. I dived to the sand and rolled on the ground to snuff the flames. So much for my grand entrance.

36

I SPENT MY FIRST HOURS back cocooned in an excited babble of all my friends and family. Everyone except Valek. But I knew I would see him when the horde dispersed.

Once my fire had finished its macabre task of burning the traitors to ash, it was doused. Thick smoke boiled from it and clung to the ground until Gale Stormdance created a fresh breeze to whisk it away.

I noted with much interest how fast life resumed. Though glad I had returned, the Councilors left for a meeting, and Fisk and his guild hurried off to work in the market.

Before he left, Fisk flashed me a wide smile and said, "Lovely Yelena, you'll need new clothes for the hot season. I know the best seamstress in the Citadel. Come find me when you're ready."

The hot season? Ari told me it had just started. I had lived in the underworld for seventy-one days, missing the entire warming season. I viewed the time with mixed emotions: glad my perceptions in the underworld didn't match reality, especially if I ever needed to go back; and upset I wasn't here to help clean up the mess left behind by the Vermin.

Ari and Janco grumbled over the hot, sticky weather and confessed their desire to go home to Ixia.

"We had fun rooting out all those Daviians," Janco said. "But I'm sure Maren misses us."

Ari looked doubtful. He had washed the black dye from his hair, and his light skin had burned in the Sitian sun. Janco's skin had tanned, matching his Sitian clothes.

"Oh this?" Janco said, when I mentioned his new coloring. "You missed some beautiful days."

"Janco's been sunning himself every chance he gets," Ari said with obvious disdain. "He claimed he kept the fire going, but I caught him snoozing in the sand a few times."

"Once!" Janco said.

They began to bicker. I laughed and moved away, but heard Ari call out, "Training yard, five o'clock."

Kiki's urgent summons had nagged me the whole time I'd been back. I hurried over to the stable to spend an hour with her. Perhaps Valek would show up and we could get reacquainted in the straw.

I scratched her ears, fed her peppermints and ducked behind a stack of hay bales when the Stable Master came looking for me, probably to give me a lecture about borrowing Garnet for so long.

Lavender Lady not go again, Kiki said in my mind.

I'll try to avoid it. No promises, though.

She huffed. *Next time Kiki go.*

A Horsefinder?

Help Lavender Lady, Kiki said, as if that ended the discussion.

Even though I longed to return to my rooms in Irys's tower, my parents insisted I come to their quarters in the Keep's guest wing after I visited the stables. Leif, Irys and Bain followed me, and the six of us sat in the living room, sipping tea. Wedged tightly between my father and mother on the couch, I was held prisoner. My desire to seek Valek would have to wait.

Bain and Irys were most interested in what had happened in the fire and shadow worlds. After giving them a brief sketch, Bain made me promise to visit him and recite the details for his book.

"You passed the Master-level test," Irys said.

"What?" Caught off guard by this sudden change in topic, I choked on my tea.

"You entered the underworld and returned with a spirit guide. Your encounter with the Fire Warper was your challenge, and his defeat your success."

"But I don't have a spirit guide."

Leif laughed. "Your bat! I thought he was strange. Beside the obvious fact that he wanted to hang out with you."

"Leif. That's not nice, considering all your sister has done for you," Perl admonished.

"Oh, right. How can I forget that she made me bait for a snake, left me under house arrest in Ixia and smuggled me into the Keep in a coffin. And don't forget the time…"

I ignored Leif's rant. I wondered, why a bat? Why not something fearsome like a fire dragon or necklace snake? Irys had a hawk, Bain a wind leopard and Zitora a unicorn. Thinking of Zitora, I reminded myself to go visit her in the infirmary. She had been severely wounded during the fight with the Warpers, and her recovery had been slow.

I kept glancing out the window, hoping to see Valek. My mind circled through various excuses for me to leave everyone to search for him.

Bain interrupted Leif's list of grievances against me. "According to our policies, Yelena is Fourth Magician."

I raised my hand to prevent any more wild speculation. "No. I can't light fires or move objects like the Masters can. I'm a Soulfinder. My job is to find lost souls and send them home, including the souls of Ixia. There is still need for a Liaison between the two countries. I plan to reassume the role."

And the first order of business would be to assess Cahil's intentions. His help in defeating Roze and uncovering all the Vermin nests had proven invaluable to the Council, but I wasn't convinced his new role meant he wouldn't try some way to claim Ixia's throne.

Leif asked, "What do we do with those glass prisons? They're under guard, but we don't want them falling into the wrong hands."

"What would happen if they break?" Perl asked.

They all looked at me. "If the souls are freed, they will go to the fire world, unless there is another Soulfinder to place them elsewhere."

"Elsewhere?" Leif raised his eyebrows.

"Into another body or to the sky." I sighed. "We will have to find a place to protect and to hide them."

"The Keep," Bain said.

"The Illiais Jungle has some deep caves," Esau suggested.

"Under the Emerald Mountains," Irys said.

"Sunken in the deepest part of the sea," Leif said.

"Buried under the northern ice," Perl recommended.

"All good ideas, but the Council will need to debate the issue and decide."

My gaze met Irys's. She gave me a wry smile. We both knew the Council would argue for months, and it was up to me to find a home for them.

I spent the rest of the afternoon with my family. Perl and Esau made me promise to come visit them.

"A nice relaxing visit," Perl ordered. "No chasing Vermin or saving anyone. We'll sit and talk and I'll make you a new perfume."

"Yes, Mother."

She made me eat before I could leave. I hurried to the training yard, hoping Valek would be there.

He was not. The man must be torturing me on purpose. I had made him wait over two months. Perhaps he was returning the favor.

Ari and Janco sparred with swords. And although Janco sang his rhymes and Ari used his brute strength, they were equally matched in skill. They stopped when they saw me.

"Come on," Janco said. "Ari wants to make sure you're in good fighting shape before we leave."

"I do?"

"Yes, you do. Otherwise you'll worry about her."

"I will?"

"Of course." Janco waved away Ari's comments. "Besides, this is just a lull before the next storm. We need to be ready!"

This time I piped in. "The next storm?"

Janco sighed dramatically. "There's always another storm. It's the way the world works. Snowstorms, rainstorms, windstorms, sandstorms and firestorms. Some are fierce and others are small. You have to deal with each one separately, but you need to always keep an eye on what's brewing for tomorrow."

Ari rolled his eyes. "Janco's unique view of life. Yesterday he compared living to food."

"That's because some food leaves you full while others—"

"Janco," I said. "Prepare for *my* storm." I swept my bow toward his feet.

He jumped over it with a nimble grace. Dropping his sword, he reached for his bow and our match began.

Since I had returned from the underworld, I could see everyone with a new sight. With a blink of my eyes, I saw through their bodies and directly into their souls. I knew their thoughts, feelings and intentions as if they were my own. Before I had to pull power for the source and project myself to them. Now the connection was there the second I thought about it.

Janco's comical surprise when I dumped him on the ground in three moves was almost worth my trip through the underworld. Almost.

He huffed and blustered and tried to make excuses. I stopped our second fight to guide a soul to the sky. Many hung around the Keep and I knew I would have to do a sweep of the Citadel.

Janco viewed my magical actions as if they were distasteful to him. "At least you're expending energy. You'll be easier to beat," he smirked.

"Wishful thinking," I said.

After losing the next four matches, Janco finally conceded.

"Am I ready for the next storm?" I asked him, smiling sweetly.

"You *are* the next storm."

Bruised ego aside, Janco and Ari were pleased with my fighting skills.

"You found your center," Ari said with a note of approval in his voice. "You're not afraid to embrace who you are. Now Janco won't have to worry anymore."

"I'll let Ari do all the worrying for both of us. Oh wait! He already does."

"I do not. You're the one who moaned and fussed about Yelena all these weeks."

"I did not."

They launched into another round of bickering. I never thought I would enjoy listening to them, but I did. Until I saw Cahil walking toward the training yard.

He held his long broadsword. I watched him approach, preparing to defend myself if need be. I studied his emotions with my other sight. Hate, determination and anxiety dominated his feelings.

Cahil stopped at the fence. "I didn't come here to fight," he said. "I want to talk to you."

Ari and Janco didn't seem concerned by his presence, and continued their debate. But they hadn't been on the wrong side of Cahil's wrath. I moved closer with my bow in hand, keeping the wooden fence between us.

"What do you want to talk about?" I demanded.

Cahil pulled in a deep breath and let the air out fast. "I wanted to…"

"Go on. Say it."

Irritation flared in Cahil's light blue eyes, but he stifled it. "I wanted to explain."

"Explain why you're nasty, ruthless, opportunistic—"

"Yelena! Will you shut up."

My expression must have warned him, because he rushed to continue. "You bring out the worst in me. Can you listen?" A pause. "Please?"

"All right."

"When I found out that I didn't have royal blood, that my whole purpose in life was a sham, I refused to believe it. Even when Marrok admitted I was just a soldier's son, I didn't want to hear it. Instead, I transferred my anger to you and Valek and decided I would find a way to make the Council support an attack on Ixia to reclaim the throne." Cahil looked down at the sword in his hand. "You know what I did after. I lost my way and swallowed every morsel of Roze's lies."

Cahil handed me his sword. It had been the King of Ixia's sword. Rescued after the King had been assassinated, the sword had been given to Cahil as part of the ruse to make him believe he was the King's nephew.

"Give it to the Commander for me," Cahil said. "By rights, it should be his."

"Have you given up your desire to rule Ixia?"

He looked at me and I saw a renewed sense of purpose in his soul. "No. I still seek to free Ixia from the Commander's strict rule. But I no longer feel I should inherit the throne. I plan to *earn* the privilege."

"Then that's going to make for some interesting discussions between us." I held his gaze.

"You can count on it."

The summons from Ambassador Signe came after a long soak in a hot bath. I exchanged my damaged cape and smoky clothes for a clean pair of cotton pants and shirt. My hair hadn't grown while I was in the underworld. The inch-long strands, though, were long enough to lay flat on my head.

The Ambassador waited in the Keep's administration building. She had the use of a meeting room and an office during her stay. I hurried up the stairs and into the marble building, hoping to see Valek there. My disappointment churned in my stomach and I wondered if Valek was avoiding me.

Ambassador Signe greeted me warmly, inquiring about my health. I studied her face. So similar to the Commander's almost delicate features, yet missing the full force of the powerful spark residing in his gold eyes. With my new vision, I saw the two souls that struggled for dominance. They took turns, but I could see the red spiral of conflict within.

"Irys Jewelrose informed me you wish to resume your duties as Liaison. Is this true?"

"Yes. Becoming an adviser to the Commander is very tempting, but I feel my skills should serve both Ixia and Sitia by keeping relations open and fostering an understanding between the two nations."

"I see. Then your first order of business should be to negotiate a salary."

"A salary?"

"You can not be paid by the magicians or the Council. You must receive equal wages from Sitia and Ixia to maintain your neutrality." She smiled. "For all that you have done recently, I would suggest you barter for a considerable amount."

"Obviously, there are many things I need to think about in my new role."

"I trust, then, your education is complete?"

I laughed. "There will never be a time when it's complete, but I've reached an understanding with my abilities."

"Good. I look forward to our negotiations."

Before the Ambassador could dismiss me, I said, "I have something for the Commander."

She looked at me expectantly.

"It's with your guard. He wouldn't let me bring it in."

Rising from her desk, she opened the door and returned with the King's sword.

"May I speak to the Commander?" I asked.

The transformation from the Ambassador to the Commander happened in a heartbeat. Even the physical features changed from a woman to a man. I had seen it before, but this time I watched with my other sight. It revealed much.

"What is this for?" the Commander asked. He studied the weapon in his hand.

"Cahil is returning it to you. You won the right to wield it over seventeen years ago."

A thoughtful expression settled on his face as he placed the sword on the desk. "Cahil. What should I do about him?"

I told the Commander about his plans. "He could cause trouble for you in the future, although I hope my efforts will change his mind."

"I know Valek would be happy to assassinate him." He considered that scenario. "But he might prove useful, especially in dealing with the younger generation." He saw my confused frown. "It'll give them something to do."

"Or give them someone to rally behind."

"All part of the fun, I suppose. Is that all?"

"No." I gave the Commander one of Opal's glass animals.

He admired the tree leopard and thanked me for the gift.

"The glow you see is magic," I said.

His gaze pierced me and I felt his sense of betrayal as if I poisoned him. He placed the statue on the desk. I explained why he could view the fire.

"I can see two souls within your body. Your mother didn't want to leave you alone when she died so she stayed with you. Her magic lets you see the glow. And it's her fear of discovery that has made you afraid of magic in all its forms."

Commander Ambrose held his body as if any movement would crack it into a thousand pieces. "How do you know this?"

"I'm a Soulfinder. I find lost souls and send them to the sky. Does she want to go? Do you want her to go?"

"I don't know. I…"

"Think about it. You know where to find me. There's no time limit."

I glanced back before I left. He stared at the tree leopard, lost in his thoughts.

Night had fallen while I talked with the Commander. Walking across the silent campus, I inhaled the warm breeze, soaking in the smells of life and the feel of air on my skin. I scanned my surroundings, searching for some sign of Valek.

Irys had lit all the lanterns in her tower. Even though she had given me three floors of the structure for my use, I found myself thinking about a salary, and my mind drifted to Valek's cottage in the Featherstone lands. It would be nice to be close to Kiki and get away from the Council's and Commander's politics each night. The cottage was near the Ixian border, too. It would be neutral territory.

A place of my own. I couldn't claim any room, cell or dwelling as my own. It would be the first time. My excitement grew.

I trudged up three floors of the tower to my bedroom. The sparse furnishings and layer of dust made for an unwelcoming sight, although the bedding was fresh.

I opened the shutters to let in clean air and felt a presence behind me. Without turning, I demanded, "What took you so long?"

Valek pressed against my back. His arms wrapped around my stomach. "I could ask you the same thing." He spun me to face him. "I didn't want to share you, love. We have a lot of catching up to do."

He leaned in and kissed me. I drank in his essence, it soothed my soul.

Eventually, I pulled away, and laid my head on his chest, content to just feel his heartbeat against my cheek.

"That's the second time I lost you," he said. "You would think it would be easier, but I couldn't douse the burning pain. I felt like my heart had been pierced by a spit and was cooking over a fire."

His arms tightened around me as if he worried I would slip from his grip. "I would beg you to promise never to disappear again, but I know you won't."

"I can't. Just like you can't promise to stop being loyal to the Commander. We both have other duties."

He huffed with amusement. "We could retire."

"From being a Liaison, but not a Soulfinder. There are many lost souls to guide."

Ever the analyst, Valek drew back enough to study me.

"How many? It's been a hundred–and–twenty–five years since Sitia crisped the last Soulfinder. Hundreds?"

"I don't know. The Soulfinders documented in the history books were really Soulstealers. Guyan could have been the only one in the last two thousand years. Bain would delight in helping me with that assignment. But I will need to travel around Sitia and Ixia to help them all. Do you want to come? It could be fun."

"You, me and a couple thousand ghosts? Sounds crowded," he teased. "At least you already found one soul, love."

"Moon Man's?"

"Mine. And I trust you not to lose it."

"The only magic to affect the infamous Valek." It reminded me of a question I had. While in the shadow world, I had had plenty of time to contemplate every single facet of him. "How old were you when the King's men killed your brothers?"

I ignored his questioning look. "How old?"

"Thirteen." An old sorrow pulled at the corners of his mouth.

"That explains it!"

"Explains what?"

"Why you're resistant to magic. Thirteen is around the age when people can access the power source. The trauma of seeing your brothers killed probably caused you to pull so much power you formed a null shield. A shield so impenetrable you can no longer access magic."

"After a season in the underworld, you're now an expert in all things magical?"

Although he was quick to dismiss the notion, the shock of the revelation was evident in his wide eyes.

"I'm an expert in all things Valek."

"Analyze this, love." He drew me in and kissed me.

When his hands pulled at the fabric of my shirt, I stopped him. "Valek, as much as I want you to stay, I need you to do a favor for me."

"Anything, love."

I smiled at his loyalty. He agreed without hesitation, without knowing what I needed. "I want you to steal those glass prisons. Hide them in a safe place where no one will find them. Don't tell me or anyone else where you put them."

"You don't want to know. Are you sure?"

"Yes. I can still be corrupted by magic. And if I ever ask you for their location you are *not* to tell me. No matter what. Promise."

"Yes, sir."

"Good." I felt relieved.

"It may take me a few days or weeks. Where will you be?"

I told him about staying on as the Liaison. "I plan to commandeer a certain cottage in the Featherstone lands and declare that parcel of land neutral territory."

"Commandeer?" He smiled.

"Yes. Having safe houses for Ixian spies in Sitia is not very friendly. Spying on each other is not conducive to the type of open dialogue I want between the two nations."

"You'll need to rebuild the stable. Hire a lad," Valek teased.

"Don't worry. I already have a houseboy in mind. A loyal and handsome fellow, who will be at my beck and call."

Valek raised an eyebrow as desire danced in his eyes. "Indeed. I'm sure the boy is most anxious to attend to his duties."

He slid a hand under my shirt and along my skin. Warmth spread across my stomach and chest. I tried to move away, but his other arm snaked behind my back. "You need to finish one job before you begin another," I said.

"The night has just begun." He pulled my shirt off. "Plenty of time to take care of my lady before I run her errand."

His lips found mine, then he nuzzled my neck. "I must." He paused to place a line of kisses down my chest. "Help my lady." He picked me up and laid me down. "To bed."

Then he removed the rest of my garments and all concerns about the glass prisons disappeared as Valek's caress took control of my senses. My entire being focused on the musky smell and smooth feel of him. My lungs filled with Valek's breath. My heart pumped Valek's blood. I thought his thoughts and shared his pleasure.

The feelings of contentment, peace and joy flowed through our bodies. Locked tight together, we owned a piece of the sky.

CHOOSE:
A QUICK DEATH…
OR A SLOW POISON…

About to be executed for murder, Yelena is offered the chance to become a food taster. She'll eat the best meals, have rooms in the palace – and risk assassination by anyone trying to kill the Commander of Ixia.

But disasters keep mounting as rebels plot to seize Ixia and Yelena develops magical powers she can't control. Her life is threatened again and choices must be made. But this time the outcomes aren't so clear…

www.mirabooks.co.uk

CONFRONTING THE PAST, CONTROLLING THE FUTURE

With an execution order on her head, Yelena must escape to Sitia, the land of her birth. She has only a year to master her magic — or face death. But nothing in Sitia is familiar. As she struggles to understand where she belongs and how to control her rare powers, a rogue magician emerges — and Yelena catches his eye.

Suddenly she is embroiled in a battle between good and evil. And once again it will be her magical abilities that will either save her life…or be her downfall.

www.mirabooks.co.uk